All Out War

ALSO BY SEAN PARNELL

Nonfiction
Outlaw Platoon

Fiction
Man of War

All Out War

An Eric Steele Novel

Sean Parnell

HARPER LUXE

An Imprint of HarperCollinsPublishers

HarperCollins books may be purchased for educational, business, or sales promotional use. For information, please e-mail the Special Markets Department at SPsales@harpercollins.com.

FIRST HARPERLUXE EDITION

ISBN: 978-0-06-294422-1

HarperLuxe™ is a trademark of HarperCollins Publishers.

Library of Congress Cataloging-in-Publication Data is available upon request.

19 20 21 22 23 LSC 10 9 8 7 6 5 4 3 2 1

To all those who've risen
in defense of America, past,
present, and future.

All Out War

Prologue

Four Months Prior
Sol-Iletsk, Russia

Major Mikhail Petrov stood at the window, smoking a cigarette and watching the snow collect on the triple strands of razor wire that stretched around the perimeter. At thirty-nine, Petrov was the youngest warden in the Russian Federal Penitentiary Service. He was also the most corrupt, which made him the perfect man to run Black Dolphin prison.

Located a rifle shot from the Kazakhstan border, Black Dolphin was an isolated, austere fortress on the steppes. A place where an escapee could run in any direction and his lungs would freeze before he saw another face.

It was the last place any of the bureaucrats from the Penitentiary Service would ever choose to visit, which was exactly why Petrov had chosen the assignment.

A knock at the door drew him from his reverie. Petrov checked the time on the Jaeger-LeCoultre strapped to his wrist and crushed the cigarette into the marble ashtray on his desk. The Jaeger cost two million rubles, more than a year's salary, and while he rarely took it off, today was not the day to flaunt his success. He replaced the watch with the Russian-made Raketa, grabbed his gray greatcoat and peaked uniform hat from the hook by the door, and stepped into the hall.

"My instructions were followed?" Petrov asked his aide, Captain Ruslan Girkin.

"There will be no problems today," Girkin assured him, taking his boss's greatcoat.

"Good," Petrov said.

They walked down a hallway lined with faded pictures of past wardens until they stopped at the main entrance.

"And prisoner thirty-seven?" Petrov asked, stepping into the greatcoat.

Girkin flashed him a feral smile. "I spoke with him

personally," he said, displaying a pair of freshly scabbed knuckles as proof. "He will not be an issue."

Petrov pulled his cap over his head and stepped outside. The cold air blazed his face and numbed his ears, but even with the howling wind he could hear the *thump, thump, thump* of an approaching helicopter. The Kazan Ansat came in at treetop level and hovered over the pad. The downdraft kicked up the fallen snow, obscuring the helo in a white curtain as it settled on its skids.

Petrov ducked his head against the blowing clouds. A tall Arab, dressed in black, stepped out of the blasting mist. Petrov locked on the man's face, and a hint of annoyance crept into Petrov's eyes.

He'd used every asset at his disposal to find out more about the man, but it wasn't until he reached out to an old friend at Russian Intelligence, paid the fifteen thousand euros the man asked for, that he'd finally made headway.

According the FSB databases, the man's name was Gabriel and he was from Saudi Arabia.

A glint of metal from Gabriel's wrist turned his attention to the silver handcuff that secured a leather attaché case.

You, Mikhail, are about to be a very rich man, Petrov thought.

"Welcome to Black Dolphin. I hope your—"

"The pilot will wait for exactly thirty minutes," Gabriel answered in flawless Russian. "Not a moment more. Do you have what I requested?"

"Yes, of course," Petrov said, taking the morning's report from a pocket and handing it over.

Gabriel checked the date and nodded. "Take me to him," he ordered.

Three floors below, Aleksandr Zakayev—prisoner thirty-seven—sat in his cell, head bowed, throwing his torso in a long shadow cast by the bare bulb hanging from the ceiling. The cell was a gray cube of concrete walls and floors. The only color came from the green bucket in the corner that smelled of piss and shit.

Girkin had come last night, using the squeak of the food cart to mask his approach. In the pit you had ten seconds from the moment the metal slit hinged open to grab your food or the guards would snatch it back. Zakayev had gotten to his feet when he heard the cart stop outside his cell. But instead of the metal tray with its meager portion of food, this time he was offered a flashbang.

The flash and subsequent concussion sent Zakayev to the floor. When he looked up, Girkin was standing at the door. The nozzle of the fire hose was pointed at his chest.

"Time for your bath, little dog," Girkin cackled.

A blast of icy well water pummeled Zakayev in the side, pushing him across the floor and pinning him to the wall. The cold sucked the air from his lungs.

When the water stopped, Zakayev caught his breath and then vomited. Feeling wretched, he tried to get to his knees, but Girkin kicked him in the stomach.

"We have a guest tomorrow," Girkin said, grabbing Zakayev by the hair. "And . . . you . . . will . . . behave." Girkin punctuated each word with a fist to the face. Delivered to four quadrants, like a diseased prayer.

Before Zakayev passed out, he made a promise to himself. No matter who came through that door tomorrow, he was going to kill Girkin.

Now, he stirred as he heard voices in the hall and boots growing closer. They were coming again. Someone inserted a key into the ancient lock and the door creaked open.

"Get on your feet, you swine," Girkin ordered.

Girkin entered the cell first, followed by two guards, Petrov, and a stranger in black. One was armed with an AK-47 and the second with a Caucasian *ovcharka:* a mountain dog bred to fight wolves. The dog instantly sensed a fellow predator and lunged for Zakayev.

The sudden yank caught its handler off guard, and he stumbled forward.

"Get control of that animal," Petrov ordered.

The guard tugged on the *ovcharka*'s leash. "Heel, you bitch," he commanded.

Zakayev never moved. He kept his head down and waited.

He knew every inch of the cell and exactly how many steps it took from where he was sitting to the door. Zakayev heard the whisper of wood scraping the metal ring. He knew Girkin had pulled out his baton, but still he did not move.

He pictured the captain in his mind, counted the steps as he crossed from the door to where he sat on the floor. *One, two, three.*

The footfalls stopped. Girkin was standing right above him.

With a savage kick Zakayev drove his right heel into Girkin's kneecap, snapping the joint backward with a wet *pop.* Before anyone could react, he sprang to his feet.

Zakayev drove the web of his left hand into Girkin's chin, grabbed the baton with his right. In a single, fluid movement he spun the falling captain around and pulled the baton tight against his throat.

The *ovcharka* growled—a deep and ominous rumbling that was magnified by the cramped confines of the cell. Zakayev's black eyes went to the dog.

"*Sidet!*" he ordered.

His voice was low and harsh, barely a whisper, but it snapped with the authority of a bullwhip. The large dog immediately stopped growling, took a half step back, and sat down.

"Shoot him!" Petrov yelled to the guard, who raised his Kalashnikov and snicked it to fire.

"No," Gabriel said, slapping the barrel toward the floor. "He is of no use to me dead."

Silence fell over the cell, broken only by the pained wheeze coming from Girkin's constricted throat.

Zakayev eyed the tall Arab. Questions firing through his brain.

Who is this man? Do I know him?

He had a good memory for faces and after a moment of study Zakayev was sure that he had never seen the man before.

Which left only one option.

He wants something. He wants you to do something for him.

"Who are you?" he demanded.

"My name is Gabriel," the man said, switching to Arabic.

A Saudi, Zakayev thought. *From Jeddah by the sound of his voice.*

"I am going to take something from my pocket," Gabriel said calmly.

"Easy," Zakayev warned, tightening the choke hold on Girkin's neck. It was funny how fragile a man's windpipe really was.

The man nodded and retrieved two photographs from his pocket. He held the first up so Zakayev could see it.

"You know him, yes?" Gabriel asked.

Memories from long ago came rushing to Zakayev. *Hassan.*

"I *knew* him," Zakayev replied, his Arabic rusty from lack of use. "His name was Hassan Sitta. But he is dead."

"Is that what they told you?" Gabriel asked, a hint of a sad smile forming. "They told you he was dead?"

Something in the man's eyes made him less sure about what he'd been told.

What does it matter? Get to the point.

"What do you want?" Zakayev demanded.

"If Hassan is dead, then who is this?" Gabriel asked, moving the second picture in front of the first and holding it up with his left hand.

The photograph showed a man standing on a street corner. It was Hassan, no doubt about it.

"Look at the time stamp on the photo," Gabriel said, pausing to pull the newspaper from his pocket. When he had it out he placed the photograph beneath the date and held them both up. "Now look at the date on the paper."

Zakayev followed his directions.

According to the time stamp printed on the photo it was taken a month ago.

It is a trick.

Gabriel seemed to read his mind. "He is alive. The Americans have him in a secret prison. A place they call Cold Storage. I need you to get him out."

Zakayev's attention slid from the Arab, covering the rest of the men in the room.

He pulled the baton tighter into Girkin's throat, a wild plan forming in his mind.

You can kill them. Grab the rifle, maybe make it down the hall, over the fence.

Gabriel had already guessed his thoughts. "Why expose yourself to death? There is another way. Come with me and see for yourself if I am lying. What do you have to lose?"

It will get you out of here. Out of the cage.

Zakayev's eyes locked on Gabriel's. "If you are lying to me . . . ," he hissed.

In his growing rage he visualized the spot in Girkin's neck that he wanted to break. First things first. He jerked the baton up and back.

With a barely audible *pop*—the sound of a twig

breaking—it was done, and then Girkin went limp. "That is your only warning."

"Of course," Gabriel said. He produced a key, unlocked the cuff connecting the case to his wrist, and handed it to Petrov.

"Shall we go?" he asked, motioning toward the door.

Zakayev scooped the picture off the ground and followed him out. He kept a wary eye on the guards, not believing anything until he was free of their clutches. Just before stepping out of the cell, he took one final look at the room, saw every detail, from Girkin's hooked body on the floor to the shit pot in the corner.

No matter what happens. No matter what I have to do. They will never put me in another cage.

ACT I

Chapter 1

Present Day
Rothrock State Forest, Pennsylvania

The sun crept over the granite peaks and towering pines lining Rocky Ridge. Its heat was burning off the mist that blanketed the low ground, revealing a red dirt path.

Eric Steele followed the trail down the mountainside, his footfalls impossibly quiet for a man of his size.

At six foot two, he moved with a predatory grace, despite the weighted plate carrier on his chest. He kept his focus straight ahead, the muscles in his long legs working like pistons, propelling him down to the canyon where the day's heat was already collecting.

The trail flattened out until the air shimmered inside the narrow corridor. He pushed on, never breaking stride, despite the fact that each breath felt like he was on fire.

Keep moving, he told himself.

Then he passed through his personal death valley, reaching the trail that snaked up toward the opposite foothills. While others would take the opportunity to rest, Steele attacked the incline. Sweat poured down his face and over his arms as he beat the trail into submission.

At the apex of the hill, he switched the rifle to his left hand and followed the trail down the other side and through a break in the tree line. The shade offered a reprieve from the sun but nothing else. Beneath the trees the air was thick, and Steele had to fight for each breath. He checked the stopwatch on his wrist, saw that he had a chance to break the record, and forced himself to speed up.

Steele was an Alpha. A clandestine operative assigned to a unit known simply as "the Program."

The Program traced its lineage to World War II. A proud history that took America's best soldiers and forged them into weapons.

Weapons with a singular purpose.

To protect America from enemies that the president of the United States couldn't handle through either diplomacy or all out war.

That is exactly what Steele had been doing six months ago, when he was sent to Algiers after a CIA convoy was ambushed on the road to Tunis. Every one of the CIA personnel was killed except for Ali Breul—a level-one asset, an Iranian scientist who had recently developed an untraceable portable nuclear weapon.

The president wanted answers and sent Steele to Algiers to find them. But instead of the missing nuke, Steele found Nate West—his best friend and former mentor. A man who was reported to have died in a bombing.

Steele tracked West from Algiers to Spain, praying that there was still some good left in his old friend. But when West managed to smuggle the bomb into the United States, Steele had to make a choice between the man who had taught him everything and the country he loved.

Steele had put West down with a knife to the chest but took a beating for his troubles. He was taken off active status for six months, and the only way back was to finish this course.

Finally, he broke out of the trees and sprinted to the finish line, adjacent to a firing range.

"Time," a man with a stopwatch said as Steele crossed the line. "Twenty-five . . . and seven seconds. Not bad."

"Not bad?" Steele panted. He was pretty sure no one had ever beat that time.

"I mean it was fast," Demo said, his flip-flops smacking against his feet as he walked over, "but after six months off I was hoping for something, you know . . . more lively."

Demo was Steele's "keeper," a nonoperational asset who supported Eric on overseas operations. Built like a fireplug, with a perpetual tan that came from his Latin American roots, he was also Steele's best friend.

"Maybe you should give it a try—" Steele said.

"The *next* phase," Demo interrupted, holding up a clipboard and reading from the paper attached, "is the firearms proficiency portion. Any Alpha returning to duty after more than two months must be able to shoot. . . ."

Broke the record and all he can say is "not bad."

Steele shook his head and walked over to the firing line, where Demo stood fiddling with a blue shot timer.

"Frangibles are marked blue," Demo said, handing him a pair of loaded magazines.

Steele shoved the magazine with the blue tape into the holder on his belt and the second mag into the rifle.

"You need a drink of water or anything?" Demo asked.

"I'm good," Steele replied, yanking the charging handle to the rear.

"You sure?"

"Yes, Mom."

Demo shrugged and fell back into his instructor role.

"You will have three minutes to work the line. Tangos are the brown targets and friendlies are the white. *Any* marks on the white and you are an automatic no go. Any questions?"

"Let's do this," Steele said.

"Shooter ready?" Demo asked.

Steele turned his back to the kill house, the rifle up and ready.

"Stand by. . . ."

Beeeep.

Steele turned around and approached the kill house, a simple cinder block building with a roof that was vented to let out the gun smoke. He advanced toward the entrance, engaging a brown target that popped up in the window with two shots to the head. At the door Steele paused, getting his breathing under control. He turned the knob carefully. He knew that in these conditions there was no such thing as a perfect shot; too fast on the trigger was a miss and too slow meant running out of time. The only way he was going to pass the test was by finding the balance between speed and accuracy. Then he shoved the door open.

The room was furnished with a discarded couch and a pair of chairs that bore scorch marks from wayward flashbangs. As Steele stepped inside, he tripped a motion sensor that activated targets to his left—one white, one brown.

He whipped about and brought the rifle to bear, fighting the reticle that bounced across the target in time with his ragged breathing.

Get it together, he told himself.

He fired a controlled pair into the hostile target and hustled through the door behind it into an office setup. The first target popped up before he fully breached the doorway. It was a no-shoot, and Steele knew Demo had set it up to provoke a reactionary shot.

"You are going to have to try harder than that," Steele said, shoving the target to the ground.

Overhead on the catwalk he heard Demo chuckle.

A pair of targets popped up behind the desk, a no-shoot in front of a brown hostile. Steele could only see an inch of brown showing behind the white target. He knew it was all he was going to get and took the shot before moving on.

The final stage had a Post-it-size sign on the door. The writing was so small that Steele had to squint to read it. WELCOME TO DEMO AIRLINES.

Uh, okay. He was about to open the door when he realized why Demo had given him the second magazine.

The first mag was loaded with hollow points. Rounds designed to tear big holes in flesh. They were perfect for environments where you didn't have to worry about overpenetration. But not for the pressurized cabin of a commercial airliner. *Demo Airlines.*

Steele quickly changed magazines—trading the hollow points for the mag loaded up with frangibles. Bullets that were designed to disintegrate on impact.

"Dammit," Demo cursed from overhead.

Steele stepped inside and found himself looking up the center aisle of a mock airliner. To his right and left were rows of seats filled with no-shoots. A target popped up halfway to the front, a sliver of brown in the sea of white. Steele engaged, but when a second target activated, the rifle jammed after the first shot.

The problem was obvious; Demo had loaded a yellow training round into the magazine, which caused a malfunction.

"I got ya now." Demo laughed.

Steele knew his keeper was expecting him to clear the malfunction, but he had a plan of his own. He dropped the rifle and yanked his 1911 from the holster and put the last round in the target's head.

"Time," Demo announced.

Steele holstered the pistol, satisfied with his quick thinking.

His keeper climbed down from the catwalk and checked the targets.

"Oh no," Demo said, holding up the final target. "I only see one hole, looks like you missed."

"Check again," Steele said, shaking his head.

"What?"

"Check it again."

Demo frowned but did as instructed.

"Damn, you stacked both rounds in the same hole."

"All in a day's work," Steele shrugged.

"Never doubted you for a second," Demo said cheerfully.

"Uh-huh," Steele replied, grabbing his rifle.

They were walking to the parking lot when the cell phone on Demo's hip started ringing. "It's Pitts," his handler said before answering.

Major Mike Pitts was the senior duty officer for Cutlass Main, the Program's tactical operations center at the White House.

"Yeah, he passed. Even *with* the old dummy-round trick you mentioned," Demo said with a wink.

"You bastards," Steele said, angling toward the 1967 GTO parked next to Demo's Ford F-150 in the lot. He tugged his keys from his pocket and realized Demo wasn't walking beside him anymore.

"Well, Mike, I don't really consider that a softball mission," his handler was saying. "Why? Because it's winter in New Zealand, and if I wanted to spend my last thirty days in the Program freezing my ass off, I'd stay right in Pittsburgh."

Steele frowned at the mention of his handler's retirement date. He hadn't thought about it all day. Steele was happy for Demo—after all, the man had put in his time—but like everyone else in the Program, he didn't want to see him go. Finding someone who didn't take himself so seriously was hard.

"Everything cool?" Steele asked.

Demo covered the mouthpiece with his hand. "Pitts says there was an incident in New Zealand and wants us to go check it out."

"How bad?" Steele asked.

Demo waved him off, keeping his hand over the phone's mic. "Don't worry about it, mano. Let me deal with this knucklehead and I'll catch up with you later. Cool?"

"Roger that," Steele said, stuffing his gear into the trunk.

He was lowering himself in the driver's seat when he heard Demo's parting words: "I don't care how bad it is, Mike. Unless this op involves palm trees and drinks with umbrellas in them, we aren't taking it."

Chapter 2

Present Day
Bellevue, Pennsylvania

Eric Steele took his foot off the gas and brought the ’67 GTO to a stop at the light. Spring had finally come to Allegheny County, and the warmer days were a welcome change. He had forgotten how rough winters in Pittsburgh could be, but the previous six months had provided a painful refresher.

Steele shifted into neutral and let off the clutch when he got a text from his mother. Can you pick up wine?

He sighed. Going to the grocery store on Friday afternoon was the last thing he wanted to do, but Steele knew he didn't have a choice.

Sure, he texted, taking a right.

Just like he thought, the parking lot was packed. He spent five minutes avoiding runaway shopping carts and caffeinated soccer moms while looking for a spot. Near the back row a woman walking gave him a friendly wave. She was short, but did not appear to be struggling under the combined weight of the toddler in her left arm and the groceries in her right.

She pointed to the tail end of a vehicle ten feet to his front and wiggled the keys in her right hand.

God bless you, Steele thought.

The woman disappeared from view for a few moments while Steele sat listening to the *tick tick tick* of his blinker. Thankfully, he didn't have long to wait. The reverse lights came on, followed by an ungainly Ford Expedition.

Steele eased forward and, when he got a look at the parking spot, did a double take. "How in the hell did she get that in there?"

Cramped was the wrong word.

He was about to pull in when a beat-up Ford pickup swerved in front and buried itself between the yellow lines.

"Oh, hell no."

The driver hopped out and ambled around the bed. He was a big man with a shaved head and a Steelers shirt with cut-off sleeves that showed off his farmer's tan and bulging biceps.

"Damn, come on Krystal," he yelled back to someone in the cab and then flashed Steele an "eat shit" grin.

"Asshole," Steele muttered as he pulled away.

Steele found another spot and this time didn't hesitate. He cranked the wheel hard to the left, parked the car, and got out, his mind on Demo's conversation with Pitts.

What the hell could have happened in New Zealand? he wondered, tugging his shirttail so it covered the 1911 holstered at his hip.

Much like the parking lot, the aisles were packed with people eager to begin their weekend, most of them focused on the beer, which created a human traffic jam en route to his destination. He finally made it to the wine and after a quick scan found the placard that marked the section for cabernet sauvignon.

Near the bottom shelf he found the brand his mother requested, and Steele's left hand was closing around the bottle when he felt a tingle run up the back of his neck.

His right hand moved instinctively to his hip—thumb extended, fingers down: the first stage of a pistol grip. Steele got to his feet, searching for the threat, then he heard a woman's voice in the next aisle.

"We don't have the money for that," she said.

"Was I fuckin' askin' ya if we could afford it or tellin' ya to buy it?" a man replied, his voice trashy and slurred.

"Baby, we got rent due. . . ."

Her words ended with a hiss like air being let out of a tire. A sound Steele knew came from the sudden application of pain.

Unlike the rest of the shoppers, Steele knew his purpose in life. It was to protect those who couldn't protect themselves. Like so many others in his profession, he lived by a simple code, and though he wasn't a violent man by nature, Eric Steele did not have a problem using it on those who preyed upon the weak.

"What the hell did I tell you?" the man said.

Don't get involved.

Steele was a natural protector—a character trait that was both a blessing and a curse. While helping others was his calling, Steele knew that it was also his biggest weakness and a habit Demo had been trying to break him of for years.

"You can't save everyone in this line of work, mano."

Just walk away, Steele told himself.

He stood up, fingers white on the bottle, and started walking toward the front of the store. Steele could see the cash register directly in front of him. All he had to do was keep walking.

But then he heard the *pop* of an open hand hitting flesh.

Shit.

Steele stepped into the aisle and saw the woman stumble backward, her hand already on her cheek.

"What did I tell you about runnin' your *mouth*, Krystal?"

"You're hurtin' me," she said, trying to pull free.

He was an inch or two taller than Steele and out-weighed him by a good twenty pounds. Krystal looked at him, her eyes pleading as the man raised his hand again. Steele had seen that look before and knew that she wasn't asking for help; she was begging him to go away.

The problem was, Steele didn't know how.

"Hey," he said.

The man turned on Steele. He gave him a quick once-over and didn't appear to be impressed with what he saw.

"What the *fuck* you lookin' at?" he demanded.

"Everything is *fine*, mister," Krystal said.

"Did I tell you to talk to him, bitch?" he asked, pushing her into the shelf.

"You a cop?"

"No," Steele replied.

"Well then, I *suggest* you mind your business," the man warned, taking a step closer. "Boy."

Steele had located the cameras the moment he walked into the store and didn't have to look to know there were two mounted in the black glass domes on every aisle. Not that it really mattered. He could take this guy down right here and the local police couldn't touch him.

But he'd been ordered to keep a low profile. An order he'd followed for the last six months, and he didn't want to blow it this close to getting back into service.

You're committed now and he isn't backing down.

Steele shifted to his left and let the wine bottle fall in his hands so that he was holding it by the neck. He was going to take the man down right there when a tiny head appeared from behind the woman.

"Mamma? Who is that man?"

One look into the child's brown eyes was all it took. Steele had seen that look before in places like Iraq and Syria, places where children lost their innocence before their first teeth.

He felt the anger drain away.

"No one, sweet boy," his mother said.

The man was close enough now that Steele could smell the booze on his breath. He noticed the change in Steele's posture and smiled.

"That's right, little man. You don't want none of this."

Steele smiled at him.

He wanted to tell him that the only reason he was still standing was because of his son. But he knew there was more to it than that. Steele needed to get back in the field. Needed to get back to the action, and to do that, he had to play the game.

Steele closed his eyes, the realization that there was nothing he could do burning like bile in his throat.

"Just let him go," he heard Krystal say to her boyfriend.

"You heard the lady," the man said with a dismissive smile. "Hit the bricks."

Steele's hands were shaking when he paid for the wine. He stepped outside. Slammed the receipt into the trash can so hard that it rocked on its base.

He took a deep breath, holding the crisp air in his lungs, wishing he could go back inside and grab the man by the throat. But he knew that time had passed.

Steele settled inside the GTO, the engine coming to life with the turn of the key. He took a deep breath, closed his eyes as the immense weight of his chosen profession pushed down on him.

Steele had become an Alpha to help others.

He knew the only way to get back to that purpose was to do as he was told. Get back on active status. To do that he had to play by the rules, even when they meant walking away from a man who should have been waiting for an ambulance right now.

Steele shifted into gear, his eyes finding the rearview.

"You can't save everyone," he said and then backed the GTO out of the parking spot.

Chapter 3

Three Days Prior
New Zealand

Zakayev stuck his hands under the kitchen faucet, the water rinsing the blood from his skin. In the mirror he could see the couple sitting in the living room. Arms and legs tied to the dining room chairs.

He turned off the water, stripped a towel from the ring on the wall, and dried his hands. Finding the house had been the hard part. His target had done a hell of a job making sure nothing was in his name. Hiding his very existence by purchasing the property through various shell companies.

But Zakayev was a patient man. He had to be to survive Black Dolphin.

Besides, with the right amount of money, you could find anything.

Once he'd located the house, getting inside was easier than he could have ever imagined. Zakayev and his men had come at three in the morning.

The witching hour.

He'd cut the security alarm first and then used a bump key to open the door. Once inside it was as easy as walking to the back bedroom where Bo Nolan and his wife slept soundly on their bed.

Zakayev dropped the towel on the floor, his hand rising unbidden to the back of his head. He fingertipped the fresh scar, his mind drifting back to Black Dolphin.

Aleksandr Zakayev remembered getting into the helicopter and the slovenly Chinese man in a rumpled suit who leaned forward with an alcohol swab.

"This is Chin," Gabriel said. "He is a doctor."

"Your arm, please," Chin said.

Zakayev watched the man wipe the alcohol swab over his bicep. He produced a syringe from his jacket and popped the cap.

"This will help you sleep."

Zakayev turned to the window and watched Black Dolphin shrink as the helo gained altitude. He felt the prick of the needle, and by the time the prison was the size of a postage stamp Zakayev was unconscious.

When he came to, he was lying in a dim room. A silk sheet was draped across his torso, soft as an angel's breath. His mouth was dry and his tongue fat, like he had just come out of the desert.

"Water," Zakayev croaked.

A woman's face appeared above him. "Call the doctor," she said.

She helped Zakayev sit up and then took a pink cup from the bedside table and held the straw to his lips. The water was ice cold and stung the back of his throat, but it was the best thing he had ever tasted. He sucked greedily at the straw, quickly draining the entire cup.

"More," he gasped.

Gabriel swept into the room and pulled the blinds open. "We weren't sure you were going to make it."

The sunlight poured into the room, and Zakayev shielded his eyes from the glare.

"Where am I?" he asked, his voice barely over a whisper.

"Mersin," Gabriel replied.

Turkey? How long have I been out?

"You have been asleep for five days," Dr. Chin

added, walking into the room with a cigarette stuffed in the corner of his fat lips. He was followed by a nurse and a man in a dark suit. Zakayev's eye was drawn to a white scar that hooked from the corner of the man's mouth down to his chin.

"You had a high fever and a respectable infection," Chin added.

Zakayev's eyes never left the man in the suit.

He's a killer.

"But now you are healthy," Gabriel interjected.

"Why did you come for *me*?" Zakayev asked.

"Because you are the *only* one Sitta trusts. The only one he will talk to," Gabriel said, walking over to the bed. He gave Zakayev a once-over, grimacing like he wasn't sure this man in the hospital bed was the right guy for the job.

"What is that?" Zakayev asked as Dr. Chin walked over to the cart and pulled on a pair of latex gloves.

"You are going to let Dr. Chin implant an RF tracker in your skull," Gabriel replied.

The man in the black suit was on the move, and Zakayev tracked him out of the corner of his eyes. He read the situation: Gabriel at the foot of the bed, Dr. Chin arranging his surgical tools, and the man with the scar flanking him. Zakayev didn't like the way things were adding up.

"And if I refuse?"

The man in the suit was directly behind him now. Zakayev heard the tug of metal clearing leather, followed by the *snick* of a safety being disengaged.

"I will have to find someone else to get Hassan out of prison," Gabriel began. "But that is not your problem. Your problem is that you must decide to either allow Dr. Chin to implant the device . . ."

"Or?"

"Or my friend here implants a bullet in the back of your skull and then drops your body in a vat of acid," Gabriel said, picking a piece of lint off his pant leg.

"Not much of a choice," Zakayev said.

Let them put their tracker in, a voice in his head said. *Make them think that they can trust you. Then when the time is right, kill them.*

"Fine," Zakayev finally said. "Do it."

He closed his eyes, waiting for more medical savagery. He remembered an incident in Syria. Zakayev had seen a grenade explode behind one of his fighters. The shrapnel pierced the skull, but the man didn't notice he'd been hit until Zakayev pulled him to the ground and pressed a bandage to the wound.

The fighter said he never felt a thing.

Later one of the doctors told Zakayev that there weren't any nerve endings in the back of the head.

Maybe, Zakayev thought, *I won't notice when Dr. Chin inserts the implant.*

He realized that was a lie the moment the drill bit ripped into his skull. The pain was intense. It felt as if he'd been struck by a bolt of lightning. The current spread from the top of his head down to his toes. His muscles tensed and his body started to shake, but he refused to cry out. He saw the nurse insert a dot of metal into an oversize syringe and slip out of sight.

Then the procedure was over and Dr. Chin was standing in front of him. The man's mouth was moving, but Zakayev couldn't hear the words.

Shit, the infernal thing made me deaf.

His hearing returned after a few seconds.

"Try not to touch it too much," Chin was saying. "They are temperamental."

"Temperamental?" Zakayev gasped. "What the hell does that mean?"

Chin brought his hands together and formed them into a ball. "Temperamental," he repeated, pantomiming an explosion. "You understand, yes?"

"If you do your job, you will have nothing to worry about," Gabriel assured him.

Now Zakayev reached for the back of his head again, then stopped himself in time. His hands were clean.

He was ready to finish off the torture. He had been patient, but now he would extract the information he needed.

He entered the dining room and turned his attention to the figures zip-tied to the metal-legged chairs. The man was leaning so far forward that the only things holding him in the chair were the zip ties around his arms and legs. Zakayev guessed he was in his mid-sixties, but after the beating he'd suffered, he looked much older. Zakayev walked over, flicked open the switchblade he took from his pocket, and placed the tip against the man's chin. He slowly increased the pressure until the man raised his head.

"Well?" Zakayev asked.

The man opened his mouth and a stream of blood rolled off his lips and splattered on the floor between his feet. Defiance mixed with pain flared in his eyes as he looked up.

"Fuck you," the man replied.

Zakayev shrugged. "Very well."

He turned his attention to the woman. Her name was Emily. She was much younger than Nolan with jet-black hair, a thin nose, and pretty lips, hidden by the strip of tape over her mouth.

"Your wife is very beautiful," he began. "Or, should I say, was very beautiful."

She tried to say something, but all that came out was a series of vowel sounds.

He placed the flat of the blade against her skin and traced it down her shoulder, beneath the cloth. Turning his hand so the cutting edge was against the fabric, he deftly sliced her shirt from top to bottom. The fabric parted, revealing a lace bra.

"What do you think, Yuri?" he asked the man next to Nolan.

"Very nice," he said with a lecherous smile.

"I haven't touched a woman in almost three years." He took his time cutting her bra straps. He pulled the bra free and stepped to one side so Bo Nolan could watch him run his hands over his wife's bare breasts. How curious, he thought, that the nipples would harden despite her furious thrashing.

"When I was in Black Dolphin, they put me in the hole. Do you know what that is?"

Nolan fought against his bonds, flexing his arms and trying to snap the chair with brute strength. When he didn't answer, Yuri took a handful of salt from the table.

"He asked you a question," he said, shoving the salt into the man's wounds.

"Fuuuck!" Nolan screamed. "Solitary. They put you in solitary."

"They called it the pit. For the first two months there was no light, no sound, just you and the darkness." Zakayev grabbed two handfuls of Emily's breasts and grinned at Nolan.

"A man has nothing to do but think about the terrible things he would do if he got out."

"I am going to kill you, do you hear me?"

Zakayev dismissed the man's threat with a *tsk* and walked back to the fireplace.

"No, you won't," he said, grabbing a poker and pulling it from the coals. The white-hot tip shimmered and popped in the air. "You are a strong man, but everyone tells me what I want to know in the end. Do you know why?" Zakayev asked, walking over to Emily.

"Don't do this," Nolan said.

"He asked you a question," Yuri repeated, roughly rubbing another handful of salt against the bleeding man's face.

"Whyyyy?" he begged.

"Because no matter how tough the man is, there is always something in his life that makes him weak."

Zakayev ripped the tape from Emily's mouth.

"Let us see how much he loves you."

"Don't—don't do this," Nolan begged.

Zakayev was lost in the terror he saw in the woman's eyes. Her powerlessness infected him like morphine.

Slowly he touched the tip of the poker to her cheek. The skin sizzled and blistered, filling the room with the smell of burning flesh. Zakayev dragged the poker lazily toward her ear and watched the skin open up only to be cauterized a moment later by the superheated iron.

Emily screamed, her mouth opening wider and wider until it appeared she was trying to swallow the room. Her scream came from a primal place, sounding more like an animal than a human.

"Stop! Stop, I'll tell you," Nolan screamed.

But Zakayev didn't stop.

He ran the poker across her forehead and into her hair. "Such a shame," he said dreamily. "All that beauty, corrupted by—"

"I sent the package to America. I can give you the address."

Now that he had broken his silence, Nolan couldn't talk fast enough. His words spilled out like water from a broken dam, an unrelenting rush of classified names, places, and code words.

It was a treasure trove of information, but Zakayev didn't care about any of that.

"The man you sent it to. What was his name?"

A strange look came into his eyes. "I . . . I don't know."

Zakayev turned on his heel and swung the poker in a tight arc toward Nolan's head. Fed by oxygen as it whistled through the air, the tip glowed white, and when it struck Nolan in the side of the head, the blow sent a shower of sparks across the floor. Zakayev grabbed him by the throat before his momentum tipped over the chair and held the poker against the flesh of his exposed arm.

"Look at her face when you think about lying. I can make her pain last forever."

And in the end, like they all did, the old man gave up what he wanted.

"His name is Eric Steele."

Chapter 4

Present Day
Pittsburgh, Pennsylvania

As Eric Steele crossed the Fleming Park Bridge, the sun's rays glinted off the Ohio River below. Neville Island was a two-mile strip of land that lay in the middle of the river. Once a vital part of the local economy, it was now a scrapyard. Block after block of abandoned warehouses, overgrown lots. A rusted legacy to Pittsburgh's past, barely a stone's throw from the city center.

It was also Steele's home.

According to his grandfather, Fred, it hadn't always been this way.

"Did you know that they used to call that ol' scrap heap the 'Market Basket of Pittsburgh'?"

"No, sir," young Eric had answered.

"Farmers said the soil was so rich that they could plant a clothespin and it would grow. The strawberries and asparagus they grew were featured at most four-star hotels along the Eastern Seaboard."

"What happened?"

"Times changed, and the farmers couldn't keep up. The fields were torn up, and developers started building factories. You know when I was in the Pacific, our LSTs—"

"LSTs?" Steele had asked.

"That was the name of the boats we used during the landing at Guadalcanal. Do you know who made them?"

"No, sir."

"Dravo Corporation of Neville Island, PA."

His grandfather had rarely talked about World War II, but when he did, Eric got the feeling that he had left a part of himself behind. Steele wouldn't know what that feeling was like until he returned home from his first deployment to Afghanistan. He seemed to belong to all the violence he left behind rather than to the calm streets of his childhood.

But when his financial adviser told him that the state

was selling properties on Neville Island for pennies on the dollar, he couldn't pass up a chance to own a piece of history.

The scenery wasn't anything to write home about, but it had everything Steele needed. He pulled the GTO onto the access road and used the remote clipped to the visor to open a reinforced security gate. As Steele wheeled through, the engine's guttural rumble echoed off the bricks and abandoned spools of wire strewn atop the cobblestones.

When he reached the river, Steele turned left. The headlights played over a red brick building with DRAVO CORP written in faded white letters. By the time he turned the corner, the steel rollup door was open and the white light from the garage splayed over the scene of urban desolation.

Eric backed the muscle car in, killed the engine, and savored the smells that filled the garage. They reminded him of his childhood, before his father left.

Hank Steele was a soldier just like Fred. But instead of joining the marines, he went into the army and became a Green Beret. He deployed a great deal, and Eric treasured any time he got to spend with him.

In particular, his fondest memories were the nights they spent in the garage. Hank would teach him to rebuild a carburetor or adjust the timing of an engine.

A week before Hank's final deployment, father and son purchased a rusted-out GTO and hauled it back to their garage.

It was going to be their project, and Hank told his son that he wanted the rust gone by the time he got back. Every night after finishing his homework, Steele went out to the garage. He was almost done with the rear quarter panel the night his mom came outside, her eyes red-rimmed and wet.

"Your father . . ."

Steele brushed the memories aside. All this R&R was making him soft. He snatched the wine off the floorboard and walked inside.

The transformation of the warehouse was a testament to the fact that Steele couldn't sit still. The first time he'd inspected the building it was so filthy even the bums stayed away. But Steele was smitten.

He hired a demolition crew to gut it, remove the faulty wiring and asbestos. Another crew used pressure washers to kill the black mold and blast a quarter century of pigeon shit off the roof and facade.

When that was done, Steele hired security contractors to install cameras, motion sensors, and Krieger level-four blast doors capable of withstanding ballistic, thermal, and explosive breaches.

Steele did the rest of the work by himself. He installed the hardwood flooring, hung cabinets in the kitchen, and added marble countertops and appliances. It took four months, but now he finally had a home.

In the kitchen he lit the Viking grill and went to the refrigerator for an ice-cold Yuengling. He lifted out the steaks he'd been marinating since morning. He had just laid the first one on the grill when the panel on the wall rang.

"Answer," Steele said, his hands dripping with marinade.

His mother's face appeared on the screen in the center of the panel.

"Mom, I thought we talked about you driving and FaceTiming," he said.

"Eric, I'm not driving. I am *sitting* at a stoplight," she said, brushing him off.

A curt honk drew her attention to the rearview. "Oh, the light has changed, thank you," she said, hitting the gas and waving at the car behind her. "I'd planned to get the wine, but then a courier stopped at the house as I was pulling out. He had a package for you."

"For me?" Steele asked, not sure if he'd heard her right.

"Yep."

How is that possible?

The moment an Alpha was brought into the Program, every record of their former life was deleted. The Program had even helped Steele move the deed of his mother's house under the cover of an LLC that he'd set up so that he couldn't be tracked through her.

"Who is it from?"

A shadow passed over the screen and he knew she was entering the Squirrel Hill Tunnel. The audio and video began to distort from the interference.

"It's . . . from . . . alt . . . illings."

"You are cutting out. Text the name," Steele said.

The call froze, and the screen went black with the words CALL DROPPED in the center.

Steele was about to try and call her back when a text bubble popped up:

WALTER BILLINGS

Alarmed, Steele immediately walked into the entryway and stopped next to a metal table with mosaic panels on top. He wasn't looking for a table when his girlfriend, Meg Harden, had dragged him to an estate sale. But when the middle-aged lady running it had shown him the hidden compartment beneath the panels, he couldn't resist.

He hinged it open, revealing two rows of ammo boxes and a stack of preloaded Wilson Combat Hi Capacity mags. Steele dropped one in the 1911 and racked the slide. The ejector flipped the chambered round skyward, and he snatched it out of the air without even looking.

Walter Billings was an alias. It belonged to Bo Nolan, a man Steele had been tracking for the last seven years. He wasn't sure how Nolan had found his mother's address. Right now it didn't matter. What did matter was that Steele didn't believe in coincidences.

He believed in being prepared.

Which was why he was switching to the 9 mm Cor Bon Hollow Points.

The Cor Bons were man stoppers. While they wouldn't punch through body armor, they were guaranteed to put a man on his ass long enough for Steele to finish him with a headshot. The Hi Cap magazines held two rounds more than his everyday carry mags.

If Nolan was sending him a package, there was a chance that he wanted to meet up. If that was the case, Steele wanted to make sure he had plenty of ammo when he came face-to-face with Nolan—the last man to see his father alive.

Chapter 5

Present Day
Georgetown

Chief of Staff Ted Lansky was many things, but a morning person was not one of them. When his alarm clock woke him up at 0500, Lansky's first thought was to hit ignore and go back to sleep. But he knew that wasn't an option.

Lansky rolled over, eyes still heavy from sleep, and plucked the phone from the bedside charger. He ran his thumb over the screen, blinked his eyes into focus, and read the text he'd just received.

Volta Park 0530

Lansky thumbed his reply and then got out of bed with a "dammit." A career in the clandestine service had taken its toll, especially on his knees, and as he walked to the bathroom his gait was stiff and slow. He stepped into the shower and turned the cold water knob all the way to the left before he could talk himself out of it.

The showerhead coughed, then sprayed him in the face. The cold water cleared his mind faster than a shot of espresso.

Lansky had assumed the days of waking up before the sun to meet an off-the-books asset had ended when he left the CIA. But six months after suffering a stroke at the State of the Union address, President Denton Cole was forced to step down and Lansky's boss, Vice President John Rockford, became the acting president of the United States, so that was exactly what he was doing.

Lansky dressed quickly, pulling on a pair of black shorts, a gray T-shirt, and Brooks running shoes, and then headed for the stairs. On the first floor of his town house, the day's first light had found its way through a crack in the blinds and was slowly advancing across the den. The interior of the brownstone had come furnished with a couch, a scuffed coffee table, and a recliner that was still covered in shipping plastic.

Lansky hadn't seen the need to add anything else. Especially since the only rooms he used with any regularity were all upstairs. In the den, the only object that looked lived in was the worn go bag he passed on the way out the door.

The bag was a holdover from a past life. A testament to the saying: "Once a spy, always a spy."

Out in the street, Lansky set off on a labored trot. A mile and a half later, when his body had finally warmed up, he jogged into Volta Park. Lansky followed the path through the trees and slowed to a walk fifteen yards shy of the tennis courts.

He found Major Mike Pitts sitting on the metal bench below the sign for court number two. The first time they had met was two weeks after former president Cole's stroke. Lansky was summoned to the hospital, where he found Cole propped up in his bed surrounded by two men he'd never seen before.

Pitts looked up as he approached. "Back when I was in Ranger Battalion, I ran five miles as warm-up," he said with a grimace. "Now it damn near cripples me."

"Serves you right for waking me up at 0500," Lansky said with a smile. "What's the problem?"

"It's Bo Nolan," Pitts replied, stomping his knee into the graphite prosthetic and then rising to his feet.

"What about him?" Lansky asked.

He was used to the doom and gloom that came with intelligence briefings. In the CIA, if the sky wasn't falling, the officers considered it a boring day.

Major Mike Pitts didn't ruffle easily, though. Calmly he said, "Nolan was murdered in New Zealand two nights ago."

"Shit," Lansky cursed. "Where did you get this intel?"

"I have my sources," Pitts said, pulling out his cell phone. "These pictures are from the crime scene. He and his wife were tortured."

The pictures were graphic, but nothing Lansky hadn't seen before. He read the damaged bodies like a script and knew that the horrors committed on Nolan's wife were to get him to talk. Lansky wasn't sure what information the killers were after until he saw the last picture.

In the photo, Nolan was lying on his side, index finger pointed at two words scrawled in his own blood: COLD STORAGE.

"This is bad," Lansky said.

"No sir, bad is your girlfriend missing her period. *This*"—Pitts pointed at the photo—"is a lit match in a room full of dynamite."

On any list of America's dirty secrets, this one would

be near the top. Cold Storage was a decommissioned nuclear icebreaker that had been converted into an illegal black site prison. Manned by a small crew of contracted sailors and elite guards who were rotated out every six months, Cold Storage stayed in international waters, where it was free from international law. And it housed the worst terrorists on the face of the planet. Men and women who were too dangerous for the general population at Guantánamo Bay.

"How would Nolan know about this?" Lansky asked.

"First question I asked," Pitts said. "I ran everything we had on Nolan and Cold Storage through the system, looking for any convergence."

"And?"

"It's a stretch."

"Tell me," Lansky said.

"In the early '90s Nolan was loaned out to British Intelligence. It was a joint operation with the CIA. They wanted him to look into a Russian training camp known as 722."

"I vaguely remember Camp 722," Lansky said. "Something about the KGB turning kids into supersoldiers or something."

"It was like a sick version of the Program," Pitts replied. "We have run across a few graduates in the last couple of years. The most recent was Hassan Sitta."

Lansky stiffened at that name. "The guy behind the attempted bombing attack in Mecca?"

"Yep." Pitts nodded. "Seems we haven't heard the last of Operation Archangel."

The first time Lansky had heard about Operation Archangel was after an NSA employee on the cyber security team located a Trojan virus during a routine mainframe defrag. The virus was traced back to Tel Aviv and the national intelligence agency of Israel, more commonly known as Mossad.

Lansky immediately authorized Cutlass Main—the Program's operation center at the White House—to use whatever means necessary to find out how deep the hack had gone. During the investigation, the techs stumbled across Operation Archangel—a Mossad intelligence operation focused on Saudi prince Faisal Badr.

Prince Badr was in charge of Saudi Arabia's intelligence service, a job that many thought marked him as the next crown prince. The king had other thoughts, and when Badr's brother, the pro-Western Mohammed bin Salman, was chosen, he was stunned. Badr hated everything about his brother, from his cozy position with Israel and the United States to his lax view of

Islam. According to the Mossad file, Prince Badr decided he had to act.

He was going to kill the crown prince.

The man Badr chose to head up the operation was
his most trusted associate. The Israelis tried to identify
the operative, but the only intel they had come up with
was his code name—Gabriel.

The messenger.

The man Gabriel hired to kill the crown prince, on
the other hand, was well known. He was a Palestinian
radical named Hassan Sitta.

Sitta came up with a bold plan: plant a bomb beneath
the Sacred Mosque in Mecca and detonate it during the
crown prince's visit.

Mossad traced the money to a Hezbollah offshoot
with close ties to Iran. But instead of acting on the intelligence, the Israeli government did nothing. Lansky
had no choice but to take the intel to President Rockford, who dispatched an Alpha team to grab Sitta without notifying Israel.

"Hassan was the last person sent to Cold Storage,"
Pitts said.

"And he still isn't talking?" Lansky asked.

"Not a word, and we still haven't found the bomb."

"I want an Alpha put on standby until we figure this
thing out," Lansky ordered.

"Done, chief," the man replied.

"And Pitts, we need to keep this quiet. We don't want either the Israelis or the Saudis finding out that we have Sitta in custody—or that we haven't found the bomb."

Chapter 6

Steele had forgotten all about the steaks until he smelled them burning. He rushed back into the kitchen, grabbed the tongs from the counter, and flipped them. They were burned black around the edges but still salvageable.

Then he turned back to the business at hand. He grabbed his cell phone from the counter and activated the encryption package. While he waited for it to load, his thoughts drifted to the man he'd grown up calling Uncle Bo.

The bond between Nolan and Hank Steele went far beyond the fact that they were both Green Berets. They were also best friends. Eric couldn't remember a single BBQ or holiday that Uncle Bo didn't spend at the Steele house.

In fact, a few days before his dad and Nolan were set to go on their final "trip" together—a word Eric would later learn was their code for a military deployment—they had grilled burgers and brats on his dad's rusted Weber. Little did Eric realize it would be the last time he saw his father.

The next time Steele saw Bo was a year after his father's disappearance. Six months after the U.S. Army switched Hank Steele's status from Missing in Action to Presumed Killed in Action. Steele had been walking home, head ducked into his jacket to ward off the cold air whipping through the leafless trees, when a rusted pickup pulled to the curb.

The man barely resembled the Uncle Bo he knew so well. He shuffled out of the cab with the aid of a cane and as he limped over to the sidewalk, Steele saw that his hair was shaggy and streaked with gray. But the biggest change was in his eyes. They were sunken and never stopped moving.

The eyes of a man being hunted.

Eric begged Uncle Bo to come home and see his mother, but Nolan refused.

"I ain't exactly welcome at your house, partner."

"What? Why, Uncle Bo?"

Nolan tried to lower himself into a crouch but failed with a painful grimace.

"No matter what you hear, your father *loves* you, Eric."

"I know, Uncle Bo. Do you . . . do you know when he is going to come home?"

"Goddammit," Nolan whispered, covering his face. His shoulders shook, and if Nolan had been any other man, Eric would have thought he was crying. But Green Berets didn't cry. His dad had told him that.

Nolan grabbed his shoulder and pulled him close. Eric could feel his stomach muscles tighten. The few leaked tears on Uncle Bo's face told him that he had been crying.

Did I say something wrong?

"I want you to listen to me, partner. You might hear some terrible things about Uncle Bo, but I want you to know that I am going to bring your daddy home. I promise you that."

"I didn't mean to make you sad."

"You didn't do anything wrong. Now, I need you to go on home. Don't tell anyone that you saw me."

Steele ran home as fast as he could. He wanted to keep his promise, but at the same time he could see how bad his mother was hurting. Besides losing her husband, she'd had to take a second job just to keep the house.

That night when his mom walked in the door, after working the second shift at Mona's, Eric was waiting.

"Mom, guess what?"

He could tell that she'd had a rough day. She smelled of cigarettes and grease, the front of her apron was stained and her hair frizzy from the heat of the diner. He followed her into the den, where she dropped onto the couch and kicked her feet up on the table.

"What is it, my baby boy?" she asked with a weary smile.

"I saw Uncle Bo today."

The smile vanished.

"What did you say?" she asked, unfolding abruptly and sitting up.

Eric tried to finish the story but stopped when his mother's countenance shifted from anger to outright hatred. She was pissed, which only confused Eric more.

"I asked him to come over, but he said—"

"What did that son of a bitch say?" she said.

"He said you won't let him."

It was the first time he had ever heard her curse, and it shocked him into silence.

But she wasn't done yet. She grabbed him by the shoulders, so hard her fingernails threatened to punch through his skin.

"I want you to listen to me, Eric. I've told Bo Nolan

that he can come over anytime he wants. Do you know why he won't?"

"No, ma'am."

"Because he knows that as soon as he steps foot in this house, I am going to blow him back outside with your daddy's shotgun. Bo Nolan is *not* your friend or your father's friend."

"What?" Eric said, his mind reeling. "Why, Mom?"

"Because he is the reason your father is never coming home."

Whenever Steele remembered that awful night, he could feel his skin burn cold. Trying to get rid of that feeling altogether, he punched out Demo's number on his phone.

"What's up, mano?" Demo answered.

"I'm sitting on a situation here," Steele said.

When Steele finished bringing his keeper up to speed, the line went silent.

Finally, Demo spoke. "Where is your mom right now?" he demanded.

Steele knew that tone very well but had never heard it outside of an Alpha operation. Why was Demo asking about his mother?

"She is on her way over. What's wrong?"

"Did she call you from her cell?"

"Yes . . ."

"Good. Stand by," Demo said.

Steele heard the sound of keystrokes on the other end of the line.

"Dude, what are you doing?" he asked.

"I'm pinging her phone," Demo said, like it was the most natural thing in the world.

"Demo, you have a tracker on my mom's phone?" Steele asked in disbelief.

"Yeah, I've got one on yours too," his keeper responded.

"I am pretty sure that it is illegal to track a private citizen's phone," Steele said, but by now he was laughing.

"According to the Supreme Court the federal government can track a phone without a warrant when there is reasonable suspicion that the citizen is in imminent danger of bodily harm."

Steele felt the cold grip of fear grab the back of his neck.

Imminent danger of bodily harm?

"She is half a mile out from you." Demo sighed.

"You aren't telling me something. Why is my mom in imminent danger of bodily harm?"

"You remember the guy I was telling you about in Greece, the one they found three months ago?"

"Yeah, your buddy from MI6 sent you the intel, said the guy had been tortured and wanted you to keep an ear out."

"That's the one. Turned out he was a former spook who had been disavowed."

"Okay. What does that have to do with my mother?"

"Last night a report came in from New Zealand. The authorities found two bodies, a male and a female, in a burned-up house. The preliminary autopsy says he was tortured. Eric, they just identified the body."

The screen on the wall blinked to life, and the gate camera showed a brand-new Audi pulling up. It was his mother's car, the one he had bought for her.

"Anyone we know?" Steele asked, opening the gate from the panel.

"It was Bo Nolan."

He had just been thinking about Uncle Bo. "Say that again," Steele said, frozen in place.

"Someone tortured Nolan to death. I'm not saying this is connected to you, but what are the odds that you get a package from a dead guy the day after he is tortured to death?"

"I'm hearing you," Steele said.

"I can send a team to get you guys. Have you in a safehouse up in the mountains in an hour."

It was the smart move, but Steele hesitated. He had

never directly lied to his mother and didn't want to start now. He knew that if a blacked-out helicopter landed at his house and whisked them off to the mountains, his mother would have questions.

Questions that Steele wasn't in a position to answer.

"Send me the file. I don't want to spook my mom unless I know there is a problem."

"You sure about that?" Demo asked.

He wasn't.

"I'm going to let it play out," Steele said a moment later.

"Roger that."

Steele pulled the steaks off the grill—not too bad— and shoved the phone back in his pocket. He remained in place, standing in the silence of the kitchen, wondering if he'd made the right choice. He had learned long ago that there was no such thing as a safe answer. But on the way to unlock the back door, Steele wondered if he'd just made a mistake.

Chapter 7

Steele knew the risks that came with being an Alpha. Everyone in the Program did. It was why they trained so hard for operations. But threats like this weren't supposed to follow you home to the States.

He brushed the thought out of his mind and opened the door. Outside, Steele heard his mother slam a car door. She was humming to herself and he recognized Nina Simone's "Feeling Good."

It was one of her favorites. The one she listened to when she was in a great mood.

Susan Steele came around the corner, and her face stretched into a smile when she saw her son. The grin was infectious, and Eric opened his arms wide for a hug.

His mother hadn't had the easiest life, but you could

never tell by looking at her. She was blessed with a timeless beauty, which made it difficult to guess her real age. The time she'd invested with her personal trainer, plus her fresh Bahamian tan, didn't hurt.

"There's my baby boy," she said.

"Mom, it's good to see you," he said, wrapping his arms around her, his eyes drifting to her purse.

She caught his glance and Steele saw the stern look, the same one he'd gotten when he was a kid and tried to pull something over on his mom.

"You hungry?" he asked, trying to divert her attention.

"Starving," she said.

Steele was pleasantly surprised that the steaks turned out as well as they did. He typically liked his medium rare, but considering everything that had happened today he was content with well done.

"So how was the cruise?" he asked, eyeing her purse again, which she had left in the kitchen.

"Wonderful," his mother replied. "You know," she said, picking up the glass of wine he had poured for her, "you should take Meg on a cruise."

Here we go, Steele thought.

"Women like that don't come around very often. She's a keeper, and I would hate to see you lose her. She's not like some of the others."

"Mom, please," Steele said, gathering the plates and carrying them into the kitchen. His mother wasn't subtle about the fact that she wanted him to settle down, and ever since he'd introduced her to Meg, her *suggestions* had become less subtle.

"Eric, all I'm saying is that you aren't getting any younger."

"Uh-huh."

"Eric, what is going on?"

"What do you mean?" he asked, feigning surprise.

"You have been staring at my purse since I got here."

"I thought that—"

"Eric Steele," she said, cutting him off.

Dammit. Steele winced. *You blew it.*

It was the same tone she'd used on him growing up, the one that told him she was serious, and he knew without looking that she had her hands on her hips.

"Yes, ma'am?"

"You want to tell me the truth?"

Steele shut off the water and slowly turned around to find his mother standing just as he'd imagined.

"I need to see that package," he said.

Susan opened her purse and pulled it out.

The package was the size of a book and wrapped in brown paper, with Steele's name written in bold black letters. According to the postmark the package had been mailed in Wellington, New Zealand, two weeks prior.

Steele held it up to the light. He inspected the top and bottom first, looking for any hints of wires or subtle bulges that would signal any type of device. Next, he checked the tape along the seams to see if it had been opened. In the center of the front edge he found a single hair. It had been placed vertically over the seam and then taped over.

"What are you looking at?" his mother asked.

Steele answered without thinking. "You see that hair?" he asked, lowering the parcel so his mother could see.

"Yes," she said.

"It's old school."

"Looks like a hair to me," she replied.

Steele smiled. "That's the point. You see, I looked this up. During the seventeenth century more commoners were learning how to read and write, and they started sending letters. This was prior to envelopes that were sealed with glue. Before long people realized that the postmen were reading their letters before delivering them."

"Really?" Susan asked indignantly.

"Yeah." Steele laughed. "I mean, what else did they have to do?"

"Their job, maybe?"

"Long story short, they developed a tamperproof wax that they would stick on the letter and seal it with specially designed rings." Steele pantomimed, stamping his ring finger down on the package. "That way you could tell if anyone opened it."

"Fascinating story, Eric, but you still haven't answered my question. What is going on?"

"Mom, you remember when I said that I worked for an import-export company?" Steele said, tugging the preloaded go bag from the compartment and dropping it on the floor.

"Go on."

"Well, I, ah—"

Before he could finish his sentence, Steele was interrupted by the alarm panel on the wall.

"Perimeter breach Zone One. Perimeter breach Zone One," the digital voice warned.

The monitor flashed to life, filling the room with the last sound he ever expected to hear in the States—the unmistakable shriek of an RPG-7 leaving its launcher.

Chapter 8

Steele turned to the monitor in time to see the RPG flash past the camera, the rocket motor leaving a white trail behind it. As the warhead hit the gate and exploded, the fireball flared in the camera view.

The detonation rang like distant thunder. Vibrating the warehouse walls and knocking plaster loose from the ceiling. The overhead lights flickered, then came back on. They were barely able to cut through the shroud of dust hanging in the air.

Steele coughed and yelled, "Master arm."

"Arming," the panel answered, tripping the door locks with a resounding *thunk*. "Doors and windows secure. Motion sensors armed."

"Lockdown," Steele ordered. Dismounting the security monitor from the wall, he grabbed his mother by the hand and pulled her through the kitchen and into the living room.

"Eric, wha—?"

He hurried her into the den. He noticed his mother's breathing was fast and her eyes wide. He knew she was hyperventilating.

"Mom, look at me." Her eyes danced, and his big hand gently grabbed her face. "Look at my eyes and breathe."

She took a deep breath and slowly exhaled. She was tough, but she hadn't ever encountered anything like this. Steele had to ignore the rage that came from seeing his mother this way.

He had lost count of how many men had tried to kill him. He had been shot, stabbed, blown up, and almost drowned, but his training had always kept him alive. Yet he was totally unprepared for how to keep his mother calm when men were trying to kill him.

"Wh-what is happening? I-I can't stop shaking . . . ," she stuttered.

"There are men out there who are trying to get that package," Steele explained patiently. "You are shaking because your body is dumping adrenaline into your blood, getting you ready to run."

"What do we do?"

"Just look at me. I'm here, and I am not going to let

them hurt you. Just look in my eyes and breathe like I am."

He repeated the process, a deep inhalation followed by a slow exhale.

"Just breathe. You are in control."

He didn't have time to coach her. He set the monitor on the hardwood floor and examined what was happening outside.

The security camera for the front gate had been blown out in the explosion, and he toggled over to the secondary camera in time to watch a dump truck roar through the smoke that hung over the driveway and ram his five-thousand-dollar gate.

The gate was made of reinforced iron composite. Steel support pillars were buried under four feet of concrete. It was rated to withstand three thousand pounds, and even after the blast of the RPG, the dump truck almost didn't make it through.

The impact crumpled the front end, sending a shower of sparks cascading over the hood. The dump truck buckled the gate but didn't rip it from its moorings. As a cloud of steam rushed up from the injured engine block, it rolled a few feet and came to a halt.

Two vans made it through the breach, and Steele saw them skid to a stop, side cargo doors already open. Two teams of assailants dressed in black BDUs and ballistic vests jumped from the vehicles and angled toward the warehouse.

In the den, Steele pressed on the wall right beside the shelf holding his military warfare books, and a hinged compartment clicked open. Inside was a palm reader. He pressed his hand against it and the wall safe clicked open. His memory touched upon the class on dealing with assets in stressful situations. He could hear the instructor's voice: "Give them something to do. It takes their mind off the now."

"Take this, Mom," he said, handing her the monitor. He explained how the buttons worked. Then he pulled a ballistic vest from the vault.

"Duck your head and tell me what they are doing."

She complied, allowing him to slide her head through the opening and secure the Velcro straps that closed the vest around her chest. "I see them," she said, her voice oddly choked.

"How many?"

"One, three, five," she counted, growing more alarmed. "Eight, I see eight men in black. I think they are splitting up, Eric."

Simo breach.

"They are going to hit the front and back doors at the same time."

Steele took out a second vest. This one was his. He

had worn it in Algiers, and the cloth was faded and stained with sweat and dried blood. He shrugged it across his shoulders and pulled it tight. The final piece of kit was a magazine-fed shotgun.

He'd been so impressed the first time he shot the FosTech Origin 12 that he'd bought one for home defense. Not only was the recoil manageable, but it was also deadly accurate at close range. The true selling point for Steele, though, was that it was magazine fed, which allowed him to reload just as quickly as he could with a rifle.

Steele had two preloaded magazines with rounds he'd borrowed from the Program's R & D department. They were hypervelocity sabot rounds capable of penetrating any body armor on the market.

Steele inserted the magazine and pulled the charging handle to the rear. The bolt carrier raced forward, stripped the slug from the magazine, and thunked it into the chamber.

"The first team is coming toward the back door." Her voice was gaining more confidence. The instructor had been right about that role advice.

"Hit the two buttons on top at the same time. It will show both cameras," he instructed. "Can you do that?"

The image shifted, showing the front and back doors.

Her breathing had slowed to almost normal, but her hands were still shaking because of the adrenaline coursing through her veins.

"Hey!" she shouted.

"What's wrong?" Steele said, turning toward the back door.

"That asshole is shooting my tires out."

The fact that he didn't hear the shots told him that they were using a suppressor. Not that it mattered. The only people out on Neville Island at this hour were bums and winos, and they weren't going to call the cops.

"Why would he do that?" she said, outraged.

"They must dislike Audis," he deadpanned.

"Eric, that is not funny, you bought it for me."

He couldn't help but smile. It was a typical response from a woman who'd worked two jobs and had never bought much of anything for herself.

"We have insurance, Mom. We will get the car fixed."

"That's not the point, *Eric*," she huffed. "Those tires were brand-new, and now I am going to have to go down to—"

"Mom, this is not the time," he said. He grabbed her by the hand, hard enough to show that she had to pay attention, and started for the stairs.

Tactically speaking, taking the high ground gave him the advantage because it allowed him to engage his attackers from above. If they maneuvered under a base of fire and tried to pin him down, Steele could simply break contact and move to another position. But first he had to get his mother to the saferoom. His major fear was that he would get pinned down before he could get her there.

"Eric, they are putting something on the back door."

Breaching charge. Time to move.

He took a final piece of gear from his bag: a pair of full-spectrum goggles.

Unlike night vision, which amplified only the ambient light, full-spectrum goggles allowed Steele to fight in any environment. If there was not enough light, the goggles were able to pick up the heat energy a living body radiated. Steele flipped the switch and ordered the security system to "blackout."

The room went dark.

Under the night vision everything was eerie green but clearly visible.

"Owww," his mother said, knocking into a lamp. "Eric, I can't see. Slow down."

"Sorry," he said, looking back at her.

The glare from the monitor flared his goggles and

he was reaching down to put it on night mode, but his mom turned away from his hand.

"Wait, that wasn't the back door. It was the—"

Steele had just enough time to shove his mother out of the way, and then the front door exploded. The over-pressure buckled the Krieger blast door at the hinges and sent him sprawling to the floor.

He landed awkwardly and lost control of the Origin 12. Steele looked up just in time to see the three-hundred-pound blast door flying straight at him. He forced himself flat a second before the Krieger skipped off the floor on its way into the dining room.

A cloud of dust and grit enveloped the room, blinding him. Before he could take a breath, the dust filled his lungs. It burned them, leaving a sweet residue on his tongue: the telltale sign that they had used C-4 to blow his front door.

Steele got to his knees and started searching for the shotgun like a kid playing blindman's bluff. *Who are these guys?* His hands closed around the shotgun, and he grabbed it by the pistol grip. He was getting to his feet when he heard the distinctive *tink* of a flashbang hitting the floor.

The exhaust fans had kicked on and scattered enough of the cloud that Steele was able to pick out the flashbang skittering toward him. There were two schools of thought when it came to deploying a "bang." The safest and more popular method was to toss the "bang," wait for it to explode, and then enter the structure.

The lesser-used technique was known as crashing the bang, a tactic reserved for only the best-trained teams. The idea was to time an entry so that you had two men entering the room at the exact moment the device exploded. It required precise timing and extensive training but maximized the effectiveness of the device.

Neither method accounted for what Steele did next.

Instead of trying to get away, he ran toward the flashbang, scooped it off the floor, and sidearmed it toward the breach.

The flashbang exploded just as the first two of the assault team were coming through the door. The point man stumbled into the wall, the blast knocking his helmet to the side. Steele centered the reticle on the side of the man's head and fired.

Boom.

Steele swept to his right, placing his body between the door and the stairwell where his mother was hiding. The second shooter reeled drunkenly into his field of view, and Steele dumped him with a shot to the center of the chest.

The others were pouring through the door, and

Steele knew that if they got a foothold it was over. He shot the next man in the chest, and the heavy twelve-gauge sabot shoved him back through the door. For a moment Steele thought they were going to keep coming and he had every intention of wiping out the entire team. Then the fourth man appeared with a ballistic shield.

Steele fired into the center of the shield, hoping the slug would penetrate. It punched through the front but did not have enough ass to kill the man holding it because he didn't fall. Steele was lining up for a second shot when a muzzle appeared over the lip of the shield.

"No freaking way," he said, recognizing the weapon from its heat shield.

It was an M249 Squad Automatic Weapon.

Steele threw himself out of the line of fire a second before the light machine gun opened up on full auto.

Chapter 9

The shooter worked the SAW across the room at chest level, and Steele knew the only reason he was still alive was because the man didn't know exactly where he was.

"Mom, stay down," he yelled.

Steele crawled under the wall of lead, the bullets zipping over his head like a swarm of angry hornets. He managed to crawl around the stairwell, pulling his feet in a second before a tracer round hit the metal and shot skyward.

He grabbed his mother by the shoulders and pushed her flat. She had her hands clamped over her ears, mouth open in a scream that was blocked out by the roar of the SAW sending six hundred rounds a minute into the house.

Steele knew they had no chance of making it to the saferoom now because the moment they stood up, the gunner would cut them down. They were going to have to wait for the man to reload and then try for the garage.

The SAW fell silent, and Steele grabbed his mother by the hand and pulled her up to her feet. "Go to the garage," he said and then stepped around the pillar and unloaded the Origin 12 on the men in the doorway.

Steele didn't wait to see if he'd hit them. All he cared about was keeping their heads down. He ran the shotgun dry, shoved a fresh magazine in, and sprinted after his mother.

A second explosion in the kitchen was followed by the sound of glass shattering. "Keep going, Mom," Steele yelled.

A figure appeared through the doorway that led from the kitchen into the dining room. Steele fired from the hip. The first round hit the man in the thigh, spraying blood over the wall. The assaulter tumbled to the ground, but the man behind him fired as he leaped over his fallen comrade.

A bullet clanged off the shotgun, ripping it from Steele's hand.

He ducked behind one of the pillars and yanked the 1911 from its holster. He now had attackers on his flanks. One team had entered through the back door and had him under fire from the kitchen.

At the front door the machine gunner kept him from maneuvering toward the stairs. He couldn't fire without risking hitting his own men, but Steele knew that wouldn't last long.

Steele looked over his right shoulder just as the assaulter came abreast of the pillar. The man raised his rifle, the sights on his mother's back. Steele grabbed the barrel with his left hand and wrenched it skyward a moment before the man fired.

The rifle recoiled, the superheated gas burning Steele's hand. He fired into the man's foot, blowing a hole in the top of the boot.

"*Der'mo!*" Shit.

He's Russian? What the hell?

Still holding the man's rifle, Steele tried to jam the 1911 into his gut, but the man hit him with a short jab to the face. Steele let go of the rifle and stomped on the man's shredded foot. He bellowed in pain, reached for Steele's night-vision goggles, and tried to drive them into his eyes.

Steele ducked out of the goggles and yelled, "Lights!"

The house lights blazed to life, and the attacker faltered, needing to adjust his own NODs. It was the opening Steele needed. He drove his forearm into the man's nose, and the cartilage gave way with a flash of warm blood. The attacker stepped backward, trying to create space, and Steele delivered a thrust kick to his chest. Simultaneously, his right hand dropped to the 1911 at his waist. He fired the instant the barrel cleared the holster, two shots into the man's gut. Steele knew the 9 mm wouldn't get through the body armor, but it knocked the breath out of the attacker, which gave Steele time to center his sights on his target's forehead and deliver the kill shot.

"*Benzin,*" a voice ordered. Gas.

Well, that's my cue.

Steele stripped two grenades from the dead assaulter's kit. A gas launcher *thoop-thooped* while he shoved one grenade under the dead man's leg, pulled the pin, and ran for the garage.

"Eric, hurry," his mother urged, already seated in his car.

Steele pulled the door closed and jammed the second frag between the bottom of the door and the metal lip. Steele made sure it was going to hold before jumping into the car and shoving the key into the ignition.

"I've still got it," his mom said.

"Got what?"

She held up her bag as the engine roared to life— reminding him just how tough his mother really was.

She wasn't exactly enjoying this, but she hadn't panicked. Steele threw the GTO into gear and punched the gas. The tires yelped on the concrete and the car shot from the garage a moment before the door to the warehouse was yanked open. Steele glanced in the rearview and saw two muzzle flashes blinking from the shadows of the garage. The bullets shattered the back window. Then the frag detonated.

Off to his right one of the fighters lifted a stubby launcher onto his shoulder and aimed it at the warehouse. Steele got only a quick glance, but it was enough for him to recognize it as an M141 SMAW-D. Built by McDonnell Douglas, the shoulder-launched multipurpose assault weapon disposable fired an 83 mm thermobaric warhead. It had only one purpose—to destroy bunkers. It was state-of-the-art gear, not something any gangbanger with a pile of money could get his hands on.

"Let's get out of here," he said as he centered the grille on the chain-link fence. As the mercenary with the SMAW-D continued to fire into the warehouse, one of his buddies lined up on the GTO and opened up.

A moment later the warehouse's windows exploded and the building shuddered. The roof caved in, letting out a plume of fire. With a defiant roar the walls collapsed.

The front wheels hit the curb and then the hood burst through the fence, sending crossed-wire edges flying. The GTO rose and fell on its springs, but Steele didn't have time to worry if she would hold together. He jumped the curb and drove across the parking lot. On the street he took a left onto Neville Road—it led to the bridge that would take them over the Ohio River and into the city.

He had no idea what was in the parcel. All he knew was that someone had gone to great expense to get it.

"Put your seat belt on," he said, flipping on the headlights. He blew through two stop signs before cranking the wheel hard over to the left. The GTO cornered like it was on rails. He let the back end come around and drifted onto the on-ramp. Neville Road took him south, and once he was on the straightaway, he stomped the accelerator to the floor. The V8 spooling up crunched a quarter mile in less than thirty seconds.

On the other end of the bridge, he reached for his cell phone. He needed to let someone know that he had been attacked. Without letting off the gas, he unlocked the phone and typed in his passcode. Then he saw a pair of blacked-out street bikes racing after him.

"Where the hell did they come from?" He spun the wheel hard left, seeking safety in the city. In its heyday the GTO could have taken anything on the road, but rebuilding a classic wasn't like buying a car off the showroom. You had to break in the engine and be prepared for any hiccups that appeared along the way. And running the car wide open like this was not in Steele's plans when he took her out of the garage that afternoon. But what choice did he have?

He saw one of the bikes coming up on his right and tried to swerve into it. Steele didn't realize it was a bluff until the rider let off the throttle. He was out of position and couldn't maneuver the GTO as nimbly as the riders could their motorcycles. The second bike took advantage and came up on his right side. All Steele could do was yell at his mom to "Get down!"

The rider reached out toward the window and fired a short burst into the side of the car. Steele saw the finger of flame and yanked on the emergency brake. It was called a moonshiner's turn, and as soon as the back wheels locked up he spun the steering wheel hard to the right.

The back end came around 180 degrees so they were facing the direction they'd come from. Steele disengaged the brake and shifted into gear. The road ahead was clear and all he had to do to escape was hit the gas.

Steele floored it and was just letting out the clutch when the engine coughed and died.

Chapter 10

Six Hours Earlier

The Airbus A380 was the world's largest airliner, but that didn't keep Aleksandr Zakayev from feeling that the walls were closing in on him. Neither did the fact that at a cruising altitude of forty-three thousand feet there was no way off the plane. *Stop being a child,* he told himself harshly as he downed the second single-serve bottle of vodka. He grimaced at his next-door seat mate, who had a Yorkshire terrier that looked like it wanted to bite his head off.

He'd killed a dog when he was eleven, snapped its spine right at the neck. It belonged to a camp guard who would make him march in bare feet in the freezing cold. He smiled as he remembered the guard's face when he found the dead mutt jacked up on the flagpole in the center of the parade ground.

Those days weren't all bad, he thought as he recalled Camp 722. That was also where he'd met Hassan.

The first week was the worst. They woke up before dawn for a five-mile run. The only time anyone spoke was when an Afghan boy fell out of the run.

"Get up," a tall soldier said.

The boy shook his head, and the soldier beat him with the wooden club he carried until he broke the boy's leg. Welcome to Camp 722.

After a small breakfast they were taken out to the "deck," where they learned hand-to-hand combatives and how to use joint locks and chokes. There was never enough sleep or food, but Zakayev had been hungry before.

He met Hassan during the second week. Zakayev had just come in from the "deck" and his lip was busted. He went into the bathroom to clean the blood from his clothes and found a tall, blond-haired boy and two of his friends beating on a skinny Arab.

"Please, help me," the boy said in terrible Russian.

"Get out of here, dog," the boy named Slavin said.

"Let him go," Zakayev told them, not sure why he was getting involved.

"What did you say, dog?" Slavin demanded, shoving the Arab to the ground.

"I said, let him go."

Slavin looked at him, his brown eyes promising violence. Zakayev let him get closer. He had been on the street long enough to know that if he took Slavin down fast, the rest of the boys would scatter.

"How dare you—"

Zakayev didn't give him a chance to finish. He grabbed the boy by his hair and slammed his face into the sink. Then he kicked him in the side of the knee like they had taught him on the "deck."

Slavin went down and Zakayev jumped on top of him. He started pounding the boy in the face and didn't stop until a soldier came in, grabbed him by the shirt, and dragged him outside.

They chained him to a pipe and left him there, but when the sun went down, the little Arab came outside with an apple and a cup of water.

"My name is Hassan. Hassan Sitta," the boy said. "We are brothers now."

A kick to the back of his seat ripped him from his memories. Zakayev turned to look behind him and saw a fat child glaring at him while stuffing cookies in his mouth.

"Mommy, that man is looking at me."

Fucking brat.

"Johnny, please," his mother implored.

They were American. That much was easy to ascertain because the child and the mother were fat pigs. Zakayev got to his feet and headed for the restroom, scowling at the boy and his mother as he passed. Inside the lavatory he washed his hands and pulled out the passport identifying him as Lars Zimmer—a computer programmer from Helsinki.

Gabriel had given it to him before he was driven to the airport. Zakayev studied it and was immediately impressed with the quality.

"This is the best work I have ever seen," he said.

"I hope so," Gabriel replied, "because it's real."

"Real?" Zakayev asked, not comprehending what his employer was telling him. "How did you . . . ?" Then he remembered what Gabriel had told him back in Turkey.

"I work for the Saudi government." Specifically, for GIP—General Intelligence Presidency. The Saudi version of the CIA.

Zakayev landed at Pittsburgh International Airport and followed his fellow passengers to the baggage area. It felt good to know that for once in his life, he wasn't traveling on forged papers. Still, he didn't relax until he breezed through customs.

A man was waiting for him at the bottom of the escalator. He held a sign with the name LARS ZIMMER written in black marker. They exchanged bona fides in Russian, and the man took Zakayev's bag and led him to a black Lincoln Town Car.

He climbed in the back and found a box waiting for him on the seat. Zakayev found a Ruger Mark IV .22 caliber pistol inside. The Mark IV was a popular pistol for weekend shooters because of the cheap ammo and manageable recoil. He flipped the pistol over and checked the spot where the serial number should have been.

It was gone.

"The address you sent earlier, it is in a bad part of town," the driver advised.

When they were a few miles away from the location, Zakayev saw what he meant. The neighborhood was a shit hole, and this was coming from a man who'd spent his time in some of the most run-down places in the world.

"I've seen nicer places in Chechnya," he said.

"The police don't even come here unless they have a SWAT team," the driver added.

The moment they pulled onto the block, Zakayev knew they were being watched. The Town Car pulled past a pair of black teens standing on the corner. One of them pulled out a cell phone, typed a number, and held it to his ear.

He knew the boy was calling the men they were going to see.

The address belonged to a sagging duplex with boarded-up windows and overgrown grass. Zakayev shoved the pistol and its makeshift suppressor in the waistband of his pants and got out. He made his way carefully up the steps, avoiding the nails sticking out of the porch.

The front door had been bashed in so many times that it didn't even have a knob, just a metal plate someone had screwed over the hole.

Zakayev knocked.

"Who the hell is it?" a voice yelled.

"Open the door," he snapped.

He heard a chain rattle and then the door cracked open. A muscular black man peeked his head out and looked around before opening the door the rest of the way. He was holding a sawed-off shotgun.

"What the hell you want, white boy?" he demanded.

"What is your name?" Zakayev asked, lowering his sunglasses so the man could see his eyes.

"Marquez," the man said.

"I am here for a package, Marquez."

"All right, all right."

The den was the only room that had any furniture in it. A slab of wood straddled a pair of cinder blocks, two couches, and a massive TV with a game system attached.

"Where is it?" Zakayev asked, not wanting to spend any more time in the house than he needed to.

"She has it," Marquez said, holding up his cell phone and showing a picture of an attractive middle-aged brunette.

"You were hired to get it from her, yes?" Zakayev asked with a hiss.

"Look, man, I don't know what you want us to do. The delivery dude was late, and by the time my man saw him, he was handing off the package. Shit," he said, lighting up a cigarette. "Didn't think you wanted us to smoke two white people in the middle of suburbia."

"Hell, naw. Ain't nobody gettin' paid enough for all *that*," a second man said from the couch.

Zakayev could read between the lines. He knew behind the man's bullshit was a much simpler reason they didn't have the package. They were fuckups.

"Where is it now?" he asked.

"I've got someone tailing her," Marquez said.

That was when Zakayev knew it was time to take control.

"I need to make a call." He stepped out onto the porch to call Gabriel.

"Yes?"

"They didn't get the package," Zakayev said.

"Explain."

"They let her get away. But the man Marquez says they have someone following her."

"Can they get it?" Gabriel wanted to know.

Zakayev had known it was a mistake to use the gangbangers in the first place. But Gabriel had overruled him. The Saudi wanted to keep a low profile and thought that using local toughs to steal a package from a middle-aged woman wouldn't arouse police attention.

But just as Zakayev thought, they had failed. Which meant he had to fix their screwup.

Still a pawn, the voice in his head hissed. *A dog with a leash implanted in his head.*

"Are you there?" Gabriel asked.

Zakayev bit down on his anger. He was growing tired of Gabriel's games. The way the man kept all of his cards so tight to his chest. But until he got that implant out of his head, Zakayev knew he had to remain civil.

"*Nyet*—no."

This time the pause was on the other end of the line.

"You are certain?"

"Yes."

"I will call you back."

A minute later the phone vibrated in his hand.

"Yuri is on his way with a team. Clean up and go," Gabriel said and then hung up.

Zakayev opened the door and stepped inside.

The shotgun Marquez had carried earlier was leaning against the wall, and Zakayev grabbed it on his way to the den, where Marquez and his crew were huddled around the TV, playing a video game.

"Call your man and find out where the woman is, right now," Zakayev ordered.

"We ain't doing shit else until we get paid," a thug with a shaved head said from the couch without looking up.

"For real," Marquez echoed. "No money, no . . ." He paused when he saw the shotgun in Zakayev's hand. "Awww, shit."

The man with the shaved head looked up from the TV. "What the hell are you going to do with—?"

Zakayev didn't give him a chance to finish. He leveled the shotgun and blasted the man in the chest.

Boom. Cha-chunk.

He racked the pump and turned on the second man and fired again.

Boom. Cha-chunk.

Zakayev took a step forward and shoved the smoking barrel beneath Marquez's chin. The barrel sizzled against the man's skin and he tried to scoot away, but there was nowhere to go.

"Call your man. Now," he told Marquez. "I won't ask you again."

Marquez picked up the phone, his fingers shaking as he dialed.

"Hey man, where you . . . ?"

Zakayev ripped the phone from his hand. "Turn on the GPS function on your phone," he told the man.

"Who is this?" the voice on the other end asked.

"The man who will pay you twenty thousand dollars to keep following the woman and call me when she stops."

There was a pause.

"What about Marquez?"

"You work for me now," Zakayev said, pulling the trigger.

An hour later, he was standing atop a parking garage a half a mile from Neville Island. A pair of black sports bikes pulled up behind him. Yuri pulled off his helmet and walked over.

He and Yuri had been the only Chechens at Camp 722—orphans who'd lost their family during the Russian attack on Grozny. But that was where the similarities ended.

Zakayev was a preternatural predator, picking up the dark arts faster than any of the other boys at the camp.

This naturally caused friction, but not with Yuri. After they graduated, Yuri was sent to join the Spetsnaz where *he* learned the finer points of killing a man.

Zakayev, on the other hand, was born with the knowledge.

He lifted the night-vision binoculars to his eyes just as the second breaching charge went off. The flash was followed by the concussion that rumbled across the Ohio River and up to the garage.

Zakayev was a connoisseur of violence and closed his eyes to savor the belligerent symphony unfolding three hundred yards to his east. The rate of fire rose but stopped short of a crescendo.

Something was off.

"Go find out what's wrong," he told Yuri.

Chapter 11

Steele saw the bikes' headlights in his rearview. They were turning around.

"C'mon, c'mon," he begged while twisting the key.

The engine turned over with a roar, and Steele shifted into first and took off, with the bikes in hot pursuit. He wanted to cut through a side street, but when he tried to go wide, the rider appeared with his submachine gun.

Dammit.

He dialed a number from memory and thumbed the speaker button before making a sweeping turn back onto Neville Road.

"Code in," a robotic voice answered.

Steele rattled off the identification code and heard the encryption package activate with two clicks. A moment later he was on a secure line with Cutlass Main.

"Go ahead, Stalker Seven."

"Road Runner. I say again, Road—"

One of the riders opened up on the GTO and sent a stream of bullets through the back glass. Steele dropped the phone and grabbed the wheel with both hands.

He wasn't the kind of man who was used to calling for help. Usually when the bullets started flying, Steele was the cavalry and he decided it was time to do what he did best.

Steele turned in his seat, the 1911 in his right hand, steering with his left.

"Cover your ears," he told his mother.

He made a small adjustment to the wheel, using the car to bring one of the riders in his sights. He fired twice and then turned around. In the rearview he saw the bike wobble and knew that he'd hit his target.

There was no time to celebrate, though. The second rider pulled up behind him and Steele could hear the rounds hitting the trunk. He checked the mirror, watched the man drift from right to left, but couldn't figure out what he was shooting at.

Realization came in the *thunk, thunk* sound of rubber shards bouncing against the wheel well and a violent wobble in the back end.

They shot out my tires. What a bitch move.

Steele let off the gas, knowing that speed and flat tires were a recipe for disaster. He checked the speedometer and saw the needle falling toward sixty miles per hour. *Way too fast.*

He needed to slow the GTO down, but it took every ounce of strength and concentration just to keep the car on the road. The right rear rim found the pavement, and the back end started to slide. Steele pumped the brakes and turned into it. He checked his speed—thirty miles an hour.

Beside him his mother was screaming.

"Are you hit?" he shouted.

Zakayev sat behind the wheel of the pickup and watched the two blips on the GPS coming closer. He was dressed in mechanics coveralls that he'd found in the auto shop where he had stolen the truck. According to the Internet the truck was called a "dually" because it had two pairs of rear tires. It was banged up and the tires needed to be replaced, but all that Zakayev cared about was the engine and the metal bumper on the front.

He listened to the riders talking back and forth on the radio. "Block the left. Yes, good."

It was almost time. Zakayev lifted the Heckler &

Koch MP7 from the bag lying on the seat next to him and shoved the magazine into the handle. Even with the attached suppressor the submachine gun was barely thirty-five inches in length, so small that the first time Zakayev had ever seen one he thought it was a toy.

There was nothing innocent about the forty 4.6×30 mm armor-piercing rounds loaded into the magazine.

He wedged it between the seats and then pulled the straps of the four-point harness over his shoulders and buckled them into the center adapter. He cinched them tight and pulled a white ATV helmet over his head. Then he started the truck and put it in gear.

The dually was sluggish at first, weighed down by the bags of concrete his men had placed in the back. On the open road the truck would have proved unwieldly, but Zakayev didn't have far to go.

He kept the lights off, made a slow turn onto the side street paralleling Neville Road, and waited.

"We are a half kilometer away," the radio announced.

Zakayev consulted the GPS, did the calculations in his head. *Go now.*

He let off the brakes and let the truck's momentum carry him down the hill.

The voice on the radio started the countdown. Zakayev made a slight adjustment with the accelerator before grabbing the mouthpiece off the dashboard and shoving it between his teeth.

Ten, nine, eight, seven . . . , he counted to himself.

Zakayev glanced to the right. He could see Steele's car and the motorcycles trailing behind it.

. . . six, five, four . . .

The rider fired a burst from his submachine gun. He didn't see the tires come apart, but the sparks that erupted when the rim hit the road were impossible to miss.

. . . three, two, one.

Steele had turned to check on his mother when he saw a shape hurtling out of the dark. In that instant it was as if someone had hit the slow-motion button on the remote. The headlights flashed on and Steele saw the truck rushing toward them. It was so close that he could make out the emblem on the grille, the pit marks on the massive bumper welded to the front, and the man with the white helmet behind the wheel.

Then the truck slammed into the passenger-side door.

The collision shattered his mother's window, and glass sprayed into the interior. His mother's door bent inward, and her head whiplashed to the left. The glass hit Steele in the face, and warm blood flashed over his skin.

Then the GTO soared into the air.

The car rolled three times, and when it stopped Steele was hanging upside down. He tried to move his head, but he was pinned. Out of the corner of his eye he saw the glint of the 1911. It was lying on the pavement, just out of reach.

Steele heard the sound of boots crunching on glass. Someone was coming. He reached for the pistol, his finger grazing the butt and causing it to spin. A pair of boots stepped into view, and Steele found it strange that whoever was coming after him wasn't in more of a rush.

A man spoke.

Russian, Steele thought.

He reached for the pistol again and felt something sharp poke against his ribs. Steele ignored it, driving himself into the object, which cut through his shirt and pierced the skin. He didn't give a damn about the pain. All he cared about was getting the gun. Steele hooked his finger, clawed at the trigger guard, and almost had it when a boot slammed down on his open hand.

Shiiiit.

The boot kicked the gun away and then the man slowly lowered himself into a squat. Steele stared at his attacker, taking in his thin face and the cold, dark eyes. One look into them and Steele knew this was the end. He would get no pity from this man.

The man reached for the handle, gave it a tug, but the door was stuck firmly in place. He took a breath and this time he ripped the door free from its hinges and threw it on the ground. The man bent down to reach inside the overturned car, where Steele was still trapped.

Steele grabbed his arm from inside the car. He was trying to sink a wrist lock when the man yanked his arm away and ducked free of Steele's grip. The man stood up and punched Steele in the head.

The first punch dazed him. The second smashed his nose flat against his face. Steele tried to fight back, but he was upside down and unable to defend himself. The man kicked him a second time, and Steele choked on a rush of his own blood. He felt himself passing out.

In the distance he thought he heard sirens but couldn't be sure if they were real or his ears ringing from the attack.

"*Politsiya.*" Police.

"*Idti,*" the man ordered.

The man reached back into the car and grabbed the package off the roof. Steele could see the paper was streaked with his mother's blood.

"Mom?"

The sirens were getting closer. The cops less than a mile away.

The man leaned to his left, looking past Steele, and shook his head.

"*Mertva,*" he hissed. Dead.

"No. No, she's not," Steele said.

The man shrugged and leveled the pistol at his chest.

Steele could see the reflection of the blue lights in the man's cold eyes. The cops were getting closer. The man's finger closed around the trigger.

"*Dolxhny uti seychas,*" the other man yelled. We have to leave *now*.

The man glanced up at the street, his finger curling around the trigger with a curse.

And then he fired.

Chapter 12

Jerusalem

Costas Kaidas was at a bar, working his way through a bottle of Johnnie Walker, when his phone rang.

Kaidas glanced at his phone and grimaced when he saw that it was Angelo, his foreman, calling. *Shit, what now?*

"Yeah?" he said, answering the call.

"You need to get down to the tunnel. I found something."

Kaidas glanced at the clock. It was a quarter to ten in the evening. "Can't it wait?"

"No," Angelo replied.

Dammit.

"I'm on my way."

Kaidas carried the bottle out to his white Toyota pickup with the Sterling Mining logo painted on the side and climbed in. He shoved the bottle between his thighs, started the engine, and drove west toward the dig site.

His route took him past the Temple Mount, where a group of Israeli police stood guard. Kaidas nodded at the men as he passed but didn't stop, continuing down the street until he came to the stop sign.

He activated his left blinker, rolled down the window, and checked his rearview. The coast was clear, and he lifted the bottle, drained the contents in one long pull, and tossed it out the window.

"Ahhhh," he said, smacking his lips.

The road ran south, giving him a clear view of the Silwan neighborhood.

Silwan started out small. A stony collection of sun-bleached houses built on the eastern slope of the Kidron Valley. The first inhabitants were Jewish farmers who settled the area in the seventh century.

Since then the neighborhood had grown and its current population was primarily Palestinian. A mix of working-class families who lived in apartments above their concrete gray shops, and the younger, more militant generation who spray-painted anti-Israeli graffiti on the shopkeepers' metal security gates.

Kaidas palmed a handful of mints, hoping they would mask the smell of the booze before stopping at the IDF checkpoint at the bottom of the hill. He checked his breath. Blowing it into his hand as he took his foot off the gas.

Minty fresh.

Kaidas took his papers from the visor and watched the soldier approach. *C'mon, c'mon.*

"Don't see you around here this late," the soldier said, flashing him an easy smile.

"Always something with this project," Kaidas said.

The Israeli soldier gave his papers a cursory glance, but Kaidas noticed his eyes never left the carton of cigarettes on the passenger seat.

"Almost forgot," he said. "I picked this up from the duty-free shop," he said, handing over the smokes.

"Bribery will get you everything," the IDF soldier said with a smile. He took the gift and slid it into his cargo pocket.

"I was hoping that if I passed out enough cigarettes, I might be able to get to work on time. Doesn't seem to be working, though," he said, nodding to the checkpoint. "Seems like you guys put up a new checkpoint every week," Kaidas joked, checking the clock on the dash.

It was ten fifteen.

Kaidas had been working the young soldier for the past few months, plying him with cigarettes and playing the friendly foreigner. He was eager to learn anything about the IDF's security posture, but Adam remained tight-lipped.

Of all the days you pick to open up, it has to be to-night?

"It is going to get worse before it gets better, I'm afraid."

"Really, why is that?" Kaidas asked.

The soldier looked back down the road and, seeing there were no other vehicles, leaned in and laid his forearms on the windowsill.

"Rumor has it," he said with a conspiratorial smile, "a very important man is coming to visit."

Kaidas forgot all about the foreman's late-night call.

"Like Shakira important?" he asked, playing on Adam's infatuation for the Colombian singer.

"Bigger," he said, lowering his voice. "The president of the United States."

"The president is coming to Silwan?" He laughed. "Why? Did he find out your government is illegally evicting all the Palestinians in the neighborhood?"

"Please," the guard scoffed. "If my country was

doing anything illegal would we allow your mining company to come in and work?"

Kaidas had to agree that he had a point, but before he could reply a second voice cut through the night.

"Are we paying you to work or talk?" Sergeant Ariel Levy's voice barked from the shadows.

Fuck.

Sergeant Levy had never tried to hide his feelings about Sterling Mining or Kaidas for that matter.

He hated them both, but for different reasons.

Levy's problem with Sterling came from the fact that the mining giant's large trucks and earthmovers were always clogging the roads. Causing traffic to back up around the checkpoints, which made his life more difficult.

He wanted them to finish the irrigation tunnel under the Silwan neighborhood, get it connected to the new desalinization plant on the north side of the city, and get the hell out of town.

Naturally, Levy blamed Kaidas every time there was a delay.

Sergeant Levy came marching out of the guard shack, a scowl etched on his face.

"Why is it that every time I come out here you two are chatting away like girls at the beauty shop?"

"Just being friendly," Kaidas replied.

"Get back to your post," Levy told Adam, never taking his eyes off Kaidas. "What is a Sterling big shot doing out after dark? Shouldn't you be out working on your next hangover?"

"Got a drill problem," Kaidas lied.

"A drill problem?" Sergeant Levy said, rolling his eyes. "How many delays are you guys going to have this month?"

Sergeant Levy, like most of the soldiers manning the checkpoints, didn't have a problem with the Palestinians living in the Silwan neighborhood. Like many in the army, Levy had grown up in a more tolerant age than the older hardliners.

"We'll get it sorted out," Kaidas said, hoping to head the sergeant off and knowing immediately that it hadn't worked.

"I find it strange that Sterling is having so many issues so close to completing the project."

"Just bad luck. We will get it done on time."

"Well I'd suggest you get to work, Mr. Kaidas," he said, waving him through.

"Don't work too hard, *sergeant*," he replied, shifting the Hilux in gear.

He followed the road north, the headlights dancing over the hilly landscape dotted with scrub brush and withered olive trees. The Silwan district was predominantly Palestinian and it was no secret that the Israeli government had never been supportive of the water pipeline project.

Kaidas hadn't understood the reasoning at first, but as he got to know the guards in the area he got a better sense of what was going on. Foreign land developers had been eyeing a corridor that cut through the Silwan neighborhood for years. They had attempted to buy the land, offering twice the actual amount, but the occupants weren't interested in selling.

One of the developers hired a savvy surveyor out of Germany and had him look at the parcels in question. The man found that a large majority of structures inside the corridor had been built illegally.

Not only were the buildings a safety hazard, but according to the survey they were also built on land owned by the State.

The developers filed an eviction notice on behalf of the Israeli government and the high court authorized the finding. The initial uproar threatened violence. But since then things had settled down.

However, the presence of Sterling Mining plus the fact that the land developers were trying to buy the land so they could build luxury apartments once the low-rent apartments were bulldozed had reignited the issue.

Kaidas drove through the gate, past the sign that read STERLING MINING—*SILWAN PROJECT*, parked in front of the converted conex box that served as the foreman's office, and got out. The job site was a hive of activity in the daytime, and seeing it so quiet gave Kaidas an eerie feeling.

"Angelo?" he said, stepping inside the office.

He wasn't there, so Kaidas picked up the desk phone and dialed his cell.

"Where are you?" he asked.

"Main tunnel. Get down here, you aren't going to believe what I found."

Kaidas hopped back in the truck and followed the metal tracks past the excavators and dozers parked on the left side of the site. On the far north end the headlights revealed a large hole cut in the side of the hill. Kaidas tapped the brakes, guiding the Hilux down into the tunnel.

Angelo's truck was parked at the end, next to a shipping container with the word PARTS stenciled on the side. The box was leaning against the wall, but it was the open door and the portable work light shining inside that made Kaidas's guts knot up.

Angelo stepped out of the container and raised his hand to shade his eyes from the headlights' glare.

"You have *got* to see this," he said.

Kaidas shifted into park and cut the engine. "What are you doing down here?"

"Taking core samples," Angelo replied.

"At night?"

"Yeah, I do all the samples at night. But I needed a pick, thought the dig team might have one in the box."

"Where did you get a key to the dig team's box?" Kaidas asked.

"From the office," Angelo said.

The interior of the box was laid out like the rest of the storage containers, rows of wooden shelving on both sides loaded with spare parts for the temperamental machines.

"Like I said, I was looking for a pick and when I got to the back, I felt a draft," Angelo said, walking to a sheet of plywood at the end with belts hanging from it. "These things go on cargo ships, so they are supposed to be sealed."

"Yeah, sure. Go on," Kaidas said.

"Check this out."

He grabbed the corner and tugged. The plywood hinged free and Kaidas found himself staring at a six-foot hole.

"What in the hell?" Kaidas said.

"Someone has been very busy." Angelo grinned, snapping on his flashlight.

"How far does it go back?"

"C'mon, I'll show you."

Kaidas estimated that the tunnel was at least two hundred yards long and well built. The sides and room were reinforced with metal beams.

"Shine the light at this beam," Kaidas said. A quick look at the stamp told him they weren't from the work site.

At the end of the tunnel they found bare concrete and an exposed metal pipe. In the corner a pair of wheelbarrows leaned against the wall next to four shovels and an acetylene cutting torch.

"Ho-ly shit," Kaidas said.

His surprise was genuine, but not for the reasons Angelo thought.

Kaidas knew the tunnel was there. He knew, because he'd brought in the crew that dug it.

He was surprised because he'd thought they had done a better job of *hiding* it.

Should have checked the entrance before you sent them home.

Kaidas knew it was too late for that now.

His mind went back to Saudi Arabia and the tunnel Sterling had dug there.

It was Kaidas's second dig as site engineer, the culmination of fifteen years of kissing the right ass and taking the shitty assignments. Digs in places like Peru, Mongolia, and Mali.

Kaidas had always liked to drink, but it wasn't until his wife left, took their two kids and half of his paycheck to move to Florida with her new boyfriend, that Kaidas became a drunk.

Everything came to a head a month into the Jeddah dig.

It was midnight and the job site was quiet. The drill crews had left after washing their equipment and making sure it was ready for the next day.

Kaidas was in the office with a fresh bottle of Jack Daniel's. He needed to write his quarterly progress report, which was due in the morning.

He finished the report at twelve thirty and the bottle ten minutes later.

Kaidas didn't *feel* drunk when he got into the truck and pointed it toward the Sterling Housing complex three miles away. He didn't feel drunk when the yellow lines on the road started to blur. Or when his eyes started to droop.

The last thing he remembered was trying to find something on the radio and then everything went black.

Kaidas woke up handcuffed to the hospital bed. Two burly Saudi policemen guarding the door and the man in the black suit sitting in the corner of the room.

"Who are you?" he'd asked.

"You can call me Gabriel, and I just became your best friend."

Back in Silwan, Angelo was looking at him.

"Did you hear what I said?" he asked.

"No," Kaidas answered.

"This tunnel, do you know where it goes?"

"No," Kaidas lied.

"It goes all the way to the Temple Mount," Angelo said. "Do you know what the Israelis would do if they found out about this?"

"What would they do?" Kaidas asked, picking up the shovel and tapping the concrete sewer line.

"Well first they would put us all in jail," Angelo said.

"Jail?"

"*If* we were lucky . . . ," Angelo said, turning back to the pipe.

The moment his head was turned, Kaidas swung the shovel. The blade hit the engineer in the back of the head with a resounding *thwang,* pitching him into the wall.

Angelo's skull bounced off the pipe and then he slid down to the floor with a grunt. He lay there twitching while Kaidas placed the blade against the back of his neck.

Kaidas closed his eyes, his mind going back to the

hospital in Saudi Arabia. The cold metal of the hand-cuffs around his wrist, the pictures in Gabriel's hand of Kaidas's mangled truck and the car with the dead man behind the wheel.

"You passed out behind the wheel, crossed into the other lane, and hit him head-on. He was a good man, with a family, and you killed him."

"No," Kaidas said, feeling the bile rising in his throat.

"Yes," Gabriel said, "and you will spend your life in jail for what you have done. Unless you do as I say."

Kaidas stomped down on the shovel, driving the blade into Angelo's vertebrae, killing him in an instant.

"You nosy piece of shit," Kaidas said, tossing the shovel to the ground.

He grabbed the man's flashlight and walked back to the box. Kaidas shut the false wall and went to his truck for a fresh padlock. After securing the box he drove back up top and checked the clock on the dash.

It was ten forty-five.

Kaidas knew that if he hurried, he could still get a few drinks in before last call.

Chapter 13

Washington, D.C.

The sun was on its way down when Meg Harden left Peet's Coffee on the corner of Seventeenth Street, carrying two cups of coffee to-go. While most Washingtonians were ending their day, Meg Harden was just beginning hers.

She stopped at the deserted crosswalk, waited for the light to change, and then crossed onto Pennsylvania Ave.

Meg passed the Eisenhower Executive Office Building, the foot traffic thinning around her as she followed the black iron fence to the white guard shack blocking the entrance to her office.

A guard in a white uniform stood off to one side, a rifle slung across his front. He offered Meg a nod as she got in line and then turned his attention back to the street.

"Have your credentials out," the guard at the booth was telling the people ahead of her.

Crap, Meg said to herself. Realizing that she'd left her credentials in her purse.

"Sorry, Robert," she said, stepping up to the guard post.

"Card in your bag again?" the man said with a smile.

"Yeah, but I brought you an Americano. Extra shot, right?" She smiled, placing the cups on the counter before grabbing her purse.

"Ms. Harden, you can put your creds anywhere you want as long as you keep bringing me my java." Robert smiled.

Meg found the card and handed it over. Robert grabbed it, his fingers brushing hers, and then it was falling.

"Shoot. I'm . . . I'm sorry," he said, bending to retrieve it.

At five foot five, Meg wasn't a typical White House staffer. And even with her shoulder-length black hair pulled into its customary ponytail, she was stunning. She graciously looked away, not wanting to embarrass

Robert, and when he finally picked her creds off the floor and scanned them his face was bright red.

"You are good to go," Robert said.

"Try not to work too hard," Meg said, clipping her badge onto her lapel and angling toward the West Wing. She still couldn't believe how much her life had changed in the past six months.

Before coming to the Program, Meg had spent ten years in the army, eight of those with ISA or Intelligence Support Activity, a clandestine unit tasked with collecting actionable intel for Tier 1 assets. Meg loved operating in the field, but after being passed over for promotion twice, she decided to get out.

A month later the CIA came calling.

On paper the job they offered was exactly what she had been looking for: more action and less paperwork. It wasn't until she went to Algiers that she saw the truth—the Agency wasn't interested in her tactical expertise. They had plenty of spies and shooters, what they *wanted* was someone with Special Access Program clearance.

Before 2001, a top secret clearance was all an intelligence operative needed to get in the game. But as the War on Terror dragged on, the government started relying on black projects and off-the-books operations to combat the enemy. These programs were extremely sensitive, and classification protocols slowly shifted from shades of gray to matte black.

In Algiers Meg worked on a Special Access Program known as the Gatehouse—an off-the-books repository for compartmentalized intelligence that was so secret only Meg and the CIA chief of station knew of its existence.

Meg came to the Program's attention after she helped Eric Steele track Nathaniel West down. President Rockford was impressed by her boots-on-the-ground experience and out-of-the-box thinking and brought her on board to assist with Keyhole.

The Keyhole Surveillance and Global Target System was a program that mined all forms of digital data, such as cell phones, security feeds, and audio sources. The system was so powerful, it could track targets in real time, anywhere in the world.

Meg dropped the half-empty cup in the trash and continued down the hall until she came to a silver door guarded by two men in suits. She placed her eye in front of the biometric reader and the door slid open.

Cutlass Main's operations center was staffed by the best and the brightest the United States had to offer. The techs and analysts had one job: to track and support Alphas and their keepers in the field. The techs were responsible for coordinating land, air, and sea assets as well as monitoring and maintaining the myriad of Intelligence, Surveillance, and Reconnaissance assets the Program used for operation.

The Keyhole section wasn't on the main floor. It was tucked in one of the cubbies that lined the walls of Cutlass Main and required a second biometric scan to gain access.

She sat down at her workstation and was about to log in when one of the techs said, "Boss wants to see you."

Shit, what did I screw up now?

Meg threaded her way past the rows of desks crammed with monitors and analysts to the duty officer's hooch and knocked on the door.

"Come in," a firm voice ordered.

Meg found the senior duty officer, Mike Pitts, sitting behind his desk.

"What's up, chief?" she asked.

"I called you in here to see how you are getting on," he began.

"It is an adjustment to be sure," Meg replied.

"You are doing a hell of a job," Mike said, rotating his chair and pointing up at the whiteboard mounted on the wall.

The other techs joked that he just liked to play with markers, but Meg knew differently. The board told Pitts everything he needed to know at a glance, and unlike the supercomputers, it couldn't be hacked. Meg knew that the board was law, which was why she was shocked when she saw her name written over the section marked KEYHOLE.

That can't be right.

"Everyone is very impressed. I want you to run the—"

Before he could finish the alert sounded, and a flashing red box popped up on the main screen.

"We've got a hot one," someone said.

Meg followed Pitts to the door, her eyes drawn to the flashing red alert on the main screen. It was the "hot box"—a signal that somewhere an Alpha was in trouble.

"Someone get me a grid," Mike said. "And I want that call on speaker, now."

"Got it," a tech said, flashing the data on-screen.

CODE: ALPHA ALERT
ORIGINATION HIT: 87032863
40.494453, -80.073958

"That can't be right," Meg said.

"Why?" Pitts asked.

"Because it is in the States."

The audio came up next, and Meg froze when she heard the voice.

"Cutlass, this is Stalker Seven."

"Go ahead, Stalker Seven."

"Road Runner. I say again, Road—"

"Road Runner, I've never heard that one," Meg said.

"No one has," Pitts replied, his voice flat. "It's the code for an Alpha under attack in the States."

Chapter 14

Eric Steele came to and found himself strapped to a spinal board.

Gloved fingers touched his face and then probed toward his eyes. His eyelids were pulled open, and the glare of a penlight sent a bolt of pain through his head. Steele tried to move, but something mechanical had him clamped in place.

"Pupils are blown," the man said after checking both eyes.

"W-what is going on?" Steele said, trying to turn his head to get a look at the shadowy figures just out of his line of sight. "Someone answer me."

"Shit, he's awake."

"Sir, do you know what day it is?" the man asked, placing his hand on Steele's chest.

The pressure of the hand sent a shock wave of pain rushing through Steele's nervous system and he twisted to avoid it.

"Sir, I need you to relax," the voice ordered.

Steele could only lift his arm a few inches and knew they had restrained him. But why? What the hell had happened?

The man's face came back into view. He was holding an oxygen mask and his gloves were covered in blood.

"Whose blood is that?" Steele asked.

The man ignored him and pulled the mask over his face.

"Whose blood is that?" Steele demanded, louder this time, but his voice was muffled behind the oxygen mask.

He jerked against the restraints, felt some slack, and pulled harder. He burst through a flash of pain and ripped his arm free. He grabbed the man by the front of his flight suit.

"Whose blood is that?"

The voice had become frightened. "Shit, someone dose this guy."

"Grab his arm."

Gloved hands closed around his wrist. Steele shook them free, pulled the man in the flight suit toward him, and then shoved him across the room.

"We need some help over here."

Steele tried to jerk his other hand free, arching his back in an attempt to get off the table. He felt the prick of a needle in his arm, grabbed the gloved hand by the wrist.

"Eric, mano, relax," a familiar voice said.

"Demo, is that you?"

His handler shoved the man out of the way and grabbed Steele's hand. "I'm here, brother."

"Okay. That's what I needed to know."

The drugs worked fast. The edges of his vision began to blur and then everything went black.

"Mr. Steele, can you hear me?"

The voice was calm, standing out amid the whirring and clicking of a machine. "My name is Ava. I was told to say Diamond."

Diamond.

It was the Program's countersign, a word that told Steele he was safe. But why couldn't he move?

Ava answered the question before he had a chance to ask.

"Mr. Steele, the reason you can't move is because you became agitated on the Life Flight. The flight surgeon was afraid you would exacerbate your condition and gave you succinylcholine."

Steele knew that succinylcholine was a short-term paralytic. He had used it on prisoners to get them onto helicopters before. It would wear off in time.

"How did I get here?"

"Mr. Steele, you were in a serious accident."

"I can't remember."

The machine clicked and whirred, and the pad he was lying on vibrated—pulling him slowly into the light.

A middle-aged woman and Demo were waiting for him at the opening of the MRI capsule. The look on his keeper's face told Steele everything he needed to know. Something was terribly wrong.

"The doctor will go over the results, but I didn't see any bleeding. There is some swelling, which might explain the memory loss."

Steele kept his gaze on Demo, who refused to look him in the eye.

"Tell me what's what."

"Mano, it's . . ." He trailed off, rather than coming up with his usual quips. "It's your mom, mano." When he finally looked up, there were tears in his eyes. "She is hurt bad, brother."

Steele felt a sudden surge of memories: the truck barreling toward them, the violent impact on the passenger side, his mother's side, her door bent in badly. . . .

"I want to see her. Can I do that?" he asked.

Demo looked at the nurse, who nodded gravely.

"Okay, mano, okay," he said.

Demo rolled him to the intensive care unit and helped him stand up.

A pair of nurses were working on his mother, and all Steele could see was her arms. Her right hand had a catheter taped to the skin and a clear line running to the IV bag hanging over her shoulder. Her left wrist was already in a cast.

Steele heard the ventilator before he saw it. The dry sucking sound told him that his mother wasn't breathing on her own. One of the nurses stepped out of the way and Steele got his first glance at her face. Her skin was pale and her lips gray.

"Oh Jesus," he said.

Demo steadied him. "She is a fighter, just like you."

"Who would do this?" Steele asked, tears in his eyes.

"We don't know, mano."

A monitor started beeping erratically and a red light flashed above the door. A moment later the trauma team came running down the hall. They rushed inside, the nurses already pulling the curtains closed.

"Let's go," Demo said, easing Steele back into the wheelchair.

"But I have to—"

"You can't do anything," Demo said harshly. "Your mom, she's beyond your ability to help her."

Chapter 15

Green Bank Facility

Steele sat on the hospital bed, listening to the *scratch scratch* of the doctor's pen on his chart, eyes fixed on the bit of twisted metal in a specimen jar. The bullet was a 9 mm Cor Bon, but the only reason Steele knew that was because he had loaded it in the magazine of his 1911 himself. The doctors had pulled it out of his bulletproof vest before the CAT scan.

He knew that the hollow point had left the barrel at 1,350 feet per second and traveled a very short distance before hitting him in the chest. On impact the copper jacket did exactly what it was designed to do. It mushroomed. Peeled back on itself, exposing the lead core.

Steele knew that the rapid expansion had saved his life. If he'd loaded the 1911 with a full metal jacket—a bullet that *didn't* expand on impact—it would have punched through his Kevlar.

And he'd be dead.

Steele closed his eyes and focused on the box where he kept the pain from past missions. Where he stuffed all the loss, fear, and anger. He couldn't remember how many times they had told him: "Emotion can get you killed faster than a bullet."

Steele turned his attention back to the reports from New Zealand that Demo had printed out for him. One was from the fire investigator and the second was from the lead investigator.

NEW ZEALAND POLICE

Crime Scene Notes

Reporting Officer: Detective Constable Caldwell, Thomas

Crime Scene Notes: D/C Caldwell was called to the scene after responding officers located victims in the living room. **Victim 1:** (unknown white female) was found seated in a chair. The body was badly burned and contained melted black substance on wrist and chair. **Victim 2:** (unknown white male) was found on floor near computer with remains of wooden chair close to body. Melted black substance was found on chair and left wrist.

Crime Scene Tech identified melted black substance as plastic. Notes forwarded to Homicide.

Initial medical examiner's assessment

Assessment of **Vic 1** (unknown white female) shows extensive antemortem bruising, including third-degree facial burns and ligature marks on wrist and ankles.

Vic 2 (unknown white male) also showed extensive antemortem bruising, broken nose, broken jaw, and broken ribs. **Vic 2** also shared ligature pattern of **Vic 1.**

Presence of melted substance on wrist, ankles, and chair (of both Vic 1 and 2) was identified as polymeric material, specifically Nylon 6/6. Nylon 6/6 is primary substance used in cable ties and consistent with ligature bruising.

The report was devoid of emotion. Given the clinically detached prose, the man could have been speaking about a broken-down car instead of a human being. Steele flipped to the autopsy photos, knowing that was where he'd find what he was looking for. Unlike the report, there was nothing detached about the enclosed eight-by-eleven stills. They were graphic and unflinching.

Steele wasn't a doctor, but he was an expert in death and violence. He had seen horrors in the service of his country that would haunt his dreams for the rest of his life, and he knew without a doubt what had happened to Nolan and his wife.

"Someone tortured them both and left them to die," Steele commented.

"Skip to picture five," Demo said.

The photo was a close-up of Nolan's right forearm and hand. The thumb was broken and the skin around the wrist torn where Nolan had ripped his hand free of the zip tie. His forefinger was outstretched, pointing at the floor, where written in his own blood were the words COLD STORAGE.

"Cold Storage," Steele read aloud. "That mean anything to you?"

"No," Demo replied.

Steele stared at the picture until the image was

burned into his mind. Whatever Cold Storage meant, it had to be important. Important enough to make a dying man break his thumb and flay his own arm to pass it along.

Steele rose swiftly to his feet, ready to take action. Instead, the room started spinning. He shut his eyes, focused on staying upright. "Easy, brother," he heard Demo say.

When he opened his eyes, his keeper was standing a foot away, ready to catch him if he fell.

"Mr. Steele . . . ," Dr. Thomas began.

"Cut the Mr. crap, my name is Eric," he grunted, easing himself back onto the bed. "I just stood up too fast, that's all."

"Eric, I've been a trauma surgeon in Iraq *and* Afghanistan. After that I spent two years at Walter Reed. I've worked on operators before—SEALs, Rangers, Delta, you name it."

Steele's head was pounding from standing up too fast, and he hoped the doctor would get to his point sooner rather than later.

"The Program came to *me*. Do you want to know *why*?"

"Because you are hot shit."

"No, they sent me to Walter Reed because I was

hot shit. The Program brought me here, let me pick my own equipment, and vet my own staff, because when it comes to brain injuries, I am the best in the world. You want to get back in the fight and would do it if you are ten percent or a hundred. Part of it is the training, but mostly it is the way you are wired. Someone hurt your mother and you want to go kick some ass."

Steele bristled at the mention of his mother, but the doctor ignored it and kept on talking. "I'm not here to stop you. I am here to help you."

It was not the answer Steele had been expecting.

"You have a plan?"

"The traditional course of action is time and rest, but we have the ability to get aggressive if you—"

"Hold on, doc," Demo interrupted. "You just said the traditional course of action is for Eric to take it easy. If that is what—"

It was Eric's turn to interrupt. "I've been *taking it easy.*"

The look in his eye made his handler recoil. His hands came up like Eric had just thrown a haymaker. As he stepped back, Steele realized he had a clear view of the mirror. It was his first time seeing his face since the accident.

The damage was extensive. His nose was bruised, face swollen, and a ragged laceration ran from his right ear to his mouth. But he knew it was his eyes that caused Demo to step away.

They were hot and feral: the eyes of a killer.

"Eric . . . ," he began, "this is *not* a good idea."

"I don't remember *asking* you if it was a *good* idea," Steele snapped.

Demo's eyes went flat and his jaw took on a hard edge. Steele watched him open and close his fist and then let out a long breath.

"There is a right way and a wrong way to do this, mano."

"You know I love you, brother, but on this one, you're either *in* my corner or you are in *my way*," Steele said.

"Heard another man say that once," Demo said.

The barb was well aimed, for he was referring to his former mentor, Nate West. And he could see that his handler wished he could take the words back as soon as they left his lips.

"Gentlemen, I . . ."

Steele's body began to shake from the rage building inside him, and when he spoke there was ice in his voice.

"Get out."

"Eric, mano . . ."

But Steele wasn't listening. "Get the hell out, and if you come back, you better have the name of who did this."

Chapter 16

Cutlass Main

As much as Meg wanted to see Eric, she had no idea where they had taken him. The only information Mike Pitts passed down was that Steele and his mother had been transported to a secure facility.

"He is good."

At home Meg was a self-professed control freak. Everything had its place, which was one of the reasons she had flourished in the army. Eric said she had OCD, and she had often wondered how she ever ended up in intelligence, where chaos was the norm. Before she met Eric, randomness hadn't been a problem, but after almost being killed by Nate West, she'd started having panic attacks.

Meg was having one right now as she approached the gray metal door that marked the entrance to the Keyhole section ahead. The tingle that preceded a panic attack rolled up her face. She picked up the pace, keeping her eyes focused on the black number 2 painted in the center of the door.

Just get inside.

She leaned into the biometric reader, her breathing coming faster and faster as she waited for the lock to disengage.

Cutlass Main was the world's most advanced tactical operations center, but it being located at the White House came with unique challenges. Outside 1600 Pennsylvania Avenue, threats against the United States expanded across the globe at an exponential rate, but there was simply no room for Cutlass Main to expand inside the White House.

Before the Program inherited Keyhole, the TOC, or "floor," as it was known to the techs, was the nerve center, and all available space was used to support the mission. The supercomputers and server banks were originally housed inside a pair of secure vaults built into the west wall. When Keyhole moved in, the servers were consolidated into one vault and Keyhole personnel into vault number two.

Finally, the lock beeped and the door slid open.

Meg stepped inside and scanned the room. The space, not much larger than her dining room, was arranged on two tiers like a movie theater. Thick concrete walls blocked any outside noise, and the muted overhead lights lent a tomblike feel.

Meg headed to her desk, which was in perfect order. She idly lined up the rows of pencils and Post-it notes while surveying the room. Near the wall, the audio and visual team were seated at their stations, mining a cluster of feeds. Next to them was the Keyhole database. On the dais above it all was the master terminal.

Meg glanced up and saw Lauren Wilks smile and wave for her to come up.

Lauren had been the lead engineer for Keyhole back when it was under the NSA and had forgotten more about the system than Meg had learned.

"Thank you soooo much," Lauren whispered.

"For what?" Meg asked.

"For taking that damn job. I'd already turned Mike down three times and I was worried he was going to fire me if I said no again."

"I haven't had a chance to accept it yet," Meg said.

"But you will, right? Please?"

"I don't know if I am ready for—"

The encrypted phone on the desk interrupted Meg in midsentence and Lauren picked it up.

"Yeah, just a second. It's for you."

"For me?" Meg asked, reaching for the phone.

Lauren nodded.

It was the first call she had received since coming to Cutlass Main, and Meg wasn't sure how to answer. The best she could come up with was "This is Harden."

"It's Demo. Look, I, uh—"

"Just tell me that he's okay," she whispered.

Meg could feel her pulse hammering in her ears and the squirm in the pit of her stomach. She searched for somewhere to sit down, not realizing that Lauren had gotten to her feet or that she was now sitting in her chair.

"Oh shit. Meg, he's fine," Demo said weakly.

"Jesus, you can't do that to me," she exclaimed.

"I didn't mean to scare you. I'm just frazzled."

Meg collected herself and nodded to Lauren. "He's fine," she mouthed.

Demo continued, "Eric is good, just banged up. His mom, though. She is in bad shape and he isn't taking it well."

"I can come to you," Meg offered, suddenly hopeful.

"I don't think Eric is going to be staying very long.

There is this doc here who has some treatment he can use to get him back on his feet."

She knew Demo well enough to know that he was holding something back.

"What *aren't* you telling me?" she asked.

"He's not thinking straight, Meg. You know how much his mom means to him. He is going to go after whoever did this to her and . . ."

"You need my help."

"Yeah," Demo said, letting out a breath.

The last six months of Meg and Steele's budding relationship had been difficult. He wasn't used to being in one place for so long. After merely the second week he started climbing the walls.

They went out, did the normal things couples did, but Meg could see that Eric was restless. Jokingly, she told him he was like a cougar, pacing around, searching for prey, but he just glared at her. That, combined with the uncertainty of when he'd be back on active status, hung over their lives like an axe.

At least she had one comfort. While they weren't technically exclusive, they weren't exactly interested in seeing anyone else.

"Eric is a big boy, and I know if it were my family, I'd want to go after them too. How can I help?"

"He is totally not ready for a mission."

"That's it. I'm coming down there."

"I'm serious. That would not be a good idea."

"And why the hell not?" Meg had fully recovered from her earlier shock and was back on her feet. She didn't realize that she was getting loud until Lauren mouthed, "Calm dooown."

"Sorry," she mouthed back.

"Can you work your magic, find out who did this? I'll pull some strings, hopefully get this sorted out before he decides to go Rambo on these people."

"Let me see what I can do," Meg said. She hung up the phone and turned to Lauren. "It is time to get to work."

Lauren pulled her chair back to her station and tapped her code into the rectangle of black glass that acted as the keyboard. The only way Lauren had agreed to come to Cutlass Main was if they allowed her to redesign the interface. At the NSA they used the traditional monitor and keyboard setup. The system worked, but it would have kept Keyhole locked into a two-dimensional space.

The way she had explained it to Meg was: Imagine the difference between a map and a globe. Keyhole, she said, was a three-dimensional engine, and if the Program wanted to harness its true capabilities, they needed to let her design a new interface.

The first step was to get rid of the keyboard and monitor. Lauren was given access to both MIT and DARPA labs, and what she came up with was truly revolutionary. Instead of a traditional screen, Keyhole's visual feeds were holographic and projected into whatever the workspace tech wanted. Lauren preferred a curved focal point similar to a theater. The control board was nothing more than an array of motion-capture cameras embedded beneath the glass. All a tech had to do was stand over the control board and launch the calibration system. The control board would run the tech through a typical data-capture session and synch the cameras to the tech's movements.

Under Lauren's tutelage, Meg had passed the initial familiarization phase and was able to putter through either an audio or visual search. The best way she could explain it was that while she was learning to play chopsticks, Lauren was capable of conducting the Philharmonic.

Origin Grid 40.494453, -80.073958 flashed on the monitor, and Lauren hit enter. The screen came alive with a collection of all the CCTV, cell phones, and ATM feeds from the area. Keyhole's supercomputer fused all of the signals into one seamless feed, which gave the appearance she was looking at the intersection in real time.

"The call came in at 19:34," Lauren said, typing the time into the search bar.

Meg didn't have an official Program order, but she knew it was only a matter of time. "Take me back."

Lauren hit enter, and the feed morphed back in time until it showed the same intersection at 6:30 P.M., thirty minutes before the ambush.

"Pan out," Meg said.

She worked the controls and Keyhole started mining every available signal. Traffic was light at that hour, but sporadic cars passed back and forth. At 6:45 a vehicle appeared at the top of the screen.

"There."

Lauren lassoed the truck and the feed became sporadic as the amount of digital data lessened.

"Not a lot of cameras. I can run a full panel if you want."

"Let's see what happens."

The truck cut its lights and the picture bounced like a drunk trying to focus. The computer acquired a weak audio signal that sounded like it came from a handheld radio. A voice squawked and then it was gone.

They lost time, the picture going black for three minutes, and when it came back on she saw Steele's GTO. He was being chased by two motorcycles.

"His phone was on, wasn't it?"

"Yes, we have the lock."

"Okay, shift."

Using Steele's phone, which was connected to Cutlass Main at the time of the attack, Meg was able to hear what was happening. The computer identified the voices and sounds stored in its database and showed them on a second screen like closed captions.

CUTLASS MAIN: "Code in."

STALKER 7: "Cutlass, this is Stalker Seven."

MIKE PITTS: "Go ahead, Stalker Seven."

STALKER 7: "Road Runner. I say again, Road—"

UNKNOWN FEMALE: screaming.

STALKER 7: "Cover your ears."

The collision, glass shattering, the car rolling. A grunt of pain followed by a woman's screams and then silence.

STALKER 7: "Are you hit?"

STALKER 7: "Mom."

Grunts. Sound of boots on glass.

UNKNOWN MALE: Language . . . Russian. "Politsiya." Translation: Police.

UNKNOWN MALE 2: Language . . . Russian. "Mertva." Translation: She is dead.

STALKER 7: "No. No, she's not."

Pistol shot.

Meg had closed her eyes, so she jumped when the gun went off. In the distance she could hear helicopters coming in, along with sirens. The sound grew louder and she heard Demo call out Steele's name.

"Back it up to the Russians," Meg said. *Russians? What would they be doing in Pittsburgh, Pennsylvania?*

Lauren ran them both through the system and they listened while the computer searched. The first voice belonged to a younger man. The second sounded older, and the fact that he was speaking to Steele made Meg think that he was in charge.

"Mom?"

"*Mertva.*" Dead.

"We need to ID those voices, and I don't care if we have to beg, borrow, or steal to get it. Do what you have to do, but I want this guy by the end of the day," Meg said.

Chapter 17

Neville Island

Usually Zakayev didn't care who he killed, but the thread between Nolan and Steele, that intrigued him.

Who is this man Steele?

He definitely wanted to know more about him. Mainly because he could tell that Steele was the kind of man who would come after him.

Which was why Zakayev drove the rented minivan to the Fairfield Inn & Suites to conduct counterintelligence on the house he'd hit on Neville Island.

He had reserved the room online. He parked the van and grabbed one of the roller bags from the back and headed inside to check in. His room was on the top floor, facing east, just as he had asked. Zakayev paused outside the door and snapped a pair of latex gloves over his hands. He swiped the keycard and entered the room, leaving the lights off.

Zakayev opened the window and set up the camera— a Nikon with a Sigma 150–600 mm telephoto lens. He screwed the camera into the tripod and backed away from the window until he was sure he would not be silhouetted. Then he looked through the viewfinder.

From his vantage point, Zakayev had a bird's-eye view of the forensics teams working through what was left of Steele's house on Neville Island. Just as he had been told, the local police were gone and in their place was a team dressed in white Tyvek suits. They had marked the scene with white engineer's tape, breaking it down into a grid. The clarity of the Sigma telephoto lens allowed Zakayev to read the numbers on the yellow placards that marked the spent shell casings.

Fifteen minutes into the surveillance, a Bell JetRanger helicopter flared for landing. Zakayev snapped a picture of the tail number, then focused on the two men who got out. It was the second man who grabbed his attention. He was short and stocky, obviously Latin American. He walked around the site, allowing the other man to do the talking.

Zakayev recognized a fellow trigger puller when he saw one, which begged the question: Who was this guy? His suspicions were confirmed when the mystery man knelt next to a pile of expended brass and picked up one of the casings. He flipped it over to read the head stamp on the casing and then shoved it into his pocket.

The man got to his feet and pulled the sunglasses off his face. Zakayev watched his eyes narrow through the telephoto lens. He knew the man could not possibly see him without a pair of binoculars, but Zakayev had the unexplainable sense that the man knew he was there.

It was time to get the hell out of the United States while he still had the chance.

Chapter 18

Green Bank Facility

The nurses woke Steele up every two hours to check his vitals and pupils. His body was exhausted, but his mind was still racing, and after a few hours of staring up at the ceiling, wishing the memory loss had taken away the bad memories too, he gave up the idea of sleep and wheeled himself to his mother's room in the ICU.

His mother lay still in the bed, machines breathing for her, monitoring her heart rate and respiration.

This is all my fault, he thought, reaching for his mother's hand.

Steele could deal with the pain of being shot, along

with the aches and bruises of the beating. He could shoulder the fact that Demo was pissed at him, because he knew it would pass.

But no amount of training could ever prepare him for seeing his mother like this. The sight broke Steele's heart.

"Mom, I'm going to make this right," he whispered, hot tears forming in his eyes.

His nurse found him sitting beside his mother's bedside when she came on shift at 0700.

"I've been looking all over for you, Mr. Steele," she whispered.

"Sorry, I . . ."

The nurse grabbed the handles of his chair and wheeled him out into the hall.

"My name is Maria," she said, introducing herself.

She wheeled him back to his room, where a light breakfast was waiting. "I'd ask you how you slept, but according to the charts, it appears that they were evaluating you for a concussion all night long."

Steele drained the coffee but only picked at the eggs and fruit. Seeing his mom in a coma had taken away his appetite.

He pushed the plate away. "I'm ready when you are."

Maria pushed him out into the hall, aiming for the

elevator at the far end. She swiped her card before picking the floor and then the elevator began its soundless descent. When the doors opened, the sign read AD-VANCED TREATMENT.

Steele glanced out the window, hoping for a clue as to where the hospital was. The landscape was dominated by rolling hills and a canopy of dark green as far as the eye could see. Off to the left, a fog-filled valley stretched toward the horizon, but the only other break in the sea of green was the strip of black snaking through the hills.

A road.

"Where am I?" he finally asked.

"Green Bank Medical Facility."

"West Virginia?"

"Mm-hmmm."

At the end of the hall she turned into a glass-fronted room that looked more like a laboratory than a doctor's office. Maria stopped the wheelchair next to a black recliner. A second nurse appeared, followed by the doctor. The nurse pulled on a pair of gloves and then started an IV.

"Rough night?" the doc asked.

"I've had worse."

Steele wasn't in the mood for small talk, and luckily,

neither was the doctor. He got right to the point and started outlining the treatment plan.

"We are going to start off with steroids, one of the best tools we have for swelling. Usually we would give you pills, but I think we agreed that time is of the essence."

Steele nodded.

The machine beeped as the nurse typed in the dosage rate and time. Then it hummed to life.

"Could you lie back please?" she asked.

Steele complied and she started attaching sensor pads to his head, chest, and neck.

"Oral steroids take a few days to be absorbed by the body. We are speeding that up, but it still could take three days to get maximum results."

"Three days?"

"Don't worry, we are going to speed that up by using hyperbaric oxygen therapy."

"How is that going to help?"

"For the brain to regenerate it requires additional energy. The chamber will increase the oxygen levels in the body, and the increasing blood flow will trigger the development of new blood vessels and promote neuroplasticity—which is a fancy way of saying it helps the brain rewire itself. We used the same treatment on President Cole."

The last comment grabbed Steele's attention. "You treated Cole?"

"Yes, of course. In fact, he is here right now."

Steele felt a surge of hope. If anyone could help him figure out what was going on, it was Denton Cole.

"Can I see him?"

The doctor frowned, but after Steele pressed him, he said, "I don't think it can hurt."

Steele stood in the hall and watched the nurses fussing over former president Denton Cole while his wife, Nancy, tried to stifle a smile.

"I can fluff my own pillows, thank you," Cole said.

"Why is it that you old men are the worst patients?" one of the nurses asked.

The first time Steele had checked in on Cole, he was still in a medically induced coma while the doctors tried to figure out what had caused the stroke. The initial prognosis was grim because the specialists had to stop Cole's chemo treatment while he was in the coma.

"The cancer is spreading, and the doctors don't know which one is going to kill him first," Nancy had told Eric on one of his visits.

Then one day he woke up.

From the hallway Eric could hardly tell the old man was sick. Sure, he had lost some weight and his hair had a lot more gray now than a year ago, but the famous smile was back, and from the laughs he shared with the nurses it sounded like his sense of humor was too.

Nancy must have sensed his presence because she got up and came out into the hall, with a beaming smile that couldn't hide the sadness in her eyes.

"Eric, I am so sorry to hear about your mother," she said, opening her arms and pulling him into a hug.

"She's . . ."

"She is going to be fine. Your mother is a strong woman. I've known her for years, and she is much stronger than you know."

He hoped she was right.

She let go of the hug and held him at arm's length.

"I must say that I am looking forward to the day when you do not look like you just got into a bar fight."

"Yes, ma'am." Steele grinned. "How is the old man doing?"

"Good days and bad, but you'd never know it by the way he's acting," she said. "That man is just too stubborn to die."

"I need to ask him a few questions. It is about work."

It wasn't a secret how protective Nancy was of her husband. She had always been that way. Stories abounded in Washington about those who had slighted

Cole in one way or another, only to face the wrath of Mrs. Cole.

Steele could feel that instinct kicking in now as she studied him.

"I don't know, Eric."

"He might be able to help me find out who attacked us."

"Eric, my boy." Cole's voice carried out into the hall. "Don't just stand there like a stranger, come in."

Steele kept his eyes locked on Nancy, waiting for her answer before he did anything.

"Okay," she whispered. "Just this once."

Steele moved to the door and watched the wide smile dawn on Cole's face.

"Good morning, sir."

"Not by the looks of your face. I can't wait to hear this one."

"I was going to bring roses, sir, but the gift shop was all out," Steele joked, stepping into the room.

"Never was a big fan."

He waited patiently for the nurses to prop the former president on his pillows, and when they left, Cole asked, "So, what brings you to the circus?" The smile faltered when he saw the admittance bracelet on Steele's wrist.

Steele filled him in on the attack and his mother's condition.

Eric had always looked up to Cole when he was president, and to see him in his current state was almost as hard as the time spent at his mother's bedside.

"Sir," Steele finally ventured, "I need your help."

"Don't know how much help I can be, but what can I do for you?"

Steele laid out everything he knew, including the mysterious package and Bo Nolan's murder. "He wrote the words *Cold Storage* in his own blood. Any idea what that means?"

"Dammit," Cole said softly.

"Sir?"

"Son, what I am about to tell you is something that only four other people in the world know. I'm not proud of it, but I think you better than anyone can appreciate the fact that sometimes we have to do things to keep this country safe that we would never do otherwise."

Steele didn't like where this was headed but offered a hesitant nod. He knew that just because he had an Alpha clearance didn't mean that he had access to every secret the United States government had.

"In 2002 the CIA was pulling high-value targets out of Afghanistan, Pakistan, Europe, you name it, but they weren't getting any actionable intel out of them. The agents were under considerable pressure from Washington to stop any future terror attacks, but the HVTs weren't talking. The CIA wanted these guys classified as enemy combatants, so they could ship them to countries that practiced enhanced interrogation."

Steele knew the feeling well. He had captured many terrorists whose cells were still in the planning stages of an operation. There was nothing more frustrating than knowing that an attack was imminent and the only person who could help you stop it was some dirtbag jihadist who wouldn't talk.

"They wanted permission to ship these guys to countries that allowed torture," Steele said just to make sure he was tracking.

Cole gave him a weary nod. "That's right. I was on the Senate Intelligence Committee when this came up. Nine-eleven was fresh in everyone's mind, and despite my fears that extraordinary rendition and enhanced interrogation were going to come back and bite us, I signed off on the request," Cole continued.

"So, what is Cold Storage?"

Steele could tell by his profile that he was carefully examining his answer. When he turned back his face was serious.

"Over the course of the War on Terror the United States and our allies have amassed quite a collection of scumbags. Places like Guantánamo Bay were fine for the low-hanging fruit, financiers, to midlevel planners and some commanders, but a lot of people wanted to know what we were going to do with the hardliners." Cole paused and nodded toward the pitcher of water on the table.

Steele got to his feet and retrieved a cup. He had asked himself the same question Cole just posed more times than he could remember. While the media loved to paint Guantánamo Bay in the harshest light possible, the fact was that terrorists sent to Cuba were allowed lawyers and books and even luxury privileges like multimillion-dollar soccer fields equipped with lights, so they could play games at night. All funded by the U.S. taxpayer. But worst of all, they were allowed to communicate with other terrorists. The left called it a torture factory, but Steele had been to Guantánamo, and it was Club Med compared to some of the other prisons he had seen.

Steele filled the cup with ice water, tore the wrapping off a straw, and helped his old friend sit up.

Cole took a long drink and nodded his appreciation.

When he continued, his voice was raspy and his color gray. Steele realized Cole was getting tired.

"Cold Storage was the answer to that problem. During a summit in Geneva, a secret decision was made to use a decommissioned icebreaker as an unsanctioned black site prison. It would be used to house the worst of the worst: men who had nothing but evil in their heart."

Jesus.

Black sites were nothing new, but they only stayed secret for so long. The fact that the United States and her allies had been running a floating black site since 2002 and he hadn't heard a single rumor was beyond his comprehension.

"Respectfully, sir, it is hard to believe that something like Cold Storage exists and I have never heard of it."

Cole gave him an understanding nod. "Believe it or not, it is real."

"But why would Nolan think that has anything to do with me?"

"I don't have the answer to that one, but I know who will."

Steele felt a glimmer of hope but cautioned himself. "Rockford?"

"No!" Cole said, wincing from the force of his reply. He squeezed his eyes shut against the pain, and Steele took a step closer, unsure of how to help.

"No," he repeated, softer this time. When Cole opened his eyes, there was a hint of shame. "I want you to keep John out of this."

"Sir, he is the president of the United States. How can I possibly keep him out of this?" Steele asked, confused.

"Did you know that John Rockford turned me down the first time I asked him to run with me?"

"No sir, I didn't."

"I figured he would," Cole said with a smile, "which was why I had to have him. All men want power, so if you find one who doesn't, that is the guy I'd want running things."

It was the same way Steele felt about Demo, and the words reminded him of the fight they'd had the night before. He felt a sickening cocktail of guilt and shame, but he pushed it away. Steele was determined to get Cole to answer his question.

"Sir, what does that have to do with keeping Cold Storage from President Rockford?"

"What is your primary job as an Alpha?"

The question came out of nowhere and would have caused Steele to falter if not for the fact that just like every Alpha, he'd begun his training at the Program's remote facility in the backwoods of Fort Bragg.

It was known as the Salt Pit.

A name that came from the fact that for security and budgetary reasons, the training facility was listed as an actual salt mine under the Department of Energy's budget. And from the moment Steele started Indoc, the cadre had hammered the answer to Cole's question into his head.

"An Alpha offers the president of the United States a third option. A way to protect America from enemies that can't be handled with diplomacy or all out war."

"And what happens if an Alpha is compromised or captured on an operation?" Cole asked.

Again, the answer came without having to think.

"If an Alpha is compromised or captured, he is disavowed. Denied. Forgotten."

"Seems harsh, doesn't it?" Cole asked.

"My job is to give my life so the president can do his job."

"They call that plausible deniability. And like it or not, it is a vital component to keeping this country free."

Cole rubbed his hand over his face, and Steele could tell he was summoning the last of his energy to finish the conversation.

"Rockford never wanted to be president," he continued, "and I suspect that if he'd known I was grooming him to one day take my job, he would have never accepted the vice president job in the first place. But now that he is the president, his first priority is to protect the office, because without that there is no United States."

"Tell me what to do," Steele said.

"Just like I was grooming Rockford, I was also grooming you."

"Me, for what?"

"I needed to know there were people John could lean on. You were one of them. Ted Lansky is the other."

"The chief of staff? He has been read in on the Program?" Steele asked.

A smile crept across Cole's chapped lips, and briefly Steele could have been looking at a healthier, younger man. But just as quickly as it had appeared, the smile was gone.

"Nathaniel West got too close . . . much too close," Cole said. "It made me realize just how much smoke and mirrors come with the Program." He paused and nodded toward the water cup.

Steele lifted the straw to his lips, and after a drink, Cole continued in a tired voice.

"Lansky is the only person John trusts one hundred percent. He knows about Cold Storage and can put you in contact with people who can help."

Cole's voice started to falter, and Steele knew their time together was coming to an end.

"What people?" he asked.

"They are called Cemetery Whisper," Cole mumbled.

Cemetery Whisper? What is that, a place, a person, a code name?

"Sir, I don't know what that is," Steele said.

"Lansky," Cole whispered. "Talk to Lansky."

Chapter 19

The White House

A red folder under his arm, Ted Lansky walked beneath the breezeway, heading for the Oval Office. It was his favorite time of year. When the temperatures in D.C. were just right and life was returning to the city.

It had rained the night before and his eyes drifted over the White House lawn. The air was fresh, and drops of water clung to the dogwood blooms—glinting like diamonds in the sun.

Lansky stopped near the door, wanting to savor the sight. He was a realist and knew these rare moments of beauty never lasted. In a few weeks it would be so humid that even the short walk down the colonnade would require a new shirt afterward.

His thoughts shifted to how he had gotten here in the first place. The call from Cole that had changed his life.

Lansky was at home, his retirement date from the CIA three days away. He had given his life to the Agency. Refused to compromise or cut corners in defense of the nation.

This hard-nose style had earned Lansky more than his share of enemies. It was no secret that the powers that be had already made sure Lansky was blackballed inside the Beltway. All the Beltway buzzards were waiting for Lansky to turn in his credentials, and then it would be time to settle their old scores.

The only thing he knew for certain was when the dust settled, there was no way in hell he was going to find a job anywhere near D.C.

Then the phone rang.

"Hello?"

"Ted, this is Denton Cole."

Denton Cole?

Lansky had met the man at a few parties. They had made polite small talk, but Lansky never remembered giving him his home number.

"I'm going to get right to the point," Cole said. "I

am running for president and I want Rockford as my number two."

Lansky wasn't sure how that had anything to do with him.

"Ted, it's not a secret that you don't have a lot of friends."

Oddly enough, Lansky found himself nodding in agreement.

He'd heard that Cole had a preternatural ability to be brutally honest, but not insulting. A skill that allowed him to say things like "It's no secret you don't have a lot of friends" without sounding like an asshole.

"That is true, sir," Lansky agreed.

"Well *I* want to be your friend," Cole replied.

Denton Cole had never expressed any public interest in running for president. Lansky knew that there were powerful men in Washington who wanted him to run. Those same men had been quietly working in the shadows for the past six months. They were making moves: fund-raising, calling in political favors, and neutralizing potential enemies.

Moves that got people talking, and Lansky had made a career out of being a good listener.

His first thought was that Cole wanted him to get dirt on someone, but he quickly rejected that notion. Playing dirty wasn't Cole's style.

"Do you want to be *my* friend, Ted?"

Lansky had enough experience to know that men like Cole didn't announce that they were running for president unless they knew they were going to win. He also knew that when a potential president of the United States asked you for something, there was only one answer.

"Yes, sir. How can I help?"

"You and John Rockford have been friends for fifteen years. He trusts you," Cole said. "I need you to get him to reconsider about being my running mate."

"Well, sir, you know how he can be when he makes up his mind."

"You're damn right I do. That's why I'm asking for your help."

But today, before knocking on the door, Lansky thought, *Wonder where I'd be if I'd said no?*

"Come in," a strong voice commanded.

Lansky found Rockford seated behind a massive oak desk. His shirtsleeves were rolled up as he plowed through the briefs and binders stacked before him. It was a sight he would never get used to.

Physically Rockford was an imposing man. With his wide shoulders and thick arms, he looked more like an all-American linebacker than the leader of the free world.

"Someone in North Korea actually took the time to write this," he said, holding up a binder. "Twenty-two-page letter on why we should lift sanctions." He dropped the binder with a *thump.* "This comes a month after they shot a missile over Guam. Blows my mind."

"Are you going to do it?" Lansky asked with a smirk.

"Putting it in my to-do box right now," Rockford said, dropping the binder in the oversize trash can. He leaned back and placed his hands atop his head.

He looks tired, Lansky thought as he walked to the center of the room.

"Mr. President, I need to talk to you about something."

"C'mon, Teddy, not today."

"I wouldn't be here if it wasn't important," Lansky said, holding up the red folder.

Rockford shut his eyes and rubbed his hands across his face. "Please tell me that is the only folder you had in your office and not an Alpha flash."

"Wish I could," Lansky said honestly.

"I should have known," Rockford muttered, opening his eyes. "Give me the highlights. Is it the Syrians, Iranians, Koreans . . . Chinese?" he asked.

"Last night someone tried to kill Stalker Seven."

That got Rockford's attention.

"How is that possible, he just came back on active status."

"They hit his house. Steele is banged up but fine. His mother . . . "

"His mother was there? Is she okay?" Rockford asked.

"She was transported to Green Bank. Doctors have her in a medically induced coma."

"Jesus . . . ," Rockford said, motioning for the folder.

Lansky handed it over, and as always, the president turned right to the synopsis. He didn't even make it past the first paragraph before he slammed his hand on the table and jumped to his feet.

"HOLY SHIT, Ted! Fifty feet down the hall is the most advanced intelligence operation in the world. In the WORLD, Ted," he yelled. "But somehow a disavowed Alpha manages to send a mysterious package to the United States. *Before* he and his wife are tortured. And how do we find out about this, Ted? From the INTERNET. Tell me how that happens, Ted?"

"Sir, when we were at the CIA, how many times did something like this pop up?" Lansky asked. "How many times did you tell me that intelligence work isn't an exact science? We read and we react the best way we can. That is why I'm here *now*."

Rockford walked over to the window overlooking the Rose Garden. He took a deep breath, and Lansky knew he was mulling over his response.

"The first time I felt the full weight of the responsibility that came with this job I was standing right here, looking out this window. I realized at that moment that the average American is certain that tomorrow will look just like today."

He turned around.

"And they expect me to make it happen."

"You have made it happen and you *will* continue to."

"Sometimes I wonder," Rockford said, walking back to his desk.

He dropped himself into his chair and picked up the red folder. "Right now, the United States is all alone in the world. The UK is trying to sort out Brexit, the rest of Europe is worried about Russia, and Israel—well right now, they wouldn't trust us to deliver a letter."

"They'll come around," Lansky said.

"You think Israel is going to come around if they find out about Archangel and the fact that I authorized Cutlass Main to spy on them?"

"Sir, if I may speak frankly."

Rockford nodded his assent.

"Out of all of our allies, Israel has time and time again shown that they will do what is necessary to protect themselves. They have spied on us, stolen from us, and lied to us, but they know we are in this together."

"Funny you say that. Do you know who I was talking to before you walked in here?"

"No."

"Prime Minister Bitton of Israel," the president answered. "He is willing to put everything behind us. . . ."

Lansky knew Rockford was desperate to fix the United States' strained relationship with the only ally in the Middle East. He also knew Bitton's offer would come with a price tag.

"If we do what, sir?" Lansky asked.

"If we open an embassy in Jerusalem."

"WHAT?" Lansky asked, unable to contain his shock.

"Right now, the biggest threat in the Middle East is Iran. Both Israel and Saudi Arabia agree. In fact, Crown Prince Salman will be at the ceremony in Jerusalem."

"But, sir, opening an embassy—"

"Will send a clear signal to Iran that Israel, the Saudis, and the United States are firm in their commitment to stop the rise of Shia extremism in the Middle East," Rockford said, grabbing a pen from the desk and cutting Lansky off with a wave of his hand.

He turned to the last page of the Alpha flash and signed his name below the authorization order.

"We leave for Jerusalem in five days," Rockford said, closing the folder and handing it over. "This situation better be handled *before* I get on that plane. Is that clear?"

"Yes, sir," Lansky said, taking the folder and heading for the door.

He crossed the hall to his office and found Pitts sitting in front of his desk.

"It's signed," Lansky said, passing Pitts the folder with the Alpha flash inside on his way to the minibar.

He poured himself a healthy shot of whiskey, and when he turned, Pitts was on his feet.

"I'll put Stalker Eight on it," Pitts said.

Lansky took a long swallow and shook his head. "No. Call Stalker Seven and tell him I want to meet."

Chapter 20

Washington, D.C.

Steele pulled the Chevy Astro van onto Thirty-fifth at 10:30 A.M. Traffic had finally started to ease up in Georgetown now that the majority of commuters had made it to their desks. But Steele knew finding a place to park was a whole other challenge.

Demo was sitting beside him, munching on a bag of pretzels. They hadn't spoken since Steele checked out of Green Bank, and he knew from experience that when Demo got quiet, there was no forcing him to open up.

Steele caught a break at the end of the street, finding an open spot next to Dixie Liquors. He pulled past, tapped the brakes, and expertly backed the van to the curb. All that was left for him to do was dry-swallow a pain pill.

The pill left an acrid taste in the back of his mouth. He glanced at the mirror, noting the difference after three days of treatment. Steele had spent most of the time hooked up to an IV loaded with steroids and anti-inflammatories. He'd been doubtful of the doctor's claims, but the results were nothing short of miraculous.

Not only had the swelling gone down, but the stiffness in his joints also was gone, and the bruising had started to fade. Steele settled back in his seat, resolved to wait in silence until Demo finally spoke.

"Look, mano . . . ," he began, only to stop just as quickly as he had started.

Steele waited for his keeper to find the words he was looking for.

"This thing with your mom and the hospital, it's . . ." Demo's voice was soft and vulnerable, something neither man was used to. "I want you to know that I'm with you no matter what. But the fact is, you aren't in any shape to be going on an operation. Especially not one this personal."

"Pitts doesn't think so."

Demo sighed and shook his head. "Did you actually talk to Pitts?"

"I responded to his text," Steele said with a frown.

"Well, I actually talked to him, you know, on the phone, like a civilized person."

"Text, call, it's the same thing, man," Steele said.

"Did he tell you on his text that he wanted to send Stalker Eight, but Lansky overruled him?"

"Stalker Eight—Collins?" Steele said.

"Yeah, you weren't his first choice for the mission."

Steele tried to undercut the serious point Demo was making by cracking a joke. "See, Cole was right. Lansky knows what he is doing."

"Lansky," Demo said, rolling his eyes. "I'm not sure what exactly you *think* that you know about the guy, but just because he wanted you on this op doesn't mean he is right."

"What exactly is your problem?" Steele snapped.

"Well, first off," Demo said, counting off his points with fingers dusted with pretzel salt. "Someone just tried to kill you. Second, we have no idea who that person was or what he wanted. And when I go to the pile of rubble that used to be your house, guess what I find."

"Jimmy Hoffa?" Steele said, praying the pain pill would kick in soon.

"No, smart-ass," Demo said, refusing to back down.

His handler jammed his hand into the pocket of his

faded jeans, came out with a dented brass shell casing, and tossed it at him.

"A casing?"

"'A casing?'" Demo mimicked. "Turn it over and look at the head stamp, genius."

Steele followed his instructions and read the number etched on the bottom of the brass. 5.45 × 39. That told him not only the bullet's caliber but also where it had been manufactured.

Russia.

"You're a gun guy. Would you call that a common caliber to see in the U.S.?"

"No," Steele said, shaking his head.

"And why not?"

"Because it's Russian military."

"The defense rests," Demo said, lifting a can of Coke from the paper grocery sack he'd brought with him and cracking the top with a flourish.

"All right, I'm listening," Steele conceded.

"I'm sure Lansky is a salt-of-the-earth kind of guy, but he isn't one of us, which means I don't trust him. If this thing goes sideways, it is going to be me, not Lansky, who has to face your mom."

"Okay, what's the plan?" Steele asked.

"We take it easy," Demo said, handing him an RF scanner. "Run it by the numbers."

"Fine," he said, stepping out.

"One more thing, man," Demo said, picking up the paper sack and handing it to Steele.

"What's this for?"

"The meter. Put it over the top. I don't want to get towed while watching your back."

Steele pulled the paper sack over the meter at the back of the van, put an earpiece into his ear, and pulled the Cannondale EVO mountain bike from the back. He clipped the transmitter to the collar of his hoodie and hopped on.

"Radio check," Steele said, putting his right foot on the pedal.

"Lima Charlie," Demo said.

Steele took off down the hill, keeping the mountain bike close to the curb. It felt good to have the breeze racing through his hair. Biking always felt like freedom to him. He pedaled west on M Street and took a left at the Ukrainian embassy. Steele coasted down the hill and over the footbridge that led to the Capital Crescent Trail.

The Aqueduct Bridge was built in 1830 to connect Arlington and Georgetown. In 1916 the Army Corps of Engineers dubbed it the Francis Scott Key Bridge, in honor of the man who had written "The Star-Spangled Banner." Despite its illustrious name, the project was plagued by problems that included cost overruns and structural deterioration. Four years after opening, it was replaced by Key Bridge, and now all that was left was a section known as the ruins.

Tactically, it was the perfect spot for a meet. The Potomac River took the south side out of play, and the bike paths offered two egress routes should trouble arise. Steele coasted beneath the stone arches and hopped off the bike. The river current was furiously beating against a tree limb that had lodged against one of the pillars below. He pulled his cell phone from his pocket and walked deeper into the tunnel.

The signal bars on the phone disappeared, because the granite construction blocked the reception.

Back at the opening, Steele rotated the messenger bag to the front of his body and removed the repeater. The black box fit in the palm of his hand, which made it easy to conceal. Steele thumbed the power switch to receive. He knew that as long as the repeater was in the open and he stayed within line of sight, he'd be able to communicate with Demo.

"Target coming off the Key Bridge," Demo advised. "Roger."

He checked the Rolex Submariner on his wrist. Just like he thought, Lansky was ten minutes early.

Steele took a SIG P365 from the bag. SIG called the

pistol a Micro Compact and the first time he'd held one Steele had thought it was a purse gun. Generally, he avoided subcompact pistols, preferring to stick with the 1911.

But he'd been intrigued by the fact that it came with a ten-round magazine, and since carrying a firearm in D.C. was illegal he didn't need a concerned citizen calling D.C. Metro about a man with a gun.

He booted up the RF scanner, leaving the flap of the messenger bag open so he could see the screen. Steele was fairly certain that Lansky didn't have time to send a team to bug the meet, but he wanted to make sure.

Steele turned his body in a slow circle, pretending to stretch out after a long ride, and when he didn't pick up any signals outside of the aqueduct, he moved beneath the arch.

"He's on the footbridge. Black suit, blue tie."

Steele was about to respond when two women, one pushing a stroller, entered the arch from behind him. Not wanting to be the crazy guy talking to himself under the bridge, he clicked the transmitter button once and then let it go. The technique was called breaking squelch, and Steele knew that when Demo heard the *click-hiss* signal he would know that Steele had received his transmission but couldn't talk.

He waited for the women to pass and then he saw Lansky coming toward him.

"I've got him. Loop in channel two. Listen only," he told Demo. There was a moment of silence. The second channel allowed Demo to record the conversation, but if anything were to go sideways, it would disappear anytime he or Demo transmitted over channel one.

"You're hot," Demo replied.

Steele broke squelch and watched the chief of staff approach.

"You expecting trouble?" Lansky asked, stopping at the aqueduct's opening.

"Well, someone did just try to kill me," Steele replied.

Lansky nodded, but when he came closer Steele stopped him.

"Not so fast, Ted," Steele warned. "Lift your jacket, lose the phone."

Lansky frowned but complied. He lifted the edge of his coat and made a slow circle, allowing Steele to see that he was unarmed.

"Where's the trust?" he asked, unclipping his cell phone and placing it on the Cannondale's seat before walking toward him.

"C'mon, Ted, you've been in the game long enough to know that you've got to earn it, just like Rockford did," he said, motioning Lansky forward. As the chief of staff approached, Steele glanced at the RF scanner.

The needle stayed locked to zero.

When he was sure that he wasn't transmitting, Steele pulled the casing out of his pocket and tossed it to Lansky.

"Take a look at this."

The chief of staff caught it in the air and flipped it over. His eyebrows arched as he glanced at the head stamp.

"Russian and brand-new by the looks of it," Lansky said.

"Welcome to the circus," Demo said over the radio.

"Where did you get it?"

"From what's left of my house."

"This is starting to feel like I'm in a Gray Man novel," Lansky said. "According to the report I read they also collected a SMAW-D."

"And all because Bo Nolan sent a package to my mom's house? What don't I know?" Steele asked, cutting to the chase. "What is the connection between Nolan and Cold Storage?"

"While you were off active status, we learned that Mossad had gained illegal access to the NSA database."

"A hack?"

Lansky nodded.

"Why would they risk hacking an ally?"

"All goes back to Nate West and that damn Iranian nuke that got loose last year. Former CIA director Styles tried to save her ass by making a deal with Israel."

"That didn't work out too well, seeing how that bitch is in prison," Demo quipped.

Steele ignored him. He was trying to digest what Lansky was telling him.

"Standard protocol is to investigate the hack with counter intel assets," he said.

"That is exactly what Rockford did. He authorized Cutlass Main to look into it, and that is the first time we heard about an operation Mossad was running in Saudi Arabia. It was called Archangel—they had credible intelligence of a bombing plot to kill the Saudi crown prince."

"Who was behind it, Iran?" Steele asked with a whistle.

"Not this time," Lansky replied. "It was an internal power struggle. Prince Badr trying to take out his brother, the crown prince. Badr didn't like how cozy he was getting with the West."

"What happened?" Steele asked.

"We sent Stalker Eight in. She found the tunnel and even grabbed a Tango."

"Sounds like a success to me," Steele said.

"It would have been if they had located the bomb."

"I assume this Tango got a one-way ticket to Cold Storage?" Steele asked.

Lansky nodded. "His name is Hassan Sitta. Some kind of Hezbollah super bomber. But he's not talking."

Steele quickly changed subjects, trying to catch Lansky off guard. "Tell me about Cemetery Whisper."

Lansky's eyes went flat, like someone had flipped off the light switch to his soul. Steele could see the wheels turning in the old spy's head.

Don't get cagey on me, Ted, Steele thought.

"Where did you hear that?" Lansky asked.

"A friend."

Lansky tried to brush him off. "I'm not here to talk about ancient history."

"Nolan getting disavowed might be ancient history," Steele countered. "But there is a connection to what you are telling me and Cold Storage."

"Nolan was working with Cemetery Whisper when he was killed."

"Who are they?" Steele asked.

"Officially, Cemetery Whisper is a collection of disavowed Western intelligence agents. Guys who bled for their countries but were cut loose for one reason or another. They are castoffs. Ronin," Lansky said.

Steele knew that the Ronin were samurai of feudal Japan whose masters had been killed. They were warriors forced to roam the country looking for work.

"And unofficially?" Steele asked.

"They are spies who grew tired of seeing their brothers and sisters betrayed by the countries they served and decided to do something about it," Lansky answered.

"You need to go to London. I will set up a meeting there," Lansky said.

"What if things get messy?"

"Why do you think I asked for you?" Lansky said, retrieving his phone. "I'll be in touch."

ACT II

Chapter 21

Leipzig, Germany

Under a slate-gray sky, the wind was cold and biting as Zakayev cut through the housing tenement. His boots echoed off the concrete block walls. His destination was two blocks south, but he wanted to keep off the streets. Stay away from the cameras the Germans had on every street corner.

Europe had changed in the past five years. Borders were being tightened, battle lines drawn. Tension was brewing in the air, a feeling that unknown threats were mounting in the distance.

From the open windows of the low-rent apartments came the smells of unwashed bodies and stale foods.

Scents that reminded Zakayev of the days leading up to his capture in Syria and being sent to Black Dolphin.

Zakayev had been working for the Russian foreign intelligence or the FSB since graduating from Camp 722. He was tasked with assisting insurgents fighting against America in countries like Iraq and Afghanistan.

He had been sent to Syria three months before Russia's first troops started to arrive. In that time Zakayev had taken a ragtag group of fighters who were still loyal to President Assad's faltering regime and turned them into a lethal combat force.

Then the Russian commandos showed up with orders from Moscow putting Zakayev under Captain Dusan's control.

It didn't take long for Zakayev to realize that Captain Dusan was an idiot. The kind of man who went to war to get promoted off his soldiers' blood, sweat, and tears.

But it wasn't until Dusan started using Zakayev and his men as bait that the Chechen decided to kill him.

He found his opportunity a few days later, after a long day of patrols. The sun had just dropped behind the shattered mound of rubble that had once been Aleppo's skyline. They were heading back to their camp, one of the Spetsnaz commandos leading them south. The man stopped at a corner to pull his night vision out of his pouch when a shot rang out.

Zakayev saw the flash from a building across the street, but before he could say anything a machine gun opened up from a second position.

"Ambush," Dusan yelled.

The commandos returned fire, and Zakayev yelled for his men to seek shelter in the building across the street.

"This way," he said.

Behind him Dusan screamed, "The Chechen coward is running away."

The captain's first shot snapped over Zakayev's head, the second hit the point man, Nizar, in the back. The bullet punching through his spine.

Zakayev watched the man fall face-first to the ground.

"*Nizar,*" he screamed.

Then a towering rage took over. His world turned red, his body burning hot like he was on fire.

Zakayev turned, flipped the selector of his Kalashnikov to auto, and leveled it at Captain Dusan's chest.

Die, you son of a bitch.

The rifle bucked against him, and the bullets left a line of perfect red holes across Dusan's chest.

"He killed the captain," one of the commandos yelled.

Zakayev pivoted toward the voice and fired. The first round hit the commando under the jaw, blowing his brains into his helmet.

Kill them all, the voice in his head commanded.

Zakayev raked the AK-47 across the commandos until the bolt locked back.

He dropped the rifle and had the pistol halfway out of the holster when they rushed him.

Back in Leipzig, Zakayev stepped out of the alley and onto the street lined with bars and hotels that rented rooms for an hour. He stopped at the first one he came to. Paid the man at the front desk in cash and took the key and went upstairs.

He locked the door behind him, dropped his bag on a table scarred with cigarette burns, and went to the sink. He twisted the hot water knob, and the pipes started vibrating in the walls. The faucet released a trickle of brackish water, but as the pressure built, the sound grew more violent.

Zakayev stepped back, concerned that the sink might explode. Finally, the faucet vomited a ball of black-and-gray residue into the drain. The water that filled the sink was pale yellow and smelled of sulfur. But it was hot, and that was all he cared about.

He placed the stopper in the sink and walked over to the bag. Zakayev pulled out a magnifying glass, an X-Acto knife, and the box of rubber gloves he'd bought at the store and laid them on the table.

Zakayev couldn't stop thinking about the packet Gabriel had emailed to him. It showed Steele boarding a plane at Washington Dulles. Worse than the fact that Steele wasn't dead was the few tidbits of information Gabriel had been able to dig up on the man.

The information didn't even fill up a full page, mostly circumstantial claptrap, grainy photos from places like Algiers and Tunisia, rumors of an American operative with green eyes—an unstoppable killer. Zakayev had heard enough ghost stories to separate fact from bullshit, and he knew that the only way to stop a man like Steele from hunting you down was to kill him, which meant Zakayev had to keep moving.

He wasn't afraid of Gabriel or death.

Zakayev knew he was going to die, but *he* was going to be the one who chose the when and where. Not some chickenshit Saudi who stuck a bomb in his head.

With that purpose in mind, he stretched a pair of rubber gloves over his hands and took the package he'd taken from the GTO out of the bag.

Besides the rust-colored spots dotting the brown paper and the tears around the edges, the wrapping was relatively unharmed. He held it up to the light and inspected it.

The paper was too thick, and Zakayev knew better than to simply rip it open.

Spies always had little tricks.

He carried it to the sink and held it over the steam, making sure each side was saturated and the tape had pulled free. Zakayev took it back to the table and used the magnifying glass to inspect every inch for the outline of wires or other antitamper devices. When he was sure that it was clean, he cut the tape free and peeled back the paper, revealing the contents.

A fucking book?

Of all the things he'd imagined could be inside the package, a faded 1993 *National Geographic Atlas* was not one of them. Zakayev inspected every inch of the book, starting with the spine. He held it upside down, fanned the pages to see if anything fell out.

Nothing.

He checked the cover for any seams or bulges— anything that would indicate something hidden. But there was nothing.

Nolan wouldn't send this book for no reason.

What was Nolan's story? Zakayev wondered.

His gaze drifted to the tattoos covering his hands and arms. At Black Dolphin a man wore his history on his body, but it hadn't always been that way. Before being processed into the penal system, Zakayev's skin had been clean. The prisoners at Black Dolphin called him a virgin. His lack of tattoos caused him to get into countless fights, for reasons Zakayev didn't understand until one of the older convicts broke it down for him.

"The tattoos come from the old days when the guards branded prisoners. Escapees got the *B* for *begly*—escapee—branded on their backs so the guards knew who to keep an eye on," he began with a knowing smile. "If you were serving hard labor, they branded *SK* on your arms, but the worst"—he leaned in conspiratorially—"the worst were the *thieves*. No one can stand a thief. They branded them on the foreheads."

"I had no idea."

"Yes, yes, it is true. The government"—the old man paused to spit on the ground— "outlawed the branding, but they had started something, you see. The one thing they cannot take from you is your *mast*—your suit."

"Suit? I don't understand," he admitted.

The man pointed at his arm. "Your skin," he said. "Mark a thief's skin and everyone knows he is a thief, yes?"

Zakayev flipped idly through the atlas, taking his

time with each page, searching for anything out of the ordinary. He was about to give up when he found the answer.

He picked up the phone and dialed the number Gabriel had given him.

"Yes," a man answered. The scrambler made his voice sound metallic.

"I found it," Zakayev said. "I need to go to Buda-pest."

"Go to the train station. Green trash can. Your contact will have a blue umbrella and your papers."

Ten minutes later, Zakayev bought a ticket to Buda-pest at the window and headed down the stairs.

The station was a holdover of the Soviet Union: in-stitutional gray walls, dirty tiles, and the biting scent of cologne that failed to mask the unwashed stench of the masses.

To Aleksandr Zakayev it smelled like home.

At the bottom of the stairs he found two soldiers posted up. He eyed them warily, but when he drew abreast, he realized that they were not a threat.

Fresh-faced boys, he thought. *Not old enough to shave, much less carry a rifle.*

Zakayev could have killed them both before they had a chance to use the AK-74s draped nonchalantly across their chests. But there was no need. The soldiers were too busy searching for attractive girls in the crowd of drab-suited men and pinch-faced women to pay him any mind.

He angled past the soldiers and seamlessly blended into the crowd. His roving eyes searched for the green trash can and the contact with the blue umbrella. Zakayev found the trash can but not the umbrella. He'd thought that spotting color in the monochromatic sea of grays and blacks would have been easier.

"Aleksandr," a voice cooed behind him.

Zakayev recognized the voice and felt a jolt of fear creep up his spine. If Gabriel was going to send an assassin, he had picked the right one.

The woman standing there was blond and just as beautiful as he remembered.

"Irena," he said.

"I heard that you were dead," she said, a hint of a smile tugging on her pouty lips.

Irena Turov came to Camp 722 a malnourished ten-year-old girl with clear green eyes, stringy hair, and lips that were too big for her face. Zakayev didn't pay her the slightest bit of attention, but the commander of the camp, Colonel Kozlov, saw something in the young Ukrainian. At fourteen he sent Irena to a separate camp.

When she returned, two years later, Irena was beautiful. Zakayev learned that she had already been assigned to the FSB. They gave her the code name White Widow, and by the time she graduated from Camp 722, Irena had already amassed five high-level kills.

"Not dead yet," he said.

"Don't worry, Aleksandr," she said, reading his mind. "I am here to help you." She pressed her hand into his.

"Help me how?" he asked, feeling something metallic in his palm.

A key.

"Eric Steele is in London."

Fuck.

"Go to Budapest. Yuri is on his way to London. He and I will handle Steele." She winked and then disappeared into the crowd.

The key had the number 103 etched into the top. Zakayev angled for the lockers, watching the guards from the corner of his eye. The locker turned out to be at the end of the drab green row, third from the top. He fit the key into the lock and opened the door. Inside was an exact replica of the bag he had in his hand. Zakayev made the switch, exchanging his bag for the one containing his new identity, closed the door, and walked to the restroom.

He fed a few coins into the slot and pushed through

the turnstile. The bathroom was small and filthy. He went to the last stall, closed the door behind him, and flipped the lock. Zakayev set the bag on the toilet and then stripped out of his travel clothes. Inside the bag he found a pair of gray slacks, a long-sleeve shirt, and a fleece jacket. He dressed quickly, put the cash and train ticket into his pocket, and then checked the final object in the bag.

The OTs-38 Stechkin was a five-shot revolver developed for the Russian special forces in 2002. The pistol wasn't sexy. It had boxy lines that gave it a primitive appearance, but Zakayev didn't care about the way it looked.

He had requested the pistol because when loaded with 7.62 × 42 mm SP4—silent pistol cartridges—he could fire the pistol without a bang or a flash.

It was literally a silent killer.

Zakayev checked to make sure three boxes of SP4 ammo had been included, then put his dirty clothes back into the bag and stood up. He stashed the locker key behind the toilet and then checked the passport. It was worn but current and to his surprise even had the entry stamp with today's date affixed to the front page. He pushed the pistol into his right pocket and the cash and ticket into his left, grabbed the bag, and headed out to board the train.

Chapter 22

London

The flight to Heathrow took eight hours, and with the time change it was almost three in the morning when Steele and Demo landed. The Ambien he had taken on the flight had knocked Steele out but, as usual, failed to keep him under.

Sleep deprivation was nothing new. He was trained to push himself and knew how the body reacted. After twenty-four hours the brain has the chemical impairment of someone with a .10 blood alcohol level. Judgment was the first to go, followed by a decline in short-term memory and decision making. Reaction times were longer and hand-eye coordination worse.

Heathrow was the busiest airport in Europe. A sprawling structure that echoed with every language under the sun. After deplaning, Steele paused at a mirror to check the concealer he'd reapplied on the flight to mask the bruises on his face. It had been a few years since the last tradecraft class he'd taken at Langley, and he wasn't sure if he remembered which areas to darken and which to lighten.

He was pleasantly surprised when he saw that he hadn't lost his touch.

The signage directed them down a long hallway to a flight of stairs. When they reached the floor below, their bags were just coming out, and they knifed through the press of bodies to retrieve them.

"Guess we better get in line," Steele said, nodding at the roped-off serpentine that led to the customs booths.

"They call it a queue here," Demo said.

"Good to know," Steele replied.

Steele would have preferred to travel with just a carry-on, but two burly men with open-ended tickets and no accompanying luggage tended to garner unwanted attention. They purchased the suitcases and nondescript clothing from a box store in D.C. The tags had been removed and the fabric rumpled to look lived in, but in the end, they were still props: something to satisfy the customs agent and then be discarded.

Steele wasn't worried about clearing customs. He was worried about the man he was scheduled to meet.

"What do we know about this guy you are meeting? Ol' what's his name," Demo asked.

"Percy? He has a degree in economics from Cambridge. Fluent in German and Russian. Got scooped up by MI6 and sent to the East German desk," Steele answered.

"And then what?"

"Then he went to the private sector."

"You think it is a good idea to trust a civilian?" Demo asked.

"We aren't trusting anyone," Steele replied. "Lansky might be on the up-and-up, but since this isn't our turf and we don't know these people, we are going to take it slow," Steele said with a grin.

"I guess you do listen," Demo said, eyes wide with surprise.

"Don't get all sappy on me," Steele replied.

They had been in the line for half an hour when the customs agent finally motioned Steele forward with a flick of a finger. Eric approached, passport at the ready.

"What brings you to London, Mr. . . ." He glanced down at the passport. "Mr. Sands?"

Max Sands was a legend Steele used in Europe, a

separate identity he had created for Alpha operations. If anyone ran the legend through Interpol, they would find that Max Sands was a businessman from Toronto with an apartment, tax information, and a driver's license to match.

"I'm here on business," Steele answered honestly.

"And how long will you be staying?"

"Not sure about that one. I am heading up to Scotland to meet with some investors," Steele said, playing on the English disdain for their northern cousins. "Last trip I had to change my flight three times, so this go-round I got an open-ended ticket."

The agent smiled. "I understand *exactly* what you mean. Besides whiskey I've no idea what they bring to the UK." He handed Steele his passport. "Have a good trip."

"Thank you, sir."

On the way out, they passed the cab stations, with their peculiar tall black taxis, and took a short pause to exchange dollars for pounds, and walked down a flight of steps to the Piccadilly line, which ran from the airport to London. The Tube.

"I'll get the passes, you grab the coffee," Demo said.

"Good call," Steele replied.

He stopped at the first coffee kiosk and waited for the barista to order a brace of coffees. Steele pressed his back to the counter and scanned the crowd while waiting for his order.

Growing up, Steele had been a big fan of James Bond and loved how the British spy was able to pick out a singular threat in a sea of moving bodies. The movies made it easy. The bad guys were always in black, which made them easy to spot.

If only they were that easy to find in the real world, Steele thought.

He knew from experience that the probability of someone trying to hit him in the open was extremely low. London had too many cameras for anyone to try.

Any threat at this stage of the game would be a passive tail. To get spotted, the agent would have to make a mistake. Get too close. Make eye contact for too long.

Mistakes seasoned professionals rarely made.

Even so Steele made a sweep of the room, stopping only when the barista approached.

"Here ya are," she said.

Steele passed her a twenty-pound note, grabbed the coffees, and went to join Demo at the Tube map.

By the time he made it through the crowd a blond woman was standing a few paces from Demo's right, frowning at the map.

Steele handed the coffee to Demo, wondering how he missed her approach.

"I hate these damn maps," Demo said, taking the coffee and nodding toward the random scribble of multicolored lines. "They look like a kid's drawing."

"Looks like all roads go to Cockfosters," Steele said, taking a sip and watching the woman walk away.

"If you are done sightseeing, I'm good to go," Demo said, catching him looking at the blond woman.

Steele felt his face redden as he followed Demo down a second flight of stairs to the deserted train terminal.

Steele drained his espresso and looked around for a trash can. "Where do they dump the trash?"

Demo pointed at a man sweeping the floor with a push broom. "No rubbish bins in London, boyo. Too many memories of IRA lads depositing ticking packages."

The train arrived, the cars dented and the metal pockmarked. Steele sat down and felt the overwhelming urge to close his eyes. The espresso had taken the edge off, but he was exhausted. They rode the Tube to Barons Court and walked to a parking garage.

Inside the garage was dark except for the red LED lights attached to the security cameras. Their transportation and gear were waiting inside a black Range Rover parked in stall twenty-one. Steele took a Streamlight micro flashlight from his pocket and scanned the undercarriage while Demo kept watch.

After making sure the SUV was clean, Steele retrieved the keys from the gas tank, popped the hatch, and tossed them to Demo, who climbed behind the wheel.

Steele dug between the upholstery, found the release lever, and opened the compartment. Inside was a duffel bag and two black Pelican cases.

He opened the bag with a whistle. "Well, hello there," he said, taking out a stack of fresh hundred-pound notes. He took one of them from the stack and examined it with the flashlight. The ink and printing looked good. Next, he rubbed it between his thumb and forefinger. "Nice paper too."

Steele shoved the cash into his pocket and opened the first case. Instead of the usual Glock 19s he uncovered a pair of Browning Hi Powers and two Walther PPKs. He checked one of the Hi Powers and shoved it into his waistband. Before closing the hatch he also took out the case and then climbed into the passenger seat.

Demo had already checked the vehicle's gauges. Making sure it was gassed up and ready to go. Both men knew that when something went wrong, the cause was usually little things that someone had overlooked.

Like the time Steele had picked up a drop car in Yemen only to find that it was out of gas.

"Are we good?" he asked.

Demo nodded and pulled out of the garage. They stopped at the top lip and eased into traffic. Neither man noticed the Ducati motorcycle that pulled out a few seconds later.

Chapter 23

London

Yuri picked up the car at a chop shop near the Thames. The men inside were Eastern Europeans, bulky men wearing blue coveralls who knew better than to ask any questions.

The gray shops and rusted warehouses faded away as he neared the borough of Kensington and the address Irena had given him. Like many of the neighborhoods in central London, Kensington looked like it had a rich and storied history. The smallest of the inner London boroughs, it was a haven for the rich and powerful. Its tidy streets were lined with high-end shops, expensive cars, and resplendent banks.

It was the kind of area that frowned on people like Yuri. Which was the reason his blood ran cold when he saw the police car idling at the curb and realized that he was speeding.

"Shit." He knew that slamming on the brakes would draw the cop's attention, so he took his foot off the gas and glanced worriedly at the bag on the passenger-side floorboard.

Dammit, Irena.

She was the only person Yuri had ever met who did this to him. Just the thought of her sucked the blood from his brain and engorged a lower part of his body. Made him do stupid things to impress her like speeding through London in a stolen car with a bag of submachine guns.

Luckily, the London cop wasn't paying attention. But the scare was enough to make Yuri engage the cruise control.

He made it to the address she'd sent without any further incident and grabbed the bag off the floorboard. The apartment was nicer than he would have chosen, with a marbled lobby and a doorman in a red jacket. Yuri took the elevator to the third floor. The door was open.

"Irena?"

"You're late," she called from the other room.

Yuri closed the door and threw the dead bolt. When he turned, Irena was standing naked in the entryway. He let the bag clatter to the floor, his eyes tracing the curves of her body.

"I . . ."

"You what?" she asked, nibbling her lower lip.

Yuri stepped closer and reached for her waist. He felt the warmth of her bare skin on the palm of his hand, saw the desire in her eyes when he picked her up.

He carried her into the living room, kissing her on the neck. A moan started, low in her throat, and her hands scrambled to his belt.

"I missed you," she said.

Yuri laid her on the floor and pulled his shirt over his head, exposing the rippling muscles he knew she liked. "I missed you too," he said.

Thirty minutes later, Yuri was running his finger over the white scar above her breast while Irena smoked a cigarette and looked at the picture from the file he'd brought with him.

"This is new," he said.

She blew out a line of smoke. "Got it in France last year," she said. "So, tell me about Steele."

Yuri eyed the picture of the man with the green eyes. "His name is all that I know."

"He didn't look like much when I saw him at Heathrow," she said.

"That's what I thought the first time we went after him."

"I followed him, you know." Irena smiled.

"Please tell me that you are joking," Yuri begged.

She shook her head side to side. "Followed him all the way to his safehouse."

"What if he had seen you?"

"But he didn't." She smiled. "Never knew I was there."

"You have to be careful with this man," Yuri cautioned.

"Are you worried about me?"

"Yes. He is very dangerous."

Irena took the cigarette out of her mouth and lowered it to the photo. "So am I," she said, burning one of Steele's eyes out with the tip of the smoke.

Silence fell over the room and Yuri's gaze followed the acrid smoke up to the ceiling.

"What are you thinking about?" she asked.

"Zakayev," he answered honestly.

"What about him?"

"Do you remember the first time we all met at the camp?"

"I remember the colonel almost catching us in the woods." She giggled.

The memory still terrified Yuri. "Even then, Kozlov had a plan for all of us," he said. "He knew you would go to the FSB, Hassan would be sent to Hezbollah, and I would join the Spetsnaz."

"What is your point?"

"You knew the colonel better than anyone," Yuri said. "What was his plan for Zakayev?"

Frowning at the name, Irena sat up and snuffed the cigarette out in the ashtray. "There are only two things you need to worry about."

"And what are those?" Yuri asked.

"The first is how we are going to kill Eric Steele," she answered, climbing on top of him. "I think you can figure out the second."

Chapter 24

London

Steele's dreams were chaotic, rushes of shadowed faces, voices, and places. One moment he was meeting with Lansky in Georgetown. The chief of staff was telling him to go to London.

In the next instant he was in Heathrow, standing in front of the map. Trying to make sense of the maze of red, blue, and green lines.

"Where are you going?" the woman with the green eyes asks.

"I don't know," Steele answers.

Suddenly she has a pistol pointed at his stomach. Steele tries to move, but he is frozen in place.

"I do," the woman says. "You are going to hell."

And then she fired.

Steele's eyes flashed open. He was immediately awake, arm sweeping for the Hi Power under his pillow.

"Holy shit," he said, realizing it was just a dream.

He sat up, chest covered in sweat, and rubbed his eyes. A glance at the clock told him that he'd gotten four hours of sleep.

Steele pushed himself to his feet, went to the Pelican case, and grabbed one of the prepacked tac-wallets. Inside was a credit card, some cash, an earpiece, tracking tabs, and a set of lock picks.

He didn't plan on getting into any trouble, but Steele knew it paid to be prepared.

Steele shoved the Hi Power into his waistband and opened the door, the hardwood floor creaking under his feet despite his light step. The hall was short, the sun providing enough light that he was able to find his way to the den.

Demo was sprawled out on the leather couch, dead asleep. He had one shoe on his foot, the other lying upturned on the floor. Across from him the BBC was on the television.

"Poor guy is all tuckered out."

The previous keeper had stocked the flat with tea

but no coffee, and Steele made a mental note to stop by the store on the way back. On the street, it was a bright and cloud-free morning, but Steele knew that could change in a flash. He grabbed an espresso and stopped at a pay phone to make a call. He dialed the calling card code from memory and then the number.

"Bryan Manning," a cheery voice answered.

"Mr. Manning, it is Max Sands."

"Oh, good morning, Mr. Sands, how may I help you today?"

"I am in town on business and would like to drop by the shop to pick up some clothes that I ordered."

"Wonderful, how is ten o'clock?"

"Perfect."

He hung up the phone and walked to the nearest Tube station. At the turnstile Steele swiped the Oyster card Demo had bought when they arrived and walked downstairs to the Piccadilly line and boarded the train.

In the subway car, Steele watched the cityscape flash by the window, noting the cranes dotting the skyline. London was a city stuck in perpetual growth, constantly expanding, refurbishing, or reinventing. It reminded him of a teenager in the midst of a growth spurt—always outgrowing itself.

Twice during the ride, Steele glanced up at the map attached to the bulkhead just to reassure himself that he was on the right line. There was something about the London Tube that had always confused him.

"Next stop Piccadilly Circus," the automated system announced.

The car stopped at the station at exactly a quarter till ten and Steele slipped into the crowd, heading for the stairs. Near the top he held his breath, preparing himself for the onslaught of cigarette smoke he knew was waiting for him aboveground.

Piccadilly Circus was one of the most popular sights in London, and Steele found every nation in the world represented on the sidewalks. Everyone had their cell phones out. Some were taking pictures of the digital sign, while others snapped selfies. A brave few scrambled across the street and almost got clipped by a double-decker bus for their troubles.

Steele had rules for each city he visited. In London it was "never cross the road unless it is in the midst of a pack of locals." There had been some close calls in the past, but so far, the rule had kept him from any unnecessary trips to the emergency room.

He crossed Regent Street with the crowd, took a left, and found himself arriving at his destination.

Savile Row had been at the heart of London tailoring since 1803. It was a name synonymous with well-dressed men and the originator of the "bespoke suit." The first time Steele heard about Manning and Manning tailors he was on an operation in Paris. He was called in to assist on a routine close-target surveillance, and it never crossed his mind to pack a suit.

But when Cutlass Main learned that the handoff was going to be made at the Paris Ritz, Steele knew he needed to remedy the situation quickly. He went to a department store and bought one off the rack.

Steele's job was to monitor the handoff and avoid detection. He had run similar operations countless times, but they were usually on a dusty street in the Middle East, not the Paris Ritz.

The men and women attending the high society affair spent more money on their clothes than Steele spent on rent. He knew there was a problem when he handed his invitation to the doorman. The man looked him over, the Gallic sneer on the edge of his lips unmistakable. He took Steele's invitation between his index finger and thumb, like it was covered in shit.

Steele got the hint. In some places clothes really do make the man.

A dignified split-front building, 9–10 Savile Row had a gray stone exterior and walnut door and transom. It was equal parts good taste and modesty, the exact attributes that drew Steele to Manning and Manning in the first place.

Steele finished his coffee, dropped the container in the bin, walked inside, and took the elevator to the fifth floor.

Bryan Manning was the epitome of an English gentleman with a well-manicured white beard and an easy, good-natured smile.

"Good morning, Mr. Sands," he said, gesturing for Steele to come in.

"Mr. Manning, thank you for fitting me in on such short notice."

"Not at all. What brings you to London?" he asked while leading him to the dressing area, where a pair of suits were hanging from wooden hangers.

"Business mostly."

"Of course."

There were two suits waiting. The first in a charcoal gray. It was a replacement for a similar suit that had bullet holes in the front. The second was navy blue; both fit like a glove.

Bryan eyed them professionally, made a few minute adjustments before nodding his satisfaction.

"I've got a late dinner at the Sabers Club," Steele said, nodding to the suits.

"Wonderful establishment. May I suggest?" he said, looking at the two suits.

"Please," Steele replied. He had never been to Sabers or any other gentleman's club in London but knew their dress code was strict.

"Sabers is one of the oldest and most conservative of London's great clubs. While either suit would work, I think the navy blue would fit the bill."

"Thank you, Bryan. I'll take your word for it."

Downstairs, Steele was stepping onto the sidewalk when he had the feeling someone was watching him. His hand drifted to the Hi Power at his waist, eyes scanning the street. Looking for any threats.

Nothing.

Must be the jet lag, he thought.

But Steele knew better than to ignore his instincts. Just because he couldn't see the threat didn't mean it wasn't there. Instead of heading back the way he came, Steele took a longer route. Making a big circle that allowed him to use the glass-fronted buildings to check his back trail.

When he was sure that he was clear, he ducked into the underground station and headed back to Demo.

Chapter 25

London

Yuri stuffed steel wool into the WIX fuel filters, and when he was done, he twisted them onto the barrels of the two H&K MP5Ks. The makeshift suppressors were bigger than the real thing, but he knew they would work.

The submachine guns came without stocks and a shorter four-inch barrel, which made them perfect for what he had planned. Yuri connected a bungee sling to the frame and handed it to Irena, who slipped it over her head and then zipped it beneath the black rider's jacket.

"Good?" he asked.

"Perfect."

Yuri stowed his submachine gun and threw his leg over the Ducati. The motorcycle rumbled to life as he pulled the helmet over his head and felt Irena climb on behind him.

"Can you hear me?" he asked, speaking into the microphone installed in the helmet.

"Yes. Let's go hunting."

Steele was on his way back to the safehouse when he realized that he hadn't checked in on his mother since leaving the States.

He stopped outside the Tesco supermarket, where he planned to stop and grab some groceries for the safehouse, and checked his watch. It was almost 10:00 A.M. in London, which meant it was close to five in the morning back at Green Bank hospital.

Steele dialed the number his mother's doctor had given him.

"Dr. Thompson," the man answered.

Steele could tell from the background noise, the squawk of the PA system paging another doctor, that Thompson was making his rounds.

"Doc, it's Eric Steele, just wanted to check in on my mother's status."

"Eric, good to hear from you. Just one second," Dr. Thompson said.

His answer was followed by the rustle of the man's hand over the phone.

Steele took it as a sign that the doctor wanted to have the call in private, and he sensed that the news wasn't good.

"Are you there?" Thompson asked a moment later.

"Yeah, I'm here."

Thompson's tone was somber, and Steele prepared himself for the worst.

"Eric, your mother started running a high fever last night. I ordered blood drawn and . . ."

A hiss of static muted the end of his sentence. When the connection cleared, the first thing Steele heard was "surgery."

"The surgery went well, but we won't know anything until . . ."

"Doc, you cut out. Surgery, what surgery?" he demanded.

"We had to remove her spleen, Eric."

A wave of guilt rolled up Steele's body. It was a hopeless sick feeling that made him weak in the knees.

Dammit. I should have been there.

"Before you start blaming yourself," Thompson began, as if reading his mind, "we do lots of these every week. It sounds bad, but I don't want you beating yourself up."

"I should have been there," Steele said.

"Very important people trust you to do your job. I'm going to need you to trust me to do mine. We are going to run another blood panel tomorrow morning. I will have more news for you when you call back. Right now, however, I have to finish my rounds."

"Yes, sir," Steele said. "Thank you, doc."

"You got it," Thompson said, hanging up.

Steele shoved the phone into his pocket and stepped into the store. He already had his hands full with the suits, but Demo would be hungry.

He felt terrible about missing his mom's surgery. To make matters worse, Demo was also on his conscience. Steele knew that even though Lansky had signed off on the op, it wasn't a typical Alpha mission.

It was personal, and he'd dragged Demo into it.

He walked through the store, grabbing the needed items rapidly. He threw some coffee, two bottles of water, and some Cocoa Krispies cereal into the basket. Steele was so preoccupied that he almost forgot the milk but managed to grab a can of condensed on his way to the register.

At the register the girl asked, "Yawanna bag for four pence?"

"Excuse me?"

"A bag," the girl said, pointing at the plastic sack. She held up four fingers. "It's four pence for the bag."

"I have to *buy* a bag for the groceries I just paid for?"

She nodded.

Steele was too tired to ask why, and since he knew there was no way he could carry the loose groceries and the garment bag for the suits, he handed her the coins.

He was halfway down the block when the bag split. Cupping his hand, he managed to save most of the contents, but the condensed milk hit the sidewalk and rolled off the curb.

"Of course . . . ," Steele said, frustrated.

Draping the suits over the hood of an Aston Martin, he tied the flimsy plastic handles into a square knot and flipped the bag, carefully shifting the load until they set in their new positions. He never saw the Ducati pull onto the street.

Annoyed, Steele quickly bent down to retrieve the rogue can of milk, which had rolled behind the tire of a Peugeot.

Suddenly he heard the rear windshield explode over his head.

Chapter 26

Thwaaaaaaaap.

Steele dove behind the Peugeot and yanked the Hi Power from his waistband. He crawled toward the engine block, heart hammering in his chest at the realization that someone had just tried to kill him in broad daylight.

The Metropolitan Police didn't hide the fact that they had installed cameras on every block. They operated on the theory that if criminals knew they were being recorded, they might think twice about breaking the law.

Whoever had taken a shot at him didn't give a shit. Because instead of running away, the shooter flicked the selector switch to full auto and opened up on Steele's hiding place.

Thwaaaaaapppppp thwaaaaaaaaappppp.

The Peugeot swayed under the onslaught. The car rocked on its hinges, the bullets blasting star-shaped holes through the aluminum skin as the shooter raked the car from stem to stern.

Steele's plan was to hit him on the reload, but he never got the chance.

Before the first shooter ran through his magazine, a second opened up. The bullets cut across the hood, punching through the metal with the sound of rocks on a tin roof.

Steele judged that he had been under fire for less than thirty seconds. But in a gunfight, time was subjective. He was experienced enough not to lose his cool or give in to the irresistible urge to run. Instead he took stock of his surroundings; tried to learn as much as he could about his attackers without actually seeing them.

Despite missing the kill shot, they were obviously professionals. The first shooter had laid down a base of fire, forcing Steele to ground. Once his partner entered the fight, he was able to reload and then they attacked together. One fired while the other advanced. They were trying to keep his head down so one of them could flank him. There was only one problem. They hadn't killed him with the first shot.

And that was a mistake Steele promised was going to cost them.

He waited for a lull in the fire and leaned forward, ripped open the plastic grocery bag, and got the box of cereal. Steele placed the box between his knees and then hit the sideview mirror with the barrel of his pistol. He gingerly grabbed the largest section of broken mirror and held it up so that he could view the street from different angles.

The shooters were dressed in black motorcycle gear with matching helmets. The one closest to Steele was shorter than the other, with long blond hair that hung from the back of the helmet.

The girl from the airport. *Has she been tracking me the whole time?*

There was no time to answer the question. Not when he was pinned down, had no idea where the second shooter had gone, and needed to get the hell out of the kill zone.

He needed a distraction and wished he had a flashbang.

His eyes drifted to the box of cereal. The brightly colored box reminded him of the close-quarter shooting class at the Salt Pit and the cadre who asked if any of them had ever heard of the OODA loop.

"No one? Well, get out a pen and some paper, because it might save your life." The cadre went on to explain that the OODA loop was conceived by Major John "40-Second" Boyd, an air force fighter pilot. The letters stood for Observe, Orient, Decide, and Act, and they defined how a pilot should process stimulus in a dogfight.

"This is how we make decisions. Every one of us. And anytime the brain observes additional stimulus, the chain starts all over."

Steele grabbed the box of cereal.

It would have to do.

He arced it hard over his left shoulder, hoping the sudden flash of color would catch the shooters' eyes. Make them think their target was making a break for it.

Staying low, he hobbled toward the trunk, hoping to get a shot off before the woman reloaded. The rounds impacting the front of the car shifted off target, and Steele knew the shooter had seen the box and opened up. He slipped around the back of the Peugeot and saw the woman reloading.

Steele was lining up the shot when the woman jammed the magazine into the submachine gun and turned toward him.

She figured out your little trick.

The backdrop was shit—truly. Because a glass-fronted apartment building was the absolute worst thing to have behind someone in your sights. If he missed, there was a good chance the round would go sailing into someone's living room. Might hit a man or woman watching the morning news. But if he didn't take the shot, he was going to die.

The woman saw him and raised her submachine gun.

Steele fired.

The Browning bucked in his hand, and the front sight recoiled skyward. Steele kept his focus on the target and saw the bullet punch a hole through the plastic visor. She dropped headfirst into the street, like a marionette with cut strings.

Steele ducked back around the car, a plan forming in his head. Stay close to the dead one.

He tore the tac-wallet out of his pocket, aware of the sirens in the distance. Steele needed to get the hell out of there, but he also had to know who the hell was trying to kill him. He tore the wallet open and yanked the tracking tab from its pocket on his way to the front of the car.

"Irena!" the second shooter yelled.

Steele transferred the tab to his left hand, staying low. The shooter raked the car with bullets while rushing to his friend's side.

The sirens were getting closer. He was going to get only one shot.

The shooter stepped closer and closer. Steele waited until the last second and then chopped the Browning across the man's wrist. The MP5 clattered to the ground.

He hit his attacker in the gut, doubling him over, and chopped the pistol down on the top of the helmet. Steele knew it wouldn't hurt him, but he hoped to stun him long enough to do what he needed to do.

Steele shoved the Hi Power into his waistband and grabbed the lip of the helmet. He pulled, exposing the back of the man's neck, and slapped his left hand down on the exposed skin.

The gel cap shattered in his hand, and Steele felt his skin warm as the polymer-based biosensor reacted to open air. He wiped his hand up the man's skin, smearing the opaque transfer material on the man's neck. The binder would adhere in thirty seconds, but to make sure the man didn't wipe it off, Steele slammed him headfirst into the car.

The shooter crumpled to his knees, and Steele scrambled around the car. He crisply swept his suit bag off the Aston Martin hood before heading for an alley.

Chapter 27

The room was dim, the only lights coming from the monitors in the corner when Meg walked into the Keyhole simulation room. She'd spent most of last night thinking about Eric, hoping he was okay, wondering when he would call. Meg knew what she was getting into when they first started dating and thought she could handle it.

She was wrong.

Meg had given up trying to sleep at 0400 and come into the office. She slipped the virtual reality goggles over her head.

"Play scene one one four," she said aloud.

The Keyhole simulator kicked in, transporting her to the re-creation of Eric's crash site.

Meg found herself standing in the street, hand up,

blocking the glare of the headlights shining in her face. She moved to the right out of the beam and saw the GTO lying upside down on the asphalt like a steel turtle.

The back tires were still spinning, and the sweet scent of vaporized antifreeze hung thick in the air. Meg stepped closer, thinking she had seen movement inside the car. A shape moved in front of the headlights, casting the shadow of a leg on the ground, then moved away.

Meg squinted, leaning forward in the darkness. There. Someone was moving inside the car. She saw a hand reaching for something on the ground just outside the window. *What is that?* She stepped closer. *It's a gun.*

A finger tipped the butt of the pistol, spinning it, and then a tall thin man appeared out of the darkness. The man walked up to the car and set his boot on the hand reaching for the gun.

"Shiiit," yelled the voice in the car.

The man on the street squatted on his haunches and turned his head to the left. Meg crept closer. *Look at me,* she begged silently. *Let me see your face.*

A momentary darkness fell over the scene, as if a cloud had passed in front of the sun. When it lifted the man's arm was outstretched, the pistol in his hand pointed inside the car.

"*Mertva.*"

Then a gunshot.

"Pause," she said wearily.

"Keyhole virtual simulation paused," an electronic voice replied.

Meg removed the virtual reality goggles and stepped away from the Keyhole station. She lowered herself into the chair and rubbed her temple. She had run through the virtual simulator so many times and tried every angle, every trick, she could think of, but still she couldn't identify the man who had attacked Steele.

A beep pulled her to the black monitor that was running a vocal search.

"Don't tell me," she said, "you couldn't find anything."

Meg brought the monitor to life with a touch of the keyboard. *Holy shit.*

SEARCH 1 COMPLETE: One Result Found.

SOURCE: KEYHOLE VOICE ANALYZER.

SEARCH CODE: All.

SUBJECT IDENTIFIED: Orlov, Yuri.

MILITARY SERVICE: 2001–2006 Assigned to Spetsnaz Special Battalion Zapad. Foreign Service: Chechnya, Lebanon, Georgia.

TRANSFERRED 2007 TO FOREIGN INTELLIGENCE SERVICE: Directorate S—Zaslon.

TRAINING: Illegal Intelligence, Deep Cover Asset, Assassination, Language.

Meg knew that the Foreign Intelligence Service, or FSB, was the Russians' version of the CIA and the Directorate S was in charge of Illegal Intelligence. Zaslon was the closest unit they had to the Program, men trained for deep-cover operation in foreign countries. A guy like Yuri Orlov had the skill set to pull off a hit on Steele and whatever else he set his mind to.

SEARCH 2 COMPLETE: No Match.

Who the hell are you? Meg wondered.

Whoever the man was there was no record of him in any voice file. He was a ghost whose voice hadn't been picked up anywhere that she could think to look.

She waved her hand at the screen in frustration and Keyhole picked up the movement. "Rewinding."

"I don't want you to rewind it, I want you to help me find this asshole." She groaned.

Dammit.

One more run, she thought, putting the goggles back

on. The VR interface was still moving in reverse, the bullet going back inside the gun, sucking the muzzle blast back into the barrel.

"Wait, what was that?" Meg said aloud. "Reverse frame."

There.

"Freeze." Meg made a circular motion with her hand, and a digital lasso formed around the rectangle of flesh covered in what she had thought was oil. "Zoom in."

The computer enlarged the image, but it was still too fuzzy to see.

"Can we clean that up?" she asked.

"Stand by," the voice replied.

The image blinked, and an hourglass appeared while the computer worked on boosting the pixels. A moment later it was clear enough for Meg to see that the black stains on the hand and wrist weren't oil; they were tattoos.

"Mark frame and analyze image." Meg felt the buzz of excitement.

"Analyzing."

"Image analyzing complete."

On the screen were four tattoos, each one enlarged in its own box. Three of them were ring tattoos—a crown on the index finger, a skull on the middle, a dark square on the ring finger. On the back of the hand was a tiger with a dolphin in its mouth and the number 6.

Meg focused on the clearest image, the tattoo of the tiger on the back of the hand. It was well done but not professionally so, and the ink had already started to fade around the edges.

"Where do you get a bad tattoo? The army?"

She opened a browser and typed IMAGE SEARCH: "MILITARY TATTOO with TIGER DOLPHIN and NUMBER 6," adding the quotes so the search engine would know to focus on those exact words.

---

0 RESULTS.

Meg deleted MILITARY, dragged the rest of the images into the search bar, and tried again.

This time the search took longer, and Meg found herself rubbing her hands together in anticipation.

---

12 MATCHES FOUND.

She highlighted the tiger and the dolphin and reran the search. The first thing to pop up was an article on criminal elements in the Russian prison system with a gallery of tattoos. Under the heading Penal Colony N° 6, Meg found a tattoo similar to the one she was looking for.

She hadn't thought to consider prisons in her search parameters and ran the tattoo image and the facial scan through the Russian Prison Nexus.

Meg wasn't expecting much, but the first result was a frame from a security camera showing an emaciated and obviously sick man being led to a helicopter by a man dressed in black.

The system locked on to the hands and blew up the image.

It was the same tattoo.

The second image was a prison photo taken after a fight that he was involved in.

---

1 MATCH.

ZAKAYEV, ALEKSANDR.

INMATE: Penal Colony N° 6.

"I got him," she said, printing out both pictures. She grabbed her cell phone and badge, snatched the photos off the printer, and ran out the door.

Meg found Lansky on his way to the Oval Office. She grabbed the chief of staff by the crook of the arm and pulled him into one of the offices lining the hall.

"I need the room," she told the pair of interns at the desk.

"What are you doing?" he asked.

Meg shut the door and turned to Lansky.

"I found him," she said.

"Found who?"

"The man who attacked Eric." Meg paused to take a breath. "There were two men who attacked Steele, both Russian speakers. We got a voice lock, and ran it through the NSA's analyzer."

"You ran it through the system and what?"

"The first guy is Yuri Orlov. Former Spetsnaz, bit of a shit heel. I couldn't find anything on the second suspect until I ran his tattoos."

She handed him the printouts, Zakayev's photo on top.

"I ran his tats through the computer and got a hit from the Russian Penitentiary Service. His name is Aleksandr Zakayev. He is a Chechen, arrested in Syria and sent to Black Dolphin for killing some Russian soldiers."

Lansky's eyes narrowed as he studied the first photo.

"Don't know him, but Black Dolphin is a tough place. Most people who go in never . . . ," Lansky said, shuffling to the second photo. "Shit."

"What is it?" Meg asked.

"This guy leading him to the helo. I *know* him," he said, heading to the door.

"Where are you going?" Meg asked.

"*We* are going to brief the president."

"The president?" Meg followed Lansky into the hall. "Hold on, I need—"

"Meet me at the Oval," Lansky said.

Meg was flustered and stood in the hall, not sure what to do.

"Hey," Lansky said, grabbing her attention from the end of the hall.

"Yeah?" she asked.

"Whatever you need to do, you might want to hurry. Making the president of the United States wait isn't the best introduction."

Oh God, Meg thought, ducking into the bathroom and checking her reflection in the mirror.

Meg wasn't in the habit of wearing a lot of makeup. In fact, all she carried in her purse was a compact, lip gloss, and an old tube of mascara.

Why didn't I bring my purse?

All she could do was fix her hair, and when she was

done, Meg was turning to leave when she heard someone vomiting in one of the stalls.

"Are you okay?" Meg asked, pulling a fresh paper towel and wetting it with water from the sink.

"I think so," came a shaky reply, followed by the flush of the toilet. The door swung open and Meg found herself standing face-to-face with Lisa Rockford, the First Lady of the United States.

Meg handed her the wet towel, and Lisa wiped her mouth and offered a weak smile.

"I'm forty-two years old. Never imagined that I'd get pregnant this late," Lisa said.

Meg could tell she immediately regretted saying it by the look on her face.

"I have no idea why I just said that," she said, her hand moving to her mouth.

"Ummmm, congratulations," Meg offered. "I'm sure the president is thrilled."

"I haven't told him yet. I don't even know why I am telling you. I don't even know you." She laughed. "He has been working so hard on this Israel thing, I don't want him to have to stress about this too."

Chapter 28

Budapest

Zakayev sat next to the window, the Hungarian countryside flashing by the window. His eyes traced the landscape. Drifting over the fields of wheat and rye that shimmered in the lowlands.

He followed the terrain north, where vineyards clung to the side of the foothills. Rectangles of cleared earth below ridgelines of thick pines.

It was the pine trees that reminded him of Camp 722, and the first time Hassan saw snow.

Zakayev had been cleaning his boots when Hassan ran to his bed, eyes full of wonder.

"Come look," Hassan said, grabbing his arm and pulling him off his bed.

"What? What is it?" he asked.

"I-I don't know."

Zakayev followed him to the door, not sure what to expect when he looked outside.

"What?" he asked, eyes looking past the snow for whatever had grabbed his friend's attention.

"It is all *white*," Hassan said.

Then it hit him. *He's never seen snow.*

Hassan was one of the few at the camp from outside of Europe. He'd grown up in the Gaza Strip, at the Jabalia refugee camp. A harsh place where there was an abundance of diseases, but never enough food.

"Snow?" Hassan said, working the word around in his mouth.

"Yes, it is frozen rain," Zakayev said, stepping outside. He reached down and scooped up a pile of snow, mashing it into a ball.

"It won't hurt you," he said, throwing the snowball at Hassan.

A smile slowly played over his friend's face and he finally stepped outside, reaching down to make a snowball of his own.

Thirty minutes later Hassan had the entire barracks

outside. The boys broke into two teams and set up opposing forts for the snowball war.

Zakayev was defending his position when he saw a man dressed in all white appear at the top of the hill outside the camp. He was waving his arms in the air. Shouting into what looked like a radio.

"Who is that?" Hassan asked.

Before Zakayev could answer, one of the guards was blowing his whistle. Yelling at them to get back inside.

Zakayev glanced up at the guard tower, saw the guards raising their rifles. "I don't know, but we need to get inside."

He was moving toward the barrack, thinking that Hassan was with him, when the first shot rang out.

"Hurry," Zakayev said. He was about to break into a jog when he realized that he was alone.

Hassan?

He turned and found Hassan running toward the man.

"Don't shoot him," Zakayev yelled at the guards, running after his friend.

He caught up with Hassan at the fence and heard the man yelling into the radio, "Abort, abort. There are children here."

Another shot rang out, the bullet landing short, kicking up snow at the man's feet. Hassan, seemingly oblivious to the danger, ran through the gate and out into the open.

"Run," the man in white yelled.

Run?

Why would *they* run? The man was the intruder.

A second rifle barked, Zakayev recognizing the distinct crack of the Dragunov sniper rifle.

The man tumbled to the ground, and when he pushed himself to his knees the snow near his thigh was stained crimson.

"Hassan, they will shoot you," Zakayev yelled.

But his friend was too busy staring at the man to pay attention to him.

"Look at his eyes," Hassan said when Zakayev came to a halt beside his friend.

They were bright green.

"You have to run," the man spoke, his Russian clipped through gritted teeth. "There is a bomb and I can't stop it."

Zakayev grabbed Hassan's jacket and was trying to pull him away when the air was filled with a rushing whistle. The first time he'd heard the sound was in Chechnya. Zakayev had thought it was a train. Now he knew better.

It was the sound of a bomb cutting through the air.

In an instant the world went orange and black.

The explosion lifted Zakayev and threw him across the yard. When he finally looked up his world was on fire.

Back in Budapest, the train bumped into the station, and Zakayev got off. He waited outside for Yuri to pick him up. After ten minutes he pulled his cell from his pocket and called the Russian.

When there was no answer he began to worry.

Had the Americans found the safehouse? Was Yuri alive?

There was only one way to find out.

He typed a quick text to Gabriel, asking for the directions to the Budapest safehouse. He hailed a cab and gave the directions to the driver.

"I will take you as far as Baross Street," the man said.

Zakayev was tired and in no mood to barter. He passed the man another thousand Hungarian forints.

"It is not the money," the man said, passing it back. "Too dangerous."

"Just get me close."

The drive was only six kilometers straight line, but because of traffic in the city it took thirty minutes. The driver let him out at the cemetery—four blocks north of his destination.

He stepped out of the cab, got his bearings, and

walked east, ducking under a chain-link fence and stepping onto a seemingly abandoned street.

"Hey, you."

He glanced in the direction of the shout.

"Fucking Johnny Prague," Zakayev cursed when he saw the three military-aged males leaning against the wall, drinking from a bottle. They looked Muslim and he guessed they were part of the recent influx of refugees.

Johnny Prague was a local gangster and club owner who was being paid to get them a safehouse and weapons needed for the assault on the target. He obviously hadn't put the word out on the street to leave Zakayev alone.

"Hey ass-face," the youth yelled, taking the bottle and pushing off the wall with his foot. "I'm talking to you," he said, throwing the bottle at Zakayev. The missile landed harmlessly off to his right.

"Nice throw," one of the other boys said, laughing.

Zakayev had spent most of his life on the street and knew that respect was the coin of the realm. All over the world, in neighborhoods just like this one, more blood had been shed over perceived insults than real ones.

Part of him felt sorry for the boys. After all, he'd been one of them once.

Just let it go, he urged silently.

But his time on the street had also told him that it wouldn't happen. The boy had to save face, and that meant a confrontation.

Whether Zakayev wanted one or not.

"Get him," the tough yelled, breaking into a run.

Zakayev angled for the alley, the *slap-slap* of their shoes on the pavement growing closer.

Little bastards, the voice in his head snarled.

If there was going to be a fight, Zakayev couldn't afford for it to be in the middle of the street. He was too close to the end and wouldn't allow a vengeance-seeking family member or a chance encounter with the police to derail his plans.

No, if he was going to deal with them it would be on ground of *his* choosing.

"Run old man," the leader yelled, thinking he was in control.

Zakayev stepped into the alley, taking in every detail with a quick glance.

It was wider than he expected and littered with trash and the smells you'd expect to find in this part of the city. A brick wall with razor wire strung across the top blocked him from exiting the other side, and Zakayev knew there was no way to get over it without needing a tetanus shot after.

He stopped and turned around just as the boys stepped into the alley.

"Where are you going, old man?" the bottle thrower asked, his eyes dancing with impending violence.

The boy was taller than Zakayev and dressed in a ratty pair of jeans, faded Reebok high-tops, and a Tupac tank top; not yet old enough to shave, but ready to kill a man he had just met.

Just kill them and be done with it, the voice urged.

It was Zakayev's normal reaction, but something about the boy reminded him of Hassan, and instead of a bullet he found himself trying to reason with the boy.

"What do you want, I am just passing through," he said, switching to Arabic.

The boy was surprised, but he recovered quickly.

"This is our street, old man."

"Go back to your corner, boy," Zakayev snapped.

"Fuck you, old man," the bottle thrower spat.

He knew intimidation wouldn't work on the boys. They belonged to a generation raised in the midst of civil war. Death was their mother and she had weaned them on violence.

To them kindness wasn't a virtue, it was a weakness.

"Let's cut his throat, Ali," the second boy said, producing a length of chain.

"I want his jacket," the third stated.

The pack spread out, one boy moving to his left, the second to the right like wolves circling the kill.

"Last chance," Zakayev hissed. "Take it while you *still* can."

Ali smiled and moved closer. He pulled a box cutter from his pants and extended the blade with his thumb. "Like I said, old man, this is our street and if you don't pay the toll—"

You tried. Now kill them, the voice said.

Zakayev snatched the OTs from his waistband. The pistol came out smoothly, the suppressor sliding free of his waistline and coming up on target. Ali froze, and his face went blank at the realization of his fatal error.

Zakayev shoved the OTs in Ali's face and pulled the trigger. The subsonic bullet punching through the bridge of the boy's nose, vaporizing his cranial vault. Ali was dead before he hit the pavement.

The OTs worked as advertised, and the two other boys didn't realize their friend had been shot in the face until his knees buckled and he fell to the ground. Zakayev shot the second boy in the throat and swung the pistol to the third boy.

He had already turned toward the street, hoping he could outrun the bullet. Zakayev took his time and lined up the shot. He placed the sights on the middle of his back and shot him through the spine.

The OTs worked better than he could have imagined. He'd heard pellet guns that were louder, but still, he stepped to the edge of the alleyway and peeked out. He watched the street, counting to sixty in his head, but nothing moved.

Zakayev stepped back into the alley and started dragging the bodies to the back wall. The one he had shot in the back moaned when he grabbed his arm.

"I can't feel my legs," he said.

Zakayev spied the length of chain the other kid had dropped and picked it up off the ground. He looped it around his throat, dropped a knee into his back, and pulled. The boy flopped beneath him, but without the use of his lower extremities it was a short fight. Zakayev pulled on the chain until he heard the unmistakable sound of his death gurgle and the boy went still. Then he dragged the body to join the others.

Zakayev covered them with trash and used a sheet of newspaper to wipe the blood off his hands. Killing the boys didn't bother him, but he was annoyed that they had wasted his time. Zakayev looked around to ensure he wasn't leaving a trace of evidence, but he knew there would be no investigation. When he finished he turned and jogged to the safehouse, hoping that Yuri was there.

Chapter 29

London

Following the attempt on Steele's life, Steele and Demo had changed locations to the Savoy. Located in Westminster, the Savoy Hotel was the first luxury hotel in London and the first public building with electric lights.

Up in their room, Steele strapped the holster holding the Walther PPK to his ankle and gave it a tug to make sure it was secure. He shrugged into the Manning and Manning suit coat that went with the pants he'd picked up that morning and then checked his Submariner.

It was a quarter to seven.

Demo walked into the room and took a massive bite

from the apple he'd found on the table. "I 'alked 'o 'itts," he said.

"I have no idea what you just said."

Demo chewed and after swallowing said, "You want me to come with you?"

"No," Steele said with a shake of his head. "As much as I'd like the backup, you stay here, keep an eye on our rabbit," he said, nodding toward the computer that was tracking the man who'd attacked him.

"I would ask Pitts for a takedown team, but I already know what he would say." Steele smiled, and did his best Pitts impression. "'You are an Alpha, you *are* the tactical team.'"

Demo laughed and shook his head. "I am *not* going to miss this bullshit."

"Don't get into retirement mode just yet."

"Oh, don't worry, I'll be ready to move when you get back," Demo said, picking up the controller and turning on the television. "Just as long as you don't come back in the middle of my stories."

Steele took the elevator down to the lobby, an art deco masterpiece with vaulted ceilings, marble columns, and a checkerboard tile floor.

He walked to the front entrance, where a town car was waiting to take him to the Sabers Club.

Sabers, like the Savoy, was a holdover from another

era, a time when all-male clubs were the norm as opposed to the exception. A place where middle-aged professionals and stodgy landowners drank scotch in their oversize leather chairs and spoke longingly about the long-lost British Empire.

The driver stopped the car in front of a three-story building whose stone blocks had been weathered by time. The Palladian facade and burnished bronze fittings made it look more like a bank than an exclusive club.

A severe-looking gatekeeper met Steele at the door.

"Mr. Sands, I presume?"

"That's right."

"If you will follow me, Mr. Norman is expecting you," he announced.

The gatekeeper gave Steele a miniature tour as they walked, his voice strong and carrying over the *tap-tap* of their shoes on the waxed marble floors.

"Sabers was founded in 1674, which makes it the second-oldest club in London," the man said. He motioned to the south wall, where a bank of photos lined up beneath two crossed cavalry swords.

He led Steele through an archway and into a large room that had a sitting area, complete with bar and billiard tables near the front and toward the back a row of smaller, private dining rooms with curtained windows.

Most of the tables were already occupied by men talking over lowballs of amber-colored liquor, but near the east wall a man sat alone, legs crossed, a copy of the London *Times* open before him. From a distance Steele would have guessed he was in his late thirties, but on closer inspection he saw the age lines around his eyes and wrinkles crisscrossing his brow. He wore his blond hair slicked back and had a neat mustache above thin lips.

The man saw Steele coming, ground the cigarette into the ashtray, and neatly folded the paper before getting to his feet.

"Mr. Max Sands," the gatekeeper announced.

"Thank you, Geoffrey," the man said. "Percy Norman." He crossed over to Steele and extended his hand.

"Thank you for meeting with me."

"My pleasure, I've reserved a room, shall we?"

Steele hadn't even gotten comfortable when a waiter appeared with a pair of menus.

"What'll you have to drink?" Percy asked.

"Bourbon if you have it," Steele replied.

"Two Blanton's," Percy said, waiting until the waiter had left the room before getting down to business. "Heard you had a bit of a scuffle today. Nasty bit of business you've got yourself into."

"Feels like someone is trying to tell me something."

The waiter returned with their drinks and Percy pulled out a silver cigarette case. "Do you mind?" he asked.

"No," Steele said, taking a sip of the bourbon.

Percy lit the cigarette with a match and blew a jet of graphite smoke toward the ceiling. "How may I help you?"

"Tell me about Cemetery Whisper," Steele said.

The mask fell away and Percy leaned in, his eyes cold as a hawk's. His right hand began inching toward the lip of the table. Steele flicked at a piece of lint on the cuff of his pants and in one smooth motion skinned the Walther from the ankle holster.

"Let's not get hasty, Mr. Norman."

"Bloody Lansky," Percy swore. "Who are you?"

"My name is Eric Steele. We had a mutual friend in the late Bo Nolan."

"Of course, can't believe I missed it. You are the *spitting image* of your father."

It was Steele's turn to be surprised.

"You knew my father?"

"Yes, I did. He was a good man. And you can put that away." Percy nodded to the pistol.

For some reason Steele found himself trusting him.

"So about . . ."

"Not here."

Percy got to his feet and Steele followed him into the hallway and down a flight of stairs to what appeared to be a cellar.

"They built this bunker during the Blitz," Percy explained. "No chance of anyone hearing us down here."

"What can you tell me about Cemetery Whisper?" Steele asked again, getting right to the point.

"During the Cold War, MI6, the CIA, and your Program were all working together to defeat the Soviets. From the start it was clear that this relationship wasn't built to last, but there was a war on, and everyone was willing to do their part."

"How did it work?" Steele asked.

"MI6 and Langley did most of the intel work and the Program handled most of the heavy lifting."

"They were using Alphas as assassins?" Steele asked.

"Well, things were different back then. The CIA was still working under that *asinine* executive order that kept them from assassinating, which limited their usefulness. We would have preferred to deal directly with the Program, but Langley made it clear that it wasn't an option."

"How did it all fall apart?" Steele asked.

"It was the mid '90s and we had a chap in Moscow who kept hearing about Camp 722."

"Never heard of it," Steele said.

"No one had, which is the point. Our man did some digging and found that the camp was built in 1942 for tank training in preparation for the winter counteroffensive. The Russian High Command wanted it built in the middle of nowhere, well out of range of German Luftwaffe and invisible from the air. They brought in five thousand prisoners from Siberia and built the place in three months."

"Many hands make light work," Steele said.

Percy nodded. "The benefits of a totalitarian government. Our man went to Moscow and found a few records that said Camp 722 was decommissioned after the war, but he wasn't buying it."

"What happened next?" Steele asked, not sure where Percy was going with the story but sure the man had a point.

"Our man's cover was blown, and we asked Langley for a Russian expert. They sent us Bo Nolan."

Now Steele was hooked.

"Nolan learned that after WW II, Stalin sent a KGB officer named Colonel Vadim Kozlov to tour the countries that had been annexed by the Soviet Union. Stalin was still reeling from the fact that Hitler's invasion of Russia had blindsided him and charged the KGB with making sure nothing like that happened again."

"And Kozlov found the answer," Steele said.

"He did indeed. When Kozlov saw how many displaced children there were—kids who had lost both their families and their countries—he realized that with the right training, these children could be taught to fit in anywhere. Kozlov grabbed a few dozen, sent them to Camp 722 for training."

"What kind of training?" Steele asked.

"At first they were trained how to act like Americans or Brits. Taught the language, the habits, how to dress and act. When they turned eighteen the KGB sent them to their assigned countries with papers and new lives. By now the Cold War had started and Kozlov decided to weaponize his next class. He added demolition training, hand-to-hand combat, sabotage, intel collection, assassination, and eventually murder for hire."

"Jesus, that is sick," Steele said.

"Without a doubt. In fact, it was so sick that Nolan's report was immediately classified 'Need to Know,' but when these kids started showing up in places like Serbia, Chechnya, Colombia, and the West Bank, the decision was made to shut Camp 722 down.

"Nolan requested an Alpha to assist in taking the camp down, and that's when things went sideways." Percy paused for another cigarette.

"You see," he said, blowing out a lungful of smoke, "the CIA didn't bother sharing with the Program that the camp was full of children. When your father saw this, he called for an abort."

"Then what happened?" Steele demanded, his voice growing cold.

"Someone at the CIA vectored in a couple of fast movers. When your father realized they were calling in an airstrike he broke cover and tried to warn the children. Got himself shot and captured for his troubles."

Steele, like every other Alpha, knew what would happen if they were captured. Since an Alpha didn't exist, there was no need for the country to disavow them.

The Program simply cut the string.

"Nolan was wounded trying to get to your father. Not sure how he made it out to be honest, but he was never the same after that," Percy said with a sad shake of his head. "The guilt ate him alive, and he just wouldn't let it go. Kept telling everyone that your father was still alive."

"He came to visit me a year after my father went missing. I see what he was trying to tell me now," Steele said softly.

"Your father wasn't the first one we lost," Percy said, taking another drag, "and we both know he won't be the last. But the way they just abandoned him, it wasn't right. That is how Cemetery Whisper started.

Just a handful of blokes trying to do what was needed to recover our own."

Steele ached to hear more about his father but knew this wasn't the time or the place, especially with the man who attacked his mother still on the loose.

"I was able to put a tracker on one of the men who attacked me today."

"Now that *is* a spot of good news," Percy said.

Steele pulled out a PDA, their target a dot blinking over a map of the city.

Percy leaned over and looked at the map.

"Budapest, that's Johnny Prague's territory."

"That psycho is still alive?"

"Very much so."

"Look, I need some trigger pullers who know their way around Budapest. Can you help me out?"

"Thought you would never ask." Percy smiled.

Chapter 30

Falls Church, Virginia

Meg stood in the kitchen of her apartment, a pair of yellow gloves and a bucket of cleaning supplies sitting on the counter. She took a sip of pinot, set the glass on the kitchen table, and glanced outside.

It was dark, and in the distance she could see the twinkle of lights that marked Alexandria, where she had lived while working for the CIA.

Meg had fallen in love with Falls Church the first time she visited. Located twenty minutes from D.C., it had somehow managed to hold on to its small-town feel despite its proximity to the Beltway.

When Steele was recovering, they had spent their

days wandering through the farmers' market. Tasting the locally grown Gala apples that exploded in your mouth when you took a bite. Or Meg would drag him to the Eden Center, where she lost herself among the eclectic shops lining the street.

To her, Falls Church felt like home.

She knew how lucky she was to get the apartment at Wexford Manor. A sought-after complex of red brick apartments with dark shingled roofs and a black lamppost that flickered at night.

The first time she visited, Meg learned that the next vacancy was a year away. On Steele's urging she'd put her name on the list, and six months later she got a call.

The kitchen, like the rest of her apartment, was spotless. But Meg still couldn't get the meeting with Lansky and President Rockford out of her mind. And the only way she knew how to unwind was with a glass of pinot and a bottle of Clorox kitchen spray.

Meg tugged the gloves over her hands, her mind drifting back to the meeting.

She'd half sprinted to the waiting area outside of the Oval Office, heart hammering in her chest when she arrived. The first thing she saw was the woman sitting behind the oak desk next to the closed door that led into Rockford's inner sanctum.

Behind the desk, Mary, the president's secretary, looked up from the computer monitor.

"My name is Meg Harden and I am here to see President Rockford," she said, eyes widening at the explosion of angry voices coming from behind the closed door.

"May-maybe I should come back later," Meg offered with a weak smile.

"Doesn't work like that, honey," Mary replied with a smile. "They are waiting for you inside."

Meg walked over to the door. She could hear Rockford's voice clearly through the wall.

"Ted, I don't care what the intelligence says," he shouted.

"Don't worry, his bark is much worse than his bite," Mary said, waving her through.

Meg opened the door and stepped inside.

Rockford and Lansky were squared off at the center of the room. The president had the pictures she had printed out in his right hand.

Meg could count on one hand how many times she'd seen Rockford in person. He was an imposing presence. But his size was usually tempered by the smile on his face.

Not this time.

This time, Rockford was visibly angry.

"Sir, this is Meg Harden, she works at Cutlass Main."

"I know who she is," Rockford said, regaining his composure. "Tell me about this Zakayev," he said.

You've done this before, Meg told herself.

It was true. During her time in the military and the CIA Meg had held countless high-level briefings. But never to the leader of the free world, and when she opened her mouth to speak, her mouth was bone dry.

"Sir, I, uh."

Her mind flashed back to the restroom and the bomb the First Lady had dropped on her. That she was pregnant but hadn't told her husband yet.

"Just run me through it," Rockford said, his voice softening.

Meg took a breath and ran through what had happened since Steele was attacked.

Rockford listened to the entire briefing, waiting until she was finished before speaking.

"This is great work, Meg. Really well done," Rockford said.

"So you will cancel the trip?" Lansky asked.

"No," Rockford replied.

"No?" Lansky said, eyes wide in disbelief.

"That's right, Ted. I am NOT canceling the trip to Israel. The peace accord is too important."

"Sir, this is a credible threat," Lansky interjected.

Rockford walked over to his desk and picked up a bulging red folder with a blue border.

"You know what this is, Ted?" he asked, holding the folder aloft and giving it a shake.

Meg recognized the folder. When she first came to Cutlass Main and was still learning the ropes, she'd helped compile one just like it. Pitts called it the Red Ball, and inside the folder was every threat relating to President Rockford that the Program had intercepted that week.

"I get one of these every Monday," Rockford was saying. "Every *week*, Ted, I get a folder just like this full of threats on my life."

"Sir, that is not the same thing, and you know it," Lansky said, looking to Meg to back him up.

"Sir, he is right, we use a very wide net when compiling a Red Ball."

Rockford acted like he hadn't heard her.

"We are going to Israel," he said. "If this guy is a threat, then you two need to figure it out."

How could he blow us off like that? Meg wondered that night. But as she was reaching for a second roll of paper towels her phone rang.

She stripped off the gloves and looked at the screen.

It was Lansky, and as usual he cut right to the point.

"I need you to be at Joint Base Andrews in thirty minutes," he said.

"Hold on," Meg stammered. "Say that again."

"We are going on a trip. Plane leaves in an hour and I need you there," Lansky answered.

"But—"

"Look, I've got to go. Just get your stuff and meet me at Andrews," he said before the line went dead.

Meg ran to the hall closet and pulled her carry-on suitcase from the shelf before rushing to the bedroom.

Thirty minutes. Plenty of time.

She opened the closet and felt her OCD kick in at the sight of the clothes neatly arranged on color-coded hangers.

You can do this, she told herself. *You did it in the army.*

In the army, Meg had been on a six-hour recall, which meant she had to be out the door and ready to go in four hours. She had adapted by packing two separate bags. For official operations she had one bag filled with uniforms, tan shirts, green socks, boots, plus her shower kit. She had a second bag for clandestine work. It had her civilian clothes, shoes and hiking boots, and its own shower kit.

One bag was black and the other green. She had

kept them both packed and in her trunk at all times. But now she had no packed bag at the ready.

Meg opened her drawer and was instantly overwhelmed by the neat piles she found inside. Lansky hadn't told her how long they were going to be gone or where they were going, which left her with an infinite number of possibilities.

She started with shirts, socks, and underwear. Meg put each one in a separate Ziploc bag, which she labeled with a Sharpie. And then she checked her watch.

Shit. How long did that take, ten minutes?

"To hell with this!" Meg yelled. She started grabbing clothes at random, a couple pairs of pants, shirts, a jacket plus a pullover, and then jammed them all into the bag. Five minutes later she zipped the case and headed for the door.

When Meg arrived at the base, she flashed her badge to the gate guard, who told her where to go. This was the second time she had been to Joint Base Andrews; the first was when she had flown home from Morón, Spain, in an F-15. For some reason this was way more stressful.

Meg parked near the hangar, where another MP was waiting for her.

"Ma'am, we need you to go through a security check."

"Uh, okay. Do you have any idea where I am going?"

"No, ma'am," he replied, waving her inside the hangar.

The MP took her bag to one of the scanners, while a female directed her to walk through the X-ray machine. The machine beeped, and Meg winced when she realized she had forgotten to take off her pistol.

"I am so—"

"Hands off the weapon, ma'am," the female MP said. Off to the right side a German shepherd uttered a low growl and shook its head.

The woman unclipped Meg's Glock from her hip, dropped the magazine, and ejected the round.

"Hey, hey." Lansky's voice carried across the hangar. "She's on the cleared list," he said, his feet *tap tapping* across the concrete floor.

"What is going on?" she demanded.

"Grab your gear. I can show you better than I can tell you."

Meg retrieved her bag.

"This will be placed in a lockbox on the aircraft," the female guard said, holding up Meg's gun.

Meg shot her a fake smile.

"I have the highest security clearance in the room and I can't carry a freaking gun on a plane?"

Lansky was waiting for her at the door.

"Not on this plane," he said, pushing the door open.

Meg stepped outside and immediately forgot all about her problems when she saw Air Force One sitting on the tarmac fifty yards away.

"Ever been to Jerusalem?"

Chapter 31

Budapest

The pilot of the Harbin Y-12 lowered the gear and reduced his airspeed in preparation for landing. In the back of the twin-engine turboprop, Percy leaned forward and shouted over the engine noise.

"Now these blokes don't look like the chaps you two are used to dealing with," he began, "but they are switched on. I can promise you that."

"You got us a bunch of fat bodies, didn't you," Demo said. "Great."

Steele suppressed a grin.

"You guys better buckle up," the pilot yelled.

Steele glanced toward the cockpit and saw the flicker of lights that marked the landing zone. *I hope these guys know what they're doing.*

The pilot executed a flawless landing and had the ramp coming down before the plane reached the end of the makeshift runway. He had told them before taking off that he would drop them off but couldn't risk waiting around.

"You two stop fighting," Steele said, grabbing the Pelican cases he'd brought with him from London and getting to his feet.

The moment the plane came to a halt the three men walked off the ramp and hustled to the edge of the runway. In the cockpit the pilot had advanced the throttles and a moment later was racing back the way he'd come.

Steele looked around and realized they were in the middle of a cow pasture.

"That guy can fly his ass off," he said.

"My guys *always* come through," Demo said in the darkness.

Steele didn't need to see his handler's face to know he was looking at Percy.

"Good for you," the Brit said, holding up a red-lensed flashlight, which he flashed twice in the darkness.

Across the field there were two return flashes and then Steele heard an engine start. The Mitsubishi SUV bumped across the pasture and came to a halt next to them. Two men got out of the vehicle and walked around.

"Thanks for meeting us," Percy said, shaking hands with the driver, a short, rough-looking man with a gray newsboy hat crushed atop his head.

"Anytime," the driver said.

"Jesus, where did Percy dig up these relics, the Members Only club?" Demo whispered.

"Do you need a snack or something?" Steele asked, keeping his voice low.

"What? This is how retired people talk," Demo replied. "I'm just trying to get ready."

"And who are these lovely lassies?" the second man, a taller and heavier version of the first, asked.

"See, I told you," Demo said.

"I'm Eric and this is Demo," Steele replied, ignoring his handler.

"Nice to meet you," the driver said, shaking Steele's hand. "Red's the name, and this tubby fucker is Phillip."

"Don't let it fool ya," Phillip said, slapping his gut. "I can still crack skulls when I need ta."

"Good to know," Demo said, rolling his eyes.

"If you ladies are done bumping your gums, we can get a move on," Red said.

"Bunch of grumpy old shits," Demo said, opening the door of the SUV and climbing inside.

An hour later they were parked in an alley across from the target building.

"What a shit hole," Demo said, looking up from the PalmPilot that allowed him to track their target from the gel Steele had smeared on him.

"I've been here a few times. Used to be a nice place," Red said, "until Johnny Prague bought it and set up shop."

"Any friendlies inside?" Steele asked.

"Junkies and hookers but . . . mostly a bunch of punks with guns. No one the police will miss."

They got out of the SUV and walked around to the back.

"What's the play?" Phillip asked, pulling on a pair of black leather gloves before opening the hatch.

Steele quickly filled them in on the attack back in the States and how he'd managed to tag one of his attackers in London.

"This guy is the only link we have to the man who attacked me in the States," Steele continued. "He is on the third floor. Red, since you've been inside, you can take point," Steele said, dropping the bolt on the H&K UMP.

"That means don't kill him, gramps, because we need to know what *he* knows," Demo added.

"I know what it means, junior," Red said, flipping up the blanket that covered the floor of the cargo area and revealing a pair of weathered Sterling MK4s.

Steele immediately nudged Demo, hoping he wouldn't say anything, but it was too late.

"C'mon, guys."

"What?" Phillip asked, shoving a magazine into the weapon.

"Have you guys cleaned those since you stormed Normandy?" Demo asked without a trace of a smile.

"Don't judge a book by its cover, junior," Red said. "Phillip and I were sneaking over the Berlin Wall and killing Communists with these things while you were still tugging on your crank."

"Well, shit." Demo smiled. "That's all you had to say."

Steele passed out the radios and earpieces and after a commo check turned to Percy.

"Be ready in case we have to pull out in a hurry."

"Will do," he said.

Red led them across the street and down a flight

of stairs to the basement. The door was chained, and Steele moved up. He shoved the suppressor against the lock, blasted it free, and held the door for the rest of the team.

The basement was dark and smelled of water and fresh earth, silent except for the distant *drip, splat, drip, splat* of a leaking pipe. Steele climbed in, the movement sending a hissing rat clawing through a hole in the wall. Red led them to a door and down a short hall to a flight of stairs covered in graffiti and beer bottles.

Red held his finger up to his ear and then pointed upward.

Steele could hear it too—voices.

Red handed his rifle off to Phillip and pulled a thin dagger from his belt.

"Stay close, but give me room to work," he said, starting up the stairs.

Steele heard a pair of voices say something in Hungarian. Red must have agitated the native speakers because Steele heard a curse, followed by the sound of a fist hitting flesh.

Demo was already moving, and by the time Steele made it to the top there were two men lying dead on the ground and Red dropped an empty magazine from a Hungarian FEG.

"Nice work," Demo said.

"Bloody idiot had the safety on," Red replied, taking his weapon from Phillip.

They stacked up on the door, Steele taking the number two spot, and entered the hallway, whose dim light revealed peeling wallpaper and water-stained carpets.

A tall man with a cutoff AK-47 sat on the arm of a stained couch that sat a few feet to the right of door number three. A rail-thin girl sat on the couch, playing with his chest hair. When she saw the men with rifles, she let out a scream, but before the man could bring his rifle into play, Steele dropped him with a headshot.

"Red, take long, Demo, flashbang on me," Steele said, grabbing Red by the shoulder and driving him across the threshold. Red covered the hallway, allowing Steele to turn toward the door. By the time he turned, Demo had the bang prepped and was holding it up.

Steele knew any element of surprise had been blown when the junkie started screaming, which meant they were going to have to take the room dynamic. He booted the door, paused to let Demo toss the bang into the room before stepping inside.

The place was a wreck, beat-up tables covered with take-out wrappers, piles of filthy clothes, and overflowing ashtrays. Steele's first target was a man in a blue track suit, sitting in a folding chair to his right.

The man raised a silver revolver and Steele double tapped him in the chest.

The bang went off behind him, and Demo was firing a moment later.

Thwap. Thwap.

Steele dug the corner and pivoted to cover the room. He saw a man dive into the closet and went to pursue when a burst of gunfire erupted from the bathroom on his left. Steele moved across the room, knowing the gunman had seen him.

"Come to me," he told Demo, pointing at the bullets cutting through the drywall. His keeper nodded that he understood and ducked low.

Safely in the middle of the room, Steele ripped a mini frag from Demo's war belt, and while the shooter continued firing toward the opposite corner, he pulled the pin and hooked it into the bathroom.

Thoomp.

Steele drove toward the closet, already knowing what had happened. He tore down the clothes rack and found a crudely cut hole in the brick.

"Shit."

Their target was gone.

"We've got a runner, let's wrap this up," he said over the radio.

Demo was already taking documents from the table and shoving them into his pouch.

"Thirty seconds, Demo, and then we are moving," Steele said, pulling a camera from his kit and snapping headshots of the dead men. When he was finished he went through their pockets, finding a business card, some loose change, but nothing else.

"Ready when you are," his keeper replied, moving to the door.

"Stack up," Steele said, putting Red and Phillip behind Demo and taking the rear for himself.

"I'm up," Demo said.

"Stand by." Steele switched the camera for a can of teargas and then said, "Move." Demo stepped out into the hall, heading back toward the stairs, and Steele tossed the gas to cover their rear.

"Percy, we are coming out the north side of the building. Might be a hot extract."

"Copy, on my way."

"That was a spot of fun," Red said after they had all piled into the SUV. "Besides the bad guy getting away. Am I right?"

Steele held up the business card he had taken from one of the men's pockets.

"The Last Drop. Didn't know this hellhole was still around," Steele said.

"Oh yes. Very much so. And it's owned by Johnny Prague," Percy replied.

Shit. This just got more complicated.

"Target is heading toward the river," Demo said, holding up the PalmPilot.

"If Johnny Prague is protecting him, the Last Drop is his *last chance*."

"Which means, we need a change of clothes and a new car," Steele said, settling back into the seat.

We are getting close.

Chapter 32

Budapest

The Last Drop had started out as a KGB hangout during the Cold War—a spot where the KGB and their underlings plotted against the West over rakija, a popular fruit brandy. Located on the banks of the river Danube, it became *the* intelligence hub for the Balkans. Now it was owned by a Russian gangster who called himself Johnny Prague.

"This used to be the Wild West," Percy said with a wave that encompassed the entire waterfront. "Russian rules all the way."

Steele had heard stories. Back in the 1980s radical Islam was still in the cradle and the top spies were working in and around East Germany. There were rules in Germany, an agreed-upon give-and-take, but the closer you got to Moscow the wilder things became. It sounded a lot like Afghanistan in 2001 and Iraq in 2003. Before the brass arrived. Back when an operative could make his own rules.

"When the wall came down, the Drop became a haven for journalists covering the fighting between the Serbs and Croats. One of the only places you could find cheap beer and girls who wouldn't try to steal your wallet," Percy said.

"Sounds like my kind of place," Demo replied.

Steele had expected some renovation, but for some reason he assumed the Drop would remain unchanged, so when they came over the rise, he realized how wrong he had been.

"Ho-ly shit," he said.

Renovation was an understatement. The waterfront had been transformed, and in its place was an oasis of neon and shimmering incandescence. Searchlights cut across the horizon, advertising a new club, and the streets were packed with bright red brake lights.

"Yeah," Demo said. "Wasn't expecting that."

"Peace had always been the one elusive commodity the Balkans needed to come into the twenty-first century. Now that they have it, they are taking advantage," Percy added.

Steele had seen it before—stability brought prosperity, and prosperity brought outside investors. Nowhere was this more evident than on the waterfront, which was in the midst of massive revitalization.

The Drop had undergone a metamorphosis. What was once a somber building with filthy windows and a faded metal sign hanging over a gunmetal-gray door was now a neon-clad butterfly.

The street in front of the bar had been ripped up and replaced with cobblestones and a small fountain. Off to the right, a line of Bentleys and Mercedes dropped off smartly clad Serbs, who followed the red carpet past a pair of searchlights to the mirrored front door. Above it all a neon marquee proudly displayed the club's new name: KOMRADES AND KOMMISSARS.

Steele pressed the microreceiver into his ear, wishing he had worn a jacket.

"So, what's the plan?" Demo asked, handing off the transmitter.

"Percy you stay with the car, Red, you and Phillip are on containment. Demo you are with me."

Steele checked the pistol one last time and opened the door.

"Hey, mano," Demo said, getting out.

"Yeah?"

"You got a plan?" he asked, checking the tracking monitor.

"Yeah." Steele nodded, lifting the case from the backseat. "We're going to do it live."

"How many times do I have to tell you—that's not a plan," Demo said.

"Sure it is," Steele said.

They left the car and walked toward the door in the alley with the single light mounted to the wall. Beneath its halo, a thick-necked bouncer sat on a stool by the open door. When he sensed Steele's approach, he pivoted in his direction.

Steele jerked his chin upward, a slight nod that the man pointedly ignored.

"I'm here to see Johnny Prague. I've got a reservation," he said.

The man didn't bother getting to his feet. He lazily rolled the toothpick to the corner of his mouth, gave him a quick once-over, then said, "Never heard of him."

"Maybe you should check with your boss."

"Hit the bricks, mate," he said, jerking his thumb toward the street.

Steele set the case on the ground and stepped closer.

"Listen, fat boy, I've had a shitty week. You can go find your boss or you can go to the hospital and have them remove that toothpick from your ass."

"So much for subtle," Demo said.

The bouncer let out a long sigh and got to his feet. Standing up he towered over Steele by a good foot and a half, his large shoulders taking up much of the space. He rolled the toothpick across his fat lips and opened his jacket to show a silver automatic in a shoulder holster.

"Like I said, fuck off."

"Fair enough."

Steele stomped down on the man's instep as hard as he could, his right hand snaking inside the bouncer's jacket. The giant bellowed a curse in Hungarian and instinctively reached down for his injured foot. Steele ripped the pistol from the holster and, in one smooth motion, buffaloed the man with his own gun.

The bouncer went down, and Steele retrieved the case, shoved the pistol in the back of his pants, and stepped through the door.

The outside wasn't the only thing that had changed. Steele had heard about the famous teak tables that were hand buffed every morning until they shone like glass. They were gone, ripped up to make room for a massive dance floor. There was a large bar near the entrance and two smaller ones on each side. Steele saw the staircase to the left, and he and Demo took it up to a landing.

"I'm here to see Johnny," he told the guard.

The man pointed to the camera on the wall. "He sees you," he said.

Steele turned his head and flashed his best smile.

The man touched his finger to his ear and said, "Got it." Then he said, "This way."

He pushed open the door, leading Steele down a hall with rooms on either side.

"Our guy is at the end of the hall," Demo said, glancing at the monitor.

"There," the man said, pointing to the door at the end of the hall.

They stepped inside and found themselves in a rectangular room. To the left, Johnny Prague sat between two scantily clad women, a pair of large bodyguards standing to his right and left.

Steele was crossing toward Johnny Prague when he noticed a half-opened door on the right side of the room. There were three men inside; one was standing with his back to the door and one on the couch. But it was the man who turned from the window who drew Steele's attention.

He was tall and gaunt. The tattoos told him the man

could be Russian Mafia—the crowns and skulls on his fingers, that he was a killer.

There was something familiar about the man's face. Steele felt like he had seen him before but couldn't place it. They locked eyes, the man's gaze dark and threatening.

The man in the door felt Steele's presence and glanced over his shoulder and then closed the door.

According to the tracker, their target was in that room, which meant one of those men had gone after his mother.

It took everything Steele had to keep moving toward Prague when all he wanted to do was kick the door in and start firing.

"What the hell do you want?" Prague yelled.

The two men had history, and none of it was good. The first time their paths crossed was in 2011. Johnny was running a contract crew of South African mercs and Serbian guns for hire. He'd accepted a contract to protect Mu'ammar Gaddhafi, but when the Libyan dictator's fortunes began to falter, the Russian sold him out.

Gaddhafi's body wasn't even in the ground when Johnny agreed to betray the dictator's second son, Saif, who'd been too busy selling his father's weapons to get out of Libya.

The Program wanted to know what Saif had sold, and to whom, and sent Steele to track him down. He caught up with the men in a town named Ubari, and when Johnny refused to play ball, Steele put a bullet in his hip.

"I was in the neighborhood and heard that you were still alive and thought, hey, I should go see my buddy Johnny Prague."

Johnny motioned for the guard to let him pass, who then bumped Steele with his shoulder before stepping away.

"Easy fella," Steele said before placing the case flat on the table and then slammed the bouncer's pistol on top. "You might want to get one of your Dobermans to go check on their buddy."

One of the women ran her eyes lasciviously over Steele and licked her lips.

"What is that?" Johnny asked, looking at the case.

"Money and lots of it."

"For what?"

"For you to tell me who is behind that door," Steele said.

"Take your money and go," Johnny said with a flip of his hand.

"Demo, this is exactly what I am talking about. Johnny here thinks that since he is king shit of turd island, he can just tell us to pound sand. That is just rude."

"He said for you to leave," the bodyguard said.

"Easy, Ivan, I don't want to have to blow you and your friend there through the wall."

Johnny slammed his fist down on the table, his face turning bright red. Two empty glasses fell over and his bodyguard took a step toward the table.

"You've got a lot of balls threatening me in my own place."

"It's not a threat."

Steele watched Johnny's hand drop below the table and when it returned, he was looking down the barrel of a silver revolver.

Chapter 33

Budapest

Zakayev didn't know why the American didn't seem to recognize him, but he knew immediately how he'd found him.

He turned on Yuri, the man's eyes glassy from the vodka he'd been chugging since showing up.

"You led them here," he said, rounding on Yuri.

"Irena," the Russian whimpered.

"She is dead, forget her," Zakayev snapped, ripping the bottle from Yuri's hands. "You need to get your head out of your ass."

"I wasn't followed," he said, the sweat beading up on his forehead.

Things were unraveling too fast.

Zakayev didn't believe him for a second.

The attack at the second safehouse had occurred thirty minutes ago. And there was only one way that Yuri could have covered the distance that fast.

He came right here, the voice said. *Led them straight to us. Kill him.*

Zakayev knew he should have sent Yuri away the moment he learned about Irena's death. He'd told the men who took him to the apartment to keep their eyes on him.

Keep him quiet and sober, but they had failed.

And now Yuri was a liability.

Think.

"We can kill them right now. Right now," Yuri said. "They are in the next room. Pavil, tell him," he said, turning to the man on the couch.

Zakayev knew what he had to do.

"No," he said, turning on Yuri. "You sit down and shut your fucking mouth." He moved to the window, the paint around the frame cracking when he shoved it open. Zakayev looked down to the alley and saw the Dumpster.

It was his way out.

"Pavil, grab Cyril from downstairs. Get the car but do it quietly. No shooting, understand?"

"Yes, boss."

Yuri was sitting on the couch, his head buried in his hands. "I messed up. I'm sorry," he said.

Zakayev sat down beside him and wrapped his arm around his shoulder.

"Yuri, what's done is done. Calm down," he said, right hand creeping to his belt.

"I don't know how they followed me." Yuri was sobbing now. "Ever since Irena, I can't . . ."

"Yes, yes." Zakayev clamped his left hand over Yuri's mouth, twisted his head away from him, and buried the blade in his ear. Yuri convulsed against him and Zakayev pushed him away before he pissed himself.

Thirty seconds later his old friend was dead.

"We all pay what we owe," Zakayev said, pulling the knife free.

Zakayev nodded, shoved the atlas into his back pocket, grabbed a grenade from the backpack under the couch, and went over to the door. He pulled the pin and jammed it between the crack at the bottom and then moved to the window.

He tossed the bag out of the window and jumped

after it. His feet clattered off the Dumpster, and then he was on the street. Zakayev shouldered the bag, checked behind him, and pulled the phone from his pocket.

"Change in plans. The American is here," he told Gabriel when he answered. "We go tonight, send me some men."

Chapter 34

Budapest

"Everyone just take it easy," Demo said. "Everything is cool."

"You think this is cool?" Johnny asked Steele. "You know what would happen if I slotted you right here, mate?"

"You would have to clean up the mess?"

"Nothing would happen. Not a thing. This is my club, my rules."

Steele took stock of the situation. Johnny was directly in front of him, a pistol pointed at his stomach, Johnny's two goons circling to the right, blocking the door to the Russians. He heard Demo moving to the left, saw one of the bodyguards' eyes tracking him across the room.

Tensions were high, and Steele knew the situation could go to shit in a heartbeat.

It was his cell phone that ended up saving Eric.

A few months ago, Demo had downloaded "Escape" by Rupert Holmes and saved it as his ringtone. Steele had tried everything to turn it off, but his friend had used some kind of password protection that he couldn't crack.

The phone vibrated in his pocket and then the ringtone kicked in. "If you like piña coladas and getting caught in the rain . . ."

"What in the hell is that?" Johnny demanded.

"It's my girlfriend," Steele replied.

He held up his hands, palms facing out. "I am not trying to disrespect the gun you have pointed at me, but I haven't called her in three days and unless you want a *serious* situation on your hands, I need to answer it."

"This isn't serious enough?" Johnny demanded, jabbing the pistol in his direction.

"I am just reaching for my phone," Steele said, lowering his right hand. "Just my phone."

"You think this is a fooking joke, do ya?" Johnny demanded, his face getting red.

"Either *you* are going to kill me, or *she* is," Steele said, slowly pulling the phone out of his pocket with two fingers. "Johnny, why don't you put that thing down, let me talk to my lady, and when we are done, we'll pick right back up where we left off."

"I will blow your fooking head off," Johnny said, cocking the hammer. "Put the phone down."

"Okay, okay, I get it." Steele hit the end button and set the phone on his lap. "She's just going to call back," he said with a shrug.

Instead of a call Meg sent a text.

"Great, now she is sending me a text. Thanks a lot, Johnny."

He unlocked the phone with a swipe of his finger and read: This is the man who attacked you. His name is Aleksandr Zakayev. Steele opened the message and found himself looking at the man with the tattooed hands. Rage rippled across his body like the return stroke of a lightning bolt.

Johnny slipped his finger inside the pistol's trigger guard. The girls sensed the change in Steele and edged away from Johnny. The two men stared at each other in silence.

Steele felt the Browning Hi Power holstered on his hip. *You're fast, but not that fast,* he thought.

"What's it going to be, Johnny? You going to help

me out?" Steele asked, gesturing with the cell phone in his left hand. He pulled his feet in and got them set beneath the chair. Steele's leg muscles coiled, the tension building like springs.

One of the girls whimpered, and Johnny's eyes involuntarily sought the source of the noise. *It's now or never.*

Steele flicked the phone at Johnny like he was trying to bury a playing card in a sheet of plywood. He jumped to his feet, knocking the chair over, and side-kicked the bodyguard in the chest. The blow drove the man backward, and he slammed into the closed door.

The impact cracked the frame and popped the lock free from the jamb. The door came open and the bodyguard tumbled inside the room. Steele was about to follow him into the room when there was an explosion.

He covered his face with his arm and saw the second bodyguard rushing toward him.

Steele grabbed his wrist and slung him toward his boss. Johnny panicked and reflexively pulled the trigger. The guard took the bullet in the gut and tumbled across the table. Steele stepped into the second room, clearing it from the threshold.

He assumed the man lying dead on the couch was the man he'd been chasing, which meant his target had gotten away.

"He's gone," Steele yelled to Demo.

"On it," his handler said.

The hallway door burst open and three more guards rushed in.

Demo hit the first man with a controlled pair to the chest. He fell, and the second guard hurtled his body. Steele kicked the chair toward the man, tripping him in midair. The man went down but managed to roll over his shoulder and jumped to his feet.

Steele backhanded him across the face. It wasn't enough to break his nose, but it got his eyes watering and allowed Steele to get closer.

He slapped his hands over his attacker's ears, grabbed the back of the head, and jerked his knee into his face, but the man wouldn't go down.

The hell with this.

Steele hit him with a tight left and skinned the Browning from its holster. He fired two shots from the hip. Demo had taken care of the final guard and was stepping into the hall, leaving Steele to deal with Johnny, who had untangled himself from the dead bodyguard, raised his revolver, and fired.

The bullet went high, blasting the sconce off the wall and showering the room with shards of glass.

Steele centered the Hi Power on Johnny's forehead. "Game over," he said, pulling the trigger.

He stepped inside the room and saw the two bodies and the open window. Steele holstered the pistol, climbed through the window, and jumped down to the Dumpster.

"Percy, Demo is on the move, meet me on the east side of the building."

Chapter 35

Steele jumped into the SUV.

"Where are Red and Phillip?" he asked.

"Figured we might need another set of wheels, told them to go find some transportation," Percy replied.

"Good call." Steele lifted his radio and keyed the button. "Demo, where you at, buddy?"

Nothing.

Steele pulled out his phone, his imagination working through the worst-case scenarios. Was Demo compromised? Hurt? Or worse, was his keeper dead? *Lock it down. Focus on what you know.* Steele leaned forward in the seat, scanning the alleys and shadows of the street. Demo was a pro, he knew how to handle himself. Steele's finger hovered over the call button.

He had a choice to make: let Demo work or make the call and possibly blow his cover.

Steele forced himself to wait.

Percy slammed on the brakes, throwing Steele forward in his seat. He caught himself on the dash. "What the hell?" he demanded.

The Englishman pulled over to the side of the road, nodding to the street corner where Demo stood with his thumb out.

"Is this my Uber?" he asked, jumping in the backseat.

The tension drained off Steele's shoulders and he felt ten pounds lighter knowing that his friend was okay.

"Good to know I've still got it," Demo said.

"Got what?" Steele asked.

"My skills." Demo cracked before he placed his cell phone in the SUV's cup holder.

The tracking app was open on the screen and it showed a dot moving through the city.

"How did you manage that?" Steele asked.

"Because I'm a ninja. If I'd had more time I would have taken them all out," Demo said with a grin, "but I didn't want to ruin your fun, so I just got the plate off their car."

"And then he sent it to me." Meg's voice came through the phone.

It felt good to hear her voice, and a goofy grin crept across Steele's face.

"Nice to hear your voice, stranger."

"You too."

Meg got back on task.

"Demo sent the plate and I used Keyhole to grab the VIN and log in to the nav system. The track is real time."

A moment later a shining black Mercedes pulled up next to the SUV, and Steele saw Red smiling from behind the wheel.

"Always wanted one of these," he said.

"Did you just steal that?" Demo asked.

"Borrowed, mate. Where are we headed?"

"Demo, send them the tracking info. I'm ready to put this rabid dog down."

Chapter 36

Budapest

The neighborhood was an older section on the outskirts of town. A comfortable distance from the busy city center but not far enough to escape the creep of gentrification. The buildings stood in a row, most of the windows had been removed, and the open spaces reminded Zakayev of sockets with no eyes. Some of them were covered in scaffolding, others with clear plastic sheets that flapped in the breeze like a funeral shroud.

His mind wandered back to the day his life was changed forever. It was January of 1995, a new year that brought new hopes and dreams to the people of

Grozny. Zakayev remembered the day well, the bare trees, the dark gray clouds in the east threatening snow, but most of all the cold.

It was bitterly cold outside, and he stopped in a doorway to warm his freezing hands. There was a red balloon stuck in one of the trees and he was looking at it when he saw the first Sukhoi Su-24. The warplane rolled silently out of the clouds, its wings extended for better control at low altitude. The pilot brought it lower and lower to the ground and then two black dots fell from its wings.

The pilot pulled up, hitting the afterburner, and the sound was the loudest thing Zakayev had ever heard. Everyone on the street stopped and looked up as the plane rose higher and higher. Zakayev kept his eyes on the specks, watching them tumble end over end toward the apartment complex where he lived with his family.

He was twelve.

Later he would learn to tell the difference between a five-hundred-pound bomb and the bigger two thousand pounders. But at the time he was still a child, still innocent in the ways of war and man's brutality.

The explosion ripped the top six floors from the rest of the building, enveloping the street in black smoke and the smell of burning flesh. Zakayev wandered out into the street as five more Su-24s rolled in, dropped their payload, and disappeared.

Zakayev now lit a cigarette and glanced down the street, where the driver waited with the Audi, and then turned his attention to the way station. A shape flittered across the front of the target building. It was Cyril. The man crept up on the porch and then there was a hammering sound followed by the clang of falling metal.

Fucking Russian. Can't even break into an abandoned building without making noise.

The thought brought Yuri to the forefront of his mind.

He was weak. A liability, the voice said.

Yes, Zakayev said to himself, *he was also my friend.*

Friend? the voice screeched. *A friend that would have got you killed. Or worse, put back in the hole.*

The thought of Black Dolphin and the hole sent a shiver up Zakayev's spine.

"I am never going back," he said.

You will if you don't wake up. Don't you realize that it is us versus them?

A beam of a white-lensed flashlight from across the street snapped him back to the now. It was the signal.

Time to move.

He crossed the street and went into the building, an

old three-story department store that was being turned into apartments.

Zakayev pulled a headlamp over his forehead and headed to the stairs. He followed the map he'd found in the package, taking the long hallway covered in spiderwebs until it came to a T. He took a left, counting the doors until he came to the fifth one. Zakayev shoved the small prybar between the door and the frame and popped the lock.

It was a boiler room.

He had to duck to keep from hitting the pipes and made his way to the back, where he found the panel hiding the ladder. At the bottom, just as the map had indicated, was a metal door with a combination lock.

Zakayev dropped his pack and pulled out a suction cup, which he attached to the dial. He connected a cord to the laptop and hit enter. The dial began to turn, the screen showing a diagram of the lock. Each time a tumbler fell into place the computer made a notation until finally the lock clicked open.

He disconnected the device and stepped into the room.

The way stations were safehouses the Alphas had used during the Cold War. Places where a spy could rest, refit, or hide out. Zakayev was the first person to visit this one in twenty-five years.

The room contained what had been the most cutting-edge equipment in its day—maps, documents, passports, even a stack of MREs or Meals Ready to Eat. There was a desk covered in a foot of dust, a radio set on the far wall, and Zakayev's target: an ancient-looking computer.

Compared to what was on the market today the system was laughable, but in the '90s it was state-of-the-art, the most advanced system in Europe.

The way stations were technically still operational, which meant that the terminal had an open link to the files he was hired to retrieve. Miraculously the computer still worked.

Zakayev knew nothing about computers, but according to Gabriel all he had to do was follow the instructions on the printed card he had in his pocket. The card was laid out like the safety information in the back pocket of an airplane seat. Little cartoon boxes that guided him through the process. He flipped the computer on, listened to it hum and beep, and when the screen showed the prompt on the card he hit enter on the Toughbook.

Do you want to enable remote desktop?

Zakayev looked at the card, following the blocks to Step 3, which said *Enable remote desktop.*

He moved the curser over the OK block and clicked the touch pad.

Gabriel had told him what would happen when he hit enter.

"Once you are connected to the computer, our man will use a program to break the sixty-four-bit encryption and log on to the network. By piggybacking onto the secure server, the American software won't realize what is happening. All you have to do is wait."

Five minutes later Transfer Complete flashed on the computer.

Zakayev was done, he had what he'd come for. Now it was time to get out.

One step closer to getting free of Gabriel, the voice sneered.

Chapter 37

Budapest

"Why here?" Steele asked, looking at the blinking red dot that marked the position of Zakayev's Audi.

On the screen the route the Audi had taken was marked by a blue squiggly line. The driver had cut south after leaving the Last Drop and hopped on Motor Highway Zero, or M0, as it was labeled on the map.

The M0 was known as the ring road and formed a lazy circle around the city, connecting all of the outlying highways.

Steele had asked Percy to "give them room," knowing that Zakayev would be checking for tails. His suspicions were affirmed by the countless tiny circles on the screen. "Crazy Ivans" Percy called them.

"Name came from a maneuver the Soviet submarine captains during the Cold War would use if they thought they were being followed. They would order the sub helmsman to bring the sub around a hundred eighty so they could use the sonar to check their back trail."

"Smart," Demo said.

After fifteen aimless minutes of cruising around the left bank of the city, the Audi hopped back on the M0. This time their path was straight and it led them to their current position on the outskirts of the Fourth District.

The area still bore the scars of the Russian occupation of Hungary that followed World War II. Mainly the *panelház*, the drab prefabricated apartment tenements the Soviets built throughout the Eastern Bloc.

To Steele, they looked like a stack of pillboxes, similar to the ones he'd seen on the beaches of Normandy. Except the structures weren't for keeping invaders out. They were built as affordable housing for the Communist Party.

Percy pulled over and shoved the transmission into park. His phone rang and he picked it up, the light from the screen illuminating his face.

"It's Red," he said aloud. "They found the car.

Wants to know if you want them to do a drive-by of the area?"

"No. Tell them to hang back," Steele said. "We need to make sure this is their final stop."

"Demo, run the grid through Cutlass Main, see if we can find out—"

"Already on it," Demo said, eyes glued to the PDA in his hand.

"Maybe he's stopped for a spot of tea," Percy suggested.

"Zakayev is crazy, but he is also calculating. He is after something, we just need to find out what it is."

"No active locations," Demo muttered. "Let's check the archives."

They sat in silence for almost a minute and then:

"Bingo."

"Whatcha got?" Steele turned to Demo.

"This building here," he said, showing him the screen. "Was a way station during the Cold War. According to the archives the Program managed to get an asset into the city and he set one up in the basement of that building."

"Way station?" Percy asked.

"A secure facility our guys could use to refit or send encrypted information back to the States," Steele answered. "When was it deactivated?" he asked Demo.

"Give me a second, mano."

Steele pulled a road map of the area out of his pocket and found their position.

"We are here," he said, pointing, marking it with a dot. "This is the way station," he said, making a second mark two streets to the north.

"Think I found what he wants," Demo said.

Steele could tell by the tone of his voice that it wasn't good.

"They never deactivated the station."

"I can't imagine there is anything inside that he would want, unless he likes old MREs."

"No, you don't understand. That way station is still on the ARPANET," Demo said.

"English, please."

"Back in the 1960s the Department of Defense started a project they called the ARPANET. They built a network of government servers so they could communicate in case of a nuclear attack. The Program had one of the servers built inside Cutlass Main, all of the old way stations were hardwired in."

"Demo, I don't speak geek. What does that mean?"

"It means that Zakayev can hack into Cutlass Main using the old-ass computer inside *that* way station," Demo said. "Is that plain enough for you?"

"Uh, yeah," Steele said.

"Red, I need you guys to find a spot close to the building. Set up an overwatch position, we are coming to you," Steele ordered.

"Right-o," the man replied.

"Percy, you are going to find the phone lines," Steele said, lifting the H&K UMP from the floorboards and ducking into the sling. "And when I give you the call you are going to shut them down."

"Got it," Percy replied.

Steele and Demo were getting out of the SUV when the radio crackled to life. This time it was Phillip.

"Found one, north side of the road, three houses to the left of the target building."

"Roger that. We are coming to you. I'll signal with a red lens, let's keep it nice and quiet."

"Will do," Phillip replied.

"Mano, I'm not sure what you are going to do without me," Demo said as they stepped off.

Even though the streets were empty, they tucked their submachine guns into their jackets and angled into the shadows of the buildings that lined the street.

Steele climbed over a low wall and landed in a cluttered garden area. It was dark, a sea of gray and black with bits of trash and stacks of brick littering the high grass. The only light came from the luminous dial of the compass attached to the buttstock.

They threaded their way north, creeping through the alleys, one man pulling cover while the other moved. Steele had memorized the map and came to a halt at the end of one of the alleyways.

He pulled out his red lens flashlight and thumbed the endcap.

"Got you," Red said over the radio.

"We are coming in," Steele replied.

Demo slipped past him and crossed the street with Steele covering his six. He stopped in the doorway and covered Steele when he crossed.

Inside the building, Red and Phillip were at the window. They had set up their position to cover the southwest of the building.

Steele moved to the window and observed the target building. The safehouse was directly across the street, just like it was on the map. The two men had a good position.

"I've found the box. Ready when you are," Percy said.

"All right, here's the plan, we are going to take the south side. You guys handle anyone coming out the front. Containment is key. If the perimeter opens up, we will lose these guys."

"You want sneaky sneaky," Phillip asked, holding up a suppressed submachine gun, "or life of the party?"

He nodded to the M79 grenade launcher propped near the window.

"Whatever you need. Just don't let them out."

"Don't you worry. I've got that Russian fucker on the porch, I can smell him from here," Red promised.

Demo and Steele exchanged worried glances.

"Let's make it happen."

Demo led them back the way they had come, back-tracking to the alley where they slipped through another yard and entered the rear of an abandoned building.

They were now in position directly across the street from the target building.

"We are set," he told Percy. "Go ahead and cut the phone lines."

"Done."

"You sure this is going to work?"

He had no idea what the man was doing inside, but if he was accessing Cutlass Main, waiting wasn't an option he could afford.

"If the phone lines are cut there is no way that he is going to be able to transmit. If he can't transmit there is no reason to hang around."

Makes sense, Steele thought, leaning closer to the open window.

The silence was deafening and made worse by the pounding of Steele's heart in the darkness. He thought he saw movement at the back of the house and raised the H&K, lining up the dot of the Aimpoint micro on the spot he wanted to shoot. He forced himself to look away and then back on target.

Nothing.

Steele was well aware of autokinesis, the involuntary twitches of the eyes that tricked the brain into thinking something was moving. He had seen it plenty of times in Afghanistan and Iraq, but it was still unsettling.

Waiting was the hardest part because it gave the mind time to go through the hundreds of ways things could go wrong.

What if they came out the front, what if there was another way out? What if . . . ?

A single crack of a gunshot cut through the night and Steele knew the time for questions was over.

Chapter 38

"Who is shooting?" Steele asked, his line of sight to Red and Phillip's position blocked by a scaffolding.

"My money," Demo said, pausing for effect, "says it was the fat one."

A second shot rang out and Steele found himself regretting the decision to move. They were on the back side of the target and couldn't see what was going on.

"I'm going to the roof," he said, turning to the stairs.

In an instant, the probing shots turned into a full-on firefight. A burst of automatic fire streaked through the night and Steele saw a handful of tracers bouncing skyward. He knew it was too late to move.

"Stay in your lane," Demo said.

Holding your sector of fire was *the* most basic of all

infantry tenets. It was a concept drummed into every private who had ever held a rifle. One meant to curtail a warrior's natural inclination to get into the fight.

Running toward the sound of battle was natural, but Steele knew that once you were given a field of fire you held it, no matter what. It was day one stuff and he had almost violated it.

A grenade exploded with a low *cruuummp,* the sound telling Steele that Phillip had finally gotten to use his M79.

"Taking heavy fire," Red said over the radio. "Could use a hand."

"On it," Demo said.

Steele now had two sectors to watch. He had to keep his eyes on Demo and watch the back door, which meant he had to push outside of the house and take a position behind a stack of roofing shingles.

He glanced to his left and saw Demo fire a burst, the muzzle flash silhouetting him in the dark. Steele turned back to the target house just as a second grenade detonated on the roof. He shaded his eyes from the explosion, which cast premature daylight over the scene. At that instant a figure walked out of the target building and Steele saw his face clearly in the firelight.

Their eyes met and the fog that had masked all of the memories from the attack lifted. Steele saw the man standing over him, pointing the pistol at his chest. He heard his voice, "*Mertva.*" Dead.

Light him up.

The man raised his rifle and Steele flicked the selector switch from safe to fire. The guns went off at the same time, two jets of fire, two bullets, and then Steele was falling backward.

"Eric!" Demo yelled.

Steele saw his target jerk and fired two more shots on his way to the ground. Steele landed on his side, the pain in his chest taking the breath from his lungs.

The man cursed in Russian before spraying the yard with automatic fire.

Steele curled up behind the bags of concrete, trying to get air into his lungs. He was aware of Demo rushing toward him, firing on the move, and the sound of tires squealing on the street.

"Help me up," he yelled to Demo.

His handler shoved him to the ground and started checking him for any wounds.

"The vest . . ." Steele gasped. He was trying to tell him that the vest had stopped the bullet.

That's when the target house exploded.

"The crazy fucker Zakayev killed his own guys!" Demo yelled as they ran around the corner of the house, dodging the falling debris the explosion had kicked into the air. In the distance Steele heard the wail of sirens. The cops were on their way.

"Percy, come on."

Steele brought the H&K to his shoulder and fired a burst at the retreating Audi carrying Zakayev down the street. The burning way station made it too bright for Steele to see the red dot inside his optic so his shots were low. He adjusted and reengaged and walked the rounds up the trunk, the back window shattering in a spray of glass.

The SUV screeched around the opposite corner and slid to a halt. Percy leaned across the seat and threw open the passenger-side door. Steele jumped into the front, followed by Demo, and Percy was off.

Steele opened the front of his shirt, revealing a black Kevlar vest, the 7.62 round a flattened brass disk on the front.

"You hit?"

He ran his hand beneath the vest and let out a relieved sigh when his hand came back free of blood.

"Seat belts, gents," Percy ordered over the growl of the SUV engine. He raced through the gears and followed the Audi.

"That was him," Steele said. "I remember all of it." He yanked the belt over his chest and clipped it in. "Son of a bitch shot me in the chest with my own pistol."

"Can't wait to have a few words with him myself," Demo replied, rubbing the soot off his collar. "This was my favorite shirt."

The Audi raced through the town center, almost hitting a white-and-blue police cruiser that was crossing through the intersection. The car immediately flipped on the lights and set off in pursuit of them.

"This ought to be interesting," Percy said.

Steele took the opportunity to glance back the way they had come.

The fire that had started in the way station had spread from the basement. Now the entire building was aflame. Steele could see the flicker of the red and gold flames and a jet-black pillar of smoke rising above Budapest's ancient skyline.

Farther to the south there was already a line of firetrucks on their way to battle the blaze.

"Are you wearing driving gloves?" Demo asked.

"Of course," Percy replied, like it was the most natural thing in the world, and Steele wasn't sure how to reply.

"Whatever floats your boat," Demo remarked.

"This little car can move," Steele said, glancing at the speedometer. They were traveling at 112 kilometers per hour, which converted to 70 miles per hour.

The Skoda police cruiser was gaining on the Audi

when a head popped out of the Audi's sunroof, followed by a torso. It was Zakayev, and the tube he hoisted on his shoulder left no question as to his intentions.

"Is that a LAW?" Demo asked.

Steele had seen the Lightweight Anti-Armor Weapon or LAW in action, and despite the fact that it had been around since 1960, its collapsible design made it highly portable. He had seen them used against all types of vehicles, but this marked the first time Steele had seen one fired from a *moving* vehicle.

Steele doubted the police officer knew exactly what was being pointed at him, but his driver obviously had the common sense to know it wasn't good. He jerked the wheel to the left, but the Skoda was too close to miss at this range. All Zakayev had to do was shift to his right and fire.

The 66 mm rocket leaped from the tube and hit the Skoda in the center of the hood. The detonation shoved the front end straight down and sent the car tumbling off the road.

Chapter 39

Budapest

The SUV sped down the street lined with office buildings and shops. Steele rolled down the window. He shoved a fresh magazine into the rifle, leaned out, and fired. Zakayev let go of the expended launcher and dropped back inside the Audi.

"He is going for—"

Steele had settled the Aimpoint on the broken rear window and hammered through the magazine.

"What was that?" he asked, ducking inside, his eyes watering from the slipstream.

"He is going for the highway," Percy responded, pointing toward the on-ramp to the M1 ahead.

The driver of the Audi waited until the very last second before committing.

"Nice try," Percy muttered.

There was traffic on the highway. Not the usual rush, but enough to provide sections of cover for the Audi, which weaved in and out of the cars. Steele had to wait for a clean shot, and when he finally took it, the driver quickly jerked the Audi across traffic and cut in front of a truck, blocking any additional shots.

"There is an exit coming up in half a kilometer," Demo said from the back.

"I can't see around this wanker," Percy replied and swung into oncoming traffic, headlights filling the car. The engine was a high-pitched hum, the RPM rising toward the red as he pushed the gas to the floor.

"There are cars coming," Steele said.

Percy ignored him and kept the car on track.

"They are coming right at us."

In the back Demo started praying in Spanish and Steele scrambled to connect the seat belt. He wasn't sure why he bothered. A head-on collision at this speed was going to kill him with or without the belt.

"Suck it in," Percy said, cutting the wheel back to the right and slicing in front of the semi.

The driver laid down on the horn and Steele let out a long breath.

"Never doubted him," Demo said weakly from the backseat.

"There," Steele said, pointing at the exit and the rapidly fading taillights.

Percy pumped the brakes and cut toward the ramp with a quick look in the mirror.

"I do love a good ride."

Steele glanced at the GPS as they flashed off the highway, Percy following the Audi south. They crested a small hill, the moon high and full in the sky. In the rearview, Steele could see the distant city lights winking behind them.

Then the road dipped down, coiling like a snake toward a cut in the trees. The Audi hugged the corner, disappearing into the gloom, with the SUV tight on its tail.

The moment they entered the tree line, the moon disappeared, its sallow light blocked by the thick curtain of ancient trees.

Percy activated the high beams, with a flick of his fingers. The LEDs threw a rectangle of white light across their path and sparked off the reflective squares embedded in the center of the asphalt.

"Don't lose them," Demo urged, the Audi's taillights disappearing around the curve.

Percy's jaw was set, his fingers deft on the wheel.

He took the turn, foot pressing on the accelerator, tires chirping against the centrifugal force trying to pull the SUV off the road.

A quick glance at the speedometer told Steele that they were doing sixty-five per hour, an impossibly fast speed for the curve. But somehow Percy kept them on the road.

They came out of the turn with a full head of steam, and up ahead Steele saw the lights bounce off a white road sign. The sign was there to warn the drivers that they were entering a switchback.

Alarm bells were going off in Steele's head but before he could offer a warning, Percy was twisting the wheel to the left and Steele felt the SUV squatting on its springs.

His eyes sought the apex of the turn, the spot where the road would begin to straighten, but the road kept bending to the left. The SUV's weight shifting farther and farther from center.

We are going to crash.

Percy downshifted, the engine absorbing the RPMs with a roar.

"C'mon you bitch," the Englishman hissed.

Just when the back tires started to slide, the road leveled out and Steele could see the Audi's brake lights glowing bright red a quarter mile ahead of them.

"Holy shit we—" Demo began, but before he finished the sentence a pair of machine guns opened up from either side of the road.

"Contact," Steele yelled, watching the line of yellow tracers coil toward the car.

The bullets lashed across the hood and blasted through the windshield.

The first blast caught Percy full-on, shredding his chest. Steele felt the warm spatter of blood splash across his face and he raised his arm to shield his eyes from the exploding windshield.

"Grab the wheel," Demo yelled.

Steele opened his eyes, and saw Percy slumped over the wheel.

Another burst hit the SUV. The rounds chewed through the aluminum, showering the interior with chunks of insulation.

Steele saw a clearing in the trees and shoved the wheel over.

"Hold on," he yelled to Demo.

The sudden change in direction confused the gunners, and they mercifully avoided a broadside attack. The front tires hit the embankment and the car was airborne. The only thing that kept them alive was the barbed wire fence. It caught the grille, slowing the car enough for Steele to yank up on the emergency brake, and then they nosed into the pasture.

The car skidded across the field, barely missing a cow, and then buried itself into the ground. Steele unhooked himself and reached over to check Percy's pulse.

He was dead.

Steele threw the door open and climbed out of the car.

In the backseat Demo shook glass out of his hair with a curse. He tried to get the door open, but it was stuck.

"How in the hell," he muttered, kicking at the back door, "did that tatted-up motherfucker get a team ahead of us?" Demo demanded.

Finally clear of the car he untangled the sling and laid the submachine gun over the trunk.

Steele leaned over the seat and grabbed the bag off the floor. He unzipped the flap, answering Demo's questions while pulling out a pair of PVS-17s.

"Easy," he began. "Zakayev called up his boys, told him he had a car full of suckers on his tail."

Steele mounted the night vision behind the optic of the submachine gun and with the flip of a switch the darkness was replaced by the emerald-green hue of the night vision.

"And then he led us right into the kill zone."

"I really hate that guy," Demo said.

Join the club, Steele thought, scanning the area.

They were in a pasture—a postage stamp–size clearing in the midst of the woods. Off to the right, he could see the road through a line of skinny trees.

"Well, unless you are planning on calling for Triple A," Demo said, attaching his own night vision to his rifle. "Or you got a boat to get through that swamp," he said, pointing back the way they had come, "we need to move north."

Steele stripped two mini frags from the bag and tossed one to Demo.

"That bad?" he said, looking back the way they had come.

"Nothing but brambles and water."

"Well let's not make it easy for them," Steele said, knowing that whatever additional men Zakayev had picked up would be closing in for the kill.

They moved north, skirting the trees that ran the length of the road, leaving the smoking car and Percy's body behind them.

"I've got movement on the right. Machine gun team crossing the road," Demo hissed.

Steele froze, the two men taking a knee in the overgrowth.

"Light 'em up," Steele hissed.

Demo snicked the selector to fire and cracked three shots at the targets Steele couldn't see.

There was a yelp of pain and then the machine gunner opened up, firing a long burst from the hip.

Steele wished they had long guns. The small sub guns, with their limited range and small caliber, were not the best weapon for an open field encounter.

Out in the road, the machine gunner was laying down a lot of lead, but his fire was inaccurate because he was shooting freehand.

Steele's first thought was to rush him. Take the men out before they got their position set.

Then the second machine gun opened up on their flank.

"Contact left," said Steele, ripping the pin from the mini frag and hurling it like a baseball at the first machine gun team.

Demo moved up, taking cover behind a tree, waiting for the frag to blow.

The machine gun chattered for a second, then the mini frag exploded.

Steele ran forward, closing the ten feet of distance with the SMG up at his shoulder. One of the men was out of the fight, and so was the gun, but the second was on his hands and knees. Steele clubbed him in the back of the head, knocking him out.

Demo yelled as the second machine gun fired a long burst from the trees to their left.

Steele yanked the man's boots off his feet and left him lying there. Barefoot and unconscious.

"Flanking right," Demo yelled, sprinting down the road.

He made it ten feet when he came under fire.

"Little help," Demo yelled.

Steele ran straight at the gun, the SMG pressed into his shoulder. He saw a figure, flipped the gun from safe to fire, and settled the reticle on the man's chest.

He fired two shots, and saw the man drop to the ground.

A second fighter took his place.

Steele transitioned and pulled the trigger. The gun bucked, but the shot was low and then the bolt locked back.

He was out of ammo.

Yanking the Browning from its holster, he dumped the empty submachine gun, not liking the fact that he was charging a machine gun with a pistol.

On the road he could hear Demo firing. Steele prayed his keeper's shots would keep the men's heads down.

Steele charged, pistol up, mouth wide as he screamed at the top of his lungs.

He fired, keeping count of the rounds in his head.

One, two, three, four . . .

Through a break in the trees he saw the gunner turn the belt-fed machine gun toward him. He kept running and firing, praying Demo had a shot.

Five, six . . . c'mon, Demo. Seven, eight . . .

At the last second, Steele dove to the left, his shoulder hitting the ground a moment before the gunner opened up. Shredding the area he had just vacated.

He rolled, feeling the bullets sweeping toward him, and then Steele heard a single shot from Demo's position and the firing stopped.

"All clear," Demo yelled.

Steele got to his feet and walked over to check out the body. Besides the tattoo on his finger there was nothing.

They headed back to where Steele had left the other men he'd shot. One of them was just coming to.

"Hey," Steele said in Russian as he placed the barrel against his neck. "I've got a question and you *better* have an answer."

Chapter 40

Vienna

Eric Steele stripped off his bloody clothes, dropping them in a pile next to the sink. The steam from the shower drifted over the mirror. The fog slowly obscured his tired eyes, sunken cheeks, and blood-plastered hair.

He stepped into the shower, pulling the door closed behind him, and ducked his head under the water.

The water rolled off his body, down his legs, staining the porcelain crimson on its way to the drain. Steele closed his eyes, a wave of exhaustion consuming him. But his mind wouldn't rest. It slipped back to Budapest and the man Steele had interrogated on the side of the road.

"What do you want to do with him?" Demo asked.

Steele shrugged. "You got another mag?" he asked. "I'm empty."

Demo passed him a fresh magazine and Steele walked over to the man on the side of the road and lowered himself into a crouch.

"You speak English?" Steele asked, dropping the empty mag from the Browning.

"I know nothing," the man replied.

"That's not what I asked," Steele said. "I want you to know that, usually, I'm a pretty patient guy."

The man watched him reload the pistol, his eyes wide in the moonlight.

"But I've had a pretty shitty week." Steele press checked the Browning, making sure there was a bullet in the chamber.

"Your boss, Zakayev, he came to my house. Shot the place up, wrecked my car, and put my mom in the hospital." Steele raised the pistol. "Do you understand what I'm telling you?"

"Y-yes," the man replied, sweat beading up on his forehead.

Steele glanced at his watch and then pressed the pistol into the center of the man's forehead.

"You have ten seconds to decide. Either you answer my questions . . ." Steele flicked off the safety, and the man flinched at the metallic *snick*. "Or you die on the side of the road."

The man told him everything he knew.

His name was Gavrie and he was an enforcer for a local Russian crew that called themselves the Brotherhood.

"We received a call from a man I'd worked with before."

Steele let him talk, knowing better than to interrupt.

"The man gave me an address to a warehouse, said the guns, money, and a phone were inside. All we had to do was wait for another call. That is all I know."

"What was the man's name?" Steele asked.

Gavrie paused, fear in his eyes.

"I . . ."

"His name?" Steele demanded, pushing the muzzle deeper into the man's skin.

"Gabriel," Gavrie said.

Steele wanted to kill the man. He deserved it. But Gavrie was unarmed, and Steele wasn't an executioner. So, he zip-tied him to a tree, took his phone and the van they'd left down the road.

Inside the shower Steele scrubbed until his skin was raw-pink like a medium rare steak. Finally, when he felt clean, he cut the water. The bathroom was humid and the air thick when he stepped out. He toweled off, wrapped the towel around his waist, and twisted the cap of the sweating bottle of beer.

Damn that tastes good.

He drained half the bottle in a long gulp and leaned against the counter. The marble felt cool through the towel. Steele was tired. Tired of death, tired of fighting, and most of all tired of men like Zakayev. He gave himself exactly thirty seconds to feel sorry for himself. He thought of Percy. He thought of the dead cop who'd been blown up with the LAW. And all the other innocents who had needlessly died because they were in the wrong place, at the wrong time.

The cost is always high. Too high.

Then he locked the painful memories away.

Steele finished the beer, tossed it in the trash, and opened the door.

Demo sat at the table hunched over the charred remains of the computer Red had somehow recovered from the way station. They had managed to link up in Tatabánya, a small town thirty miles west of Budapest.

"This hard drive is fried," Demo said.

"What about the phone we took off Gavrie?" Steele asked.

"I downloaded everything and sent it to Pitts."

"And?" Steele asked.

"And, that Gabriel cat is a real piece of shit. You remember our little meeting with Lansky?"

"Yeah," Steele said, pulling on a pair of dark jeans and a T-shirt, his mind going back to the bridge in Georgetown where Lansky had told him what they knew about the attack that put his mother in the hospital.

"Gabriel is Prince Badr's right-hand man. He is the one who found Sitta, came up with the plot to assassinate the crown prince at Mecca."

Steele pulled two bottles of beer from the minifridge and walked over to Demo.

"Here you go," he said, handing one of the bottles to his keeper.

"Gracias," Demo said.

"De nada."

Steele glanced down at the computer Red had retrieved, hardly believing that the melted black square of plastic had once been a computer. Demo had the guts of the Toughbook that Red had retrieved from the way station's ashes spread out on the table.

The screen was shattered and black where the LCD had leaked out of its cells. The keyboard reminded him of a dental experiment. The keys were twisted and stuck up at odd angles. Demo had everything in a neat little row so he could focus all of his attention on the hard drive.

The drive had gray heat marks across the casing, and the edges were melted. Steele couldn't believe that it had actually survived.

Demo connected the drive to his laptop by a red-and-white cord, and after a few keystrokes it made a pathetic humming sound.

"C'mon baby, give me something," he coaxed.

Steele walked to the window and felt the pieces starting to fall into place.

The first time Steele had heard about Prince Badr and his hatred for the West was after a Program operation was compromised in Yemen. It wasn't his op, but Steele had read the after-action report and knew the operation was supposed to be a simple smash and grab.

The target was a bomb maker with ties to Hezbollah who was targeting Saudi forces operating in Yemen. Using IEDs on their convoys.

The Saudis had tried and failed to find the guy and finally reached out to the United States for assistance.

The op was supposed to have been run by the CIA, but this was after Director Styles's fall from grace, and Rockford wanted all high-level missions passed through Cutlass Main. The target intel was on the money and the Alphas on the ground had cut into the terrorist's communications.

They had a lock on the target and were ready to hit

the house when Cutlass Main intercepted an incoming call. The voice instructing the terrorists that the Americans were on the way was encrypted. Cutlass Main never could get a voice ID.

But they were able to track the phone and found it was linked to Prince Badr.

Steele had wondered at the time why Badr would want to tip off a terrorist. Now he wondered if the target was Hassan Sitta.

"That operation in Yemen, the one where the target got the call," Steele said, turning back to Demo.

"What about it?" his keeper asked, without looking up from his work.

Demo was a wizard, able to do things with computers that he had neither the skill set nor inclination to understand. In many ways Demo was the brains of the operation. He kept things tidy and organized, freeing Steele to do what he did best: execute.

"I always wondered why Badr would tip the guy off. I mean, the Saudis hate the Iranians as much as Israel."

Before Demo could answer, the screen flashed to life.

"Okay, here we go," Demo said. "These files are everything Zakayev accessed at the way station. This file here is for some kind of remote link. The files were uploaded to . . ."

Demo opened the folder, which was followed by a message that said:

File path corrupted.

"Son of a bitch."

"The Saudis are Sunni. Why would they want to help an Iranian, a Shia bomb maker?"

Demo drained the beer, his Adam's apple bouncing as he poured it down his throat. "No clue. But what I do know is that when I retire, I'm going to open a microbrewery," he said, smacking his lips. "Going to call it Neck Oil."

"Neck Oil?"

"Yeah, the beer oils the neck, get it?"

"Not really."

"Just get me another beer and leave the thinking to me. If I need something smashed I will give you a call."

"Fair enough," Steele said, leaving the question in the air and returning to the fridge.

What was Zakayev after? What did he get from the way station?

He needed help and knew exactly the person to call.

"I'm calling Meg," Steele said, handing off the second beer and dialing the number.

The phone rang twice and then went straight to voicemail.

He hung up and was shoving the phone back into his pocket when Demo's computer dinged.

It was Meg on the secure chat network.

Can't talk right now. Kind of busy flying on A F 1.

"Did I read that right?" said Demo.

A F 1? Demo typed back.

Yeah that big blue 747 with the presidential seal on it.

"Well, look at her. Flying super first class."

Not sure how you pulled that off. But can you help us peons? Demo wrote.

LOL. What do u need?

Got a fried drive. Going to send you the raw data. See what you can find.

Send it ☺

"She never sends me a smiley face."

"What can I say, mano, women like me more than you."

ACT III

Chapter 41

Air Force One

Meg found the dining room in the middle section of Air Force One was not being used and stepped inside. She opened her laptop and waited a moment for the Wi-Fi to reconnect.

You there? she typed on the chat bar.

Yep.

Opening data packet now.

The antivirus program scanned the zip file, and after the green check mark popped up, she dragged the program onto her desktop. *Let's see what we have here,* she thought.

Meg used EnCase, a computer forensic tool that allowed her to retrieve the data and convert it into a digital map. Once the map was populated, she was able to re-create the digital timeline. The uploaded file immediately grabbed her attention.

The data painted a clear picture. Once the computer was connected to the drive a third party took control. Whoever that person was bounced the signal off a half a dozen servers in an attempt to hide his location. The breach itself was simple. The operator used the way station's antiquated system to get into Cutlass Main's server and download information.

Whoever was at the console knew exactly what they were looking for. Meg could tell because they spent less than two minutes inside the server. She determined their target was a file labeled Cold Storage. Inside the file, Meg found thousands of dated subfolders. She opened the most recent one and found herself looking at a long list of numbers.

"What in the world is this?"

Meg saw that there was a pattern to the numbers and at first thought it was some kind of code. Knowing that time was not on their side, she cut the first few lines and pasted them into the search bar.

A hit came back identifying the numbers as latitude and longitude coordinates.

Geotags, but of what? she wondered.

I've got a list of grids. What am I looking for? she typed.

A ship. Demo replied.

OK. Hold on.

Meg dragged the coordinates into the mapping software, the map centering on the Arctic Ocean. She dragged five complete files into the mapping software and waited for it to autopopulate.

The map that came up detailed the vessel's path for the last five years. The ship's path was orbital—one continuous loop. But what stuck out was that it never went close to land.

A ship that never goes into port. How does that work? she asked herself.

"Let's take a look," she said, accessing the Keyhole icon on her laptop. She checked her watch and found the corresponding time on the files. According to the coordinates from the mapping software the vessel had not changed course in five years.

She typed the grid into the computer and hit enter.

No feed.

"Of course," Meg said. "There aren't any satellites in the area the one time I need them." She opened Keyhole's orbital and found the first satellite that would intersect with the spot. There was a civilian satellite that would pass over in fifteen minutes.

She typed out a quick message to Demo telling him what she had found.

We need a location and fast, Demo typed back.

Well, unless you have a satellite in your back pocket, you two are going to have to wait, she thought.

Working on it, Meg typed back.

While she waited for the satellite to align, Meg opened a new folder on her laptop and copied the route for the past year into the new file. It was busy work, but it never hurt to have a backup just in case.

Do you know how to use screen share? she typed. You have to be on the Cutlass Interweb, but that shouldn't be a problem.

Yep, wait a second.

Screen share allowed Demo and Steele to see what was on her screen. In essence they would all be able to see the target at the same time. It was easier.

Allow User Demo 993? the prompt asked. She clicked the yes button.

The satellite feed they were waiting for was from World View-3, a commercial Earth observation satellite owned by a company named DigitalGlobe.

Meg had just saved the data to her computer when the feed finally came up. Instead of the dark gray of the ocean she had expected to see, the screen was all white.

Is there something wrong with the lens? she wondered.

And then she saw it.

Chapter 42

Vienna

"There she is. Cold Storage," Steele said.

Staring down at the massive ship made him feel like the discoverer of a lost world. Like Indiana Jones finding the Holy Grail.

"I've never seen anything like it," Demo said, awed by the sheer size of the ship.

It was massive, so big in fact that Steele wasn't sure how it stayed afloat.

They were looking at it from an angle, the satellite's lens giving them a clear view of the sheet of ice covering the thick plated hull.

Snow was carpeted across the deck, and icicles hung

like claws from the metal guide wires that stretched from the three-story superstructure.

"The ship hid it in plain sight," Steele said. "Very smart."

"What do you mean?" Demo asked.

"The Russians call this the Northern Sea Route. It is an important shipping lane not only for them but also for the Canadians and the U.S. No one would ever notice one more icebreaker."

The gray-and-white paint scheme blended in perfectly with the ice. That combined with it moving so slowly had made it almost impossible to see, but there it was.

"That's where he is going," Steele said, tapping the screen. "Cold Storage."

"Hey man, don't touch the—" Demo said, but before the words were out of his mouth the feed disappeared and the monitor went black.

C:\Users\SystemDP894>Admin
Admin-Termination Flash 7/19/2018 21:30:18
c:\Cutlass.Remote Shutdown
Access Is Denied

"Oh shit," Demo said, grabbing the blue Internet cable plugged into the computer and ripping it out.

"Hey, what the hell?"

"We have to go, NOW," Demo ordered.

Steele and Demo had been working together long enough that they knew when to jump and when to ask questions. Steele knew this was not the time to ask why. He shoved the weapons into the duffel, zipped it up, and conducted a quick scan of the room on his way to the door.

Steele had long ago disciplined himself to only take what he needed out of his bag and to put it back when he was done. He scooped up his pack, shouldered the duffel, and moved to the door.

Demo opened the microwave, slid the laptop inside, and closed the door. He cranked the dial to the right, and thirty seconds later they were in the garage. Demo jumped into the driver's seat, cranked the engine, and shifted into gear.

"You mind telling me what that was all about?" Steele asked when they were on the road.

"Those memos we get from time to time, have you ever bothered to read them?"

"Memos? Wait, you mean all that spam stuff they send every month?"

"That's not spam, Eric."

"I read the one about our insurance premiums going up," Steele replied honestly.

"Eric, they don't just send those out because they are bored. They send them out because they contain important information. Information like the Program instituting the Termination Protocol."

"Okay, I might have missed that one."

"Color me surprised," Demo grumbled.

"Give me a break, they literally send *hundreds* of those things a month."

"No excuse."

Steele went wide eyed and started feeling around in his pockets.

"What are you looking for?"

"My bullshit flag, Demo," Steele said, straight-faced. "Because I know for a *fact* that back when you were operational you didn't have time to sit around and read *every* memo Cutlass sent you."

"Valid point."

"So, how about you get off your high horse and fill me in." Steele smiled.

"Cutlass Main's cyber security starts with a primary firewall—"

"Okay, back it up," Steele interjected. "You lost me at firewall," Steele said.

"It is like talking to a child," Demo said.

"Why can't you just *use* English? I mean, it is a language we both understand," Steele suggested.

"There is this thing called an encrypted server—think of it as a giant thumb drive where Cutlass Main stores all of its data," Demo began.

"Huge thumb drive, got it."

"Think of it like the mailboxes in an apartment. Everyone who lives in the building has a key to the door. They all have access to the mailboxes. Each resident has a specific key that opens their mailbox, tracking?" Demo asked.

"Yep." Steele nodded.

"Now that setup is just like Cutlass Main's server. We all have access, but you need the proper clearance to open certain boxes."

"I'm with ya."

"In our little apartment building analogy, the first level of security is the outside door. Then the individual key. Well, Cutlass Main added an additional layer after the data hack on the NSA."

"Keep going, I'm still with you," Steele said.

"Yep," Demo said. "The termination flash adds a third layer of security to highly classified boxes. It tracks the keywords someone might use when looking for a certain file. Say someone hacked in and was looking for a nuke. They manage to get all the way to the part where they type *nuke* into the search engine and hit the enter key. If what they typed is a 'flagged word' and they *do not* have the security clearance, the system starts an automatic lockdown protocol."

"And what does that lockdown entail?" Steele asked.

"Well, everything," Demo answered.

"Like *everything,* everything?" Steele demanded.

"Tactical frequencies, service and support channels, mission codes, all have to be reset," Demo said, counting them off on his fingers, the other hand still on the wheel. "Not to mention all the nonofficial covers, code words, all while trying to locate the source of the breach. That is a lot of data."

"How long does it take for Cutlass Main to come back online?"

"Man, I don't know," Demo said, throwing his arms in the air.

"Take a guess," Steele demanded.

"If I had to guess, eight to ten hours."

"You have to be shitting me."

"We don't have half that much time."

Chapter 43

Arctic Ocean

Inside the cramped confines of the four-engine Antonov AN-12, the ramp snapped open, flooding
the cargo hold with the Arctic air. Zakayev was wearing a dry suit rated for ten below zero, but it wasn't
enough. He was freezing.

After the machine gun ambush he earlier set up outside of Budapest, he had told Cyril to drive southwest.

"Where are we going?" the Russian asked.

"A town called Kaposvár, there will be a car waiting
for us," Zakayev replied.

An hour later they slowed near a gravel drive. Cyril
made the turn, the Audi bouncing off the street, its tires

crunching over the rocks. They followed the drive over a small stream and down a hill where a small farmhouse sat next to a metal barn.

"I'll get the door," Zakayev said.

He hopped out of the Audi and swung the bay door open. The Audi pulled inside and Zakayev followed, pulling the door closed behind him.

Cyril cut the lights and turned off the engine, darkness settling over the interior of the barn. Zakayev ran his hands over the wall until he found the light switch.

The lights came on and he blinked against the glare. When he could see he saw Cyril scanning the interior.

"Where is the car?" the Russian asked.

The barn was empty except for a few hay bales and the bridles hanging next to the horse stalls.

"It's over here," Zakayev said, pulling the OTs from the back of his pants.

Cyril turned, his eyes widening when he saw the muzzle pointed at his face.

"What are you doing?" the Russian asked.

"Nothing personal, but you work for Gabriel so . . . ," Zakayev said with a shrug.

"So, what?"

"So, this is as far as you go."

The OTs coughed. The bullet hitting Cyril in the

center of the forehead. Snapping his head back. Dropping him where he stood.

Zakayev holstered the pistol and walked to the door on the far side of the barn. He stepped outside and called Gabriel's number.

"I'm at the rendezvous, send the helicopter," he said.

"How many passengers?" Gabriel asked.

"Just me. The rest didn't make it."

The helicopter flew him to a small airfield outside of Nitra, Slovakia, where a twin-engine Piper Aerostar was waiting to ferry him to a military training camp outside of Murmansk. On the ground the team leader of the seven-man assault element was waiting.

Inside the Antonov, now flying over the Arctic Ocean, Zakayev watched the men checking the motor and waterproof bag strapped inside an inflatable Zodiac assault boat. While they worked, the team leader waddled over to Zakayev, the swim fins strapped to his feet *slap slapping* on the metal floor.

Zakayev hadn't jumped out of a plane in ten years and as he pulled his helmet over his head and fumbled with the buckle, he tried to remember the class he'd received at the FSB's training facility.

"Jumping is the easy part," the FSB instructor had said. "It is what follows that will kill you."

The cadre thought it was hilarious. Zakayev had not.

"Once you are out, you must keep a stable body position, or you will start to spin." If you find yourself in a spin, "fuck the sky," the instructor had told the recruits.

Zakayev had come to learn "fucking the sky" was the instructor's answer to everything. After his first jump, he learned that the man meant for them to arch their backs and bring their arms in tight.

"If you can't control the spin, pull this," the instructor had told them, pointing to the rip cord.

Fifty seconds. That is all the time you have.

Zakayev had seen what happened to men who waited past that. They had passed out—a death sentence when it happened at twenty thousand feet above Earth.

We will be fine, the voice said as Zakayev finished buckling his helmet.

"Five minutes," the team leader said, *slapping* from the front of the plane.

The team had been waiting for Zakayev in Murmansk, a once proud port city located sixty-seven miles from the Norwegian border. Any hesitation he felt about being back in Russia was tempered by his knowing that following the events in Budapest, it was probably the safest place he could go. He had no doubt that Interpol and the Americans were looking for him.

Zakayev watched one of the men take the drogue parachute from the Zodiac, careful that it didn't catch air, while the rest of the team unhooked the mooring lines from the boat. The men started shuffling toward the door, the team leader falling in behind Zakayev to make sure he went out with the rest of them.

Zakayev stopped at the foot of the ramp and looked down. They were too high for his eyes to make out any detail through the gray cloud bank that hung over the drop zone. He couldn't see the target, which meant he was forced to trust the man with the GPS.

"Go," the team leader yelled.

The man holding the drogue chute threw it from the cargo hold. The slipstream caught it and inflated the chute to the size of a beach ball—big enough to yank the Zodiac out of the plane. The men fell in after it, and Zakayev felt a sudden shove from behind.

He was falling before he had time to get angry about being pushed out of the plane.

The wind grabbed his body, and just like the FSB instructor had warned, Zakayev started to spin. His first reaction was the same as it had been the first time he had been thrown into the water. He tried to fight it.

Zakayev caught a brief glance of the AN 12 banking back toward Murmansk and then he started spinning faster and faster. His world became a blur of gray clouds and blue sky and then he remembered his instructions and threw his arms out and arched his back.

He was in the clouds now, and at 120 miles per hour water hit his exposed skin like rocks on the highway. The moisture started to collect on his goggles, and there was no way for him to tell if he was spinning or not.

Zakayev was about to pull his rip cord when he broke through the cloud bank and saw the team floating gracefully below him. One of the men flipped over onto his back and waved at him to "come on." Zakayev dutifully tucked his head to his chest and brought this feet and knees together and raced to their position.

It was hard for him to judge distance or speed, but when he got close enough to make out the details on the Zodiac, Zakayev threw his arms and legs out again to slow his descent. The wind tore at his clothes, pulling at his fins. The lactic acid started to build in his ankles and calves, but he ignored it, keeping his eyes on the altimeter unwinding on his wrist.

When the chute attached to the Zodiac popped, Zakayev reached for his rip cord. He yanked the metal handle and felt the canopy grab air and jerk him to a sudden stop. The screaming wind in his ears vanished and Zakayev gracefully descended into the middle of the Arctic Ocean and crashed through the water.

He tugged on the riser straps, releasing the canopy,

and kicked to get out of the way. By the time he got himself sorted out the team had the Zodiac untangled and the motor attached. They cranked the engine and steered over, one of the men scooping him out of the water.

Hassan, I am coming, Zakayev thought.

Chapter 44

Ny-Ålesund, Norway

Ny-Ålesund was the northernmost populated town on the Svalbard Islands. A harsh, windswept land strategically located midway between Norway and the North Pole. The town had a population of twenty, and one glance out the window of the single-engine bush they had chartered in Alta, Norway, told him why.

"I hate the cold," Steele muttered, zipping the Gore-Tex jacket up to his neck.

They had taken the train from Vienna to Oslo, where they were forced to stop at a way station to top off their waning funds and grab the equipment they would need.

Demo had signed out twenty thousand euros from the vault, leaving a paper hand receipt, since the computer system was still down.

They packed their gear into a pair of duffel bags and charted a series of planes north. By the time they found a pilot willing to take them to Ny-Ålesund, they had exhausted their funds.

And they still weren't near Cold Storage.

"This thing is a piece of shit," Demo proclaimed, looking up from the bilge pump.

"Will it work?" Steele asked.

The men were standing on the deck of a KingFisher, a twenty-eight-foot aluminum-hulled "coastal" that had more rust than paint.

Steele had met the man in the town's only bar and knew the boat wasn't going to come cheap.

"How much?" he had asked the captain, a salty bearded man in a faded blue cap.

The man looked at his son, who translated Steele's question.

"Eighty thousand kroner," the boy responded with a straight face.

"Great . . . boat," the man said in halting English.

Steele did the math in his head, but Demo was quicker.

"Do *not* give that man nine grand for this thing."

"You have a better option?" Steele asked.

"We could take it, write him an IOU or something."

"No, dude, we aren't stealing this guy's boat." He turned to the boy. "I don't have that much money, but this . . ." He unhooked his watch and handed it to the old man. "Tell him I will trade him for the boat, gas, and some food."

The old man instantly became a watch expert. He flipped it over, checking the inscription on the back. "Rolex," he said to the boy in much improved English. "See how the hand sweeps instead of ticks, that is how you know it is real."

"This motherfu—" Demo snapped.

"I've got this," Steele interjected.

The old man grinned, displaying a set of teeth too nice to belong on an island in the middle of the Arctic.

"We have a deal."

"That old dude hosed us," Demo said, stepping inside the cabin.

Steele glanced over his shoulder, and at the sight of his handler, a broad grin spread across his face. Demo was wearing a canary-yellow slicker, the front covered in oil.

"Did you fix it?"

"Yeah," he grunted, pulling his arm free of the slicker before tossing it to the ground.

"The old man left us some brandy," Steele said, nodding to the bottle on the ragged couch, and then turned his attention back to the control panel. The twin Mercury 300s growled as he advanced the throttle. The KingFisher surged forward with Steele behind the wheel alternating views out the windscreen and back at the RPM and oil gauges.

He glanced at the map laid out on the table and then at the compass. He made a small adjustment to the helm, bringing the KingFisher back to the correct azimuth, and then checked the battered Casio that the old man had thrown in, along with food, brandy, and some foul weather gear that stunk of fish.

The work on the engines had thrown off his timetable and forced him to replot his course, but now that they were running, he hoped to make up some of the lost time. The problem was the course took them more to the north, and he could see the ice sparkling white in the distance.

Demo took a hit of the brandy and then started assembling the gear they had brought with them. He started unpacking their firepower and asked, "You remember that time in Khartoum when we had to use that drunk pilot for a supply drop?"

"How could I forget Robbie Atlas," Steele said, adjusting the wool turtleneck that was irritating his skin.

"You think he really was a porn star?"

"I can tell you what he *wasn't* and that was a good pilot."

"Man, when he dropped that supply bundle right in the middle of those rebels, I thought we were done for sure."

Steele silently agreed. The mission was supposed to be a quick in-and-out, but when they stumbled across the command and control camp for the terrorist faction operating in the area, Cutlass Main told them to stay. The problem was that the rebels had a working T-72 tank, and the heaviest thing he and Demo had with them was an M79 grenade launcher.

He had requested a supply drop, but instead of one of the usual contractors, someone had picked Robbie Atlas, a former bush pilot who, as fate would have it, was in the middle of a weeklong bender and drunk as hell.

The rebels received the supply bundle as a gift from the gods and promptly set about celebrating with a gallon of palm wine. That night Steele and Demo had to sneak into their camp and steal back some of the gear, so they could neutralize the T-72 for the next day's operation.

"Is this your way of saying we are going in light?" Steele asked.

"You saw the size of that boat," Demo said.

Steele nodded and looked down at the gear they'd taken from the way station.

The Oslo station was tiny compared to the ones in the Middle East, and the armory had reflected the fact that there wasn't much action that far north.

"No C-4, can you believe that shit?" Demo had asked at the way station, stuffing a claymore into his pack.

"They've got teargas," Steele had said, holding up a can.

"Bring it." Demo had nodded.

They had grabbed a pair of suppressed UMP submachine guns, two sets of night vision, eight frags, two Browning Hi Powers, and three thousand rounds of .45.

Back on the boat Steele picked up the UMP. "We have gone in light before," he said.

"Not *this* light. I wouldn't rob a 7-Eleven with this junk."

"Don't forget this flare gun that Lars left us." Steele grinned.

Demo suddenly changed the subject.

"You checked in on your mom?" he asked.

"Got in a quick call from Oslo. The infection is gone, blood work is clear, but . . ." Steele went quiet.

"Your mom is a fighter. She is going to be fine. You'll see. All we have to do is save the world again first."

"Thanks, brother," Steele said.

He could see ice forming ahead. They were mostly smaller pieces, jagged shards that had calved off the icebergs. He backed off the throttle, knowing that despite their size, it wouldn't take much to rip the hull out of the boat.

Demo got to his feet and moved beside him.

"Not many people in the world ever get to see anything like this," he said.

Steele had to agree.

It was a landscape beyond compare. A frozen wasteland where the ice fields stretched from horizon to horizon, one massive plain of shimmering white. Farther to the east a lone iceberg towered skyward. Even from a distance it easily rivaled some of the largest buildings in Pittsburgh.

"We should be able to see it by now," Demo said, lifting a pair of binoculars to his face.

Steele hoped he was right. He knew that the ice he could see was only a fraction of what was below the water, and the last thing either of them wanted was to join the polar bear club right now.

"I think I've got it," Demo said, looking up from the GPS unit that was guiding them toward the coordinates Meg had sent before the computer link was cut. "Give me two degrees to port."

Steele nodded and turned the wheel, squinting at the sun despite his dark sunglasses. He cut the engines to neutral and waited.

"Yeah, half a mile," his handler said, handing over the binos.

Steele pressed them to his face and scanned the hull. The satellite hadn't done the ship justice. It was gigantic, its heavy bow and reinforced hulls three times the width of any ship he'd ever seen.

Despite the thick ice blocking its path, Cold Storage moved forward at a sluggish pace, its massive props leaving a churning whitecapped wake behind it.

Near the bow the Zodiac tied against the ship looked like a toy.

"He is already on board," Steele said, lowering the binoculars. "Last chance to call this off."

Demo was already getting his gear together.

"Sorry, mano, but nothing gets my blood flowing like a one-way trip."

Chapter 45

Meg found Lansky sitting by himself near the back of the plane. He was staring out the window, the pipe he carried but never smoked clutched between his teeth.

She had brought the pipe up to Steele one night over Chinese.

"I've never seen him smoke, but every time he wants to talk, he has that damn pipe out."

"Lansky is a shadow man," Steele told her.

"A what?" Meg had never heard the term before.

"Shadow men are the guys at the CIA who sit in dark rooms mulling over problems. They are cerebral, methodical men who look for all the angles."

"I think I am following you," Meg said, still not sure what this had to do with the pipe.

Eric flashed her a knowing smile.

If that smile had come from *anyone* else Meg would have taken it as condescending. But not Eric. When he smiled at her like that, Meg went warm and tingly inside because she knew he could see right through her.

"What happens when you flash a deer with your headlights?" Steele asked.

"It freezes," Meg answered.

"Yep." Steele nodded. "Because their eyes are optimized to work in low light."

"They can't see," Meg said, filling in the blanks.

"A shadow man is used to having time to work a problem from all angles. When you put them in the light they freeze, just like the deer."

Meg was close, but she still didn't understand what Lansky's pipe had to do with it.

"The pipe is Lansky's prop. Something that bought him time when he was put on the spot. He might have quit smoking, but he still needs the prop."

Meg quickly filled Lansky in on what she had learned from Demo and Steele. She told him about the coordinates and the ship she'd found.

"Can you override the termination flash?" she asked.

Lansky held the pipe in his right hand and ground the stem between his teeth.

"No," he said, his voice laden with frustration.

"Shit," Meg swore, slapping the side of the chair. "Zakayev breaches a way station, triggers the termination flash, and now when Eric and Demo need us the most, you are telling me that we can't do *anything*?"

"*We* can't, but Rockford can," Lansky said, getting to his feet.

Chapter 46

Cold Storage

Half a mile short of their objective, Zakayev pointed to a block of ice and told the man piloting the Zodiac to cut the engine. The silence that fell over the ocean was unnerving. While the team leader secured the boat to the surface of the ice with a hook attached to a nylon line, Zakayev lifted the spotting scope to his eye and scanned his surroundings.

Even at max magnification, he couldn't see an end to the vast bleakness that surrounded him. It appeared that he could travel endlessly in all directions and see nothing but gray water and the white-blue ice. Finally, he turned his attention north, where Cold Storage plowed determinedly through the ice field.

It was time to get ready.

Zakayev pulled his mask over his face and shoved the mouthpiece between his lips. He gave the team leader a thumbs-up and let himself fall backward into the ocean. The visibility was terrible, but he could see the ChemLight attached to the diver in front of him, and Zakayev tucked his arms against his body and started finning through the water.

Thirty minutes later his legs were burning when he saw the cloud of bubbles being kicked up by the huge screws. Zakayev surfaced and clamped the magnetic climbing handles to the hull and started his ascent. He didn't have a rope or any safety equipment to catch him if he fell. Just sheer determination. It was enough, and soon he was climbing over the rail.

He dumped his tanks and fins with the rest of the men, got his rifle into action, and moved toward the base of the bridge.

According to Gabriel, Cold Storage was largely an automated ship. Because of this the crews were small—typically six to eight men. They stayed on board for six months, never going to port or seeing anyone else. At the end of the tour a fresh crew rotated on.

The current crew had a few weeks left on their cruise.

A lucky break, Zakayev thought. *They will be lazy, thinking of all the prostitutes and booze they are going to get when they return to shore.*

Zakayev was the first to make contact. He saw a crewman ducking behind a ventilator hood, smoking a cigarette, and drew his dive knife. He slipped behind the unsuspecting crew member, placed a hand over his mouth, and buried his blade in the man's neck. He yanked the keycard from the chain around his neck and motioned for one of the assaulters to dump the body over the rail.

Zakayev swiped the card over the door lock and held it open for the rest of the assaulters. Once inside, the team leader paused to rip a diagram off the wall and glanced down at it while the first team cleared the floor and the second took the stairs.

According to the diagram, they were in the mechanical section, the floor above was wet and dry storage, followed by the sleeping quarters, galley, bathrooms, gym, and radio room.

The top floor was the bridge.

They took down the boat exactly the way they had rehearsed back at the camp in Murmansk. Breaking the boat down into two cells of three men each. Zakayev let the team leader handle the command and control and helped the first team clear the floor.

"Mechanical clear," he said over the radio, moving back to the stairs and up toward the third floor.

"Second is mostly storage. Almost finished clearing," the second team announced.

"Hold on the three," the team leader ordered.

"Good copy."

Zakayev passed the door to the second floor and glanced down the hall. The team leader and the rest of the team were halfway down the hall, moving fast but smoothly.

He continued up to the door on three and stopped.

"Holding on three," Zakayev said.

The second cell finished checking the storage and he could hear them moving up the stairs behind him. Zakayev was up front and nodded for the last man to move up and get the door.

"*Vypolnyat*." Execute.

The man opened the door and held it.

The corridor was barely wide enough for two men to stand side by side. The metal bulkheads and doors were painted off-gray; the nonslip laminated floor buffed, but not waxed, to a dull sheen.

Zakayev saw a man walking toward him, a towel

around his waist. He raised the AK-12 and fired. The bullet snapped the man's head back and he fell to the ground.

"One down," he said, dumping two of the assaulters into the first room. The next two in the stack moved up beside him and Zakayev carried them to the next room.

"Contact," another voice declared, as calm as if he were telling someone that he had to go to the restroom.

"Two down."

Zakayev was alone in the hall. He sucked up against the wall and waited for support before taking the next room. A hand squeezed his shoulder and he button hooked into the room.

The stainless steel tables and matching refrigerated lowboys told Zakayev that it was a galley.

To his right, Zakayev saw four men sitting at a table, three with their backs to him and one sitting across. One of the men was taking a sip from a glass of water, and when Zakayev centered his optic on the man's face he saw the shock in his eyes.

Before the crewman could raise the alarm, he fired. The bullet shattered the glass in his hand on its way into the man's brain. The second crewman turned toward the sound, an annoyed frown forming below his bushy mustache. Zakayev fired. Another headshot that spattered blood and brain across the man seated to his left.

"What the hell?"

The remaining crewmen tried to get to their feet, but Zakayev cut them down halfway.

The second assaulter joined the fight. He cut down a cook filling up the coffeepot, and a second holding a tray of bread.

Zakayev walked toward the kitchen, putting a bullet in the back of each man's head that he passed. He dropped his magazine, inserted a fresh one, and bent down to retrieve a roll.

"I love these things," he said, picking up a roll and taking a bite.

By the time he made it back to the hall the men were calling the floor clear.

"Moving to the bridge," the team leader said.

"We need the captain alive," Zakayev told him.

By the time he finished clearing the hall the team leader was back on the radio.

"Bridge is clear. We have the captain."

"On my way," Zakayev replied.

He took the stairs to the bridge and found the team leader standing over a middle-aged balding man.

"Bring the Zodiac," the team leader said over the radio.

"On my way," the remaining assaulter replied.

"He was hiding in his bunk," the team leader said. "Here is his access card."

"And the rest of the crewmen?" he asked.

"We have accounted for eight. The other two crewmen are standing guard down in the hold."

"Good."

Zakayev switched to English.

"What is your name?"

The captain glared at him.

"You are not a soldier, and this is not war. You are in international waters with a boat full of men your country kidnapped."

Still the man refused to speak.

Zakayev backhanded him across the face, splitting the man's lip. He walked over to the wall and lifted the fire axe from the mount. "Hold him down," he ordered.

Chapter 47

The ice sheet buckled under Cold Storage's nose, giving way with a shuddering groan like that of a dying animal. Sections of ice, some the size of small cars, banged off the steel reinforced hull and then floated away.

Behind the massive ship, Steele piloted the King-Fisher over the calm path of water Cold Storage had just cleared.

"Big son of a bitch," Demo remarked.

"*Big* doesn't even do it justice," Steele replied.

He adjusted his course, steering the smaller ship into the shadow cast by the towering superstructure. Steele knew the eclipse was a temporary break from the blinding sun. He had read somewhere that during the Arctic summer the sun never set and wondered what the first men who ventured in the lands had thought about that phenomenon.

Steele had gotten a vague sense of Cold Storage's proportions from the satellite images, but there was no comparison to seeing it in person. It was a massive ship designed with the singular purpose of transporting the most dangerous men in the world through the most spartan conditions on Earth.

Officially, Russia was the only country to have ever fielded or operated a nuclear-powered icebreaker, and Steele could see some similarities between Cold Storage and the photos he had seen online. The shipbuilders had used existing plans to lay it out, but that was where the comparison stopped.

He imagined it to be almost two football fields long and at least two hundred feet from the water to the top of the superstructure. Steele cut the engines, allowing the KingFisher's momentum to bring them closer to the ship.

"You ready to join the party?" Demo asked, taking the pneumatic gun out of the wheelhouse and pointing it toward the rail.

Steele went over his last-minute checks, donning the bump helmet and clipping his night vison to the mount. On the deck the pneumatic gun coughed, sending a line attached to a magnet grapnel skyward.

There was no turning back now.

Steele tugged the straps and made sure the helmet wouldn't slide around, checked the suppressed Hi Power on his hip, and closed his eyes. The fact that Cold Storage was full black, a term that meant there were no physical records on file, denied Steele and Demo their usual mission prep.

On most missions, he and Demo spent hours poring over the target packet, examining imagery, drone footage, and up-to-date intelligence.

They would know the layout of the structure and how many targets were on board. Unlike the movies, where the hero goes in blind, the Alphas knew that mission success often went to who was most prepared.

Steele, like the rest of the men and women in the Program, held to Benjamin Franklin's famous motto, "Failing to plan is planning to fail."

He forced all of that out of his mind and focused on the mission at hand. When he opened his eyes, Demo was waiting patiently at the doorway.

"You ready?"

Steele op slapped down on the Heckler & Koch UMP submachine gun charging handle, sending a .45 caliber hollow point into the pipe.

"Thumbs-up, let's do this," he said.

He slung the UMP and grabbed the rope, making

sure he had a good bite between his feet before starting his ascent. It was arm-burning work, even with the use of his legs. When he was almost to the rail, Steele locked the rope between his feet and unslung the submachine gun. He reached up, grabbed the rail, and muscled his way on board Cold Storage.

Steele was near the aft of the boat and took cover behind a metal manifold. He scanned the deck from close to far, senses on high alert. Other than the gentle saw of the icebreaker on the ocean, nothing moved.

Where the hell is the crew?

He heard Demo land softly behind him. His handler moved silently to his back and squeezed him on the elbow—the signal that he was ready to roll.

Both men had been in the army before joining the Program and were at a disadvantage when it came to boarding and taking a ship. This was definitely a job for a SEAL, the hardened warriors whose stock-in-trade was taking down vessels at sea.

On board the KingFisher they had talked through every scenario they could imagine. But it was all speculation. Alphas received training on ship clearing, but the scenarios weren't on a boat full of psychopathic terrorists.

Demo had suggested that they try the bridge first, which made sense to Steele. Best-case scenario they would locate a crew member or at least a diagram of the boat. Steele moved toward the metal stairs, sub gun up in case he had to take a shot.

Cold Storage continued plowing through the ice as they advanced. He assumed that they would have felt something, considering the thickness of the ice, but besides the sound and a slight vibration they could have been driving down the highway in an SUV.

Steele found blood near the doorway, a single drop, but it was large enough not to be from a cut.

"Blood," he told Demo.

Steele had assumed that the crew was highly trained but knew that no amount of training or number of readiness drills could stave off the sheer boredom that had to come with the job.

Demo shifted to point, and they moved up the stairs. They found nothing but empty rooms on the first two floors.

There is no way these guys got in here without some kind of fight.

"Shit," Demo said as soon as they stepped onto floor number three.

Steele saw a man with a towel around his waist sprawled out in the hall, crimson blood pooling on the off-white floor. He had sensed that whoever had come before them were pros, but it wasn't until they made it to the galley that he saw just how good they were. He counted six dead and Steele could tell by the neat piles of brass on either side of the door that there had been only two shooters.

"Left side did all the shooting," Demo said, checking the bodies. "All headshots."

"These guys have skills, no doubt about it," Steele said.

"Mercs?"

"Too smooth for that. They took down three floors without a scratch."

"Hell, even the dead checks are accurate. These guys are definitely pros," Demo said, reaching down and picking up one of the shell casings. He looked at the head stamp. "Russian, 5.45 by 39, same shells I found at your house," Demo said.

The Russian Federation had been modernizing their aging arsenal for the past ten years—moving away from the 7.62 for smaller and lighter rounds.

It wasn't a new argument—heavier bullets meant more weight. Lighter bullets meant you could carry more ammo. But as far as he knew there was only one unit who had the AK-12.

"Only one way to find out," Steele said.

They cleared the hall and were halfway up the stairwell when Steele held up his hand, fist closed. Hold.

Someone was screaming.

Steele unrolled a fiber optic camera from his kit, waited for it to synch with the monitor on his wrist, and then shoved it under the door to the bridge. He twisted the black cable in his hand, eyes on the screen, until he found the source of the bloodcurdling screams.

One of the crewmen was sitting in a chair, two Tangos dressed in black thermal suits looming over him. He saw a flash of gauze and then one of the men pressed an auto injector against his leg and dosed him with something Steele couldn't see.

A moment later the screaming stopped.

The Tango stepped out of the way, and when Steele finally got a clear view of the crewman, he felt bile rise up in the back of his throat.

Jesus.

The man's hand was gone, and below the tourniquet the freshly applied gauze was already stained red.

"What in the *holy fuck* did they do to that guy?" Demo whispered.

Steele had an idea, and if he was right it meant Zakayev was already in the hold. He had two options. They could go head-to-head with the assaulters, but the odds of making it through a gunfight at this close range and not taking a bullet were low.

The other option meant potentially sacrificing an innocent man.

Steele knew what he had to do, and cursed Zakayev and the men for forcing him to make the decision. He slipped the fragmentation grenade from his pouch and showed it to Demo.

His handler gave a gentle shrug, one that confessed he didn't see any other option.

Steele pulled the pin, shook his head, and released the spoon. He counted slowly in his head. *One, two . . .*

On three Steele leaned around the corner and threw the grenade.

Chapter 48

Ben Gurion Airport—Tel Aviv

Meg was waiting in the hall outside Rockford's office on Air Force One when Lansky stepped out. She could tell from the look on his face that things hadn't gone well.

"He's not budging," Lansky said after he shut the door behind him.

"Let *me* talk to him," she'd said, trying to push past Lansky and enter Rockford's sanctum."

"Doesn't work that way," Lansky said, grabbing her by the shoulder. "And you know that."

She glared at the door, her face hot with anger.

"The hell with this," Meg said, wrenching free of his grasp, and stomped off.

Meg ended up in the galley. She went to the refrigerator, pulled open the door, and grabbed a bottle of water.

That pigheaded son of a bitch, she thought, slamming the door harder than she wanted and knocking a bowl of fruit to the ground.

Dammit.

"I know the feeling," a voice said.

Meg startled. She had thought that she was alone, but when she turned around Lisa Rockford was sitting at a table nursing a club soda.

"Oh, I am so sorry," Meg said, her face flushing.

The First Lady smiled and motioned her over.

"Only person who evokes that kind of reaction is my husband. What is he up to now?" she asked, her right hand sliding over her belly.

She's protecting her baby.

Lisa's eyes locked onto hers, two pale blue searchlights. The question in the First Lady's eyes was painfully easy to read. *Is my child in danger?*

Meg forced herself to keep Lisa's gaze when all she wanted was to jump to her feet and scream, "YES your child is in danger—YOU are in danger."

But she *couldn't.*

The only thing she *could* do was offer a hint of a nod.

"I'm sure you will take care of it," Lisa said.

And just like that the spell was broken.

"I hope you feel better," Meg offered weakly.

Before Lisa could answer, one of the stewards stuck his head in the galley and told her that they were ten minutes from landing.

The First Lady got to her feet and they walked out into the hall. Meg thought she was going to say something else when she covered her mouth and started speed walking toward the lavatory.

Meg returned to her seat, feeling like a failure.

It's not my place. Not my job to tell Rockford that his wife is pregnant.

The plane landed ten minutes later and Meg followed the staff and reporters down the rear stairs and stepped onto the tarmac.

Inside the hangar, Ted Lansky was talking to Prime Minister David Bitton.

Bitton was short and handsome with thick black hair and olive skin. Before going into politics, he had been a commander of the 35th Brigade, the famous Israeli paratrooper division. He was reported to run his cabinet the same way he'd run his brigade, with military precision. So it was no surprise that the "Lion of

Judah" was not pleased with having to wait for Rockford and his wife to deplane.

She could tell Lansky was apologizing, by his obsequious gestures, and that Bitton wasn't buying it by the fire in his eyes.

When Lansky turned and started walking toward Meg, the prime minister turned angrily to his aide and pointed at his watch.

"Are you trying to piss off everyone today?" she asked.

"Bitton certainly thinks so. Claims Rockford is making him wait on purpose. Called it a 'power play.'"

The sound of cameras clicking announced that the president and First Lady were ready, and while Lansky turned toward Air Force One, Meg kept her eye on Bitton. The moment the cameras came out he was all smiles and understanding. He walked to the bottom of the stairs, and when Rockford stepped onto the tarmac Bitton smiled broadly and offered the president a warm embrace.

"You would think they were brothers," she whispered to Lansky.

"Bitton is a masterly politician. Did you know that it cost the American taxpayers ten brand-new F-22 Raptors just to get him to agree to this meeting?"

"Are you serious?"

"As a heart attack," Lansky said.

After a few moments for the cameras, the president and Bitton got into the presidential state car. On the outside "the Beast" appeared to be a bulky Cadillac STS, but it had more in common with an MRAP than a luxury vehicle. The Beast was impenetrable. Capable of withstanding bullets, RPGs, and even nerve gas, but because of the armor it had to be transported by a military C-5.

Meg followed Lansky to a second vehicle, and when she ducked inside the first person she saw was Lisa Rockford.

"Good afternoon, ma'am," she said.

Lisa looked pale and uncomfortable, her eyes wary.

"Have you two ever met?" Lansky asked.

"No, my name is Meg Harden," she said, extending her hand.

The First Lady's eyes softened, and she offered a grateful smile.

"Please, call me Lisa."

"Yes, ma'am," Meg replied.

The ride from Ben Gurion to Jerusalem was thirty-one miles, and the drive gave Meg an opportunity to rethink what she had said in the hangar. Like most Americans, every time Meg arrived in a new country, she found it hard not to compare it to the United States. The first thing that struck her was the size.

At 8,019 square miles, Israel was larger than New Jersey, but not by much. The walls, checkpoints, and fortifications that lined the road from Tel Aviv to Jerusalem made it impossible to forget that it was a country surrounded by enemies on all sides.

Military and police vehicles lined the road and cleared the streets for the presidential procession. Meg knew that the airport had been closed until the president had deplaned and the motorcade left the area. The same was true of the sky above the route. The only aircraft allowed to fly were the warplanes circling well out of sight and the attack helicopters flying directly above.

Meg knew that security was on alert because of Rockford's visit but wondered how much different it looked on a normal day.

The situation on the ground gave her a chance to see things from Bitton's perspective, helped her understand why Israel had been pissed when the former administration had signed the nuclear deal with Iran. The bomb that Nate West had stolen from Iran could have easily wiped out more than half of the country, and the fallout would have left the rest uninhabitable.

Meg brushed the thought from her mind and forced herself to think about something else. But no matter how hard she tried, Meg couldn't shake the sense of impending doom, which grew stronger the closer they got to their destination.

Chapter 49

Cold Storage

The frag hit the deck with a *tink* and one of the assaulters yelled, "Contact." But before they could respond the grenade exploded.

Steele raced up the final stairs and onto the bridge, which was enveloped by the acrid haze of Comp B. He dug the right corner, eyes and muzzle searching the smoked-out room for any sign of movement.

The scorch in the center of the room marked where the frag had detonated. It was a perfect throw, right in the middle of the assaulters. The grenade had exploded up and out, and what shrapnel hadn't hit the men in the chest left the glass lining the bridge spiderwebbed and spotted with blood.

Miraculously the assaulter directly in front of the crewman had shielded the man from the blast. He was dazed, but otherwise uninjured. One of the assaulters grunted and tried to roll to his knees; Steele shot him in the back of the head and rushed to help the crewman.

"Friendlies," Steele yelled.

The man wavered on his feet, the blood coming out of his ears telling Steele that the overpressure had ruptured his eardrums. He couldn't hear him.

Steele grabbed him by the shoulders and spoke slowly, hoping the man could read his lips. "We are Americans," he said. "Here to rescue you."

"You have to stop him," the man said weakly, blood dripping from the stump where his hand had been. "He took my keycard and . . ." He looked down at his arm. "You have to stop him."

"Go, I've got this," Demo said.

Steele moved to the door and saw the card reader. "I need a card."

"Look behind you," the man said.

Steele turned and found three crewmen stuffed in the space between the bulkhead and a metal support beam. *Jesus.* There was no time to pay his respects.

He jerked one of the cards off a dead man's shirt and slapped it over the reader.

Steele hustled down the stairs and found the man's missing hand lying on the floor next to the palm reader. The door in front of him had a sign that read:

WARNING
RESTRICTED AREA
UNAUTHORIZED ENTRY IS
PROHIBITED. NO PHOTOGRAPHY.
USE OF DEADLY FORCE AUTHORIZED.

Steele knelt down to pick up the severed hand when the door was suddenly opened from the inside and one of the assaulters stepped through.

Down in the hold, the magnetic lock clicked open and Zakayev started the stopwatch on his wrist. There was no mention of the lockdown or the self-destruct sequence in the files taken from the way station. In fact, the only reason Zakayev knew that he had exactly eighteen minutes to grab Sitta and get off the boat was because the captain had told him.

Plenty of time.

He pulled the OTs-38 from its holster and stepped inside. There was a man sitting in front of him, reading a magazine. All Zakayev could see was the back of a blond head and the tips of his boots propped up on a desk.

"Hey, Tommy, you were supposed to relieve me five minutes ago," the man said, flipping the pages in the magazine he was reading.

"Yeah, take your sweet-ass time," a second voice off to his left said.

Zakayev inclined to the right, trying to get a look at the second guard before he killed the first. He caught a glimpse of the blue coveralls and the edge of a clipboard. It was enough.

He shot the first man in the side of the head, the OTs sounding like a book closing in a library. The second guard looked up, trying to identify the source of the sound, and Zakayev shot him in the chest.

Compared to Black Dolphin the cellblock was a four-star hotel. The doors were brushed metal and soundproof, each one with a plexiglass window cut into the door. The cells themselves were ten by ten with a bed mounted to the wall, a stainless steel toilet and sink, and a clear plastic table. The inmates were clothed in orange jumpsuits, their hair shorn to their scalp and beards neatly trimmed. There was a video camera outside each cell monitoring the occupants, but Zakayev knew there was no one watching on the other end.

He ignored the men beating on the windows, their mouths moving wordlessly behind the soundproofing. He stopped at cell 22 and looked inside. Hassan Sitta was sitting on the bed, staring straight ahead.

Zakayev pulled his balaclava down, revealing his face. Then Sitta broke into a wide grin.

"Time to get you out."

Chapter 50

Cold Storage

Steele was out of position and knew it. He was standing at the door, ready to step into the hold, when the man appeared in front of him.

"Uh, hey, have you seen a guy with a lot of tattoos?"

He tried to rotate the UMP up and on target, but his attacker had already launched a kick at his head.

Steele managed to block most of the blow with the muzzle, but the force sent the SMG flying backward and knocked Steele on his ass. Instead of rolling over, he brought his knees back to his elbows, planted his hands next to his head, and then when he was fully coiled, Steele kicked straight up.

One minute he was lying flat on his back and in the next instant he was back on his feet.

The man froze at the maneuver and Steele shook his head up and down.

"That's right, Ivan, you just picked a fight with a ninja."

The Russian delivered a thrust kick to Steele's chest that wiped the smile off his face. Steele had a basic understanding of Systema, the martial art designed by Russian spec ops, and knew that it was a style that relied on kicks to keep the opponent at bay.

His best defense was to get inside the man's guard and end the fight as soon as possible. Since the man was both taller and heavier than him, Steele knew this was easier said than done.

The Russian launched another kick, but Steele was ready. He ducked his head to his chest and brought both arms up to his right side, absorbing most of the blow on his bicep. Steele tried to hook the leg and caught a knee to the chest for his trouble. It knocked the breath from his lungs, but Steele managed to stay in close. He worked the body like a boxer, a hook to the kidney followed by a compact jab to the solar plexus.

"Huumph," the man grunted, the air shooting from his lungs.

The assaulter launched a weak jab and Steele easily

batted it away, firing a right cross that caught the man in the chin.

"C'mon, Ivan, haven't you seen *Rocky IV*?" Steele taunted, hitting him with another cross.

The man tried to push him away, but he was sucking wind. He launched another jab, this one slower, and Steele grabbed his wrist, right arm locked onto his lapel, and jerked him onto his hip. It was a textbook hip toss, but instead of letting him go, Steele used the grip on his collar to drive the man's head into the concrete floor.

The impact was hollow and wet.

Steele kept a firm grip on the man's arms and placed his foot at the base of the spine. He pulled up on the arm as hard as he could and delivered a short stomp to the back of the Russian's neck.

The vertebrae broke with a dry *pop.*

Steele retrieved the UMP and stepped through the door. The cellblock was spotless, with brushed metal doors that had a plexiglass viewing screen in the center. Five paces from the door he found the first guard. He was sprawled forward, the contents of his skull spattered over the desk. To his immediate left a second crew member lay motionless in a crimson pool. His sidearm was missing, and the hook where Steele imagined the keys should have been was empty.

"*Privet-hey,*" a man yelled in Russian.

Steele fired a shot in the direction of Zakayev's voice.

Instead of returning fire the assaulter tried to warn the rest of the team, allowing Steele to line up the second shot and cut him down. A burst of rifle fire chattered from the observation deck that ran above the cells. Steele hadn't seen it, and the only thing that kept him from being hit was the metal post to his right.

Steele dove behind the desk, making himself as small as possible, while the gunman blew chunks out of the wood.

"Still alive I see," the voice Steele had been hearing in his dreams yelled.

"Missed you too, dipshit," Steele said, flipping the UMP to full auto.

"But not for long, my little *tarakan*." Cockroach.

"Uh-huh," Steele said, lifting the SMG over the table and holding the trigger down with his thumb. He hammered through the magazine, spraying the area more to gain time than anything else.

The H&K went dry and Steele pulled it down and dropped the magazine. He shoved a fresh one into the submachine gun, ignoring Zakayev's wheezing laugh, and then he heard a door slam shut.

Steele cautiously peeked out from behind the table. He was alone. *Must be a second door.*

He got to his feet and scanned the cellblock. The cell

doors were painted red, the walls an institutional gray. In the center was a twenty-foot open area with yellow footprints painted on the ground. Steele assumed this was where the prisoners were let out to walk around.

Above the cells was a metal catwalk for the guards and then bare metal beams overhead.

Steele trotted to the center of the cellblock, ignoring the men beating on the plexiglass windows.

"Demo, he's loose, there must be a second door," Steele said into the radio. When he let go of the button the receiver issued one long beep that told him the radio didn't have a signal.

His traffic hadn't gone through.

The door was recessed in the wall at the far end of the cellblock. Steele reached into the pocket where he had placed the security card. His fingers came out the bottom and Steele realized that the pocket must have gotten ripped in the fight. He looked back the way he had come and saw the card lying in the middle of the floor.

"Of course," he muttered.

Steele trotted back to retrieve the card when a red light that he had missed earlier flashed to life followed by a long buzz. He wasn't sure what the light signified, but Steele decided it best not to stick around and find out.

He picked the card up off the ground and was on his

way back to the door Zakayev had used when the buzz-
ing stopped. A short silence followed and then Steele
heard the unmistakable series of clicks that stopped
him dead in his tracks.

It was the sound of magnetic locks disengaging.

This is not good.

The first prisoner came out of his cell like a bull
after the matador. Steele fired without breaking stride
and then one after the other the doors flew open and
the prisoners converged on him. From then on it was
a simple battle drill: shoot and move, shoot and move.
He fired three quick headshots and then realized that
making a stand was not the best idea. There were too
many prisoners to kill. Mobility was the only way he
was going to make it out.

Steele's only chance was to make a hole in the human
wave.

He flipped the selector to auto, lowered the muzzle, and hosed their legs with .45. The UMP chewed
through the thirty-round magazine in a matter of seconds, and Steele dropped the magazine and hurdled
over the fallen prisoners.

He almost made it.

A hand grabbed his foot, tripping him in midair.
Steele sprawled forward, the card flying out of his hand
and skittering across the floor. He ducked his head

to his chest and when he hit rolled over his shoulder. Steele got to his feet, eyes scanning the floor for the keycard. He caught a glimpse of it and then a sandaled foot sent it spinning across the floor. Someone grabbed him from behind, fingers clawing for his neck. Another pair of hands grabbed the submachine gun by the stock and tried to yank it free.

Voices in Pashtu, Arabic, Farsi, as well as some he couldn't translate howled for his blood. Steele tucked his head, so they couldn't choke him. He was looking at the floor now and saw a pair of rubber sandals appear between his legs. Steele stomped down on the foot as hard as he could, felt the grip on his neck falter.

He ducked free of the sling, slammed the magazine across the face of a bearded terrorist. They were forcing him to the ground, grabbing his hair, hooking his eyes. Teeth locked down on his shoulder and Steele yelled, throwing a blind elbow into the man's face.

A fierce-looking giant shoved his way into the mix. He had cut the sleeves off his jumpsuit to reveal the patchwork of slashes on both arms and had a puckered mass of scar tissue that marked the spot where his left eye should have been.

"He's mine," the man yelled in broken French.

"Lucky me," Steele quipped.

Steele tried the radio again. "Demo, if you can hear me man, I could really use some help down here."

Once again, the radio signaled that his traffic had not gone through.

They were all over him now and the sheer weight of all the men was slowly driving him to the floor. Steele didn't have room to take a full swing or to throw a solid punch. He was fighting with elbows and knees, short compact blows to stomachs, groins, and necks. Steele could feel their breath on his face, smell the sweat of their bodies. He couldn't tell where he ended, and they began. He had been able to make out singular languages and dialects, but now they had merged together into one voice that cried out in unison for his death.

Steele knew that he was about to die, but he wasn't going to make it easy for them. He slipped his thumb through the ring attached to the pin of the teargas and yanked it free.

The cannister hissed and began spewing its caustic contents in a cloud of gray smoke. Steele took a breath, but the gas was already in his eyes, burning his skin and singeing the back of his throat.

Terrible idea, Eric.

The mob faltered, and Steele felt the hands holding him down recoil. He ripped the teargas cannister off his vest and threw it to the floor and pulled the Hi Power from his holster. The gas was heavier than the air and stayed low to the ground, the crush of bodies keeping it from dissipating. Steele held his breath until his vision started to tunnel and his pulse pounded in his ears. His brain screamed for him to open his mouth, to fill his lungs, but he ignored it.

Steele didn't even try to aim; he just made sure the muzzle was pointing at something orange before pulling the trigger. Bodies fell all around him and then Steele saw the keycard a few feet away. He crawled toward it, the tears distorting his vision. A leg appeared, and he jammed the white-hot suppressor against the bare skin.

The terrorist howled and leaped free.

Steele reached for the card, and actually had it in his hands when he felt himself being lifted in the air.

"Dead man," the Tuareg yelled in English.

Who is this guy?

Steele was sure he had never seen the man before in his life, but it was obvious the teargas had no effect on him. Steele clubbed the man in the top of the head with the Hi Power and the giant bellowed. He threw Steele toward the ground, trying to smash his skull open on the floor.

Steele landed on his side and managed to get a shot off. The bullet hit the man in the thigh, but instead of stopping him it appeared to enrage him even more.

He grabbed the Browning by the suppressor and Steele could smell the burning flesh over the choke of the teargas.

The Tuareg appeared not to notice and threw the pistol at Steele's head. Determined not to lose the card again, Steele shoved it between his teeth, reached behind him, and stripped the Winkler combat knife from the sheath attached to his belt.

"I kill you," the man yelled again as he charged.

Steele breathed through his nose, the teargas spreading like a wildfire inside his lungs. He choked but forced himself to keep his mouth closed and not lose the card. A second fighter rushed in from the side, and Steele kicked him in the chest.

The Tuareg slapped him in the side of the head. It was a heavy blow that threatened to burst his eardrums and knock him off-balance. Steele stumbled but managed to stay upright. The giant grabbed him by the vest and Steele raked the blade across the man's tricep.

"Auuugh," he screamed.

Steele ducked under the loping haymaker and stuck the blade in his kidney. It was a blow that would have killed a lesser man, but not the Tuareg. He somehow managed to gather him up in a bear hug and pull him close and started to squeeze. Steele's arms were trapped against his side and he could feel his ribs compress.

Steele spit the keycard out and drove his forehead into the bridge of the man's nose, but the pressure didn't release. Steele slammed his knee into the giant's groin and squirmed to get his arm free.

Still the Tuareg held him tight, squeezing the air out of his lungs. Steele headbutted him again, flattening the man's nose against his face. Finally, he managed to pull his arm free, pressing the blade against the Tuareg's bicep as his arm came up. Steele rammed the Winkler down through the collarbone, sunk the blade all the way to the hilt, and yanked it out.

The Tuareg gurgled and his grip relaxed, but he stayed on his feet.

Steele reached over the Tuareg's shoulder and hammered the blade into the man's back. He twisted the handle, trying to cut through his spine, and the giant bellowed and let him go.

"Kill, kill you," the Tuareg spat.

Steele greedily sucked the acrid air into his lungs, ignoring the burn. The giant's threat was weaker this time, blood flecking his lips. Steele scrambled for the Browning. He snatched it off the floor and turned to see his attacker was still pursuing him. Steele wasn't taking any chances this time.

He hit him with a Mozambique: two rounds to the chest and one in the head.

The Tuareg went down.

Steele was five feet from the door and knew if he was going to get out it was now or never.

He retrieved the keycard and walked backward toward the door, emptying the Hi Power as he moved. Steele ran the pistol dry, swiped the card, and heard the lock disengage. He pulled the door open, stepped through, and pressed his back against it.

But the door didn't shut.

There was something keeping it from locking. Steele looked down and saw a foot wedged in the door.

"Give me a break," he yelled.

He planted his feet and pushed against the door. Steele could feel the vibrations from the prisoners hammering, felt their collective weight shoving against him. He pushed back with everything he had. His legs started to quiver, and Steele knew he was too exhausted to hold it much longer.

The door inched open and a hand appeared.

Steele grit his teeth and pulled his last frag free from his vest. He yanked the pin free, released the spoon, and prayed that whoever had assembled the frag had used the full five seconds of time fuse.

Chapter 51

Steele shoved the grenade through the gap in the door.

There was a brief, panicked shout on the other side and then it detonated just before Steele's legs gave out. He slid to the floor, unable to hold himself up any longer.

The only sound that followed was his ragged breathing.

When Steele had caught his breath, he reloaded the Hi Power and got unsteadily to his feet. He wanted to go back for the Winkler but knew there was no time. Steele was walking unsteadily toward the square of light when the door he'd just left banged open.

A shrill voice filled the hallway.

"Allahu Akbar."

Steele turned to find a skinny jihadist running toward him with his Winkler.

"Hey, thanks bud," he said before shooting the man in the head.

He retrieved his knife, wiped the blade on the man's jumpsuit, and slid it back into his sheath. Steele followed the hallway and came to a second door. He swiped the keycard and had the door halfway opened when he heard the sounds of a gunfight. Now that the radio had a clear line of sight he depressed the button to talk.

"Demo. Demo do you read me?"

"A little busy right now."

"Where are you?" Steele asked.

"Top of the stairwell, they have me pinned down."

Armed with only the Browning Hi Power and one magazine, Steele stepped outside and followed an incline up to the deck. He peeked his head over the lip and found himself on the rear deck, near the railing where they had come aboard.

To his right a set of metal stairs led up to the bridge. Steele saw Demo crouched at the top, the door to the bridge yawning open behind him. His handler was firing down at targets that he couldn't see from his position.

"Keep their heads down, I'm moving in from your twelve o'clock."

Steele stayed low and worked his way along a row of

plastic shipping containers. He could hear the *thwap, thwap, thwap* of a suppressed rifle on the other side. Steele had to duckwalk around the container, and his muscles, still fatigued from the fight, quivered with every step.

Finally he maneuvered into a position where he could see one of the shooters firing up at Demo. It was a tough shot. Steele could see only the shooter's arm and part of his back. Usually he didn't like to shoot a man in the back, but Steele figured the time for fair play had passed when they locked him in the hold and opened the cells.

He leveled the sights on the man's forearm and fired. The round shattered the bone, but it took a moment for the pain sensor to make it to the shooter's brain. He didn't realize that his arm was no longer supporting the AK-12 until he blasted a shot into the pallet he was hiding behind.

Steele didn't wait for him to figure out what had happened. He stepped out from cover and fired a second round at him. This one hit the man in the side of the head and dropped him.

"One down," Steele reported once he had run to the man's position and got the AK into action.

Steele snagged two of the man's magazines and shoved them into his back pocket. He was looking for the second shooter when Steele saw a flash of orange move behind a manifold. He stepped out, trying to get a shot on target, but the moment he was out of cover, a bullet snapped over Steele's head. He ducked, but before he could get out of the way a second shot came in. This one was lower.

The bullet hit the deck at his feet. It cut a gouge in it and peppered his calf with fragments of metal. Steele broke contact with three blind shots and limped back to the manifold cover. When he got there the man in the orange jumpsuit was gone.

"Where the hell did he go?" Steele asked himself aloud before checking the wound.

There was blood seeping through his pants, but Steele could put pressure on his leg, which meant he was still in the fight. But he was going to have to find another way around. Steele wound his way through the section of crates to the stairwell on the other side of the bridge. He pied the corner, leading with the rifle, and just when he thought it was clear, a shot rang out. Steele jerked his head back, but not before catching some fragments of the wall, and getting a look at the shooter.

It was Zakayev.

He pressed the button to talk, planning on warning Demo, but when he pushed the button nothing happened. Steele stole a quick look at his left shoulder and quickly found the problem. The splash that had hit him in the face wasn't from the wall, it was from the bullet hitting his radio, and now there was no way he could warn Demo.

Steele stepped around the corner, fully expecting to feel the burn of a bullet finding flesh. It was a risk he was willing to take if it meant saving Demo's life. Steele skirted the base of the bridge, moving quickly toward the cough of Demo's UMP. He saw a muzzle flash spark near the top of one of the life rafts and transitioned his rifle onto target but kept moving toward the stairs.

Demo fired again, the sound closer this time.

"Watch your six!" Steele yelled, pivoting toward the life raft.

The shooter shifted his fire toward Steele's voice, but the rounds were high. Steele returned fire, aiming toward the deck, hoping to skip the rounds under the raft.

"Demo, watch your six!" Steele yelled before moving.

His handler responded by firing down at the life raft, forcing the shooter to retreat. Steele was waiting when the shooter stepped out, and hit him with a controlled pair to the chest.

The man was down, but Zakayev was still on the loose.

"I'm coming down," Demo yelled.

Steele angled around the topside deck, wanting to cover his keeper's descent down the stairs. He came around the corner in time to see a man in an orange jumpsuit disappear over the rail. Zakayev was right behind him, smiling over the AK-74 leveled at Steele's chest.

"ERIC, watch out!" Demo yelled, diving off the stairs.

His keeper's body hit him a split second before the rifle bucked against the Chechen's shoulder, and sent him tumbling across the deck.

Steele rolled over his shoulder and snapped a shot at Zakayev that sent him spinning over the railing. Steele jumped to his feet, intent on finishing him off, when he heard Demo say, "Mano, I'm hit."

Steele ran to his keeper's side, tearing the trauma bag from its pouch. Demo had his hands around his throat, his face pale except for the blood spurting onto his chin.

Steele ripped out the gauze and the QuikClot. "Let me see it, brother," he said. The moment the pressure was released he knew Demo was going to die. The blood was bright red and spurting. An artery. He packed the wound with the quick clot gauze and wrapped the bandage around Demo's neck.

"I'm going to get you out of here, just hold on."

Steele took the stairs leading up to the bridge two at a time. He shoved the door open, grabbed the radio, and entered the frequency from memory. There was something beeping on the console, but he ignored it.

"Any station this net, this is Stalker Seven on board Cold Storage, and I am requesting immediate assistance at . . ."

Where the hell are we?

He scanned the panel for the navigation display.

"Unidentified vessel, this is a secure channel," an authoritative voice said. "Get off this frequency."

Steele found the nav screen and clicked the mic. "Last calling station, my location is . . ." He read off the lat/long displayed on the screen as well as the heading and speed and then he noticed the flashing red light in the center of the console. Beside the light was a rectangular LCD screen, the words SELF-DESTRUCT Sequence Initiated above a timer rapidly counting toward zero.

"Oh shit."

Chapter 52

"Help is on the way, but we have to go," Steele said, lifting Demo onto his shoulder. According to the timer they had less than a minute to get off the boat.

Demo groaned, and his eyes fluttered. He opened his mouth and tried to tell him something but all that came out was a wet whisper. The tears in Steele's eyes reactivated the teargas, but he wiped them away and hoisted his handler onto his shoulder.

"I'm going to get you home," he lied.

Steele carried him gently down the stairs, counting backward in his head. He knew that there wasn't time to get to the boat. They were going to have to go over the side and hope someone was listening.

He set Demo down and hauled up the mooring line Zakayev had used to tie up the Zodiac. Steele tied the free end under Demo's arms, lifted him to the rail, and started lowering him into the water.

The count in his head was at thirty seconds.

Steele let the rope out faster, the line burning his palms through the gloves. He ignored the pain. The only thing he cared about was getting Demo into the water. Finally, when he was close to the surface, Steele let him fall.

Fifteen seconds.

He knew that he had to cut Demo free or the explosion would kill him. Steele yanked the Winkler from the sheath and cut the rope.

Ten seconds.

Steele climbed up on the rail, tucked the blade home, and jumped.

Steele was still falling when the boosting charge went off. The explosion grabbed him out of the air and flung him farther out to sea. Steele hit the surface and skipped like a stone across a lake. His arms and legs flailed in every direction, and then he went under.

The Arctic water was cold and unforgiving. It sucked the air from his lungs and the heat from his bones, but Steele fought it. He clawed his way toward the flickering light. When Steele finally breached the surface, the world was on fire.

He tore at the quick release on his vest and managed to yank it free. Behind him a low rumble echoed over the ocean, and Steele turned in time to see the final scuttling charges go off.

Cold Storage shuddered and screamed as her bulkheads collapsed. Black smoke rose from a jagged tear just above the waterline and Cold Storage listed to the side. The superstructure leaned awkwardly to the right and the support beams snapped. With a metallic shriek it tore free of its moorings and crashed through the deck.

"Demo!" Steele yelled, kicking his legs to get his chest out of the water. The surface was covered in debris, chunks of metal and plastic that acted as miniature pyres. He saw one of the lifeboats shoot to the surface and then Cold Storage's stern came clear of the water as the bow sunk beneath the waves. Steele knew that if he didn't find Demo soon his keeper would be sucked under with the ship.

He found him floating on his back, one side of his face black with oil. The bandage Steele had tied around his wound was still intact, but it was soaked through with blood.

Steele grabbed him under the shoulders and pulled Demo close.

"I'm here, brother."

Demo's lips were blue, his face ashen, and Steele could barely feel his pulse.

Get to the lifeboat.

It was the only thing that mattered.

Steele's clothes and boots were working against him, but he refused to quit. He kicked as hard as he could and angled toward the lifeboat. His arms turned to rubber, the lactic burn creeping from his legs to his chest, but somehow, he made it. Steele tore the lashings that held the orange panel over the boat free and, with one hand holding on to Demo, managed to climb aboard. Once inside the small lifeboat, he reached down and used the last of his strength to pull Demo over the side.

As much as he wanted to lie there, he knew that Demo was dying. Steele searched the lifeboat and found a red plastic box mounted to the side. He popped the lid and let the contents fall to the floor.

Steele talked to Demo as he worked, wanting him to know that he was still at his side.

"Let's get you wrapped up, brother," he said, taking the silver emergency blanket and wrapping it around Demo. He went back for the first aid bag.

The blood and seawater mix had soaked through the gauze and adhered to the wound, and Steele was afraid that if he tore it free the wound would start bleeding again.

"I'm just going to rewrap this thing."

When he was finished Steele pulled off his gloves and placed his fingers on Demo's wrist.

This is my fault.

"You have to fight, man, just hold on, please," Steele said.

Desperate for any way to help his friend, Steele went back to the box. There was a final item that hadn't fallen out—a PRQ-7 combat survivor/evader locator or CSEL. Steele flipped the power to on and waited for the radio to run a self-test. Once it was complete Steele activated the radio beacon and switched the setting to air-to-ground.

"This is Stalker Seven. Is there anyone out there, I need help."

Demo's eyes fluttered open and his mouth started to move. His voice was low, barely above a whisper, and Steele dropped the radio and grabbed his hand.

"Mano . . ."

Steele had to lean in to hear him. "I'm right here. Help is coming. You are going to make it."

Demo shook his head, the movement shaking the tear out of the corner of his eye.

"No . . . ," he said. "I'm . . . done."

"Don't quit on me. Please. I need you, brother. Just . . . just . . . please hold on."

"It's . . . been . . . an . . . honor," Demo gasped.

"This is my fault," Steele said. "I did this."

"No. My . . . choice. You . . . you . . . have to . . . keep going," Demo said, closing his eyes. "Code of the warrior . . . never . . . quit. Find Zakayev . . . finish this. . . ."

"Please don't go," Steele said, pressing his forehead to his best friend's.

"I . . . " Demo gasped. He closed his eyes and summoned the last of his strength. ". . . love you brother," he whispered.

And then Demo was gone.

Chapter 53

USS *Virginia*
Fifteen Miles South of Cold Storage

Captain Charles Murphy was in his stateroom aboard the USS *Virginia* when his orderly knocked on the door.

"Enter," he said without looking up from the laptop where he was working on the crew's Fitreps.

The *Virginia* had been in the Arctic for the past five months on a northern run conducting "routine submarine operations," mundane tasks that included under-ice transit and under-ice operations.

It was bullshit.

The real reason she was at sea was because seven

months ago an NSA satellite passing over the Russian sub pen in Zaozyorsk captured the telltale heat signature of a reactor coming online.

Both the CIA and the NSA were aware that Russia was spending billions of rubles to modernize their aging submarine fleet. However, as far as they knew, the only factory capable of building a nuclear submarine was based in Severodvinsk, a port city on the White Sea. The fact that there was a new submarine being launched from the reportedly deactivated submarine pens at Zaozyorsk was a call for alarm.

"What can I help you with, Jonesy?" Captain Murphy asked, finally looking up from the laptop.

"The XO wants you in the radio room."

Murphy leaned back in his chair and rubbed a hand over his lined face.

"Did he say what he needed?"

"We just got a call from COMSUBLANT."

COMSUBLANT stood for Commander, Submarine Force Atlantic, and Murphy knew that they didn't break radio silence unless there was a damn good reason.

"On my way," Murphy said with a nod.

He got to his feet and pulled a ball cap with the words USS VIRGINIA and SSN 774 embroidered in yellow around the submariner's badge over his head and walked aft to the radio room.

"What do you have, Dave?"

"This just came in," Dave Clark said, handing the message to his boss.

Murphy looked at the message.

From: Commander Submarine Force Atlantic

To: SSN 774

Proceeded Immediately to following grid.

The grid was already plotted on the map, and Murphy saw that it wasn't far.

"We picked up a distress call about thirty minutes ago. Came in on an encrypted channel that belongs to C 257," his XO said.

"Charlie 257," Clark repeated aloud, his slate-gray eyes narrowing.

Like all attack boat captains, Murphy had a top secret clearance. C 257 was one of the few Special Access Programs he'd been read in on, and the only reason for that was to make sure he didn't blow the ship out of the water.

"Go on." He nodded.

"We came up to transmission depth and heard this on Satcom."

"This is Stalker Seven, is anyone out there?"

It was all Murphy had to hear.

He picked up the phone that connected him to the control room.

"Control," a voice answered.

"Bring us to." He read the grid off the map and waited for the man on the other end to read the coordinates back.

"Aye, aye, sir."

"On me, Dave," Murphy commanded.

Chapter 54

USS *Virginia*

Steele lay in the bottom of the boat, staring at the silver emergency blanket he'd draped over Demo. A gust of wind rolled over the gunwales, freezing the tears on his cheek. The wind snapped the blanket free, revealing Demo's lifeless body.

Steele worked the radio until he couldn't feel his fingers.

All he wanted to do was sleep, but he fought the urge, knowing that if he drifted off, he was dead.

"Any station this net . . . any station this net, this is Stalker Seven," he yelled over the screaming wind.

His throat was raw from the cold, but he had to keep

trying. He couldn't let Zakayev win. Steele held his fingers in front of his mouth and was blowing on them, trying to get the feeling back, when he heard a rumbling from beneath the ice.

Steele searched the ice but saw nothing but white.

Then he heard it again. The rumbling grew stronger and he could feel the lifeboat vibrating. Steele didn't care. He was about to let go when he heard Demo's voice in his head.

"Never quit. Finish this."

Steele grabbed the side of the boat and forced himself to sit up. He scanned the ice sheet, saw the chunks of snow vibrating, and then the nose of the USS *Virginia* broke through the surface about forty yards away.

"Captain wants to see you," the crewman said, his hand never straying from the Beretta 92F holstered at his side.

Steele's hands and feet were swollen, and despite the thermals, jacket, and skullcap he wore, he couldn't stop shivering. He got to his feet and moved gingerly to the door.

"That way," the man said.

He followed his directions down the hall and up the stairs. This wasn't Steele's first time on an attack boat and knew that they were entering "officer's country," enlisted slang for the officers' living area.

"Right here," the seaman said.

Steele stopped in front of the wardroom, but the sailor shook his head and pointed at the door across the hall.

The captain's stateroom.

The seaman nodded and knocked on the door, which was pulled open from the inside. There were three men in the room and he assumed the one sitting at the table was the captain.

"I'll be outside if you need me, sir," the man said.

"Shut the door, if you wouldn't mind."

Steele guessed the captain was in his late forties with the pale skin of a man who had spent most of his time underwater. He knew that the navy didn't hand out the keys to the three-billion-dollar machines to just anyone. The captains who were chosen to command the boat were entrusted with a huge responsibility, and with it came absolute authority.

"I am Captain Charles Murphy, and the only thing I want to know is who in the hell you are?"

"My name is Eric Steele and I'm an Alpha."

"I know that you are aware that certain commanders in strategic areas are read in on the Program."

"Yes, sir, I am."

"What we are told is limited; however, we are given certain ways to check a man's credentials," he said, getting to his feet and walking over to the safe on the wall.

"You mean the green codes."

"This is correct. Do you know what happened when I ran yours?" he asked, dialing in the combination.

"I imagine when you made the call there was no one to pick up the phone."

"And why is that?" Murphy asked, taking a green plastic sleeve out of the safe.

Steele glanced at the clock on the wall and did the math in his head. The termination flash was still in effect, which meant Murphy couldn't get in contact with Cutlass to confirm his bona fides.

He was going to have to use the green codes secured inside the plastic sleeve. Something the rest of the officers in the room didn't have the clearance to witness.

"Sir, I am not sure if these men have the clearance to hear that."

"This is bullshit," one of the men said.

"But it's your boat so it is up to you," Steele said.

Murphy nodded toward the door, and the two officers stepped out. When they were alone the captain cracked the plastic sleeve in half and pulled out a laminated card. On the card was a list of active Alphas and

ALL OUT WAR • 433

the challenge and password for each. Murphy scanned the list until he came to Stalker 7.

"Alpha 778 Lima, Lima 9."

"Romeo 370 Oscar, Oscar."

Murphy nodded. "Good enough for me, son. Now what the hell is going on?"

"Eighteen hours ago, a man named Aleksandr Zakayev breached a way station and gained access to Cutlass Main's network. My keeper and I—" Steele paused and tried to clear the lump in his throat.

"Take your time, son."

"Zakayev got away with one of the prisoners."

"How can I help?" Captain Murphy asked, motioning from the chair across from him.

Steele wasn't sure.

His focus had been to locate and kill Zakayev, but he'd gotten away. Without Demo, Steele felt lost, not sure of his next play.

"I need to make a call," he said. "Can I get a secure line?"

Steele limped to the commo shack, where a seaman was already waiting with the secure phone. He dialed the number from memory and waited.

"Hello?" a female voice answered.

"Meg, it's me."

"Hello?" Meg said a second time.

Steele knew that because the signal was being bounced off a satellite there was a lag between when he spoke and when Meg heard his voice, so he waited.

"Eric, is that you?" she asked, the concern in her voice clear even on the shoddy connection.

"Yeah. It is good to hear your voice."

"Where are you, are you okay?"

"I'm sorry but I'm on a time crunch," he said. "I . . . I need to talk to Lansky."

"Oh, yeah, of course," she said.

Steele knew Meg understood, but he heard the change in her voice, the subtle shift from excitement to disappointment. And he hated to think he could be the cause of it.

As much as Steele wanted to talk to her, to tell her about Demo and everything else that had happened, he didn't have time. The mission always had to come first.

Steele could hear voices in the background and then Meg's voice and the sound of a hand being placed over the phone. When Lansky came on the line the background noise was gone.

"Steele, where are you?" Lansky asked.

"Demo is dead," Steele replied.

There was a moment of silence.

"Oh shit. I'm— I'm sorry. What happened?"

Steele fought back the tears and the rage building inside of him.

"It doesn't matter. He's gone and so are Zakayev and Sitta. You and Meg need to find out where he is going, so I can kill him and finish this."

Chapter 55

Arish, Egypt

Zakayev and Hassan had checked into the Grande Luxor hotel the night before. Zakayev had made contact with Gabriel and asked for a doctor. After cleaning up and eating his first real meal in forty-eight hours, Zakayev now sat in a chair near the balcony, watching the woman with the golden skin strolling beneath the palm trees, her bronzed complexion perfectly accentuating her white bikini.

A breeze rolled in from the Mediterranean Sea, rustling the palm fronds, cooling Zakayev's fevered forehead. He closed his eyes and tried to imagine that he was on vacation, but a sharp pain from his shoulder brought him back to reality.

"You are lucky the bullet didn't break your collarbone," the doctor said. "Are you sure you don't want any morphine?"

"Just get it out," Zakayev snapped.

Zakayev took a pull from the bottle of vodka, the liquor burning on its way down, and turned his attention to the man in the black suit.

"If we are being honest, I wasn't sure you could pull it off."

Before Zakayev could answer, a second voice broke in.

"I told you that he was the right man for the job," Hassan Sitta said from the doorway.

Sitta had trimmed his beard and colored his hair from black to a more neutral brown. It was a drastic change when combined with the light blue polo and pair of linen pants. If it weren't for his pale skin Hassan could have been just another man on vacation.

Gabriel got to his feet, but Sitta waved for him to keep his seat and walked over to Zakayev. He glanced at the wound and grimaced.

"You saved my life."

Zakayev still couldn't get past seeing his old friend alive.

"I would have come earlier, but they said you were dead."

"I know," Sitta said, patting his shoulder. "They were going to keep me there forever. Thought that one day they could break me," he said, walking over to the table where he poured himself a drink.

Zakayev had so many questions, but before he could ask them there was a single knock at the door.

Gabriel was up in an instant. He tugged an FN from the holster at his side, moved to the doorway, and leveled the pistol at the door. Three more knocks followed the first and he relaxed and moved to the door.

Two men walked into the room. They were big and carried themselves with a "don't fuck with me" attitude that Zakayev attributed to cops and soldiers.

They took in the room with a practiced ease, moving to the points of domination that would allow them to react if anyone in the room made a move.

Not cops. Soldiers, the voice said.

The mystery was solved a moment later when one of the men said something into the microphone attached to his wrist.

The third man who stepped into the room was dressed like an extra from *Lawrence of Arabia.* He wore a gold-hemmed *bisht,* the traditional outer robe of the Arabian Peninsula, over a white *thawb.*

On his head he wore a spotless white *keffiyeh,* which framed an oval face and black goatee.

Gabriel was on his feet in an instant. "Prince Badr," he said with a deferential bow.

Badr nodded at Gabriel but smiled warmly when he saw Sitta standing there.

"Allah be praised," he said, holding out his arms.

Sitta set his drink on the table and stepped into the embrace.

"Your Highness. Thank you," he said.

"Hassan, my boy—you look so pale. So thin."

"The accommodations were not the best. But thanks to you and Zakayev, I am alive."

"I have heard much about you," Badr said, turning his attention to the Chechen. He leaned in to get a look at the gunshot wound, his face crinkling with an appropriate wince of sympathy.

"Many thanks for bringing our brother home."

Zakayev nodded and took a pull from the bottle.

The doctor dug deep into the wound, the jolt of pain cutting off the voice in his head. "Got it," he exclaimed.

He pulled the forceps out, dropped what was left of the bullet into the metal tray with a *tink.*

"Your Highness, we have much to talk about," Gabriel said, leading Badr and Sitta off to one of the side rooms. He stopped before stepping out of sight and said, "Bandage him up, we will be leaving soon."

Yes, take care of my dog, the voice scoffed.

Zakayev waited until he heard the door close. They were alone.

Now is your chance.

The doctor had finished sewing up the wound and was about to put his tools away when Zakayev grabbed his arm.

"One more thing," he said.

"What is it?" the doctor asked.

"I caught a piece of shrapnel a few weeks back," he said, leaning forward.

He touched the scar on the back of his head with his forefinger. "Do you think you can get it out without too much fuss?"

The doctor leaned in. "Yes, I see it there, just below the skin."

He reached for the scalpel. "Hold still, this won't take long."

Chapter 56

King David Hotel, Jerusalem

The early-morning sun streamed through the window of the King David Hotel's presidential suite. President Rockford paced back and forth through vertical shadows cast across the plush carpet like a lion in a cage.

He was pissed.

Meg had been reprimanded more times than she could remember. As a captain in the army she had been chewed out by majors, a pair of colonels, and even a brigadier general. During her time in the CIA she'd once been lectured for an hour by the Algerian chief of station.

But this was the first time she'd ever seen anyone get their ass chewed by the president of the United States. In her experience the best thing to do was just shut up and take it, but Lansky wouldn't shut up.

"It was my call," Lansky said.

Jesus, please stop talking, Meg thought.

Rockford rounded on his chief of staff.

"You work for ME, Ted. You don't get to make those calls," Rockford bellowed. "What the hell were you thinking?"

"He was trying to protect you, sir," Meg said.

Rockford turned to her in a flash.

Why did I say that? she thought.

She was expecting him to start yelling but instead he rubbed his hand across this face.

"I know he was," Rockford said softly. He walked over to the couch and dropped himself into the cushions. "Run me through it again."

Meg and Lansky told him everything that had happened from the beginning, including Cold Storage and the attack on the way station.

"We were on Air Force One when Demo . . ."

She remembered when Lansky had told her the news, and she felt the same anguish at the memory. Meg looked away and tried to get control of her emotions. She told herself that she had barely known

Demo. It was a lie and she hated herself for wanting to believe it.

While it was true that she had only known him for less than a year, Meg knew that there wasn't a time frame you could attribute to relationships born in combat. She didn't realize she was crying until the tears ran down her cheek.

"I'm sorry," she said.

The tears weren't just for her, they were for Eric. She knew that when Demo had been killed Eric had lost the one man who had always been there for him. And that broke her heart.

Lansky saw her grief and took over.

"Demo and Steele tried to stop Zakayev on Cold Storage. Demo was killed in the ensuing firefight. Sitta and Zakayev got away."

Meg watched Rockford's face as he processed the news of Demo's death.

He cares, she thought, noting his face before he turned away.

"Mr. President, I think they are headed to Israel," Lansky said.

"Is this a hunch or do you have actionable intel?" Rockford asked with a soft voice.

"We have green-lighted missions with less," Lansky said.

Rockford turned and offered Meg a tight-lipped smile. "I know you and Demo were close. I offer my sincere condolences."

Meg nodded her acceptance.

"Sir, if I may," she said.

"Go ahead."

"I think you know that we need to get you and the First Lady out of here."

"It's not that easy." Rockford sighed.

He walked over to the couch and motioned for Meg and Lansky to sit down.

"Why?" Lansky asked. "Why *isn't* it easy?"

"This peace accord has the possibility of bringing stability to the most violent region in the world. Can you imagine how many lives can be saved? How many men like Demo *won't* have to die in the future?"

This was the first time Meg had thought of the situation from Rockford's eyes. There was logic there. But it made her wonder. *What would your answer have been if you knew that Lisa was pregnant?*

"Ted, I can make a call to Cutlass Main. Have Pitts freeze every Alpha operation. Put the entire weight of the Program, the United States military, and our allies behind him, but I have two conditions."

Of course you do.

"What are they, sir?"

"The first is that we stay for the peace summit."

"And the second?"

"The Israelis or the Saudis never find out," Rockford said.

"Do I have a choice?" Lansky asked.

"No, Ted, you don't."

Shit.

"Looks like we are in agreement then," Lansky said.

Rockford nodded and got to his feet.

He walked over to the desk, where a pair of hardwired phones sat side by side. To a casual bystander the phones were identical to the ones you would expect to see in a corporate office except these phones were made by General Dynamics, the same company that built the USS *Virginia*.

The Vipers, as they were called, had been installed by Rockford's advance team, and the voice and data encryption was state-of-the-art. One was labeled, the other was not, and Meg knew that the unlabeled one connected him straight to Cutlass Main.

Rockford picked up the handset and waited for the crypto to come online and connect him. When it did he said, "This is Eagle. I am authorizing full Alpha Authority for Stalker Seven."

Chapter 57

USS *Virginia*

"I don't know who you are, but I never thought I'd see this day," the seaman said as he snapped the buckles securing the harness over Steele's Gore-Tex jacket.

"What do you mean?"

"I was in the operations room when that call came in, skipper said we are taking the boat up to the surface in broad daylight."

Steele had been in the military for most of his adult life, and most of that in the army. But since joining the Program he'd spent time on air force bases, marine landing ships, and naval assault ships. Each branch of service had their own jargon that was full of acronyms and slang. To an outsider it sounded like a different language, but Steele had never had a problem catching on.

The moment he stepped into USS *Virginia*'s control room Steele was lost.

To date the only thing he knew about submarines was from watching *The Hunt for Red October*. In the movie, the control room was dim and quiet, full of men with headphones turning knobs and flipping dials. But the scene before him on the USS *Virginia* could have been from *Star Trek*.

It was well lit with a bank of digital monitors displaying the real-time information the crew needed to pilot the attack sub. To his right, two bowmen sat in black chairs using steering wheels to control the sub.

The seaman brought him over to the conning tower, a metal tube that came from the roof.

"So here is how this is going to go," he whispered. "The captain will bring the boat up to PD," the seaman began.

"PD?" Steele asked.

"Periscope depth." The man sighed. "When everything is clear he will bring us to the surface. Once we are on the surface the clock starts. We have five minutes. Got it?"

Steele nodded.

"I will climb up and open the hatch. If the helo is on time, which they never are, we will get you hooked up and you will be on your way."

"And if they aren't?"

"Like I said, we have five minutes," he said, slapping Steele on the shoulder.

Steele felt the floor shift beneath him as the attack sub surfaced and leveled out. The seaman pressed a button on his watch, and Steele heard the digital beep echo off the bulkhead. The seaman climbed up the metal ladder and twisted the latch. Steele was on his way up when a bucket of seawater rolled in and hit him square in the face.

He shielded his eyes from the sun, but the air on his face felt cool and refreshing. It was like being born again. Steele heard the seaman say something into the radio and then saw him produce a pair of binos and start scanning the horizon.

"Never on time," he grunted.

"What was that?"

"Disregard, sir."

Steele strained for any sign of the approaching helo, but there was nothing except the splash of the waves against the sub.

"Two minutes," a voice said over the radio. "Roger that, sir."

"What did he say?" Steele asked.

"Nothing, sir."

Finally, Steele heard a distant *thump, thump, thump* coming from the east. He squinted against the sun and thought he saw a distant speck appear on the horizon.

The SH-60 came in low and fast, the pilot hailing the *Virginia* on the radio, "USS *Virginia* this is Dolphin 115 how copy."

"Dolphin 115 this is the *Virginia* read you Lima Charlie."

The SH-60 came to a hover over the *Virginia* and Steele watched one of the crew members start to lower the hook. Beside him the seaman had the receiver pushed tight to his ears. His mouth was moving, but Steele couldn't make out what he was saying.

He put the receiver down, but instead of grabbing the grounding rod he began gesturing for the pilot to wave off.

"What the hell are you doing?" Steele asked.

"Sonar picked up a contact," the seaman yelled, pointing over the port side. "We have to go—NOW."

"NO," Steele yelled back. "You have to get me on that bird."

"I told you five minutes. . . ."

Steele wasn't listening; he climbed up on the edge of the tower and motioned for the helo to continue lowering the wire. He grabbed the yellow grounding rod and reached up for the hook, knowing that if he didn't, the moment he clipped in, the static electricity from the helo could kill him.

"Sir," the seaman yelled. "Screw it."

Steele connected the grounding rod to the hook, but then a gust of crosswind hit the helo. The pilot overcorrected, and Steele fought to keep a grip on the rod as the hook swayed out to sea. He was in danger of being pulled off the sub, so he finally let go. Steele waited for the pilot to steady the helo when he felt the *Virginia* shudder beneath him. He glanced to his left and saw that he was alone.

They are going to leave you.

The hook pendulumed in from the right; it was out of his reach but Steele was out of options. The *Virginia* began to dive, and Steele had no choice but to jump. He reached out as far as he could, felt himself falling, and then his hand closed around the hook.

Steele was hanging by one hand, the downdraft from the helo pushing him closer to the ocean. He reached up and got his right hand on the ball atop the hook and pulled himself up to the hook. Steele's hands were slipping but he finally managed to hook in.

"That was a ballsy move," the crew chief yelled after winching him aboard.

"Didn't see another way," Steele said, looking out the door and seeing no trace of the *Virginia*.

The helo flew him to Andøya, Norway, and landed right on the flight line where a British Tornado was waiting.

"This way, sir," a Norwegian sergeant yelled, motioning for Steele to follow him toward the closest building. He led him into the pilot's ready room, where a flight suit and helmet were waiting. Steele stripped out of the Gore-Tex but decided to keep the thermals on. He stepped into the flight suit and was tying his boots when he heard the start cart fire up the Tornado's engines.

Steele grabbed his helmet and stepped outside.

"That was quick, sir," the sergeant said, leading him out to the plane.

Steele climbed up the stairs and let the man strap him into the seat.

"This is a Martin-Baker MK10a ejection seat, sir. If for some reason you need to leave the aircraft while in flight, simply pull this yellow cord and the seat will take care of the rest."

"Good to know," Steele said, pulling the helmet on and then plugging into the commo jack.

"Can you hear me, sir?" the pilot asked, his Scottish brogue thick but clear in Steele's ears.

"Got ya."

Outside, the ground crew closed the canopy and pulled the steps away.

"I'm Wing Commander McCaffery of Her Majesty's Royal Air Force. Appears I will be giving you a ride today."

"Eric Steele, pleasure to meet you."

The pilot advanced the throttle and followed the ground crew's directions from the taxiway to the runway. After getting clearance to take off, he advanced the throttle and let off the brake. The Tornado powered down the runway, shoving Steele back into his seat as the jet climbed skyward.

"So where are we headed, McCaffery?"

"My orders are to take you to Cyprus," he said, making a few adjustments to the navigation display. "Total distance is two thousand three hundred miles from here. Obviously we are going to have to stop for some fuel, but I think we can make that in about two hours, maybe a bit more."

"Good. Your new call sign is Speedbird-Lima 757, you got that?" Steele said.

"Speedbird, sir? Isn't that . . . ?" McCaffery asked.

"Yep. I just turned your Tornado into a British Airways 777."

"Not sure how I feel about that," McCaffery said.

"Seeing as how I don't have time to fly around Russian airspace, and you probably don't want to get shot down by a MiG, I'm sure you can stomach it for a few hours."

"Excellent point, sir."

Chapter 58

The doctor was gone when Gabriel, Sitta, and Badr came out of the room.

"Ready to go?" Gabriel asked Zakayev.

Oh yes. We are ready, the voice said.

Zakayev smiled, his fingers touching the tracking chip in his pocket.

"Then Allah be with you," Badr said, embracing Hassan. "Just remember, my brother is the only one who dies. We cannot risk an all out war by killing the Israeli prime minister and the American president."

My God, so that is what they are planning.

"I will make sure of it, Your Highness," Sitta answered.

Zakayev followed Hassan downstairs, where they climbed into a waiting van.

"So now you know the plan," Hassan said with a wide smile. "Not bad for a Palestinian refugee, eh brother?"

If he was looking for validation, he wasn't going to get it from Zakayev. "Hassan, how could you let yourself get involved in such a thing?"

Sitta's smile faded and his face flushed with anger.

"LET myself get involved? Prince Badr chose me. Chose me to change the world because I am the best at what I do."

The outburst stunned Zakayev. *Why is he getting so angry? Doesn't he see that this is a suicide mission?*

"Jealous. That is what you are. Jealous that all the attention isn't on you," Hassan spat. "We aren't back at Camp 722, Zakayev. This is my world, where I tell you what to do."

He is insane.

Zakayev refused to back down.

"Then tell me what happened in Mecca."

"Mossad," Hassan answered, spitting on the ground. "They have eyes and ears everywhere. Somehow they found out about the plot to kill the crown prince. Then they went and cried to their American masters. But the team was too early."

"Too early?" Zakayev asked.

"Yes, the bomb was not there." Hassan grinned. "The bomb that I designed."

"That is why they put you on the boat."

Hassan nodded.

"The Americans thought they had everything figured out. They knew about the tunnel in Jeddah. Knew of our plans. They took two of us back to that boat, thought they could get us to talk."

In the front seat of the van, the driver navigated while the man in the brown shirt kept in contact with the border watchers through a pair of radios and four cell phones. Both of them ignored their passengers.

"What happened to the other man?"

"Rahim? He was weak. I couldn't trust him to keep his mouth shut so I—" He dragged his thumb across his throat. "The Americans didn't even care. Said, 'What is one more dead haj.'"

He will kill you too, given the chance.

Before Zakayev could reply, one of the passenger's cell phones rang and he brought it to his ear.

"We are not far," he said, consulting the map on his knee.

Zakayev had overheard them talking about how many extra police and military Israel had moved to the border crossings but didn't know why. The man up front closed the phone, took the sim card, and dropped it out of the window. He looked at the map on his lap and told the driver where to take the turn.

"It is time to hide," he said.

Hassan nodded and crawled to the rear of the van.

"Help me with this," he said, motioning toward the bench.

Zakayev grabbed the rear of the bench and pulled up while Hassan reached under the cushion and tripped a hidden latch. The bench rotated forward, revealing a hidden compartment large enough for the two men to squeeze into.

Hassan crawled in first and Zakayev followed, pulling the bench closed with the handle mounted to the bottom.

The darkness settled around them, the heat mixing with the smell of diesel. He felt Hassan's hand brush across his shoulder and then heard a click followed by the whir of an exhaust fan.

Hassan spoke, his voice friendly in the dark.

"It is good that you are here. You will like working for me," he said.

Zakayev knew at that moment that he was going to have to kill Hassan. The only question was how and when.

Chapter 59

Cyprus

"Shamrock 380 Charlie cleared for approach runway one zero," the E-3 Sentry AWAC advised.

"Roger that. Gimble, Speedbird, I mean . . ." McCaffery released the mic and shook his head before trying again. "Roger that. Gimble, Shamrock 380 Charlie on approach."

They had changed call signs three times since taking off as Speedbird, and McCaffery was having trouble with his new call sign.

"Bloody Shamrock," the pilot muttered.

"Tried to make it easy by using only UK airliners," Steele said.

"What?"

"Shamrock is the Aer Lingus call sign."

"You don't think the bloke at the tower will be concerned when a Tornado lands instead of whatever else he is expecting?"

"I think it will be fine." Steele grinned.

"Just, doesn't seem normal?"

"Does anything about today seem normal?"

"You've got yourself a point there, sir. But seriously, I'm not going to disappear or anything? I mean they are going to let me go home, right?"

"You signed a nondisclosure, didn't you?"

"Yes, sir."

"Did you read the last page?"

"Read it? There was more paper there than when I bought my first house. I thought some of the lads were taking the piss to be honest."

Steele smiled.

"Well I will sum it up for you. This never happened, and I was never here."

McCaffery conducted a perfect landing and followed the tug with the FOLLOW ME sign attached to the back all the way to the hangar. The ground crew raced a pair of ladders to the Tornado and popped the canopy.

"Thanks for the lift," Steele said, pulling off his helmet.

"My pleasure, sir," McCaffery said as the canopy came open.

Steele unbuckled himself from the harness and climbed down the ladder the ground crew pushed against the side of the Tornado. He walked across the tarmac to the hangar, where a woman with red hair waited in the shade.

"We are all just torn up over Demo," Collins Austin or Stalker 8 said, a sad smile on her face.

Steele nodded, fighting the lump in his throat.

"It's good to see you," he said.

At five foot seven, Collins was drop-dead gorgeous, with light blue eyes as clear as a pool of water. She was the last person in the world you'd expect to be in the Program, a fact that made her the deadliest woman Steele had ever met.

"It's good to be seen," she said, patting him on the back and turning to the hangar.

Shane Wylie, Collins's keeper, was waiting inside. The man was tall and thin, and walked with a limp from the sniper round he had taken in Iraq.

"How ya holding up, chief?" Wylie asked.

"I'm making it," Steele replied. "What do we have?"

"Typical political goat rope," Wylie began. "Prime minister is busting the boss's balls and Lansky is telling Eagle that coming clean about Archangel will screw everything up."

"So, no help from Mossad?"

"Nope," Wylie said. "Which is why we're staging up here instead of on the ground in Israel."

"The TOC is set up over here." Collins nodded, and Steele knew that she was ready to get down to business.

Chapter 60

C ollins led the way to the far side of the hangar, where there was a black conex box guarded by two men with rifles. It was the M-TOC or mobile tactical operation center that brought the power of Cutlass Main to Steele.

"Sorry about Demo," one of the men guarding the entrance said as they approached.

"Thanks, man."

"He was a solid dude," the other guard added. "Going to miss the hell out of him. You let us know if there is anything we can do."

"Yeah," Steele nodded, not sure of what else to say.

He stepped inside the M-TOC and found Pitts waiting for him.

"Mike, what the hell are you doing here?" he asked.

"Are you kidding me? When we heard about what happened and then found out you were getting full authority there was almost a riot at Cutlass Main. Shit, I had to pull rank to make sure I didn't get left out," Pitts said.

"Man, it is good to see you," Steele said as they embraced.

"We are up and ready to rock," Pitts said, slapping him on the back and pointing at the monitors.

"What about Hassan Sitta?" Steele asked. "What's his story?"

"Typical shithead," Wylie answered. "Russian-trained Palestinian extremist and terrorist for hire."

"Let's not sell him short," Collins interjected. "Sitta is a big-money, big-picture kind of guy. His expertise is explosives. Rumors are he can make a bomb so accurate it could go off in a room full of people and only kill the target."

"Operation Archangel," Steele said aloud. "Lansky said the intel pointed to Sitta planting a bomb beneath Mecca."

"That's right. We found the tunnel, took down the team, and exfiled Sitta, but no bomb."

"The tunnel . . . ," Steele began.

"What about it?" Collins asked.

"Digging something like that is a big undertaking, right? I mean it's not like they hired a handful of dudes with shovels."

"Well the one we hit was smaller than the main tunnel," Collins said.

"Main tunnel?" Steele asked.

"Oh, yeah, the tunnel we hit was just a branch line," Collins said, turning to a tech at the computer. "Can you bring up the info on the Jeddah water project?"

The man nodded, his fingers flying over the keyboard. A moment later a series of news articles popped up on the screen. The first article was from *Forbes* magazine and Steele read the headline aloud.

"'Sterling Mining submits winning bid to dig underground aquifer in Jeddah, Saudi Arabia. Project will provide millions of gallons of much-needed drinking water.' Bring up Sterling website," he said.

The tech complied and the website popped up on the screen.

"Current projects," Steele said, taking a step closer to the screen. "Click on that."

He waited for it to load and scanned the list of current digs Sterling had around the world.

"Holy shit," Collins gasped.

Steele saw it a moment later, the last-listed location turning his blood cold in his veins.

Silwan.

"We need a plane, NOW."

Chapter 61

Silwan

Zakayev was covered in sweat when the van came to a halt.

There was a click and then the compartment rotated open. "You can come out," the passenger said.

Zakayev felt the cool night air on his skin.

"Where are we?" he asked.

"The Silwan neighborhood in Jerusalem. We still have a short drive, but the Israelis don't come here during the night," he said, handing them two bottles of water.

Zakayev sat next to the door, sipping the water. The van took them deeper into the derelict neighborhood.

He saw shadows flitter across the rooftops and leaned forward to get a better look.

"There are men up there," he said.

"Local fighters," Hassan replied. "Don't worry, it is safe here."

Safe was an understatement. Zakayev saw men armed with AK-47s set up at intervals along the street and a pair of old Mitsubishi pickups with what looked like a DShK beneath a camo net stretched between two structures.

"Technicals?" he asked, looking at the trucks with the mounted machine guns on the back.

"Yes," the driver answered. "We have been planning this day for a long time."

The van slowed in front of a metal fence guarded by two men with AK-47s. When they saw the van approaching, they rushed to open the gate. Inside the compound were rows of old cars, engine blocks, and stacks of tires. Zakayev realized it was a junkyard.

The driver pulled the van into a three-bay garage nestled near the back fence and shut off the engine. Zakayev stepped out, stretched his back, and glanced around. The interior of the garage was awash with activity.

To his left a group of fighters stood cleaning rifles and machine guns on a table while a second crew applied IDF or Israeli Defense Forces stencils to a freshly painted deuce and a half. But what captured Zakayev's attention was the man in the thick glasses attaching a chain to anchor points welded onto the outside of a fifty-five-gallon oil drum.

"Careful now," he said, motioning for the bulky men dressed in blue coveralls. They pulled down on the chain, and the drum lifted free of its stand. It rotated on the chain, and when Zakayev saw the copper disk set inside he knew exactly what he was looking at.

"Have you ever seen an explosive-formed penetrator before?" Hassan asked, moving beside him.

"Once," Zakayev answered, "in Mosul. The Iranians called them EFPs. They wanted to test it against the huge up-armored trucks the American special forces team were using to get around the city."

"Yes, very deadly." Hassan nodded proudly.

"Theirs was smaller, about the size of a large coffee can," he replied.

"Hezbollah built this one for us. Five hundred pounds, the largest one ever built."

The men lowered the EFP onto a reinforced four-wheel dolly, and Zakayev stepped closer to inspect it. The sight of the bomb brought back memories of the Iranians and their explanation of how it worked.

"When the explosive goes off," the Iranian soldier had said, "the force of the explosion hits the lens."

"Lens?" Zakayev asked.

"The copper disk," the Iranian said, pointing inside the open end of the device. "The force of the explosion shapes it into a hypervelocity projectile. A molten missile powerful enough to cut any armor that Americans have."

Zakayev had his doubts, but when the MRAP came lumbering down the road and the Iranian squeezed the detonator, he became a believer.

The charge blew with a roll of smoke and thunder and was followed by a second much larger explosion. The fighters waited for the smoke to clear, hoping to cut down the survivors with their machine guns, but there was no need.

Not a single American survived the blast.

"Our Hassan is going to change the world," a voice said.

Zakayev turned and saw Gabriel standing with another man he'd never seen before.

"Who is that?" Zakayev asked.

"His name is Costas. He is the man in charge of the tunnel," Hassan answered.

Zakayev noticed the man's hands were shaking and

that he was having trouble standing still. He immediately suspected the man was a drug addict.

"What is wrong with you?" Zakayev asked, grabbing his arm and looking for track marks. "Are you drug sick?"

"I haven't had a drink in—"

A drunk. You can use that, the voice said.

Hassan interrupted Costas with a wave of his hand and turned to Zakayev.

"I know what you are thinking, brother," he said.

I seriously doubt that, the voice said.

"You do?" Zakayev answered.

"There is no one in the world who knows you as well as I," Sitta said with a smile.

Then you know that I am going to kill you.

"You are worried that his drinking will endanger me. You needn't be—our friend Costas knows what will happen if he takes another sip, isn't that right?"

"Yes." The man nodded.

"Then it is settled," Zakayev replied, a plan forming in his mind.

Chapter 62

Six Miles from the Israeli Border

It was dark on the landing strip where the C-27J Spartan sat waiting to taxi. The Spartan was smaller than the C-130, the Spartan's four-engine big brother, but just as fast and agile. Which made it a perfect fit for the mission.

Inside the troop compartment, Steele was still trying to adjust the new plate carrier he'd been issued.

"So, you ever done anything like this before?" Collins asked, strapping herself into the seat.

"All the time," Steele said. "What the hell is up with this thing?"

The plate carrier was heavier than his old Mayflower rig, and no matter how he worked the straps, he couldn't get it to sit comfortably.

"The new ones come with all the bells and whistles. Has built-in life support, pretty cool, huh?"

"I guess, but it feels like I'm carrying around the kitchen sink," Steele replied, giving up on the adjustments and strapping himself in.

But usually I do it alone.

"I really didn't expect you to come with me," he said.

"Are you kidding? And let you have all the fun?" she said.

"You say that now."

The radio crackled to life.

"Boxcar this is Sensor," a voice said.

Sensor was a C-17 Globemaster, an aircraft the air force used for transporting cargo and troops around the battlefield. The Program had gutted the bird, stripping out the cargo seats and replacing them with state-of-the-art communications, air-to-air radar, and air-to-ground infrared sensors, making it the perfect intelligence, surveillance, and reconnaissance or ISR platform.

"Go ahead, Sensor," the pilot said.

"Boxcar, vector heading zero four five and drop to one hundred feet."

The copilot turned to make sure his passengers

were strapped in, and when Steele flashed him the thumbs-up the pilot responded with, "Boxcar copies."

Here we go.

Steele had snuck into many countries before, but this time felt different. Tougher. Not only was Israel an ally, but they also had an incredible air defense network with F-15s and F-16s constantly on patrol. Not too many planes entered Israeli airspace and made it out to tell the story. But Steele had faith in the Program's pilots and in this pilot's training.

The C-27 banked into a hard turn, the maneuver pushing Steele back into his seat. Collins flashed him a dazzling smile. She was obviously enjoying herself.

Just wait, Steele thought, knowing what was coming next.

A moment later the pilot pushed the nose down hard, an aggressive maneuver to get under the Israeli ground-to-air radar.

"My Looooord," Collins shrieked.

For a moment Steele was weightless. He felt the contents of his stomach rising into his throat. He expected the maneuver to wipe the grin off Collins's face, but it did the opposite.

"Whooo-haaaa." She laughed, adjusting her helmet.

The pilot had barely leveled off when Sensor was back in the air.

"Boxcar come to zero nine five degrees."

The pilot pushed the throttle forward and Steele looked into the cockpit to see the copilot hunched over the ground radar. He immediately wished that he hadn't.

"What?"

"Trust me, you don't want to know."

After ten minutes of nap-of-the-earth twisting and turning to avoid radar detection, the pilot finally leveled off and pulled the throttles back.

"Five minutes out," the pilot said over the radio.

Steele and Collins got to their feet and checked their gear before climbing onto the modified Kawasaki KLR250-D8 dirt bikes with them on the plane. The bikes were painted desert tan, ran on diesel, and came to life with the flip of a switch.

"One minute," the pilot announced, slowing the aircraft just above stall speed.

The ramp came open and Steele yanked the quick connect and flipped down his night vision.

"Thirty seconds."

He gunned the throttle, keeping his eyes on the ramp.

The moment he felt the wheels kiss the ground Steele shifted into first and rocketed off toward the ramp. He worked the clutch with his left hand and shifted into second, ducking his head as he flew from the back of the aircraft.

Hot exhaust scorched the back of his neck. "Clear," Collins yelled over the radio.

By the time they braked to a halt the C-27 was airborne and heading back to sea. It was silent on the valley floor except for the muffled putter of the four-stroke engines.

"Sensor, Stalker Seven, we are on the ground."

"Good copy, Stalker. ISR shows you clear to the east. Good hunting."

"Let's roll."

Chapter 63

King David Hotel

At 0830 the convoy was assembled outside the King David Hotel. The trucks were lined up in front of the main door, the entrance and exits to the street blocked by armed soldiers.

Meg press checked her Glock 19, and after shoving it back into the holster noticed Ron Boggs, the Secret Service CAT or counterassault team leader, motioning her over.

She knew Ron from her time with the CIA, where he'd briefly worked with ground branch before taking the team leader gig with the Secret Service.

"What's up?"

"Harden, do you have any intel on this threat?" he asked.

"I thought you guys were briefed this morning," she said.

"C'mon, Meg, that wasn't a briefing, and you know it. All we were told is that the CIA has a credible threat in the area."

"That is all we know," she lied.

"Bullshit," Ron said, pulling her close. "My guys," he said, nodding toward the counterassault team leaders, "are walking around with their assholes glued shut. They are freaked out. They expect me to know what is going on, and I don't."

"Where is your truck?"

He motioned to one of the armored Suburbans up front.

They walked over.

"The CIA is being very tight-lipped about this," Meg lied. "All I know is that they have credible intel pointing to an attack on Eagle."

"C'mon, Meg, I might talk slow, but I'm not stupid. My boys tell me that you spent all night inside that brand-new Sensitive Compartmented Information Facility, or SCIF. Which means we aren't the only game in town. If the Agency is running an op, I need to know. Otherwise my guys will drop anyone who isn't dressed like this," he said, tugging on his gear. "My primary job is to make sure that I'm not the asshole who loses a president in Jerusalem. Same token, I also don't want to smoke any assets you have in play."

Meg trusted Ron, but he wasn't cleared to know about an ongoing Alpha operation.

"Can you tell me if it is a shooter?" he asked.

Meg checked over her shoulder to see if anyone was watching and then turned back to Ron.

"Not a shooter," she said.

"A *bomb*?" Ron hissed.

When Meg didn't respond, Ron swore under his breath.

"Command detonated or remote?" he asked.

"That I don't know," Meg said.

"Shit," Ron hissed.

"I know it's not much, but it is all that I know."

"Fair enough," he said, glancing down at her pistol. "Here, take this." He pulled an H&K 416 from inside the Suburban. "Just in case."

"Thanks," Meg said, taking the rifle.

She turned to leave and then realized that they wouldn't let her anywhere near the president or First Lady with the H&K.

"How's about a ride?" she asked.

"I've got room in truck four," he said, pointing to the rear of the convoy.

"The very last truck?" Meg asked, wanting to be closer to Rockford.

"You don't have to . . ."

"No, I'll take it," Meg said, jogging toward the rear vehicle.

The truck commander in the Suburban turned around in his seat when Meg jumped in.

"What the hell is this?" he demanded.

"Ron said I could ride," she said, showing him the H&K as proof.

He was about to argue when the radio came alive.

"Eagle is on his way."

Rockford and Lansky emerged from the hotel flanked by the president's personal protection detail, who escorted them to Stagecoach.

"I can tell them to hold up if you want," Meg told him, reaching for her radio.

"CAT One moving out," Ron said from the first Suburban.

"Just sit back there and don't touch anything," the man ordered. "This is going to be a milk run and I don't want you screwing it up."

"Won't even know I'm here," Meg replied, buckling her seat belt.

She hoped the track commander was right—that this was just an easy drop-off. But the voice in her head told her not to count on it.

Chapter 64

Israel

Steele glassed the guard post, a corrugated tin building with peeling green paint and a window frame that bore the faded scorch marks of an explosion. No one had bothered to replace the glass. Instead they had strung chicken wire across the hole and added three rows of tan sandbags.

Next to him, Collins continued trying to contact Sensor.

"Stalker Eight to Sensor," Collins whispered into the radio.

Their last check-in had been an hour ago, after they had spent the night trying to cover the fifteen miles from the drop-off point to the target area. Steele knew from the map recon that getting across the border wasn't going to be easy. But what he hadn't planned on was the increased IDF this far from the Temple Mount.

What should have taken a few hours ended up being a six-hour game of cat and mouse, and by the time they made it to the copse of trees five hundred meters short of their target area, the sun was on its way up.

"Would have been the perfect spot," Steele said.

He played the binos over the tall grass that would have covered their approach to the road. And then to the large boulders where he'd planned on crossing.

"Stalker Eight to Sensor, do you copy?" Collins tried again.

Nothing.

"Try the TOC," Steele said, turning his attention to the guard post.

"Stalker Eight to Iron Leg," Collins said, using Pitts's call sign.

Steele wasn't sure why their comms had gone to shit, but something made him look to the guard post for answers. He had started to inspect the roof when Collins said, "I think someone is jamming the radios."

"Take a look at the net on top of the roof," Steele said, handing her the binoculars.

"What's that, sugar?"

"The net on the roof, does it seem off to you?"

She took the binoculars, adjusted the focus, and followed his finger to the netting.

"Looks new."

"The IDF can't even bother to slap a fresh coat of paint or replace a blown-out window, but they can buy a new camo net," Steele said. "Seems strange to me."

"And where are the soldiers?" Collins added. "Shouldn't someone be up by now?"

"Have you actually seen any guards at this post?" he asked.

Collins shook her head.

"Let's take a look," Steele said.

They moved through the grass, and Steele set up a base of fire at the rock, his suppressed H&K 416 trained on the edge of the building. Collins crossed the road and took cover behind a shed before waving Steele across. He tapped her on the shoulder, the signal that he was ready to go, and Collins moved to the edge of the building, her rifle up and ready.

Steele heard a scuffing sound just out of sight and Collins held up a closed fist.

Halt.

Steele took a mirror with a telescoping handle out of his cargo pocket and dropped to his knee. He scooted closer to Collins, extended the metal handle, and eased the mirror around the corner.

A man in civilian clothes stood ten feet away, his back to Steele and Collins. The man was obviously not a soldier, Steele knew that much from his clothes and defensive posture. But what added to his confusion was the Israeli-issued Tavor battle rifle slung around his neck.

Something's not right.

Steele twisted the mirror toward the ground and saw what held the man's attention. He was using the toe of his boot to collect the expended brass littering the dirt into a pile.

Collins motioned with her left hand for him to turn the mirror toward the wall, and that was when he saw the blood and the pair of bare feet sticking straight up in the air.

Steele pointed to himself and then at the man around the corner—*I'll take care of this.*

Collins confirmed by grabbing his shoulder and pulling him to his feet. Steele put the mirror back into his pocket, replacing it with a coil of heavy-gauge wire with a pair of two-inch metal handles on the ends. Steele crept around the corner, leading with the balls of his feet before rolling the rest of his weight onto the soles of his boots. When he was an arm's length away,

Steele stretched the wire taut and looped it over the man's head, past his chin, and then yanked his hands in the opposite direction.

In one seamless movement Steele turned and pulled as hard as he could, yanking the sentry off-balance. Steele loaded him onto his hip, tossed him to the ground, and without letting go of the pressure, dragged him back the way he'd come.

Collins stepped out to cover him, and Steele dumped the body in the dust.

They moved along the wall to the corpse with the bare feet.

The man had been stripped of his clothes, and there were flies already crawling across his sightless eyes. He had a "meat tag" tattoo on his side that read:

O+/NKA

Steele knew this was his blood type and NKA meant that he didn't have any known allergies. The man was a soldier.

The building had two doors, and Collins passed the body and went to the first door. She tried the knob, signaling that it was locked with a thumbs-down. Steele slipped past her, his muzzle pointing at the second door. This one was open, and as he approached, he heard a slap followed by a pained moan.

"Hit him again," a voice said in Arabic.

Steele could smell the death before he reached the door. The pungent mix of copper and ammonia, but the moans told him that there was someone still alive. Knowing he didn't have time to wait, Steele took the room.

In the left corner there were two naked bodies. One a male, the other a tall female. Both had been tortured. Steele crossed the threshold and snapped to his right, eyes looking through the optic on the H&K.

He saw two men beating a third IDF soldier tied to a chair. Steele thumbed the safety to fire and killed both with a single shot to the back of the head.

He cleared the rest of the room while Collins moved to assist the soldier tied to the chair.

"Clear," Steele said.

The soldier was young, but it was hard for Steele to guess his age because the man's face was purple from the beating he had taken. Collins pulled the gag off the soldier's mouth.

"What happened here?" she asked in Hebrew.

The man's eyes rolled back in his head, and when he answered it was in short gasping sentences.

"He said they came last night. Ten men. They took their clothes," Collins translated, cutting the man's bonds. "The three men were left behind and wanted to know about the radio frequencies. He says they went up on the roof."

"You got this, I want to check the roof."

"Yeah."

Steele found the stairs and followed them up to the roof, where he got a better look at the camo net. Just like he'd thought, it was brand-new, and when he tugged it free, Steele saw an antenna mast with a small satellite dish at the top. He cut the wire with his knife and keyed the radio.

"Stalker Seven to Sensor."

"Thought we'd lost you," a voice replied.

"Just found a high-frequency disrupter at check-point Charlie," Steele said.

"That explains the commo problems."

Steele pulled the antenna down and checked the manufacturing plate on the dish.

"It's Russian and brand-new by the looks of it," Steele said.

"Copy all Stalker Seven. We have another problem."

Of course we do.

"We have been ordered to clear the airspace."

"Clear the airspace. By whose orders?" Steele asked.

"The Israeli Air Defense. They have established a twenty-mile no-fly zone over the Temple Mount."

A no-fly zone was established anytime the president was in the open. It closed the airspace over the presidential convoy to all aircraft besides those specifically attached to Rockford's detail, including Sensor, the Program's airborne command post.

"Great, no communications with anyone on the ground and no overhead assets. Looks like we are on our own."

Chapter 65

It took Steele and Collins thirty minutes to make it from the guard post where they found the jammer to the hill directly on the north side of the dig site.

"I'm going up for a look," Steele said.

"Take this," Collins said, handing him a black case the size of a water bottle.

"A DragonFly drone? You didn't think to use this back at the checkpoint?"

"It wouldn't have worked with the jammer," she said.

"Fair enough."

Steele worked his way up the hillside and stopped below the crest. He dropped to his belly and heard the *beep, beep, beep* of a large vehicle backing up. He peeked over the edge to find the apex bare of any cover. Knowing that he risked being silhouetted if he went any farther, Steele pulled the small box Collins had given him from his assault pack and opened the lid.

This was his first time using the DragonFly microdrone, and he silently thanked DARPA for printing the operating instructions on the inside of the case.

Steele took the matte black contact case, carefully unscrewed the lid with the *L* inscribed on the top. He balanced the fragile contact lens on the tip of his finger and attempted to affix it to his cornea. Steele had been born with extraordinary eyesight, and this was his first experience with a contact.

It was a painful learning curve, but after poking himself in the eye a few times he managed to affix it to his cornea.

"How's it going up there?" Collins asked.

"Feels like I've got sand in my eye," Steele replied.

He blinked a few times to make sure the contact stayed in place and, after he was sure it wasn't going to fall out, squinted at the instructions.

3-Detach controller pad from box and hit power button.

The controller pad was a flat LCD screen the size of a credit card. When Steele placed his finger over the power square, the words DRAGONFLY v 2.3 appeared in front of his left eye.

Steele closed his eye, and the image disappeared and when he opened it again there was a question posted on the HUD, or heads-up display.

Tutorial: Yes/No?

Steele figured out that he could interface with the HUD by moving his hands above the control pad.

"Those boys at DARPA sure make the coolest toys."

He clicked yes with his finger and watched a five-second tutorial on how to operate the DragonFly. When he was done it asked:

Launch?

He hit yes, and a moment later the device buzzed to life and a miniature drone that looked exactly like a dragonfly emerged from the box.

"Let's see what you can do," Steele said.

He closed his hand around the flight control and pushed the stick forward. The DragonFly whizzed down the hill. The drone's camera was set to panoramic and it gave him a bird's-eye view of the dig site on the other side of the hill.

The sound he'd heard came from a large tracked vehicle with a massive drill bit attached to the nose. A man in a white Sterling Mining polo was hopping out of the cab after parking it across the entrance to the work site. Behind him a pair of pickups with heavy machine guns mounted in the bed were unloading armed men with a mix of AK-47s, PKM light machine guns, and RPGs. While they got into position three burly men in blue coveralls muscled a wheeled cart off an ancient deuce and a half.

"Hurry up," a man yelled from the tunnel.

Steele used the DragonFly to follow the dolly into the tunnel. The feed blinked as the drone switched to the low-light camera, and when it cleared, Steele saw Zakayev and Hassan dressed in the stolen IDF uniforms.

"Stalker Eight to Iron Leg," Collins said over the radio. "I can't believe he still hasn't gotten the joke about his call sign," she said with a grin.

Collins was referring to the fact that Pitts was an amputee. An *"Iron Leg."*

Her grin faded when she saw Steele wasn't laughing.

"Oh, darlin'," she said. "I forgot."

"No, it's funny," Steele said. "I remember when Demo gave him the nickname. He said Pitts would never figure it out because Rangers aren't issued a sense of humor at Battalion." Steele said it with a tight smile.

Before Collins could say anything else the radio crackled to life.

"This is Iron Leg," Pitts answered.

"The bomb is in play. Have you made contact with Eagle?"

"Negative, comms are still down."

Steele had seen enough. He set the drone to loiter and shoved the controller back into the case, swept the contact out of his eye, and slid down the hill. At the bottom he put everything back into his pocket and clicked the radio.

"Iron Leg," Steele said, jumping on the net. "This operation just went real world. I say again, we are *confirming* an ongoing threat on Eagle's life."

"Roger that, Stalker Seven," Pitts said. "But that doesn't change the fact that we can't get Eagle on comms."

"Are you telling me that a bunch of shitheads with some bootleg Russian frequency jammer are keeping us from warning the president of the United States that he may be walking into a trap?"

Chapter 66

Jerusalem, Temple Mount Tunnel

Hassan stood in the front of the room, a map on the wall behind him. The rest of the team sat in folding chairs arrayed in a horseshoe, all eyes locked on Hassan as he explained the plan.

"At eleven thirty tonight," Hassan began, "two attack teams will engage the IDF patrols at these locations," he said, pointing to the map. "When they have drawn the soldiers away from our route, we will leave the warehouse with the device and drive south to this checkpoint. We will hit the Silwan guard post and then proceed to the tunnel."

"What about the Americans' communications?"

Zakayev asked, trying to learn as much about the plan as possible so he would know when to make his move.

"I procured two Russian high-frequency jammers from my contacts in Hezbollah. One will be set up on the roof of this apartment building," he said, pointing to an X north of the target. "The second will be emplaced at the IDF checkpoint. The jammers have internal frequency scanners that will adjust if the Americans try to jump channels."

Smart, but the Americans will figure it out. All of you are going to die.

"What happens if the Americans track the signal before they get to the target?" a man asked.

"That is why we are using two of them. The jammers are programmed to power down every five minutes. When one is deactivated, the other comes online so that they aren't on long enough to be tracked."

So far, the plan had gone exactly as briefed.

Zakayev watched the men push the bomb over the track while Costas Kaidas unlocked the red conex box.

"Push," one of the men grunted, trying to get the wheels over the lip of the conex box sitting on the ground. They rocked it back and forth but couldn't manage to bounce it over.

Two of the fighters dressed in stolen Israeli uniforms joined in.

"Puuuush," they grunted again.

They rocked the dolly back and forth. Finally, the wheels bounced over the lip and they pushed the device through the opening at the end of the box that led to the second tunnel.

"You dug this?" Zakayev asked Costas.

"I had a crew dig it before rotating them to another job."

The second tunnel was barely big enough for two men to stand on either side of the cart and close to fifty yards long. At the end, Hassan stood beneath an orange square that had been spray painted on the bare rock. There were holes drilled every few inches and blasting caps inserted and primed.

"Keep coming," a fighter said. "A little more."

The men strained, the oversize wheels supporting the cart flattening under the weight of the device.

"Stop," Hassan ordered.

He used a pneumatic jack to line the aiming wire up with the orange X on the ceiling.

"I will be outside," Zakayev said, holding up the radio. "Let me know if you need me."

He stepped out of the conex and headed out of the tunnel, looking for Kaidas. He found him near the exit, his white polo soaked with sweat and his face pale.

Zakayev had known this was going to be a problem

the first time he saw Kaidas. The man was a drunk and he'd seen what happened to the alcoholics and junkies sent to Black Dolphin. Kaidas was going through withdrawal, and the shaking and sweating was because of the DTs, or delirium tremors.

"Drink this," Zakayev said, taking a small bottle of vodka from his bag.

"But Gabriel said . . ."

"I don't care what he said. This is not the time or place for detox. And I don't want you and your shaking hands to accidentally shoot *me* in the back."

"Thank you," he said.

Kaidas took the bottle, but his fingers were shaking too much to get the cap open.

"Shit," Zakayev snapped, tearing the bottle from his hands, and opened the cap for him. "Now, drink. Is there another way out of this tunnel?"

"There is a sewer pipe at the end," Costas said, draining half the bottle in one long swallow.

"Where does it go?"

"According to the plans I saw, it leads to the storm drains."

The drains will lead to the street. You can use that.

"That is enough," Zakayev said. "I don't want you drunk."

Kaidas ignored him.

"I said enough," he said, slapping the bottle from his mouth.

Kaidas bent down and retrieved the bottle from the ground. He brushed off the neck and was going to finish the rest when Zakayev pulled a Makarov from his waist. The sight of the pistol was enough to change his mind.

"Pour it out."

The man did as he was told, and then Zakayev exchanged the empty bottle for the pistol. "Do you know how to use it?"

"Yes," Kaidas said, his hand already steady on the pistol.

"Take this, and don't let Hassan smell the liquor on your breath," Zakayev said, leaving him there.

He was about to go and get a look at the sewer pipe when he heard an explosion at the mouth of the tunnel.

Chapter 67

Jerusalem, Tunnel Entrance

"Do you have a plan?" Collins asked.

"I've got part of one," Steele said, pulling a Nemo Dakkar with a Nightforce scope mounted on top from the scabbard attached to his pack. "You are going to make sure no one shoots me," he said, nodding toward the hill.

"And what are you going to do?" Collins demanded.

Instead of answering, Steele unhooked his assault pack, laid it on the ground, and opened the flap. Inside was a H&K 320 grenade launcher, a bandolier containing four high-explosive rounds, three smoke cannisters, a star cluster, and a scabbard containing a Remington Tac-14 shotgun.

"That's your plan?" Collins asked.

"I said I had *part* of a plan." Steele grinned, positioning the scabbard so the cut-down shotgun was over his right shoulder.

"You sure you brought enough gear?"

Steele looked at the arsenal for a moment. "Yeah, you're right," he said. "Give me your grenades."

"I was kidding," Collins said, handing them over.

He clipped them to his belt. "Much better. See you soon."

It was a three-hundred-meter jog from the base of the hill to the driller blocking the gate. As a kid, Steele thought the biggest machines on earth were the huge dump trucks used to transport the coal around the mines in Pennsylvania. They were big but paled in comparison.

The driller had six eight-foot tires and a ladder that led onto a large square platform. Mounted to a massive metal arm was the drill bit. The bit was twelve feet in diameter and as long as a tractor trailer—the surface covered with ragged carbide teeth capable of chewing through rock.

He dropped to his stomach and crawled under the

machine and loaded a high explosive round into the launcher.

"I'm set," Collins said.

"Going loud," Steele said, lining up on the first technical.

The HE arced through the air, hit the hood of the pickup, and detonated. Steele ejected the spent casing and shoved a second round home. He fired before he was set, and the 40 mm grenade sailed over the truck, hit the pallet loaded with metal pipes, and exploded.

"Oops."

Steele got to his feet and grabbed the ladder while the fighters yelled and fired in every direction. He was almost to the top of the ladder when one of the fighters saw him climbing and directed the rest of the men to fire.

He wasn't worried until he heard the DShK chug to life.

The .51 caliber rounds hit the heavy plate armor with the ring of a hammer on an anvil, spraying Steele with bits of lead and slivers of metal.

"Little help," he told Collins.

"On it."

The Nemo cracked, and the gun fell silent. Steele raced up the stairs and into the cab of the driller.

The interior of the driller was big enough for two people to move around comfortably. The operator's control chair sat all the way to the front surrounded by the controls.

Steele took two steps from the door, stowed the grenade launcher in his assault pack, and set it on the ground before moving to the operator's chair. Steele wedged his rifle between the seat and the bulkhead through the thick windows encased in a metal cage.

Now that's a view.

From the cockpit he could see the entire work site. Directly in front of him the first technical burned brightly, the smoke masking the fighters from the ground. Up high, however, Steele was free to call out their movements to Collins.

"Got one guy using the smoke to get to the second technical," he said over the radio.

"Don't see him," Collins said.

"You will."

A moment later the fighter reached up for the gun. Slowly he lifted himself over the tailgate, exposing his torso.

"Shot out," Collins said.

Steele looked down in time to see the bullet hit the man in the chest. The impact bowled him over, and the two other fighters turned and fled, following the set of tracks north toward the yawning mouth of the tunnel.

"And they are off to the races," Steele said.

"Tell me you know how to drive that thing," Collins replied.

Like all Alphas Steele was trained to operate anything that rolled, floated, or flew, but this was his first time in a drill truck. He scanned the panel, found the ignition, and flipped the switch to on.

"Just letting her warm up," he said.

Once the glow plugs were heated, the light switched from red to green, and Steele twisted the switch to start.

The huge diesel engine rumbled to life, vibrating the entire vehicle. Steele flipped on the monitors that let him see the ground and shifted into drive. He was looking for the wheel when he accidentally tapped the gas and the drill truck lunged forward.

"Steering, steering," Steele said, looking for a wheel.

His elbow brushed the joystick on the arm of the seat and the drill truck responded by turning toward the remaining technical. He glanced at the camera, and a moment later he could feel the tires flattening the technical.

"You go, I'll catch up," Collins said.

"Roger that," Steele said, pivoting the drill arm.

The entire platform rotated around, the arm smashing through the conex box Sterling used as an office.

"That'll buff out," Steele said, centering up on the tunnel, ignoring the papers and blueprints scattering in the breeze.

He gently increased the throttle, and the driller rolled forward into the tunnel.

It was pitch-black inside, and Steele had to stop.

He pulled a penlight from his pocket just to see the instrument panel. *Lights, lights, where are the lights?* he asked, playing the light over the blacked-out instrument panel. *There.* Steele was reaching for the switch when a line of green tracers erupted from the shadows and slapped across the driller's cab.

Chapter 68

Zakayev heard the DShK open up and yelled for the men in the tunnel to get up top. One of the men charged to the mouth of the tunnel and stopped to raise his rifle. Before he could get a shot off he heard the snap of a high-power rifle.

A sniper.

The rest of the fighters hesitated as the driller drove into the tunnel and then inexplicably came to a stop. Zakayev wasn't sure what had happened, but he knew an opportunity when he saw one. He ripped an RPK from one of the fighters, set the machine gun on a pile of rock, and fired a long burst into the cab.

A second machine gun opened, sparking off the metal cage around the glass. Zakayev left his position, trying to flank the driller and get a shot on the engine, when the lights came on. The powerful floodlights caught him in the open, blinding him. He raised his hands to shade his eyes when Steele's voice boomed from the PA.

"*Hola,* cock-bag."

The driller lurched forward and Zakayev ditched the machine gun and dove out of the way seconds before being run down.

"RPGs," he screamed.

A fighter ducked out from behind a bulldozer, shouldered the launcher, but fired too quickly. Zakayev watched Steele jerk the stick to the right, and the rocket flew wide—detonating harmlessly in the air.

The explosion was deafening, and his ears started ringing. Zakayev could hear Steele's voice on the PA but was unable to make out what he was saying. When his hearing returned Zakayev realized the American was laughing.

"You guys suuuuck."

"The army is here, the army is here," a voice yelled over the radio.

"Zakayev, keep them away from the tunnel," Hassan ordered.

The tires.

He fired into the right tire and was rewarded with a rush of escaping air and then stripped a grenade from his belt. Zakayev pulled the pin, let the spoon fly, and cooked the grenade off for as long as he dared then lobbed it up toward the cab.

Chapter 69

"What is it with this guy and shooting out my tires?" Steele asked, trying to sideswipe Zakayev with the driller. The low tire pressure light came on a moment before the front end began to sink.

Auto inflate? the screen asked.

"Don't mind if I do," Steele replied.

He was reaching for the switch as something smacked against the cab and exploded. The lights flickered, and the driller stalled.

"You sons of bitches, you killed it," Steele yelled, smacking the flat of his hand against the glass, but then the engine caught, and the lights came back on. He flipped the inflate button on the dash and felt the vehicle level off as the pump blew fresh air into the tire.

I have to get me one of these.

"Now where did that little Chechen bitch go?" he asked.

"That is not your problem," a voice said. "Stop the vehicle."

Steele looked over his shoulder and found the man in the white polo pointing a Makarov at his head.

"How did you get . . . ?"

The man fired a shot into Steele's assault pack.

"Holy shit, man, there are grenades in there."

"Stop the driller or I will shoot you in the face."

"I'm new at this, which one is the brake?" Steele asked, eyeing the rifle to his left.

"The long pedal next to the . . . ," the man answered.

"Got it," Steele said, slapping the joystick and diving from his seat.

The vehicle veered sharply to the left, sending the rifle skidding across the floor. Steele saw the man was off-balance and was about to dive for the rifle when the man guessed his intentions and fired.

The Makarov barked, the bullet ricocheted off the metal floor, and hit the windshield.

"What is going on?" Collins asked over the radio.

Steele was too busy to answer but knew from the wind rustling past the microphone that she was on the dirt bike.

The man angled around the chair, cutting him off from the rifle. Steele kicked the accelerator, and the driller jumped as he tore the grenade launcher from the assault pack.

"I said stop," the man ordered, firing two rounds into the back of the chair.

One of the bullets punched through and slapped the side of Steele's helmet. The glancing blow left his head ringing, and as the man approached, Steele knew he was running out of time.

He shoved his hand into his pack and felt his fingers close around an HE round. Steele opened the breach and glanced up. The man in the polo was almost on him, the Makarov sweeping onto target.

Steele knew he was taking a major risk shooting a 40 mm high explosive round inside the digger. According to the manufacturer, the grenade needed at least fifteen feet to arm, but Steele had seen them arm the second they were fired. Either way he was out of time and options.

Steele and the man in the polo fired at the same time. The 9 mm left the Makarov's barrel at 1,030 feet per second and hit Steele in the center of the chest with the force of a baseball bat.

The 40 mm HE round hit the man in the face at 250 feet per second, not enough to kill, but strong enough to knock the man off his feet. Steele jumped up, ignoring the blood trickling down his arm, and grabbed the joystick. He managed to bring the machine to a halt.

"I'm coming up," Collins said.

"Roger that," he replied, taking a pair of zip ties from the pouch on his chest.

The grenade had wrecked the man's face, and the front of his polo was now covered in blood.

"Oh Lord, what happened to him?" Collins asked.

"He fell," Steele deadpanned.

Chapter 70

"Keep fighting," Zakayev yelled, motioning for the fighters dressed in the stolen IDF uniforms to follow him into the conex. The men turned, and the rest of the fighters went to follow.

"I said keep fighting," he yelled, shoving one of the fighters to the ground.

"We will die out there," a second said, trying to force his way past the Chechen.

Zakayev brought the Tavor up and shot the man in the chest. "Fight or die," he said, pointing the rifle at the next man in line.

"I will fight."

The man turned and aimed his grenade launcher toward the driller.

Zakayev stepped into the conex but before closing the door glanced around.

Wonder if Kaidas is dead yet?

There was no sight of the man, and he closed the door with a shrug.

What's one less drunk to the world?

He moved to the back of the conex and pushed the sheet of plywood out of the way, revealing a second opening. He stepped inside, found himself in a ten-foot secondary branch of the main tunnel.

They moved to the end and found Hassan standing next to the device.

"We can't stop them," Zakayev said. "You two go with Hassan."

"Aleksandr . . ."

"I will catch up," he said. "But until I do, he is your responsibility. If *he* dies, *you* die."

"Yes, sir."

"Go now," Zakayev said.

"Tonight, we will see each other in paradise," Hassan said to the men in the coveralls.

You won't see me, because I have no intention of dying here, Zakayev thought.

"*Allahu Akbar.*"

Zakayev could already see sparks from the drill tearing through the metal box bouncing inside the tunnel and he used a concussion grenade to seal it. He jogged back to the men in the blue coveralls and told them to grab the acetylene tank. Zakayev took a black duffel bag from beneath the wheeled cart.

"Follow me," he told the men.

The grenades had sealed the tunnel, but he could hear the drill on the other side. Already the rocks were vibrating, and dirt fell from the ceiling.

"Put it here," he said, helping one of the men lean the tank against the rock.

Inside the bag there were two blocks of Semtex and a timer with the blasting caps already attached. He pushed the caps into the plastic explosive and entered 1:00 on the pad then ran back to the pipe.

"Tonight, we will see each other in paradise," he said with a straight face.

Morons.

"*Allahu Akbar,*" the men said as Zakayev grabbed one of the radios and climbed into the sewer pipe after Hassan.

Chapter 71

Steele was looking down from the driller and saw Zakayev shoot one of his men standing outside the conex box before stepping inside and closing the door behind him.

Oh yeah, shut the door, that will keep me out.

A fighter raised a grenade launcher, but Steele had no intention of seeing if the machine could take the hit. He palmed the trackball that controlled the drill arm toward the man, smacking him across the tunnel before he could fire.

The rest of the fighters turned and ran for the exit of the tunnel, retreating as fast as they could.

Steele stopped the driller in front of the conex and centered the drill. He moved the ball until the arm was lined up with the reticle on the control screen, making fine adjustments with the joystick to get the vehicle into position.

Let's take a look inside.

He switched the camera from live to FLIR and the screen changed. The forward-looking infrared cameras displayed the men's heat signatures as orange blobs crowded near the back of the conex. Steele was spooling up the drill when one by one the men slipped through a black area and disappeared from view.

"Looks like we found the tunnel entrance."

When the RPMs were in the "drilling" range Steele extended the boom and engaged the clutch. The drill bit's carbide teeth contacted the metal walls and immediately started shredding them.

"Heeere's Johnny," Steele said, giving the joystick a forward nudge.

"What was that?" Collins asked when the explosion went off.

"These idiots are trying to seal the tunnel," Steele said, shoving the drill against the rocks.

He quickly realized there was a big difference between drilling through aluminum and a sheer rock face. The engine started to bog down, and Steele heard a fan kick on somewhere below him.

The man in the polo sat up with a groan. "You have

to switch gears," he said, hands fingertipping the lump on the top of his head.

"Gears? What gears?" Steele asked, the RPMs climbing toward the red.

"The black button on the track pad."

"Uh, not seeing it," Steele replied.

"You are going to burn it up," the man said.

He grabbed the side panel and pulled himself to his feet. His legs shook beneath him like a newborn colt's and he sunk back to the floor. "Pull the bit out, or you will burn it up."

Steele finally found the button, the acrid bite of burning bearings filling the cab. He pushed it, and the transmission *thunked* into gear. On the gauge the RPMs dropped back to normal.

But the damage was done.

Red warning lights flashed across the panel announcing the failing systems.

"I think we have a problem," Steele said. "Drill temp, oil pressure, dampener, are all off-line. I knew I should have read the manual."

"PULL THE DRILL OUT," the man shouted.

Steele was reaching for the trackball when the wall exploded, and he saw the drill bit hurtling toward the window.

"Get down!" he yelled.

"Collins." Steele coughed and opened his eyes. The drill bit had hit the cab and driven the metal cage and the safety glass inside the driller. Slivers of metal and shards of safety glass were stuck in the seat, and when Steele tried to stand up he felt something sticking out of his face.

He reached up and felt the splinter of glass embedded in his cheek and gingerly plucked it out.

"I think my back is broken," Collins groaned.

"Don't move," Steele said, grabbing his rifle and shuffling to the back of the cab. He knelt beside her and checked her for any holes and bulges.

"I think you are good; can you sit up?"

She grunted from the pain but managed to sit upright.

"Polo guy didn't make it," she said.

He looked over his shoulder and saw the man he'd zip-tied lying on the ground, one of the drill's teeth lodged in the center of his forehead.

"This isn't over, we need to go," Steele said, kicking the door open.

The ladder was twisted and charred black, but they managed to make it to the ground and limp over the floor of the conex box to the hole in the wall. Steele squeezed through the opening and Collins followed. It was dark inside, and he flipped down his night vision and checked his laser.

"You hear that?" Collins asked.

"What?" he asked.

"Voices."

How is anyone still alive?

Chapter 72

Steele followed the tunnel through the destroyed conex. Ahead of him he could hear a voice chanting in the darkness, *"Allahu Akbar, Allahu Akbar."*

"The bomb," he said, forcing his aching legs into a jog.

He stepped on a rock and went down to one knee and Collins shot past him.

"Collins, no," Steele said, getting back to his feet. "Get back here," he said.

There were more voices now and the chant was getting louder. Over the cries of *"Allahu Akbar,"* he could hear the beeping of the timer counting down.

. . . ten, nine, eight, seven . . .

Steele was a foot behind her when she stepped into the light. He rotated his night vision out of his eyes, saw Collins stop ahead of him, and then saw a muzzle flash from the opposite corner.

Brrraaaaap.

"Nooo," Steele yelled.

... six, five, four ...

The men were yelling now, "*ALLAHU AKBAR, ALLAHU AKBAR*," their voices echoing in the confines of the tunnel.

Steele saw Collins fall and then he was in the room, flipping the selector to full auto and working the reticle onto the man with the Skorpion submachine gun.

Thwaaap.

... three ... two ...

He worked the rifle from right to left, firing short controlled bursts. *Thwaaaap. Thwaaaap.* The bullets hammered across the targets' backs, dropping them to the ground. But the man in the middle didn't go down.

He turned, and Steele saw the detonator, a dark green cylinder topped with an orange firing button, mashed beneath the man's thumb. It was a dead man's switch, and the moment the man's thumb came off the button, the bomb would detonate.

Steele knew his only chance was to rip the firing wire out of the detonator. He dropped the H&K and dove for the bomb, hands reaching out for the green wires.

"*Allahu* . . . ," the man yelled.

. . . one.

Steele hit the ground a second before the explosion. He saw the section of the roof caving in and rolled to his left. A slab of concrete spiked with twisted rebar slammed to the ground where he'd been lying.

Across the room the bomber cursed and slapped the detonator.

"You," he said, picking Steele's H&K off the ground, "die now."

The man had him, and Steele knew there was nothing he could do. A single gunshot rang out and Steele tensed, instinctively closing his eyes. He waited for the bite of hot lead, and when it didn't come, he opened his eyes.

Collins was up on one elbow, smoke coiling from her Glock 19.

"I thought you were dead," Steele said, dropping the wires still wrapped around his fingers and crawling over to her.

"Not yet." She coughed, a speckle of blood covering her teeth. "You disarmed it?" she asked.

"I disarmed the EFP, but there must have been two charges," he said, ripping her plate carrier open. He saw a deep crimson stain spreading across her chest.

"How bad is it?" She wheezed.

"The plate stopped most of them, but one got through," Steele said, taking off his helmet and pressing his head against her chest. He could hear the air leaking from the damaged lung. "I'm going to have to turn you on your side," Steele said, cutting her shirt open with the Winkler belt knife.

"Ready?"

She nodded.

"Daaaamn," Collins cursed when he turned her.

He couldn't find an exit wound, and as he turned Collins, he laid her down and noticed that her lips were turning blue. Her breathing shallow and wet.

"Your lung is punctured, and air is leaking into the pleural space," he said. "There isn't an exit wound so . . ."

"Just get it over with."

Steele nodded and pulled a fourteen-gauge needle from her trauma kit. He popped the cap and used his free hand to find the third intercostal space. "Little stick," he said, inserting the needle into the chest wall at a ninety-degree angle.

"Shit, shit, shit," Collins said, tears forming at the corners of her eyes.

"Almost there." Steele pushed until the needle broke through the pleural space and he heard a rush of escaping air.

"Oh, sweet Jesus," Collins gasped, taking a deep breath while he taped the needle in place.

"Better?" he asked, unwrapping a fentanyl lollipop and sticking it in her mouth.

"Yes," she replied.

Zakayev was getting away, but Steele knew he had to get Collins out. *Think, dammit.*

"Just go," she said.

"I can't leave you in here," he said, trying the radio.

"Too much rock to get a signal. You have to be outside."

The DragonFly.

He reached into his pocket.

"What are you doing?"

"The DragonFly is still outside," he said, handing her the case. "You can use it like a minisatellite."

Collins shook her head and carefully put the remaining contact in her eye and brushed off the controller.

Steele gave her the frequency of the radio and waited while she typed it into the drone.

Here goes nothing.

"Iron Leg this is Stalker Eight," Collins said.

There was a slight delay, then Pitts's voice came over the radio.

"Stalker, Iron Leg, there has been an explosion on the surface. What the hell is going on?"

Steele grabbed Collins's radio.

"Stalker Eight needs a medical exfil right now. Take the grid from the DragonFly and tell them to step on it."

"Roger that, we have a dust-off in the area. What about you?"

"I am going to finish this," Steele said.

Chapter 73

Inside Stagecoach, Lansky watched one of the armored Suburbans leave the convoy to block an open intersection.

"I know we go way back, Ted," Rockford said, "but you don't have to protect me anymore."

"Old habits die hard, sir," Lansky responded.

Before Rockford could reply, his wife sat up and reached for one of the airsickness bags. "Honey, are you okay?" Rockford asked.

"I'm going to be sick," she said, holding the bag to her mouth.

Lansky saw that she was sweating and twisted the vent, so the cold air was blowing on the First Lady, whose shoulders rose as she heaved.

"I'm so sorry," she said, apologizing.

"Are you still feeling bad?" Rockford asked.

"The doctors said it was just food poisoning. I'll be fine."

"Food poisoning?" Rockford said. "Again?"

Lansky was equally as surprised. It was the same excuse Lisa had given the day they arrived in Tel Aviv. He remembered because Prime Minister Bitton thought Rockford was showboating. That was two days ago, and now she was sick again.

"What did you eat last night?" Rockford asked.

"John, I'll be fine, don't worry about me."

Lansky looked out the window. He remembered exactly what the First Lady had eaten. What stuck out in his mind was that she had avoided the wine, but Lansky knew better than to get in the middle of this one.

When he glanced back, Lansky saw the concern furrow into the look that Rockford got every time he was trying to piece together a puzzle.

"You had the same thing I did," he said. "A salad and then the hamburger and fries. In fact, you ate *my* fries too."

"One minute, Mr. President," the Secret Service agent interrupted.

"Maybe it would be best if the First Lady stayed in

the car," Lansky suggested, knowing they could figure out what they had eaten on their way back from the biggest meeting of Rockford's presidency.

"Lisa. Baby, are you . . . are you pregnant?"

On the surface, Meg had lost contact with Steele, and the convoy wasn't faring much better. They had switched channels and radios, but nothing seemed to work.

"CAT One . . . right . . . turn . . ."

"Not again," the agent in charge of truck four said. "We are running out of radios."

In the army, radio issues were a constant problem, but Meg never imagined the Secret Service had them. The advance party was the first to report the issue. They were already at the site, but when Ron tried to make contact, it was intermittent.

He'd contacted the Israeli Air Force and asked if they were running any kind of signal disruption. They advised that they were not, but they suggested pushing the signal intercept planes to twenty thousand feet.

The Israeli Air Defense vectored the planes to their higher altitudes and automatically increased the no-fly an additional ten miles. Which moved Sensor, the Program's radio intercept plane, out of the range of Meg's handheld radio.

The move fixed the communication problem, but not for long.

Meg was in the backseat, watching her side of the street. She scanned the faces, looking for anything out of place, but there were just too many people. The panic attack started with a shot of adrenaline that began climbing up her spine and made her mouth go dry. She turned to look out the back hatch, hoping the air would clear her mind.

The last time Meg had experienced this feeling she'd been in Algiers on the way to the Gatehouse. Her team had ended up driving into an ambush. She hoped her luck was better this time around.

"Could it be the anti-IED jammer?" the driver asked.

"Never had them mess with our radios before," the gunner said.

"Right turn," Ron said from the lead vehicle, the transmission clear as a bell.

She opened her eyes and saw the first vehicles start the turn, followed by Rockford's limo.

"Stage . . . coach . . . turn."

The move fixed the communication problem, but not for long.

"Any ideas?" the truck commander asked aloud.

"Switch to Tac/Sat," Meg mumbled.

"Why would we do that?"

"She's got a point," the driver said. "Tac/Sat uses satellites and not line of sight."

"You better be right," the truck commander said. "CAT One, can we switch to Tac/Sat?"

"Good . . . switch . . . Tac Two."

The convoy checked in on Tac Two, and once everyone had reestablished communications Ron said, "Good job, four. Let me know when the last truck is on the straightaway."

The Suburban slowed, and the driver smoothly worked the wheel. "Truck four has made the turn. All vehicles on the straightaway."

"Showtime in half a mile," Ron said.

"Here we go," the truck commander advised before turning to look at Meg. "Thanks for making me look good."

"No problem," she said.

"I'm not trying to insult you, so please don't get offended, but if we make contact, don't roll down the windows or get out unless I give the word."

"Got it." Meg smiled.

Here we go.

The advance party advised that they had the convoy in sight.

"We got you, bring it in," a voice said over the radio.

"Copy that," Ron replied.

Wait, what? Lansky asked himself, turning to the First Lady so fast that his neck popped. He watched her eyes grow wide, then tear up before she offered a tiny nod and a muffled, "Yes."

"Oh my God, that is great," Rockford said, grabbing her hand. "Why didn't you tell me?" he asked, a goofy grin spreading across his face.

"I don't know . . . ," Lisa said, the tears rolling down her cheeks. "I knew how much you had on your mind and I wasn't sure if . . ." She sniffled as Stagecoach came to a halt.

"Don't be silly, you know there is nothing more important to me than family," Rockford said, reaching over to hug his wife.

Lansky turned his attention to the window and the scrum of Secret Service agents holding a perimeter outside on the street. One of the agents pressed his back to the president's door.

"All clear, bring Eagle out," a voice said over the radio.

The door came open, the crowd noise filling the interior of the limo like a wave of sound.

"I'll be right back." Rockford grinned at his wife.

Lansky followed him out and was immediately enveloped by the security detail ready to move them down the red carpet where Prime Minister Bitton and the Saudi crown prince Mohammed bin Salman waited.

"Ted," Rockford said, pulling him close. "We are going to have a baby."

"Mr. President, I am so—" Lansky began.

And then the ground exploded.

Chapter 74

The explosion filled the confines of the sewer with an acrid cloud of dirt and gasoline.

"Keep going," Zakayev urged.

The smoke scalded his eyes, burning his lungs. He tried to hold his breath but knew it was no use.

Ahead of him Hassan stopped and turned around.

Zakayev couldn't believe what he was seeing. "What are you doing?" He coughed. "We have to keep moving or we will suffocate."

"Something . . . is . . . wrong." Hassan hacked, pulling his undershirt over his nose before taking the detonator out of his pocket. "The second charge should have gone off by now."

"There is nothing we can do about it now," Zakayev said.

"We have to go back," Hassan screamed.

"Go back . . . are you . . . crazy?" He could barely see Hassan through the smoke, but he managed to grab him by the shoulders. "We will die."

"Shut your mouth, dog," Hassan yelled, slapping Zakayev.

"What did you just call me?"

"I called you a dog. A Chechen dog," Hassan sneered.

He took a step back, reached into his pocket, and pulled out a black block the size of a matchbook.

"Do you know what this is?" Hassan gloated. "It is your leash."

"My leash?" Zakayev asked, stepping toward him.

"Yes, and you are going to heel. Or I'm going to put you down."

One of the men in the IDF uniforms flashed his light back down the tunnel. "What is going on?" he demanded.

"I want you to listen to me, Hassan, because I am only going to say this once. You are not thinking right. You have let those religious zealots corrupt your mind."

"You don't know what you are talking about," Hassan yelled.

"Look around you, Hassan, they are using you.

Can't you see that?" Zakayev said, ignoring the men and stepping closer to Hassan.

"I am warning you," Hassan said, flipping up the red cover in the center, revealing the firing button.

The hell with him. Kill him. KILL THEM ALL.

"After I kill you," Zakayev said, "I am going up there." He pointed toward the roof. "I am going to kill them all, the American president, the prime minister of Israel, and the crown prince, and then I am going to watch the world burn."

A slave no more.

"No, my friend, you are not," Hassan said, pushing the red button with his thumb.

"Oh no," Zakayev said, "what happened?"

Hassan's eyes grew wide. He jammed his thumb on the button a second time and then a third.

"I don't think it will work without this," Zakayev said, pulling his fisted hand out of his pocket.

He opened his hand and held it up so Hassan could see the shattered pieces of the device Gabriel had implanted in his skull and then he blew them into Sitta's face.

"No, it's . . ."

Zakayev punched him in the face, the blow knocking Hassan onto his ass.

"Kill him," Hassan yelled to the man dressed in the IDF uniform. One of the men moved behind Zakayev, the barrel of his rifle pointed at the back of his head.

"You lose." Sitta smiled.

"Really?" Zakayev asked. "Do you think I am stupid enough to leave my fate in the hands of your martyrs? Do you think this man wants to die serving your master?" he asked with a laugh.

"Shoot him," Hassan screamed.

The man stayed where he was.

"Let me try," Zakayev said, turning to the man. "Kill him."

The soldier nodded, turned the rifle on Hassan, and put a bullet in his forehead.

Chapter 75

It was pitch-black in the sewer and Steele pulled the Tac-14 shotgun from the scabbard and activated the IR flood on his night vision. The shotgun was nothing more than a Remington 870 with a cut-down barrel and a rounded handle instead of a buttstock—a perfect combination, being both portable and lethal. Steele racked the slide, thumbed another round into the bottom of the shotgun, and started after his prey.

Even with the night vision, he quickly lost all sense of time and distance. Steele knew that he'd only been in the darkness for a few minutes, but it felt like an eternity. For all he knew Zakayev could already be aboveground.

He pressed on.

He thought that he heard voices and stopped, but

after a few seconds of no sound but his beating heart, Steele realized his senses were so starved for stimulus that they were playing tricks on him.

How long is this thing?

He again heard voices up ahead and stopped. Unwilling to trust his ears. But this time he heard it clearly.

"Let me try," Zakayev said.

Steele crept forward, took the corner, and raised the shotgun.

"Kill him," Zakayev said.

The soldier turned his rifle on Hassan and fired.

Steele didn't know what was going on, but he didn't care. He pulled the Tac-14's trigger and the shotgun went off like a concussion grenade, filling the tunnel with double-aught buckshot.

Zakayev reacted in an instant. He yanked the fighter in front of him—using his body as a human shield.

The man fell, and Zakayev fired a wild burst and then ran through the brick archway. Steele trotted after him, shoving shells into the breach.

He stepped through the brick arch and found himself in a large crypt-like chamber with a river of water running from right to left. Steele panned the entrance, found the cobblestone walk twisting and then the orange blossom of Zakayev's Tavor.

Steele fired and stripped a frag from his belt. He

tore the pin free and tossed it toward the gunfire. By the time it *tinked* off the ground, Steele had the Glock 19 out of its holster.

Zakayev was almost to the stairs leading up to a landing and Steele knew that if he got to the high ground it was over. His only option was to crash the grenade. He rolled from cover, fired a shot, and saw the man stumble, and then the grenade exploded between them.

The concussion ripped the Tavor out of Zakayev's hands and bowled him over. Steele ducked his head, felt the hot gases scorch his face and the shrapnel cut into his arms and thighs.

Steele ran through the smoke, firing on the move. When he made it to the other side the only signs of Zakayev were the drops of blood leading to the pillars on his left.

"How is your friend?" Zakayev asked with a chuckle. "Last time I saw him, he didn't look so good."

Following the drops of blood on the ground, Steele shoved his last magazine into the Glock. *Keep talking asshole.*

"What are you *even* fighting for?" Zakayev asked, his voice bouncing off the stone.

"Come closer and I'll show you," Steele answered.

"Just another slave, following his master's orders." The Chechen laughed.

Steele sensed movement and turned to see Zakayev emerge from the shadows a foot to his right. The Chechen drove the pistol into Steele's chest and fired.

The bullet sledgehammered the ceramic chest plate, cracking it in half and punching the air from his lungs. Steele dropped the Glock, desperate to breathe. He grabbed the OTs by the barrel, the hot muzzle burning his palms, and when Zakayev rushed him, Steele managed to backhand him across the face with his own pistol.

The blow snapped the Chechen's head to the side but instead of stopping him only seemed to enrage the man. He grabbed Steele around the waist, lifted him off the ground, and slammed him into the pillar.

Umph.

Steele balled up his fist and slammed down on Zakayev's nose like he was hammering a nail. The cartilage crunched in a spray of blood, but the pain didn't seem to have any effect on the man.

"Your mother hit harder than that, and last I checked she is still unconscious," the Chechen leered, blood streaming over his teeth.

"Shut your MOUTH," Steele bellowed.

He drove his elbows down on the man's forearms and fell free of his grip. He dropped into a fighter's stance and hit him with two quick jabs to the body followed by an uppercut to the gut.

The blows folded Zakayev like a cheap lawn chair, and Steele kneed him in the face.

"You think we are all slaves because we fight for something that matters? For something bigger than ourselves?" Steele demanded.

Zakayev stumbled backward. "I think you are a slave because what you believe in is a lie."

Steele was finished listening to this psycho. He ducked down and speared Zakayev below the waist. Steele pushed with his legs, lifting the man high in the air, and then power bombed the Chechen into the cobblestones.

"I fight for the only thing that matters," Steele said, punching him in the face. "The right to be free from people like you."

Zakayev was choking on his own blood and knew he had to get off his back, but to get free he needed his arms, and that required a risky gamble. He lifted his chin and offered the American his throat. Zakayev knew it was too inviting a target to resist, and he was right.

Steele stopped punching him and wrapped his hands

around his throat, leaving Zakayev's hands free. He bucked up with his leg and arched his back. Zakayev knew he was seconds away from passing out when his hand closed around the handle of the knife.

He tugged it free and buried the blade in Steele's forearm.

The American screamed in pain and tried to break free, but Zakayev kept a firm grip on the handle. He twisted the blade until he felt it grinding on the bone and then bucked Steele off.

"You're weak. People like me will always beat people like *you*," Zakayev said, rolling to his knees.

He coughed the blood from his mouth and smiled at Steele.

Finish him, the voice screamed in his head.

"You are soft," Zakayev taunted, getting to his feet.

He grabbed Steele by the forearm, feeling the warm blood beneath his hand, and slashed the blade across Steele's thigh.

"Shiiit!" Steele yelled, dropping to a knee.

"And now, it's your turn to die."

Zakayev kicked him in the side of the head. It was a knockout blow, but the American was tough. It sent him to the ground but didn't knock him unconscious.

He tried to stomp Steele in the face, but the man rolled clear of his boot.

"Why fight the inevitable?" Zakayev asked. "Just give up. Try to die with some dignity, like the rest of your pathetic friends."

"Go to hell," Steele spat as he staggered to his feet, left arm tight against his body.

Zakayev grabbed him by the hair and tilted his head back.

"You first," he whispered, but before he could drive the blade home Steele grabbed him by the front of the shirt and jerked them both back into the six-foot-deep water.

Steele's body armor dragged them to the bottom of the culvert, where the current caught them. He held tight to Zakayev's shirt as they tumbled end over end through the murky water. Steele was trying to wrap his legs around Zakayev when he came to a jarring halt. The impact drove the air from his lungs in a rush of bubbles, and Steele tried to wiggle free, but his body armor was caught on something. He felt Zakayev's fingers dance across his throat, one digging into his artery. Steele tried to break free, but with only one arm it was useless.

He bucked and twisted, thrashing in the murky water while the blood hammered in his ears. Warning bells flashed in his head and the last thought that flew through his mind before he passed out was the realization that he was going to die.

Zakayev climbed out of the culvert, water pouring from his clothes and boots. He sloshed toward the stairs, grabbing the OTs off the ground on his way. He started up the stairs, the leg wound a lightning bolt of pain.

At the top of the stairs he quickly reloaded the OTs and looked down at his wounds. His soaking wet IDF uniform looked black, masking the blood from the leg wound.

It won't last long, but it will work.

Zakayev followed the walkway to an iron gate, pressed the pistol against the padlock, and fired. He ripped the busted lock free of the chain, stepped out into the courtyard.

The scene was chaotic.

Off to the right, the American, Israeli, and Saudi flags were mounted atop a stone wall that formed a natural barrier. The flags snapped in the breeze, their shadows falling over the three podiums at the front edge of the stage.

A wall of IDF soldiers hemmed in the mass of reporters and guests at the front of the stage. The soldiers were shouting at the men and women to "remain calm" while Crown Prince bin Salman's and Prime Minister Bitton's security details formed two protective squares around their principals.

The crowd opened a hole in the soldiers' line and broke free. They fled toward the scrum of Secret Service agents formed around the disabled limo on the street where two agents wrestled with the American president.

The prime minister's team was the first to get moving—to start pushing through the crowd like miniature Roman phalanxes. A moment later the crown prince's team lurched forward.

Zakayev easily discerned their objective—the armored trucks lined up twenty yards to the left of the Secret Service detail.

The road is the only way out.

But to reach it both the prime minister and the crown prince would have to pass right next to Rockford.

Go now and you can kill them all.

Zakayev stepped forward, shouldering his way through the crowd.

He got within five feet when a woman yelled, "He's got a gun."

Kill him.

Zakayev forced himself to maintain his pace, knowing that to break into a run would only draw attention.

"He's behind you," the woman yelled.

A man wearing a blue suit and holding a submachine gun was the last person between him and the president. The man started to turn, but Zakayev moved swiftly and brought the OTs to the back of the agent's head and pulled the trigger.

Chapter 76

Meg jumped out of the Suburban and ran through the smoke with the rest of the CAT team. She could hear Ron shouting at the CAT team to set up a perimeter while Rockford's detail yelled for the IDF soldiers to back off.

The smoke started to clear, and Meg saw the nose of the presidential limo protruding from a jagged hole in the ground.

"LISA!" Rockford yelled, running toward the limo.

"Get Eagle out of here!" Ron yelled.

"Sir, we have to go," one of the Secret Service agents said, but Rockford wasn't listening. He pushed past the man, clearly about to jump into the hole.

"Grab him!"

The detail swarmed around him and Rockford shoved them off. "Get off me," he ordered.

"Keep them back!" Ron yelled, pointing toward the IDF soldiers closing in on the bomb site.

"CAT Four on me!" the TC yelled. "Set up right here."

Meg fell in beside the men on the road to her left and the IDF soldiers setting up the inner cordon on her right. There were too many faces to watch, too much going on.

They need to get him out of here.

Meg was wondering if they should tie in with the IDF cordon when she saw one of their soldiers push through the ranks. She couldn't see his face, but there was something wrong about his uniform. It took her brain a moment to realize what it was.

Why is he all wet? Meg thought.

Chapter 77

Steele was underwater, trying to free himself from whatever had snagged his plate carrier. His lungs screamed for air. His thrashings grew weaker and just as the plate carrier came free from the metal grate, Steele passed out.

The moment the OLS or Operator Life Support System activated it sensed that Steele had gone into cardiac arrest and came online. The system ran an atmospheric scan. The sensor noted that Steele was underwater and inflated the vest's buoyancy regulator.

The bags filled with air and sent Steele floating to the surface. When his head cleared the water, a recorded voice issued a warning to anyone who might be standing around.

"Automated external defibrillator activating. Please clear the area."

Steele's eyes snapped open, the smell of ozone permeating his nostrils.

"Exit the water. Exit the water," the OLS instructed.

"Give a guy a second to transition back to the land of the living," he mumbled, grabbing the wall and pulling himself out of the culvert.

Steele lay on his chest, panting from the near-death experience. His head was pounding, and his muscles shook from the electrical shock that had brought him back to life.

You can rest when you're dead. Finish this.

Steele grunted and rolled onto his back. He yanked down on the vest's quick release, shedding the waterlogged OLS. Steele struggled to his feet, eyes locking on the wet footprints heading up the stairs.

Zakayev.

Steele stumbled back to the pillars and found the Glock 19 where it had been knocked from his hand. He scooped the pistol from the ground and dropped the magazine. It was empty.

He eased the slide to the rear and saw the shiny brass of the hollow point in the chamber.

"One shot, awesome," he said, following the footprints up the stairs.

The prints led up the stone steps and down a tight corridor. At the end there was a metal gate and a dead Israeli soldier, eyes frozen in surprise.

He pushed past him and stepped out.

The courtyard outside the tunnel was wide open, the temple's ancient stone walls rising up to the east. The area to Steele's front was a mass of soldiers, state officials, and security agents all converging on the street.

Steele held the pistol at his side and trotted toward the chaos. He expected someone to see the Glock, knowing the moment it happened he was dead. Unlike in the movies, in situations like this people tended to shoot first and ask questions later.

Where the hell is he? Steele thought, eyes searching for Zakayev.

He slipped through a break in the IDF perimeter, knowing that time was running out. Steele thought he heard Meg's voice. "It's Zakayev," she screamed.

But where?

Steele felt a hand on his shoulder and turned to see an IDF soldier standing beside him. He shucked free of the man's grasp and cut through the crowd, angling toward the edge of the perimeter. Steele kept his head down and knew he was close when he could smell the smoldering rubber of the limo.

Oh my God, Rockford.

He shouldered his way forward and then found himself in an open area.

The presidential limo sat off to his right, the ass end standing up at an angle, the hood buried in the crater blown out of the roadway. To Steele's left, the three security teams had merged into one.

All three teams were trying to keep their unit integrity, but with the crowd flowing around them it was impossible, and they were starting to merge.

"Get him to the truck," a voice yelled in English.

Steele ignored the sounds, focusing instead on the faces.

Where the hell is Zakayev?

Steele was getting frantic when he saw him.

The Chechen knifed into the perimeter, his stolen IDF uniform still dripping wet. The sudden movement caught the eye of a Secret Service agent and he turned, muzzle coming up.

But Zakayev already had the OTs pointed at the agent's head.

Steele didn't hear the pistol go off but saw the agent go down, giving Zakayev a clear shot at Rockford.

Steele raised the Glock, knowing that this was the most important shot of his life. He blocked everything else out and focused on the front sight. Steele was aware of the IDF soldier screaming a warning to his comrades. He felt them turn toward him, knowing that any second someone was going to open fire.

Take the shot, Steele thought.

Zakayev was within three feet of Rockford when one of the Secret Service agents saw him coming. The man opened his mouth, but before he could shout a warning, Zakayev dropped him with a shot to the forehead.

He was now a foot away from Rockford.

Steele gently took the slack out of the trigger, waiting for the pause in his breathing.

Zakayev centered his muzzle on the back of Rockford's head and was curling his finger around the trigger when Steele fired.

The Glock boomed, but before he could see if he had hit his target, Steele was tackled to the ground. Rough hands ripped the Glock from his grip and one of the soldiers shoved a barrel against the back of his head.

His arms were yanked behind his back, the movement sending a scream of pain from the knife wound as they cuffed him. Steele tried to get his head up. Tried to see around the legs and arms obscuring his view, but the soldier shoved his face into the stones.

"He is with us," Meg yelled, "back off."

"Ma'am, step back," one of the soldiers yelled.

The soldiers jerked him to his feet and were turning him when Steele saw Lansky striding toward them.

"Stand down," he barked.

Behind Lansky Prime Minister Bitton had already been loaded up, and Steele saw the crown prince ducking into an SUV, blood staining his stark white *keffiyeh*. In the next instant a group of CAT agents, rifles up, ready to engage if the Israeli soldiers tried to take Steele, blocked his view.

"Let him go," Lansky said. "He just saved the prime minister's life."

The IDF soldiers took off the cuffs and Steele rubbed his wrists as the CAT team formed up around them. They took a few steps forward, when Steele stopped and scooped something from the ground. He stood upright, saw Zakayev's body lying facedown on the ground. A bullet hole behind his right ear.

It's done.

"That was a hell of a shot," Lansky said as the CAT team led them toward the last three trucks.

Steele was too exhausted to reply. His legs buckled and Meg ducked under his arm, wedging her shoulders against him so that she was supporting his weight.

"It's okay, I've got you," she said.

"I can walk," Steele said.

"I know you can," Meg said, meeting his gaze. "But you don't have to do it alone."

Rockford stood next to the middle Suburban. The

door was open, and he leaned in, gently setting the First Lady inside. When he turned, Steele saw the pain on his face and knew something was wrong.

"What is wrong with Lisa?" he asked Meg.

"She was in the limo when the bomb went off," she answered, looking away.

"Well, is she hurt?" Steele asked.

"Minor bruises, but . . ."

"But what?" Steele asked.

"She's pregnant, Eric."

Chapter 78

Three Days Later
Green Bank Facility, West Virginia

Eric Steele sat in the back of the MH-60M Black Hawk, watching the endless green of the Allegheny Mountains passing below. The pilot banked south and Steele caught a glimpse of Snowshoe Mountain, its usually white peaks brown and gray in the summer heat.

"Starting our approach now, sir," the pilot called over the internal net.

Steele leaned forward and saw the town of Green Bank fill the windscreen. The pilot flared the Black Hawk into a hover over the roof of the Green Bank

Facility, and settled the bird onto the helipad with a gentle touch.

Steele grabbed the leather courier bag and hopped off. He ducked beneath the blades and jogged toward the door, where Dr. Thompson was waiting.

Behind him, the pilot pushed the throttle forward and then the helo leaped skyward.

"Morning, doc," Steele said, extending his hand.

"What happened this time?" Thompson asked, pointing to the blue cast covering his left arm.

"Wouldn't believe me if I told you," Steele replied, stepping into the stairwell. "How is my mom doing?"

"Remarkable recovery."

"What about Lisa Rockford?" Steele asked, knowing she'd been checked into the Green Bank.

Thompson shook his head. "She is fine, but the baby . . . there was nothing I could do."

"How is Rockford handling it?"

"I've never seen the man so angry. It's . . ."

"It's heartbreaking," Steele said.

"Exactly."

They walked down the stairs in silence, each man grieving for the Rockfords' loss.

"Here we are," Dr. Thompson said as he pushed through the metal door and onto the recovery room floor. He stopped at the charge desk in the center of the hall.

"She is in room three," he said. "I am sure you guys have some catching up to do."

"Thank you, doc," Steele said, extending his hand.

"For what?" Thompson asked.

"Keeping her alive."

Steele stopped outside of her room. He could hear the television playing and could tell by the whistling intro that she was watching Andy Griffith. It was her favorite show. He took a plastic container from the courier bag and opened the top. Inside was a bouquet of wildflowers that he'd bought when they stopped in Ireland for fuel.

His mother was sitting up in bed. The machines and the tubes were gone, and other than a cast on her wrist and some residual bruising, Susan Steele looked great. Eric felt a wave of relief wash over him and blinked away the tears of happiness that burned his eyes. He stepped into the room.

"Looking good, Mom," he said.

"Eric," she said, a massive smile spreading across her face. "Are those for me?"

He walked over to her bed and handed his mother the flowers.

"They were out of lilies," he said.

"What happened to your arm?"

"I hurt it at—" he began.

"Eric, the import-export business is getting too dangerous," she said. "I think it's time for you to find another job."

"Mom, I'm so sorry . . . ," he began.

His mother opened her arms, and Steele ducked into the hug.

"I . . . I never meant for any of this to happen," he said, unable to hold the tears back any longer. "If I'd known that something like this . . ."

"Eric, stop," she said, patting his head. "You are a protector, it's in your blood."

Her words were comforting but didn't ease his guilt.

"You did what you were born to do," she continued, holding him at arm's length and wiping the tears from his cheeks. "You are your father's son and I am proud of you."

"You're amazing," Steele said. "I don't know how I can ever make it up to you."

"I can think of a way you can start." His mother grinned.

"Oh yeah, and what is that?"

"There is a folder on the table that Dr. Thompson got for me. Would you mind bringing it over?" she asked, pointing at the table.

Steele got to his feet and walked over to the table.

"I don't see it," he said.

"It is under the newspaper."

He lifted the *West Virginia Daily* and saw a black folder lying underneath. His eyes locked on the emblem embossed on the bottom and he shook his head.

"Dr. Thompson's wife has one and he said that according to *Car and Driver*, the Mercedes G Wagon is the safest SUV on the road."

"What a *helpful* guy," Steele muttered, looking at the price tag.

"What was that?" his mother asked innocently.

"Just saying how helpful Dr. Thompson is."

"He really is a dear. In fact, he has already called the dealership and they have a black one in stock."

"Yes, ma'am." Steele smiled. "Is there anything else?"

His mother scooted over and patted beside her on the bed. "You can come sit with me," she said.

Steele settled himself beside her, enjoying the moment, seeing her recovery, just being here with her.

"I love you, Mom," he said, kissing her forehead.

"You ready?" Steele asked, buttoning the suit coat before stepping into the hall.

"Almost, can you help me with this?" Meg asked.

Steele found her in the bathroom wearing a simple black dress with the zipper open in the back. He stepped behind her, taking in the fresh smell of her hair.

"Are you okay?" she asked.

"Yeah," he answered, carefully zipping up the back of her dress. "You look good."

Meg smiled and lifted a string of pearls from the box on the counter, her eyes seeking his in the mirror.

"Mom's?" Steele asked.

"Yes, she told me to wear them today, is that okay?"

Steele was touched by the gesture and didn't trust himself to speak, so he nodded.

"Let me fix your tie," Meg said, turning.

They walked out the door and found a black Lincoln with tinted windows waiting at the curb. The driver hopped out and opened the door.

"I wanted to offer my condolences for Demo," he said before Steele got in.

"Thank you."

Thirty minutes later the driver pulled up to the Washington National Cathedral and opened the door.

Steele led Meg around the back to a small entrance hidden between a row of shrubs. Mike Pitts was waiting for them in the center of the room, and behind him, two men silently guarded a mahogany door.

"Heard the good news about your mom," Pitts said.

"She is a tough lady."

"I'll be right here waiting for you when you are done," Meg said, standing on her tiptoes and giving Eric a kiss.

"Thank you," he said.

Steele stepped through the door and down a stone staircase that led into the crypt of the cathedral. He stopped at the bottom of the stairs and took a breath before pushing open the door.

Here we go.

Steele stepped through the door and into the subterranean chapel, his eyes locked on the flag-draped casket sitting before the altar. He started down the aisle, lined with Alphas and their keepers, while two men in dark suits folded the flag back and opened the head of the casket.

He wished Meg was here to witness this, but Steele knew that not even the president of the United States had the power to bend the rules when it came to an Alpha funeral.

Steele stopped in front of the casket, tears burning at the corners of his eyes. There was so much he wanted to say, but looking down at Demo's face, the words seemed meaningless.

He reached into his pocket, hand closing around the expended brass he had taken from the Temple Mount.

"We got him, mano," he said, placing the brass on his keeper's chest.

A tear traced its way down his cheek and landed on the coffin, shining like a puddle of mercury in the candlelight.

He took a deep breath, fighting the emotion that rolled over him. "You were the best of all of us . . . ," Steele said, wiping the back of his hand across his face.

Steele stepped back from the coffin, snapped to attention, and raised his right hand to his forehead. "Until Valhalla, mano," he said, saluting his best friend. "You will be missed."

Epilogue

Dubai

The Burj Khalifa Hotel catered to the world's elites, men and women who expected the best. Everything about the hotel had been designed to impress. The building itself was an architectural marvel, a 2,700-foot jewel of glass and steel that towered above the desert floor like a gigantic tear.

The up-armored Mercedes SUV arrived at 11:30 P.M. The driver bypassed the main lobby and looped around the side to a second door guarded by two heavily armed men.

Gabriel grabbed the attaché case from the floorboard.

Prince Badr sat in the backseat, glowering like a child who knew that he was going to bed without dessert.

"I will call when it is time to bring him in," Gabriel said to the prince's bodyguard.

He stepped out and handed one of the guards a silver card embossed with a palm tree and two diamonds.

The card marked him as one of fifty members of the most exclusive club in the world: the Diamond Palms.

"This way, sir," the man said, opening the door.

Gabriel's shoes squeaked on the gleaming white marble floor, and after he cleared the biometric reader and walked through the Analogic Computed Tomography 3D scanner, a pair of armed guards allowed him to approach the check-in desk.

"Good evening sir," the concierge said. "How may I assist you?"

"My employer has a reservation," Gabriel said, handing him a card.

"Of course, sir," the concierge said, running the card through the scanner.

"Two guests for Penthouse Number Two."

Gabriel nodded, even though the prince was the only one who was actually going to be sleeping in the room. He and Badr's bodyguards had other duties. Mainly to keep Badr alive.

Penthouses One and Two were the most expensive rooms in the hotel. Rooms that made the high-roller suites of most hotels look like dumps. They cost eighty-three thousand dollars a night. But Badr wasn't there for the opulence. The prince was there because he didn't want to die.

"And how will you be paying?" the concierge asked.

Gabriel placed the attaché case on the counter, thumbed in the combination, and popped the locks.

"Cash," he said, turning the case around.

He was exhausted. Worn out from the scramble of getting clear of the Americans. But his fate was better than Zakayev's and Hassan's, who were both dead.

The operation in Israel had failed, and the crown prince was still in power.

Praise be to Allah that the American killed Zakayev before he could start a war.

He watched the concierge walk the case to the night manager's glass-fronted office and hand it off.

The thought of what could have happened sent a shiver up his spine. It was the only spot of light in an otherwise dismal failure.

"Can I offer you some champagne while you wait?" the concierge asked when he returned.

"No," Gabriel said.

The night manager closed the novel he was read-

ing and opened the case. He emptied its contents effi-
ciently, stacking banded stacks of hundred-dollar bills
on the table next to the counter.

Gabriel knew how much was in the case because
he'd put the money in there. Two hundred and fifty
thousand dollars—enough for three nights at the Burj
Khalifa. To stay any longer would be a fatal mistake.

The night manager cut the bands with a letter opener
and started feeding them into the counting machine.
When he was finished, he notated the amount in the
computer and went back to his book.

"The funds have been placed in your account," the
concierge advised.

Gabriel called the bodyguard's number and when
he answered said, "Bring him in."

Prince Badr and his bodyguard walked through the
door and fell in behind the armed escort who led them
to the elevator.

They all boarded the elevator that took them to the
room 1,918 feet above the lobby. When the doors *dinged*
open a steward was waiting in the hall. He opened the
door to the room and ushered the prince inside.

"This is your panic button," he told Gabriel. "It
is wired directly to your personal Tactical Response
Team. The staff has already run the pH test on the
water purification unit, and the nuclear biological con-

tamination filters attached to the heating and air unit. Is there anything else I can get for you?"

"No," Gabriel said.

The bodyguard escorted the steward outside, shutting the door behind them. Gabriel armed the security system, checked on the prince, and then finally allowed himself to relax.

It was pitch-black inside the twenty-foot water main buried beneath the Burj Khalifa. Eric Steele kept his eyes glued to the icon on the nav screen strapped to his wrist. Ten feet ahead a sonar imaging drone mapped the pipe and sent a 3D image back to the screen.

All Steele had to do was follow the icon.

"He just checked in," Meg said.

"Copy that," Steele replied.

The Saudis had given Cutlass Main unprecedented access in tracking down the fugitives. The crown prince went as far as to order every bank manager whose institution had money connected to the House of Saud to notify him if Badr tried to pull money from an account.

Which was how Meg knew when he withdrew the two hundred and fifty thousand dollars from a bank in Kuwait. After they pinned down their location, all Steele had to do was wait for them to stop moving.

He found his way through the water main until he

could see the soft red glow from the drone. Steele attached a magnet to the wall of the pipe and clipped his tether into the D ring. On paper Burj Khalifa was impenetrable, but Steele had learned a long time ago that there was always a way in.

Collins was the one who'd found it.

"The water main. A building that tall needs a ton of water and its own pumping station."

"Is it big enough?"

"Yes," Collins answered.

Normally Steele would have needed an Alpha flash, but not this time. President Rockford had put every Alpha operation on hold, and right now the only mission Cutlass Main was supporting was Stalker 7's.

"Divert the water to the secondary pipe," he said over the radio.

"Got it," Pitts answered.

Steele took a magnetic plasma cutter from the bag attached to his wet suit and stuck it against the pipe.

"Water diverted."

Steele pulled the welding shade over the self-enclosed Dräger Panorama mask and activated the cutter. The plasma torch bored a tiny hole to vent the pressure and then a much larger one. A minute later Steele was standing in the subbasement, watching the pumps suck water off the floor.

He stripped out of the wet suit, revealing sterile BDUs. He strapped a micro plate carrier over his chest, and took the suppressed H&K MP7 from his kit bag. Last but not least were the full-spectrum goggles, which he pulled over his head and turned to low visibility.

"I'm in."

"Take the access door, fifteen feet to your right," a voice said.

Steele followed the directions, and as he approached the door he saw the red light on the electronic lock switch from red to green.

"There is a ladder on the north wall. Do you see it?"

"Yes."

"Take it to the next access hatch."

Steele tightened the strap on the MP7 and started to climb. The hatch was unlocked when he reached it. Steele climbed through and adjusted the goggles to the darkness. The thermal lens showed the heat signatures from the pumps and boilers in bright red and the cooling units in vivid blue.

"Hold," Meg said.

Steele froze.

"Two workers on your three o'clock."

He wasn't interested in killing innocents, even now.

"Kill the lights," he ordered.

The lights went off and Steele stripped the Taser from his belt.

"That damn breaker again," one of the men said in Arabic. "I've got it."

Steele let the man pass and touched his lower back with the Taser. The worker dropped like a stone. He zip-tied the man and then repeated the process with the second worker.

"Overriding the locks," a voice said, followed by the swish of the elevator doors opening. Steele stepped inside and shot to the penthouse floor.

"One Tango in the hall. Standing in front of target door on the right."

"Kill the cameras," Steele ordered.

"They are dead."

The elevator door whispered open and Steele leaned out, centered the reticle on the guard's forehead, and fired.

Thwap.

Steele was outside the door before the man's body was on the ground. Instead of going in, he pulled a mask over his face and nose. He covered the filters with his hands and sucked in through his nose. When Steele was sure the mask was sealed to his face, he took an aerosol cannister from a second pouch and squatted in front of the door.

The cannister was filled with Sigma 1, an incapaci-
tant based off the gas the Russian special police used
in the Moscow siege. Steele worked the rubber tubing
under the door and set the time release for ten seconds.

According to Cutlass Main the mask would protect
him from the fallout. But just to be sure, Steele backed
down the hall.

The cannister expelled its contents into the room
with a hiss, and Steele looked down at his watch.

Ten seconds later Meg was on the radio.

"Targets are incapacitated."

Steele moved back to the door, turned the knob, and
stepped inside.

He went to the couch where Gabriel was slumped
into the pillows. Steele zip-tied his wrists together and
took the pistol from his holster. He set the pistol on the
counter on his way to the bedroom where Badr was
crumpled on the floor.

Steele secured the prince and dragged him roughly
into the living room.

Fat bastard, he grunted, heaving Badr onto the
couch beside Gabriel.

All that was left to do was wait.

Gabriel, the fitter of the two men, was the first to
come to.

"Morning, sunshine," Steele said when the man's eyes came open.

Gabriel started and looked down at the ties securing his wrists.

There was fear in his eyes.

"Wake up, sleepyhead," Steele said, backhanding Badr across the side of the head with his pistol. "Daylight's a-wastin'."

The blow opened a nasty gash across the man's forehead. The pain waking him instantly.

"Who . . . who are you?" he blubbered.

"Your reckoning," Steele answered.

"Please, I will pay anything."

"Not this time. But you will be happy to know that your brother sends his regards," Steele said.

Thwap.

The pistol bucked in his hand and the hollow point blew the contents of the prince's skull against the wall.

Steele turned to Gabriel. He pressed the suppressor against his forehead. The hot metal sizzling the skin.

"What about you, asshole? Anything you want to say?"

"If you kill me you will never find your father," Gabriel said.

It hit Steele like a tidal wave and pinned him in

place. He knew what Gabriel was doing: trying to save himself by offering to answer *the* question that had plagued Steele's entire adult life.

Was his father alive or dead?

"No," Steele said, finger slipping onto the trigger.

He had made his decision and would stick to it.

"This is for Demo," he said and then pulled the trigger.

Acknowledgments

To my soldiers in *Outlaw Platoon*: without you, I wouldn't have made it home from Afghanistan. Thank you for standing in the trenches and holding the line with me. Thank you for coaching and mentoring me as a young leader. Without you, a life after the war doesn't happen.

Writing fiction is difficult. It's time-consuming. It's tedious. The process lengthy. But throughout that lengthy process you get to meet some truly wonderful people who make it all worthwhile. My entire team at William Morrow is made up of people just like that. In a word, they're wonderful. But also hardworking, dedicated, loyal, kind, generous, and selfless. Like my editor David Highfill. He's a top-notch pro who knows the business side of publishing better than anyone else, but perhaps more important, understands the core elements necessary to tell a great story. He gives straightforward and honest feedback in a way that's easy to digest. I'm lucky to have him in my corner. In fact, his entire team is the best in the industry. Tavia Kowalchuk, Danielle Bartlett, and Tessa James—thank you all.

To my agent Daniel Conaway at Writers House: You've never once steered me wrong. Ever. You strike just the right balance of transactional magnificence and stellar career mentorship. Both are obviously important, but the latter is something I desperately needed. Thanks for always being there for me.

To Josh Hood and John Paine: Thank you both from the bottom of my heart for elevating this book to what it is today. I'm truly blessed beyond measure for your dedication, patience, and advice throughout this process.

To Evan West: I don't think there's a better creative person in the branding business today. You're a unique talent and a great friend. I'm thankful for all that you do for me, and believe me . . . I know it's a lot. Thank you for everything over the years.

To Lori McGoogan: To call you simply my assistant would be the understatement of the century. I travel to more than fifty events a year, and somehow you never miss a beat. You're the glue that holds my home base together! You're a jack of all trades; you keep my life on the straight and narrow. Thank you for always being there for me on a moment's notice.

To my family and friends: Mom and Dad, thank you for your love and support. You're the best parents a crazy son like me could ask for. Shannon, Scott, and Andy, my sister and brothers. I can't imagine having a better cadre of siblings. Thank you for the unconditional love and support over the years. John Rokosz, my great friend, thank you for all the late nights talking story and Steele. You made this book better through your involvement. To my Fairway Independent Mortgage family, Steve Jacobson, and Louise Thaxton (my work mom)—thank you ALL for the support. It's a great honor and privilege to be a small part of our charity, the American Warrior Initiative. Thank you for the opportunity to give back to our nation's veterans.

Last, but certainly not least, I'd like to thank my three amazing children: Ethan. Emma. Evan. My Three Es. You drive me to be the best version of myself. Each one of you inspires me every day. I'm blessed beyond measure to be your father and I look forward to watching you grow up.

HARPER LUXE

THE NEW LUXURY IN READING

We hope you enjoyed reading
our new, comfortable print size and found it
an experience you would like to repeat.

Well – you're in luck!

HarperLuxe offers the finest in fiction and
nonfiction books in this same larger print size and
paperback format. Light and easy to read, HarperLuxe
paperbacks are for book lovers who want to see
what they are reading without the strain.

For a full listing of titles and
new releases to come, please visit our website:

www.HarperLuxe.com